Something inside her seemed to swell and ache for more, as if she'd just been jolted to life from a deep stupor. Her heart beat like a bird's wing against her ribs. His tongue teased hers, and a shiver of surrender went down her spine as she opened for him. This was what she had feared and craved, all at once, and she never wanted it to end.

He tore his mouth from hers and clutched her to him so tightly she felt his ragged breath vibrate through her. "Don't go," he whispered urgently. "Please don't leave." He kissed her again, and she almost swooned into it. *No*, she wanted to say; *I don't want to leave you*. She pushed her fingers into his hair and held on, pulling him closer and kissing him back with every fiber of her being.

"Georgiana," he breathed, his arms trembling around her. "Come with me . . ."

CAROLINE LINDEN

When the Marquess Was Mine

∽ THE WAGERS OF SIN ∽

AVONBOOKS

An Imprint of HarperCollinsPublishers

WHEN THE MARQUESS WAS MINE. Copyright © 2019 by P. F. Belsley. All rights reserved. Printed in the United States of America. No part of this book may be used or reproduced in any manner whatsoever without written permission except in the case of brief quotations embodied in critical articles and reviews. For information, address HarperCollins Publishers, 195 Broadway, New York, NY 10007.

First Avon Books mass market printing: October 2019

Print Edition ISBN: 978-0-06-291359-3
Digital Edition ISBN: 978-0-06-291360-9

Cover design by Guido Caroti
Cover photo illustration by Patrick Kang

Avon, Avon & logo, and Avon Books & logo are registered trademarks of HarperCollins Publishers in the United States of America and other countries.

HarperCollins is a registered trademark of HarperCollins Publishers in the United States of America and other countries.

FIRST EDITION

19 20 21 22 23 QGM 10 9 8 7 6 5 4 3 2 1

*To everyone who's trying to make the world
a kinder and more equal place*

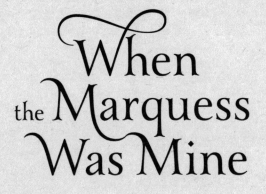

When the Marquess Was Mine

Chapter 1

1819

Iᴛ ᴡᴀs ᴛᴏ be a bacchanal for the ages.

As Heathercote remarked, a man only turned twenty-nine once. Marlow pointed out that a man also only turned twenty-eight, or thirty, once as well, but they were well used to ignoring Marlow's odd points of reason, and this one was promptly forgotten.

Heathercote planned the entire affair, inviting the most dashing, daring rogues and scoundrels in London. He declared it to be the invitation of the month, and that he'd turned away several fellows for lacking wit, style, or both. "You mean they aren't up to your standard of mayhem," said Westmorland, whose birthday it was, to which Heathercote mimed tipping his hat in acknowledgment.

After a raucous dinner at White's, they decamped for the theater. The production was well under way when they invaded the pit in search of amusement. By the time the show ended, they had drunk a great deal of brandy, thrown oranges at the stage, and lost Clifton to the company of a prostitute.

Everyone's memories ran a bit ragged after that, with vague recollections of singing in the streets and Marlow casting up his accounts somewhere in Westminster, but eventually they settled at the Vega Club. It was so late, the manager tried to dissuade them from play. Mr. Forbes knew every one of them could wager for hours, and the Vega Club closed its doors at dawn.

But Heathercote persuaded him to let them in and to give them the whist salon all to themselves. "We'll leave by noon," he promised, patting Forbes on the chest as he slid a handful of notes into the man's hand. His words were remarkably steady for a man who'd been drinking for eight hours. Grim-faced, Forbes let them in, where they commandeered the main table and called for yet more wine.

A few intrepid souls followed them from the club proper. Forbes tried to stop them at the door, but Forester recognized one and waved them in. "We don't mind winning their money," he said with a hiccup.

They played whist, then switched to loo. One loser was dared to drink off the contents of his full flask in one go, which he did. The room filled with cigar smoke and ribald language, and the wagers grew extravagant. Marlow won a prize colt off Forester. Heathercote wagered his new phaeton and ended up with someone's barouche. Sackville won the largest pot of the night, and everyone pelted him with markers.

And then one of the hangers-on spoiled it. He had the look of a country fellow new to London, with an arrogant bluster that was initially amusing but eventually turned annoying. He'd played well enough, winning a bit and losing with colorful curses that made the rest of them roar with laughter. But it became abruptly clear that Sir Charles Winston was in over his head when he wagered his house.

Marlow laughed. Heathercote picked up the scribbled note Winston had put forth and read it with one brow arched. "Can't wager property, Winslow."

The man was already ruddy from drink, and now he turned scarlet. "Can so! Your fellow wagered a horse."

"Horses are portable," said Forester, his Liverpool accent bleeding through. "Houses are not."

"Houses are worth more!"

"Aye, too much more." Heathercote flicked the note back across the table. "Markers."

"I haven't got any more markers," muttered the younger man. For a moment everyone focused in surprised silence on the empty space in front of him. None of them had run out.

"Then fold your hand," Forester told him. "You're out!"

Winston's chin set stubbornly. His mate tried to slide some markers toward him, but he angrily shoved them back. "Give me a chance to win it back."

"All the more reason to walk away, if you've lost 'em all." Marlow waved one hand, nearly toppling out of his seat. Mr. Forbes, watching grimly from the corner, came forward. "Forbes, Windermere is done."

"Sir Charles," murmured the manager. "Perhaps it's time to go."

"Not yet!" Winston scowled at them all, shaking off his friend's quiet attempts to get him to fold.

"Not now, Farley! They got a chance to turn their luck. Why shouldn't I?"

"Luck is like the wind," said a new voice. Nicholas Dashwood, the owner of the Vega Club, stepped out of the shadows. "It rarely turns propitiously."

Winston stubbornly sank lower in his seat. "I deserve 'nother chance."

Heathercote slung his arms over the back of his chair. "Well, West? What say you? Shall we let him stay and wager away everything he's got?"

Lounging in his seat, the Marquess of Westmorland looked up in irritation. "Really ought to go, Winsmore."

"Wins-less, more like," snickered Marlow.

Winston sat up straighter in his seat. "Please, my lord."

"Oh, let him ruin himself," muttered Forester, shuffling his cards restlessly.

The marquess lifted one shoulder. "Damned if I care."

"Sir Charles," said Dashwood evenly, "do not wager what you cannot afford to lose."

Winston scooped up the scribbled paper and added a line, signing his name with a flourish. "I won't, sir."

But he did. Within four hands, he'd won a bit and then lost it all—including the deed. Suddenly he did not look so belligerent or so stubborn. He looked young and quite literally green, staring at the winning hand, lying on the table.

"Should have listened," said the unsympathetic Heathercote. "Should have left."

Winston puffed up furiously. "Should have known better than to play with the likes of you!"

"Di'n't y'know that before you sa' down?" Marlow's words slurred together. "Stupid bloody fool!"

"That's my home!"

"And you risked it at loo!" Heath made a derisive noise. "Idiot."

Winston was the color of beets. "Don't call me that."

Sackville raised one brow. "No? 'S not *your* home anymore." He reached out and plucked the scrawled paper from the pile of markers and examined it, although his eyes never quite managed to focus on it. "It 'pears to be West's."

West's friends howled with laughter. "He doesn't need it," cried Winston. He made a convulsive grab for the paper before his lone remaining friend caught his arm. "He's got a dozen houses!"

"Set it up as a brothel, West," suggested Forester. "And give all your mates discounted fees."

"Free!" yelped Marlow with a wheezing laugh.

Winston drew a furious breath, but instead of continuing the fight he turned and rushed from the room, rather unsteadily; he wrestled with the door, and then almost tripped on his way out, causing more howls of laughter from the table. His friend helped him back onto his feet before the door closed on them both.

"Who invited him?" asked Heathercote in disdain.

"Marlow."

"Ballocks," mumbled Marlow, putting his head down on the table. "Never did. Was Forester."

Forester made a rude gesture. "I vouched for the other man, Farley."

"Your friends are all bad *ton*," said Sackville.

Forester's face tightened. He rose and swung

his wineglass into the air in a toast, spilling some. "Thank you all for a most exciting evening, gentlemen." Pointedly he bowed only to Viscount Heathercote and Lord Westmorland. Sackville repaid him with a rude gesture at Forester's back.

Heathercote protested, but Forester waved him off and left. With Marlow asleep on the table and Sackville still giggling drunkenly to himself, West placed his hands on the table, hesitated as if gathering strength, then heaved himself to his feet. "The carriages, Dashwood."

Stone-faced, the owner left. West—the Marquess of Westmorland—surveyed the table. "Did I win the last?"

"Aye," said Heathercote with a wide yawn.

"Credit it all, Forbes," said the marquess. "God above, I'm tired."

As expressionless as his employer, the manager stepped forward. With an air of distaste, he picked up the deed promise and held it out. "I cannot credit this, my lord."

West stared at it. "Damn. Right." He stuffed it into the pocket of his jacket and staggered out into the morning sunlight with Heathercote, never guessing the trouble that wagered deed was about to cause him.

Chapter 2

❦

Georgiana Lucas was having an absolutely splendid visit in the Derbyshire countryside when the letter arrived. That simple page of folded paper would, unwittingly and unintentionally, disturb the equilibrium of her life and send it veering wildly off course.

Of course, she did not know that at the time.

It came while they were at the breakfast table. Georgiana was idling over her tea, savoring the freedom to do so since her rather starchy chaperone, Lady Sidlow, was still in London while she rusticated in Maryfield. Her hostess and dear friend from school, Kitty, now Lady Winston, was cuddling her baby at the head of the table, rapt with adoration for little Annabel, six months old this day. Geneva, Kitty's sister-in-law, was reading aloud the amusing bits from a local parish newspaper, giggling over the tale of Mr. Pott's pigs, who had got loose in the lane and caused an uproar. The dowager Lady Winston, Geneva's mother but called Mother by all the family, was listening to her daughter while she went over the menu for that night's dinner, when the local vicar and his family were to dine with them.

Mr. Williams, the butler, brought in the post. "From Sir Charles," he said to Kitty.

"Oh!" With a pleased smile, Kitty laid the baby in the cradle at her feet. She took the letter and broke the seal.

Georgiana let Geneva pour her another cup of tea. The windows were open, and the breeze carried in the ripe, lush scent of summer and the faint buzzing of bees in the garden. It looked to be another perfect day. Georgiana considered taking a long walk, or perhaps a ride. Country life was inferior to city life in many ways, but not in the exercise opportunities available.

A clatter broke her thoughts. Kitty had dropped her teaspoon and sat bolt upright. "What is it?" Georgiana said in concern.

Kitty held the letter in a white-knuckled grip. "Charles," she said tensely.

Geneva fell silent. "What has happened to Charles?" asked Mother Winston in mild worry.

"Something dreadful." Kitty looked up, her brows drawn. *"My dearest wife,"* she read aloud. *"I do not wish to alarm you, but I write to you in great urgency and turmoil. I have had the terrible misfortune of falling in with—"* Here she broke off, her eyes dark and dismayed.

"Is he dead?" cried Geneva.

"He could hardly write a letter if he were dead," said Georgiana. She reached down to soothe the baby, who had begun whimpering at Geneva's outburst. "Go on, Kitty. What has happened?"

"He's not dead." Kitty put down the letter and stared out the window.

"Do tell us, my dear," urged Mother Winston. "Was he robbed? Is he injured? I have heard the streets of London are not safe."

Kitty didn't reply, but she took up the letter again and read on. "*I have had the terrible misfortune of falling in with some very sharp fellows, and I suffered a terrible loss at their hands, to my pride, and my dignity.*"

"Someone beat him!" cried Geneva. "Was it a boxing match?"

Kitty's face was inscrutable. "I don't think so. He writes further: *The chief scoundrel who tricked me is Lord Westmorland, and I fear he may present himself at Osbourne House. If he should arrive on your doorstep, my beloved, do not let him in. He will see us all ruined.*"

Geneva gasped. Mother Winston's mouth sagged open in shock. "What?"

Kitty flipped to the second page of the letter. "He says he is trying to prevent disaster from falling on us, and will write more later. The rest merely repeats that we must not admit Lord Westmorland or receive him at all."

"They must have fought a duel!" burst out Geneva.

"Hush," scolded her mother. "Charles would never be so rash."

"Even if he did fight a duel, he's well enough to write letters, which is a very good sign," Georgiana pointed out. "And if he were injured, he would send for Kitty immediately."

"Why on earth would Westmorland come here if he had a quarrel with Charles?" Kitty asked, almost to herself. She turned over the letter again. "Charles said he was tricked . . ."

"Perhaps a business arrangement," suggested Mother Winston. "Charles can be so trusting, I have often worried he would be preyed upon. His father worried, too."

"But what business could he have with a marquess?" Kitty frowned, one finger against her lips. "Surely he would have mentioned it. And if the marquess did something unethical, Mr. Jackson would put a stop to it." Mr. Jackson had been Kitty's family solicitor for many years, and had followed her to the Winstons on her marriage.

"I doubt the marquess has the slightest idea how to transact business of any kind," said Georgiana with a snort. "Everyone knows his father, the Duke of Rowland, manages everything."

Everyone looked at her. "Of course," said Kitty in surprise. "You must know Lord Westmorland! You've been in London these three years now."

Still patting the fretting baby, Georgiana made a face. "I don't know Westmorland himself. But I know *of* him."

They moved in the same society, after all, where it was virtually impossible not to know something about everyone else, let alone someone like the Marquess of Westmorland. Her chaperone, Lady Sidlow, had an encyclopedic knowledge of every unmarried gentleman in London, and was prone to discussing them with the avid interest of a sportsman discussing horses at Ascot.

Superficially, Georgiana could have readily answered Kitty's question. The marquess was tall and handsome, fit, and lethally charming when he wished to be. He had dark hair and glinting hazel eyes that made ladies swoon. He was heir to the Duke of Rowland, and as such would inherit one of the oldest and richest titles in all of England— not that he didn't have a large income and an estate of his own already. Superficially, Westmorland was one of the most eligible men in England, and Lady Sidlow had mentioned more than once that it was very disappointing of Georgiana to promise to wed Lord Sterling, a mere viscount, when men like Westmorland were strolling freely around, almost flaunting their bachelor status.

But Georgiana also knew something of his nature, and that was why she despised him.

"What sort of man is he?" Kitty asked, her keen gaze fixed on Georgiana. "A scoundrel?"

"Is he a cheat?" Geneva demanded.

"He sounds very dishonorable, if he would trick Charles so cruelly!" declared Mother Winston.

The Marquess of Westmorland was worse, as far as Georgiana was concerned. "I would be the last person to defend his honor."

Mother Winston's eyes rounded. "What did he do?" asked Geneva, now avidly interested.

Georgiana stirred her tea. She did not have a high opinion of the marquess, but for a purely personal reason. For a moment her conscience rebelled a little; just because she disliked him . . . intensely . . . didn't mean she should blacken his name to everyone in Derbyshire.

Then she recalled what Charles's letter had said. Westmorland had tricked him, and might be about to arrive on Kitty's doorstep—why would he do that? Charles was clearly terrified of what might happen if he did. Whatever had happened with Charles, if the marquess thought to punish Kitty and her darling child in any way, or Geneva and her mother, Georgiana was not going to stand by and let him.

"He's a notorious rogue." Nothing she could tell Kitty was worse than what she'd hear in London anyway. "He runs with a very disreputable crowd— Viscount Heathercote, and Lord Marlow, and even the very shocking Mr. Clifton. You remember him, Kitty, the gentleman who nearly broke his neck climbing the spire of St. Martin's."

"Oh my," breathed Geneva.

"How would Charles have fallen in with such a man?" fretted Mother Winston.

"It must have been a lark, and not Charles's fault at all. The marquess is quite wild," Georgiana went on. "He and his friends are in the gossip papers all the time for some prank or another. They're known for playing pranks, as a matter of fact, including putting one fellow into a boat while he was utterly foxed and sending him sailing off down the Thames. They thought it was a grand joke, even though he didn't wake up until his boat hit a pier in Greenwich. At any moment he might have fallen out and drowned."

"Oh, and they might have played a prank on Charles?" Geneva's face lit up, at once intrigued and horrified by the idea. "How dreadful that would be! Poor Charles!"

"He doesn't sound at all like Charles's usual companions," said Kitty. "But why do *you* dislike him, Georgiana?" She asked it with a look that said she knew there must be more to the story than wild, roguish behavior—which might, after all, fairly describe any number of London gentlemen whom Georgiana found charming and entertaining.

"I am trying to be discreet," Georgiana said in mock indignation.

"Really?" murmured Kitty wryly.

"Please don't be!" cried Geneva, earning a stern look from Mother Winston.

Georgiana took a sip of tea. "Well, if you insist on hearing more . . ."

"Oh yes!" Geneva leaned so far forward she almost fell off her chair.

"Geneva," said her mother in reproof.

"He may be on his way here to intimidate and alarm us," returned Geneva without blinking an eye. "I think we ought to know the worst."

Mother Winston pursed her lips. "Nevertheless, it isn't decent to look so *eager*." Geneva grinned, and even Kitty choked on a laugh.

"Westmorland *is* a scoundrel," said Georgiana, abandoning all discretion. "He's ill-mannered and mean-spirited. He and his useless friend Lord Heathercote amuse each other with spiteful little comments about other people, and they don't care who overhears them. At a soiree this spring, they stood off from the rest of the guests, looking down their noses at everyone, and mocked everything from the food to the decor. He called Joanna Hotchkiss a simpleton. He suggested Lady Telford was a poor hostess, and called her decorations headache-inducing." She paused, hating that she cared at all what a drunken rake thought of her. "He said I was nothing more than a silly, shallow flirt who reveled in teasing men." Although he'd said it in more vulgar terms.

Kitty's mouth fell open. Geneva's eyes flashed. "You, silly? How dare he!"

"Very rude!" said Mother Winston indignantly. "Abominable man!"

"He's rude and abominable, and interested solely in himself," she agreed. "Quite malicious, in my opinion."

"I hate him," declared Geneva.

"So do I," murmured Georgiana.

"And now he's abused our dear Charles." Mother Winston looked to Kitty. "What shall we do, my dear?"

"For the moment, there's nothing we can do." Poised once more, Kitty folded the letter. "How odd that Charles thinks Westmorland might come here. Why on earth would he?"

"To gloat, no doubt!" Geneva looked at her mother. "We would not be required to receive him, would we, Mother?"

"Certainly not!" Mother Winston rose to her feet, a militant look in her eye. "And neither will anyone in Maryfield. I shall warn everyone, especially Mrs. Tapp at the Bull and Dog. Not only will this wretch not be welcome here, he shan't find a room in our town, either."

"I'll help!" Geneva went with her, proposing a dozen wild ideas about how they could deter and snub the marquess.

In the silence of their wake, Georgiana looked at Kitty. "What else does Charles say?" she ventured to ask.

"Not much." Kitty's gaze fell on the letter, brooding and pensive. "That's what worries me."

"I confess I can't see them crossing paths," said

Georgiana frankly. "Westmorland is a very different sort than Charles. Whatever it was between them, Westmorland may not have noticed or cared, regardless of what Charles fears."

"We both know there is one place they might meet." Kitty pressed her fingertips to her temples as if they hurt. "Charles enjoys cards more than he ought to."

Georgiana had forgotten that. Charles wasn't the most interesting person; handsome without being arresting, amiable without being engaging. It was entirely possible to spend an evening with him and not recall a single word he'd said the next day. It had been a bit of a surprise when Kitty married him, but he was a baronet and eligible enough. Kitty had always been a forceful personality, and Georgiana supposed she'd wanted a husband who would give way to her. Kitty would hardly be the first woman to feel so, and as she'd brought a sizable fortune to her less wealthy husband, perhaps she felt entitled to have the upper hand in her marriage. She certainly had more sense than Charles.

But Georgiana wasn't about to say any of that aloud. She busied herself adjusting the baby's blanket.

"Tell me the truth. Is Westmorland a gambler?" There was tension in Kitty's question.

Georgiana smoothed Annabel's soft, fair hair. "Well, yes. I believe he is." She didn't precisely know Westmorland's habits, but several of his mates were notorious for scandalously extravagant wagers and parties. It would be shocking if he weren't the same, given how much he was seen with them.

A fierce frown touched Kitty's brow. "I worry

about that. Charles has sometimes said the stakes at our neighbors' parties here in Maryfield are so low as to make any game dull. I hope he would be too clever to get drawn into a table with men like that, but if the marquess joined a table where he was playing . . ."

Georgiana thought it very doubtful that the Marquess of Westmorland would want to join any table where Charles Winston was already playing. More likely it would be the other way around. Westmorland, with the wealth of Rowland behind him, could afford far higher and more exciting stakes than Charles could.

He also preferred gaudier, flashier company, the dashing crème de la crème of London rogues, rakes, and ne'er-do-wells. Charles Winston, simple baronet of Derbyshire, would never be dashing or outrageous enough for the jaded marquess. It really was astonishing that they'd met in the first place.

But it wasn't shocking at all that Charles hadn't come out of the encounter well.

"No matter what happened, I don't doubt for a moment that Westmorland was at fault," Georgiana said breezily. "He's a thoroughgoing scoundrel, but I'm equally certain he's forgotten all about . . . whatever it was by now. Why, he must have gone on at least two or three drunken benders since he could have met Charles."

Kitty's jaw set, her mood unchanged. "Charles mentioned suffering a loss at his hands. Not to his person, but to his dignity. It must be gambling."

Probably.

"And it's very disturbing that he thinks the man might come here," Kitty finished slowly.

Georgiana glanced at her uncertainly, but the baby began to fret louder, then to cry in earnest. Kitty's attention switched to her infant daughter. She took the child and settled her against her shoulder, patting the tiny girl until she calmed down.

"You mustn't worry about it," Georgiana tried to assure her. "Even if Westmorland has the unspeakable nerve to come here, we shall bar the door and lock him out in the rain. Pelt him with stale dinner rolls and insult his tailor. That sort of thing sends any rake worth his debauched reputation howling back to London, you know."

Kitty quirked a brow, her expression easing. "Of course you would think nothing of locking the door against a marquess."

"Against that one, I would not," Georgiana agreed with a cheeky grin. "In fact, I would enjoy it."

Finally her friend laughed. "I don't doubt it." She pressed her cheek to the baby's downy head. "But still I hope he does not come."

"Kitty," said Georgiana honestly, "I cannot imagine that he would."

Chapter 3

❦

THE HARBINGER OF the apocalypse would be a lawyer.

Robert Churchill-Gray, Marquess of Westmorland, was thoroughly convinced of this. Even more, he suspected that lawyer would be his father's solicitor, Sir Algernon Sneed, who had invaded not just his house but his dressing room. And Sneed was in the dressing room only because West's valet, Hobbes, had thrown himself in the bedroom doorway and threatened bloodshed if the solicitor advanced.

He was grateful to Hobbes for that, as small a mercy as it might have been. He was still rousted from bed and forced to sit through a painful dressing-down from his mother, delivered in Sir Algernon's cool, polished voice that stripped the passion from the duchess's words but not the import. She had heard rumors of some of his latest activities and was—to put it mildly—not pleased.

For his part, Rob barely remembered the night of debauchery that had set off his mother's ire. It had been his birthday—he remembered that well enough—and there had been a raucous celebration, plotted and carried off in high style by Heathercote. He remembered his friends, wine, excellent food, brandy, women, more wine, gambling . . . They might have sung "God Save the King" while flashing their arses at Carleton House.

Unfortunately, it was something he did not remember with any clarity that had brought Sir Algernon to his door, courtesy of some gossipy friend of his mother's writing a scandalized, and quite probably exaggerated, account to Her Grace.

"I trust you will do whatever is necessary to rectify this appalling situation," read Sir Algernon, his wire-rimmed spectacles perched on the end of his nose. *"Posthaste. I should hate to have to send your father to London to speak some sense to you, and he would be very grieved to do it, as the fishing at Salmsbury has been excellent of late."*

"That's enough. I grasp her meaning." Rob put out his hand for the letter. The moment his mother threatened to send his father, he was doomed. The Duke of Rowland was generally an amiable, affable fellow, but when his temper was roused—and it would be, by missing quality fishing—woe betide the man who got in his way, including and especially his son and heir.

Sir Algernon handed it over. "If I can be of any assistance in the matter, my lord, I would be delighted to do so."

And no doubt report it in great detail to my mother, thought Rob. "Of course."

The lawyer remained in his chair. "May I inquire how you plan to proceed, sir?"

Rob peered at him. He could almost feel his brain

sloshing gently from side to side in brandy from the night before. Another of Heathercote's ideas, last night. They'd gone to the opera with Forester and some of his mates, who could apparently drink their weight in brandy. One had to keep up, of course. If he were less tired or less drunk, he might have made a more intelligent reply to Sneed, but as it was, he could only manage to say, "I'll work it out."

Sneed was not impressed. "My lord, this is a matter of property. It cannot be papered over with a handshake and an apology."

"No?" Rob ground the heel of one hand into his eye. "Ballocks, that was my entire plan."

"Was it really?" asked Sneed dryly.

Rob snorted. "Of course not. I don't even recall this Winslow fellow—"

"Winston."

"—and I do not recall winning any deed from him, and most especially I do not recall, in any degree, telling him I would commit immoral acts in his house." That had been what set off his mother the most, he knew; someone had told her he'd not only swindled this poor Winslow person of house and home, but declared that he meant to set up a brothel on the premises.

Since the house in question was reportedly located in Derbyshire, Rob couldn't imagine wanting it, let alone going to see it. As for the brothel, who would visit a brothel in Derbyshire? It might as well be in China.

Sir Algernon removed his spectacles. "I understand Sir Charles Winston is a young man, and this property is his sole holding. He must be mired in regret and anxiety about this affair. May I suggest, if you do not recall winning this property, that you approach him about giving it back?"

Rob could not remember the slightest thing about Charles Winston. That didn't stop him from hating the fellow, though, for being so stupid as to wager his house and then so careless as to lose the bloody thing. Now Rob would have to do something, to placate his mother if for no other reason. "Mired in regret, my arse. He's gone about blackening my name, Sneed, telling people I cheated him and stole his house, and you think *I* should apologize and beg him to take it back?"

"It would be the most discreet solution to the issue."

Rob let out a crack of laughter, which made his head ring. "Would it? Winslow has painted me a cheat and a scoundrel before all of London to the point where my mother heard of it all the way in Lancashire. I don't take that sort of thing lightly."

"My lord," said Sneed severely, "I do not advise retaliation."

"Duly noted," replied Rob. "Fortunately for all, you are not my solicitor."

"His Grace your father would agree with me," warned Sneed.

Rob held up one finger. "We do not know that. Firstly, because this letter is from my mother, not His Grace. We both know there is a chance His Grace hasn't heard a word of this." Rowland was generally indifferent to gossip, even if his wife was not. "Secondly, she only instructs me to rectify matters. I assure you, I have no intention of keeping Winslow's house," he added as the solicitor drew a disapproving breath. "But I'll be damned if I'll let him slander me before the *ton* and then beg him to take back his property like a whipped dog. If he couldn't stand to lose it, he ought not to have wagered the bloody thing."

"I quite agree, my lord," said Sir Algernon, "however—"

"I'll deal with it." Rob got to his feet, keeping his balance with some difficulty. "If you are under orders to report to Her Grace, you may assure her that I will devote my entire attention to the matter."

The solicitor pinched his lips together. He was not pleased but knew his place. "Of course, my lord. If I can be of assistance—"

"Yes, yes." Rob waved one hand, already turning back toward his bedroom. "Good day, Sir Algernon."

Once on the other side of the door, though, he toppled face-first into bed. The temptation to go back to sleep was overwhelming, but the thought of his father arriving was a sobering one. His mother did not bluff; she would drag the duke back to London, and then Rob would be in the fire. God almighty. What was he going to do now?

After some thought, he decided there were three questions. One, had he actually won a property? That ought to be relatively easy to verify. There should be a note or the deed itself somewhere in his belongings. If none turned up, why, he could claim the whole thing was a tissue of lies and there was nothing more to be done about it.

Two, had this Winslow fellow really made those slanderous charges against him? Again, an easy thing to discover. His friends would be sure to know, and eager to help plot his revenge.

And third, presuming the answers to the first two questions were both yes, how could he exact the most fitting vengeance upon the man? Because Rob was no saint, but neither was he a cheat, and he wasn't about to be called one without protest.

He lurched out of bed again, cursing as his head threatened to explode, and staggered to the bell rope and pulled hard. He was still clutching his temples when Hobbes appeared. "Why was Sneed admitted?" he demanded. "I gave firm orders about visitors . . ."

"It was an impossible choice, my lord. Defy your orders, or refuse a man from Her Grace."

"I ought to sack you on the spot."

"Indeed," murmured Hobbes. "Mr. Bigby was in favor of admitting him when he first called, at half eight this morning."

God almighty. He'd have to speak to the butler about that. Rob scowled at his valet as he poured water into the basin. "Don't ever suggest that again."

"No, sir. It did require some effort to persuade him to return at ten." Hobbes stood by with the towel while Rob took a deep breath and plunged his throbbing face into the cold water. It wasn't the best remedy, but these were desperate times.

"Send for Tipton," he said when he'd pulled his dripping head from the basin. "I want him within the hour."

"Yes, my lord."

"And Heathercote," he added. If he had to be awake and thinking about his respectability, Heath could damned well help him.

"Yes, my lord."

An hour later, Rob sat at his dining table eyeing his cook's cure for drunkenness. A veritable tureen of weak tea, a cup of strong coffee, and a boiled egg sat before him, lined up in the proper order. His head still felt like it was inside a drum, so he grimly picked up the tea.

"You summoned me?" drawled Heath, strolling into the room. Only the slightest wobble in his gait gave away that he had spent the previous night as Rob had done, drinking himself blue.

"You've got me into a load of trouble." He drained the first cup of tea. The footman silently stepped up and poured another. "Go on," he told the servant, who bowed and left the room. "Did we wager houses the other night?"

"The devil if I know," said Heath, staring at the cure in disgust.

"Did you win a house?"

"No." He thought for a moment. "There's a strange barouche in my mews, though. Not quite certain where it came from."

Rob groaned. "Trade me—the barouche for the house."

"Not on your life." Heath paused, an arrested look on his face. "Wait . . . Yes, now I recall. At the Vega Club. You won Winston's house. Marlow thought you might set it up as a brothel." He laughed.

Rob cursed and drank off another cup of the tea. It wasn't helping his stomach, but his head was starting to clear. "I don't want a brothel any more than I want a house."

Heath laughed again, and Rob threw a spoon at him. Too late he realized the spoon might have been used to stir some sugar into the vile tea. It must be made of rotten vegetables and old hay from the stable, steeped through a footman's dirty stocking.

"My mother says I must make things right," he said, staring into yet another cup. Two more to go, by his calculations.

Heath stopped laughing at once. "God above. How did she find out about it?"

"Gossip." He lifted the tea to his lips. "Apparently I came off as quite the callous wastrel in the telling, and now I have to mend matters."

Heath sat as Rob choked down the tea. "That will cause trouble, West."

He snorted. "Already has."

"No, no." Heath leaned forward, his voice dropping. "My uncle has been quite pleased with our progress with Forester. He wouldn't be happy if you got distracted by some silly gossip."

Rob scowled. He did not want to disappoint Lord Beresford, Heath's uncle. He'd given the two of them a clandestine assignment: monitor Frederick Forester, a merchant out of Liverpool. Forester's shipping firm was violating an act of Parliament, but Beresford had been frustrated in all his attempts to put a stop to it. No matter how many times Forester's ships were caught with contraband, they always managed to wiggle off the hook. Beresford believed Forester had allies in the British government. He'd put his nephew on the case, to see if more subtle means could trip up the man, and Heath had asked Rob to help.

Now that the wars were over, it was about as dashing a task as a young man could find, playing a spy of sorts. It fit well with his eventual, though vague, intention of doing something in government. And all he had to do was be a rake of the first order. Rob hadn't needed to be asked twice.

"Surely Her Grace will get over her upset?" Heath pressed.

"You've never met my mother. If I must choose between her displeasure and Beresford's . . . make my apologies to your uncle." He poured more tea, wanting it done with. "The solicitor said I should give the deed back to Winslow, even though he was fool enough to lose it."

"Give it back!" Heath reared back in amazement. "It's a debt of honor!"

"Heath," said Rob with complete honesty, "I do not want the bloody house. The sooner I get rid of it, the sooner we can continue with Forester." He bolted down the last cup of tea.

"Mr. Tipton, my lord," announced the butler, not a moment too soon. The solicitor, this time his own, appeared in the doorway, and Rob waved him to a chair.

"I have a problem," he said, clutching the cup of coffee as if it were salvation. After the tea, it probably was. "It seems I have acquired the deed to a house."

"Indeed, my lord," said Tipton without blinking.

"I don't want it." He took a cautious sip of coffee and exhaled in pleasure at the taste of it. "I need to return it to the man who lost it."

Tipton's eyebrow quirked, but he only repeated, "Indeed, my lord."

Rob sipped more coffee, beginning to feel restored. "How do I do that?"

"Well." Tipton shifted in his seat and cleared his throat. "I presume this acquisition was made at the gaming tables." Rob nodded once. Tipton spread his hands. "Then it ought to be a simple act. One might wish to add a stern word about wagering valuable property, of course."

"So I can give it back to him?"

Tipton nodded. "I don't see why not."

"That's brilliant. Precisely what I needed to know." He paused, glancing at Heath, who was watching with a mixture of disbelief and dismay. "Simply handing it back makes it rather easy on the fool who lost it, don't you think?"

"Aye," muttered Heathercote.

"Especially a fool who's gone about London telling people I defrauded him of it." Rob scowled at that memory.

Tipton's eyebrows shot up. "Fraud, my lord?"

"The devil he has," exclaimed Heathercote.

"He has." Winslow deserved to squirm until he apologized and retracted his slanderous charges publicly.

"I wouldn't give him a stained handkerchief," Heath was saying. "You can't appease that sort of thing!"

"No." He stared into the coffee. That damned cure might actually work; he felt more like himself than he had in days. "I won't give it back to *him*. The idiot will probably just wager it away again. No . . . I'll give it to his family and make them aware of what he's up to." If they were anything like his own family, Winslow would suffer far more, for far longer, if his wife or mother knew what he'd done. Rob did not want that house, but he did want to make the man writhe and agonize over his actions.

Heath burst into laughter. "Oh, that's too good! West, you're positively fiendish."

He smiled over his coffee. "Tipton, find out where this Winslow lives."

AND THAT WAS HOW Rob found himself rattling northward the next day toward the hamlet of Maryfield in Derbyshire, looking forward to giving Sir Charles Winston—not Winslow—a very memorable lesson.

Tipton had tracked down Winston's solicitor and demanded the actual deed to the house, using the scribbled note Hobbes had located in the pocket of his jacket as leverage. Part of Rob had hoped the lawyer would refuse to give it, which would have let him off the hook. But, somewhat disappointingly, the lawyer had meekly handed it over.

Heath had refused to come, despite enjoying the prospect of the revenge Rob would have. Marlow pleaded family obligations. Clifton couldn't even be found, and Sackville said he'd rather take holy orders than go.

Piqued, Rob decided he did not need his friends' company; he could travel faster without them anyway. By a happy coincidence, Maryfield was less than fifty miles from Salmsbury Abbey, the Rowland seat in Lancashire. With only a small detour he could return to London by way of Salmsbury. Like his father, he also enjoyed a spot of good fishing, and after such a journey, he'd have earned it.

It would also prove to his mother how extremely attentive he'd been to her wishes, and prevent her from sending the duke after him. Rob would drive to Scotland and back in a poultry wagon to avoid facing his father in a temper.

As the miles passed, however, the diabolical pleasure of this plan began to wear thin. It was three days' journey to Derbyshire, and even though his travel coach was outfitted with every luxury, Rob had never wanted to spend three days inside any coach.

Dust drifted in the windows and the sun beat through the shade. He cursed the narrow confines of the coach. He wished for his horse, even though he'd never subject his favorite gelding to this long a trip. The road was rutted, jolting him about so hard his head banged on the cushioned wall. This was a fiendishly brilliant idea, but it had clearly rebounded and was now causing *him* enormous inconvenience.

By the morning of the third day, when there remained only twenty-some miles to go, he took one look at his carriage, which seemed to have shrunk in every dimension since he left town, and decided to risk a hired mount. The stable master led out a strong-looking animal, and he accepted it at once.

The sun still blazed, but at least he was out in the open air. He threw some necessities into the saddlebags, and told his coachman and valet to take lodging at Macclesfield, the nearest town of any significance. He expected to spend a few days in Maryfield, then continue on to Salmsbury Abbey.

It was afternoon when he reached the hamlet, barely a village at all. A brief stop at an inn called the Bull and Dog to water the horse confirmed he was nearly there; Osbourne House was only three miles distant.

He began to think he'd be doing Winston a favor by keeping this house. Not only was it leagues away from anything resembling civilization, the locals were rude and lazy. His query about the best road to take had been met with suspicion and hostility. They demanded to know who he was, and when Rob informed them, there was none of the usual eruption of solicitude, and no offers of guidance.

He was not used to that. Normally his title flattened everything in its path, spurring even the laziest lout into action. This time they all but turned up their noses. He discarded his plan to spend a few days here recuperating from the journey, rusticating with some potent country ale. He would spend the night and be on his way, even if he had to hire the sorriest nag in Derbyshire.

The road to Osbourne was a lonely stretch of narrow, sunken lane, bordered by hedgerows on one side and a wide muddy ditch in front of open meadow on the other. The sun seemed to have got hotter since he left the village. He stopped at a signpost and lingered a moment in the shade of a gnarled hawthorn to doff his hat and wipe his brow. It had been a long time since he'd been outside so much. He ought to have kept the carriage. His throat itched for a mug of ale, or a good glass of claret.

Heath had been right, damn him. This was an idiotic idea. With a sigh he set the horse back in motion. Only a mile to go.

He paid little attention to the trio of riders who came up behind him. They passed at a smart trot, one after the other, only to stop twenty feet ahead of him.

"Where be you headed, Lordship?" asked one.

He halted his horse, belatedly realizing his isolation. He wasn't afraid of a fight, but it was three on one, bad odds in any circumstance, and once again he cursed his mates for abandoning him. "Hardly your concern."

The biggest one jumped down from his horse. "That's rude. Answer the question."

"I'm afraid we've not been introduced."

The third man chortled. "We will be, guv."

The big man reached for the bridle of the horse. At the last moment Rob turned the horse's head to avoid his grasp. The fellow glowered at him. The other two dismounted.

He had a pistol, but it was in the saddlebag. He hadn't thought he'd need it, so far from the main roads and city. He eyed the meadow to his left, trying to guess whether his horse could outrun them.

It was worth a try. Rob pulled the horse sharply left and put the spurs to him, but the ruffian was too quick; he had Rob's coattail in his hand, and he yanked, causing the horse to give a shrill whinny and bolt.

And with a bone-jarring crash, the marquess hit the hard-packed dirt of the lane.

Chapter 4

～～～～

GEORGIANA URGED HER horse across the field, relishing the chance to let the animal run. In London ladies were expected to ride gentle mares and never venture past a trot, but Georgiana loved to go fast.

The weather was warm and clear, and it hadn't rained in a week so the ground was firm and dry. Geneva and her mother had gone visiting in the carriage. The baby had been fussy and unhappy all morning, and Kitty didn't want to leave her. That left Georgiana free to do as she pleased.

Adam, the groom, pulled up alongside her. She glanced at him in question, and he gave a nod and a grin. Yes, the horse could go faster. Georgiana touched the gelding's flank with her crop and leaned low over his neck as he shot forward, reveling in the rush of wind past her.

They streaked across the field, the horses taking soaring leaps over a low stone wall. *Good heavens, this is living*, she thought with glee. They tore up toward Maryfield, keeping well clear of the sunken lane that wound between the hedgerows. Finally they had to slow the horses, Georgiana doing so with a sigh. It would be wonderful to continue that way, at high speed, for an hour.

"A good run, my lady," said Adam admiringly.

"Ajax is a marvel!" She stroked her horse's neck as they turned back at a walk. "Would that I could take him with me to London."

Adam chuckled. "Sir Charles might not like that. Ajax is one of his favorites."

Georgiana shook her head in pretend despair. "Of course he is! How could he not be?"

The groom started to reply, then fell silent. He turned his head and gazed intently toward the road. "Lady Georgiana," he said quietly, "we need to make haste."

"Why?" Up ahead, a horse's frightened whinny sounded, making Ajax dance sideways into Adam's horse. "What is it?"

"Might be a spot of trouble," said Adam grimly. He flipped open a pocket on his saddle and drew out a pistol, proceeding to check it while keeping one eye on the road. He did the same for a second pistol, tucking the first back into the pocket.

Nervously Georgiana glanced that way, too. There were horses and people on the road. The road was so sunken she couldn't make them out clearly. "What is it? What's happening?"

"Robbery, most likely." Adam nudged his horse forward, blocking her view. "There's been a rash of it about lately. We ought to head back."

Maryfield was a small village, well off the turnpike. It wouldn't be travelers; it would probably be a local woman on her way to market, stopped and robbed of her coin. It had happened once to a teacher at Georgiana's school. The woman had been abused, spat upon, and relieved of a month's salary. She'd been taking it to her sister, who lived in the nearby town and was ill with four small children, and instead returned to the academy with blood on her face and a mortal terror of walking to town.

She rode around the groom. "Not yet."

"My lady," he protested, once again riding forward to put himself between her and the road. Another frantic neighing sounded from across the field. "It's not safe!"

"You have a pistol," she pointed out. "And it's far less safe for that poor victim."

"Don't go any closer," the groom pleaded. "Please, m'lady!"

Georgiana obeyed, but kept her eyes fixed on the road. There was shouting, and now more than one horse was whinnying. "Go look," she told Adam. "Please. If someone is harmed while we sat here, I could never live with myself."

He frowned. "My duty is to look over you, m'lady. Sir Charles will turn me off without a reference if I leave you defenseless."

"I shall explain to Sir Charles."

Stubbornly the groom stayed where he was. "No, ma'am. 'Tain't safe."

She hesitated, but then a horse burst over the embankment and took off across the field, riderless and clearly spooked. A shout came from the road, and then a man appeared running after the horse. He caught sight of Georgiana and the groom and stopped, then disappeared back into the road.

"Ah, saints, we're in it now," said Adam in despair. "Go catch that horse!" He spurred his own horse into a gallop, pistol in hand.

Georgiana suspected he'd told her to follow the horse because that would lead her away from the trouble in the road, but she obediently touched her crop to Ajax's flank and took off after the runaway. There came the sound of a single gunshot, hopefully Adam's, and then no more.

She caught the horse easily—he was spooked but tired—and spent a few minutes calming him before taking hold of his reins like a lead rope and heading back toward the spot of the robbery.

She approached hesitantly, but found only Adam in the road. "They run off when I took chase," he told her. He still held a pistol. "We should get home."

Beyond him a man lay facedown in the dirt. Georgiana muffled a gasp behind one hand. "Is he—? Did they—?"

Adam's eyes continued to swivel around, taking in the area. He spoke without looking toward the figure in the road. "They could come back. I'll send for a constable once we're safely back at Osbourne."

"Is he dead?" she finally managed to ask. The man in the road hadn't moved a muscle. Georgiana's stomach churned. He was dead, she knew it, and Adam wasn't looking because he knew it, too.

Then the man's hand twitched. A slight movement, but enough to indicate life. With a gasp of relief she flung herself off Ajax. "We have to take him with us," she said to Adam. "Help me get him across his horse." The runaway must be his; there were plump saddlebags over the horse's back, and the villains had let him go.

"We ought not to get involved," Adam insisted. "Those thieves might come back! He might even be one of them. I only startled them, ma'am, we must make haste—"

"And we will," she said firmly, "with him." She thrust the reins of the runaway at the groom, who took them with a ferocious scowl. "I cannot let a man bleed to death in the dirt."

There was quite a bit of blood, and she took a deep breath to keep her hands from shaking. The victim lay facedown, his hat gone and his coat torn. Blood ran over the side of his head, matting his long dark hair. Gingerly she touched his back, and felt the rise of his chest as he breathed. "Help me!" she ordered the groom, who still stood at a distance.

Grumbling, he came and took a hard look at the fellow. "This is a bad business, Lady Georgiana."

"It will be worse if we leave him." She seized the reins of the runaway horse and tied him to a sagging hawthorn branch. "We've got to take him back to Osbourne House." Town was over two miles away, while Osbourne House was less than one.

"I don't like this," muttered the groom. But he bent down and rolled the prone man over.

There was more blood down his front, running from his face to stain his collar and cravat, onto his waistcoat, which had been torn open. He'd been pummeled about the head, and his hair was plastered over his face in dark scarlet ropes. It was enough to make her stomach heave.

She tried not to look at the poor man as they heaved him to a sitting position, then Adam hauled him up facedown over the horse's back. He was a large man, tall and well built, and he weighed a ton. Georgiana pushed and shoved, helping as best she could. *What a lark*, she thought in dark humor; the first time she touched a man's thighs, he was beaten almost to death.

"Let's be off," said Adam, glancing up and down the road as if armed murderers might come racing toward them at any moment. He gave Georgiana a leg up onto Ajax's back before leaping into his own saddle and pulling the runaway horse, with its battered, bleeding burden, behind him.

Georgiana watched that inert figure all the way back to Osbourne House. One arm dangled limply toward the ground; the other must be caught beneath him. The rocking of the horse set the loose arm swaying plaintively, as if he were trying to summon help. Which of course he was not doing; he might in fact be slipping the rest of the way into death. *Please don't die*, she silently begged. Georgiana had seen her father die, and she did not want to repeat the experience ever again. By the time they reached the graceful curved drive of Osbourne House, she felt almost personally responsible for this poor man, clinging to life and helplessly dependent on her.

Williams, the butler, met them with an expression of incredulity. "What is this, Adam?"

"We came upon a terrifying scene." Georgiana flung herself out of the saddle and ran to the unconscious figure. A light touch on his back reassured her he was still breathing. "We must get him into bed and send for a doctor at once."

"My lady." The butler gazed at her in shock.

"He was attacked by villains in the road! He needs help!"

"Of course, but . . ." The butler's face broke in relief as Kitty came out of the house. "Lady Winston."

"What's happened?" Kitty demanded, rushing forward.

"We were riding and saw an altercation from a distance. Adam gallantly rode in to break it up, but not before they'd beaten this poor man half to death." To Georgiana's eyes, it seemed like his breathing had slowed. She shuddered; she did not want him to die right here on the front steps of Kitty's home.

Kitty glanced sharply at Adam. "Are you certain he wasn't one of the villains?"

The groom hesitated, but the figure hanging limply over the saddle began to slide. With an exclamation, Adam lunged forward and caught the wounded man before he could fall headfirst onto the gravel, though only enough to break his fall.

The poor fellow landed on his back, his arms flopping wide and his head resting at a drunken tilt to his shoulders. Some of the blood must have been wiped off by the saddle or the horse's side, and this time Georgiana could make out his features, despite the swelling beginning in earnest on one side of his face.

She took one look at his face and gave a strangled scream.

Kitty, who had bent down to look at him, jerked upright. "What?" she cried. "What is it?"

Georgiana could only look at her, speechless. Oh God.

Kitty, she remembered out of the blue, had a ruthless streak in her. At school once, when another girl had mocked and snubbed her for her background, Kitty had taken the abuse calmly, then somehow managed to slit the soles of that girl's dancing shoes, causing her to slip and fall during dance lessons in a horribly embarrassing way. The girl had sprawled on the floor, howling that she'd turned her ankle, and Kitty had sat quietly at the side of the room plying her fan with the faintest of smiles on her lips. To her friends she was unwaveringly loyal and generous, but to anyone who crossed her . . .

Kitty stepped over the unconscious form and seized Georgiana's arms. "Are you going to faint? What is wrong?"

"I—I know who he is," she whispered numbly.

Kitty's eyes narrowed. "Do you? Who is he?"

He would die without their help. He might already be beyond saving, with all that blood dripping slowly out of him, but any chance of survival he had rested in their hands. In *her* hands. Georgiana's chest felt tight and she wavered on her feet. She wet her lips and squeezed handfuls of her skirt so tightly, her fingers cramped.

"It's Sterling," she choked out. "My fiancé."

Kitty's eyes went wide as the name registered. "Good heavens! Oh my dear—no wonder you're overwrought! Do not despair, we shall do everything we can for him." She gave Georgiana a brief, fierce hug before whirling to her servants. "Adam, fly to the doctor at once!" The groom vaulted back into his saddle and tore off. Kitty ran to the open door of the house. "We must get him inside! John, Angus, come at once!" she cried inside, and her two footmen came running. "Gently now," Kitty commanded. "Mrs. Hill! Turn back the bed in the green bedroom! Send Lucy to heat a large pot of water, and fetch some bandages—a great many bandages, Mrs. Hill! And my sewing kit—at once!"

The footmen carried the unconscious man by his shoulders and legs into the house. Kitty hurried before them, calling out instructions to her housekeeper and answering the anxious queries of her mother-in-law and Geneva as the drama reached the rest of the household.

Outside, alone for the moment, Georgiana started to put her face in her hands, only to recoil at the sight of her bloodstained fingers. There was so much blood—on him, on her, in a dark puddle out on the sunken road where they'd found him, now on the gravel drive of Osbourne House. With jerky motions she wiped her hands on her skirt, trying not to think of what she had just done.

It was to save a life, she told herself. She was right to have done that.

But the man she'd saved was not Viscount Sterling, her charming and beloved fiancé.

It was the Marquess of Westmorland, who had come to turn Kitty out of her house and home.

Chapter 5

⹨⹨⹨

THE TRAIL OF blood led through the hall and up the stairs, seeping into the carpet. Georgiana gripped the banister and slowly climbed the stairs, avoiding each splatter of red.

In the corridor outside the sickroom she stopped. The door was open, giving her a view of Kitty and her servants, scrambling over themselves to help the man who had come to destroy their lives.

A second letter from Charles had arrived just yesterday. Kitty hadn't shared this letter with Geneva or Mother Winston, but she'd showed it to Georgiana. More despondent than in the first, Charles had confessed to Kitty that he had been duped into putting up Osbourne House as collateral in a dispute with the marquess. The marquess subsequently demanded the deed, and Mr. Willis, the family solicitor in London, had foolishly handed it over before Charles could warn him not to do so. He assured his wife he meant to fight Westmorland's claim, based as it was on nothing but deceptions and fraud, but he reiterated that they must not admit or speak to the marquess if he should present himself in Derbyshire. In a dire aside, Charles added that the marquess had spoken of turning the house into a den of vice.

He assured Kitty this would never happen, but Kitty had been deadly, calmly furious. She vowed to defend her home and family with every means at her disposal. Georgiana hadn't repeated her joke about driving off the marquess by insulting his tailor; it was no longer as amusing. She saw the thick letters Kitty posted later in the day to Charles and to Mr. Jackson, her own solicitor, and she also saw the gleaming row of guns on the wall in the small back parlor.

There was no question Charles had done something stupid. Georgiana didn't know if the Malicious Marquess could legally claim the house, but it wouldn't matter if he showed up, deed in hand, and demanded that they vacate the premises, only to be shot by a vengeful Kitty.

Whatever idiocy Charles had committed, however, would be compounded by Georgiana's own.

She swallowed the lump of anxiety in her throat. She hated being put on the spot, especially a very stressful spot, and she had panicked when the injured man rolled over onto his back. Until then she'd felt it imperative to do everything possible to help the poor soul, beaten within an inch of his life and left for dead. But when she recognized the Marquess of Westmorland, her first instinct had been horror.

She hated him. Everyone at Osbourne House hated him—and rightly so, in her opinion. But if she told Kitty who he was, she feared her friend would refuse to help him. Beaten as he was, it would take very little to allow Westmorland to quietly bleed to death.

No one, not even the Malicious Marquess, deserved to be left in the dirt to bleed to death.

And as a result, she said he was someone Kitty would unquestionably help, someone who would unquestionably *deserve* her help.

When he woke up and revealed his real name, Kitty would be enraged. She would accuse Georgiana—rightly—of bringing a viper into her nest. She would almost surely throw her out, and never speak to her again. Georgiana's stomach twisted painfully at the thought.

Or what if he never woke up? What if he died here? Kitty thought he was Sterling; she would want to write to Lord Pelham, Sterling's father, and send his body to Pelham Park. Georgiana would have to tell her that, no, it was a marquess, and instead they would have to tell the Duke of Rowland his eldest son and heir was dead. One of the few things Georgiana knew about Rowland was how devoted he was to his family. If he thought Kitty had let his son die because of the deed . . .

Oh dear heavens. She felt dizzy. She might be ill. She turned to go to her own room, wanting to hide under the covers until she thought up a way out of this nightmare.

"Georgiana!" Kitty took her arm, and Georgiana started so badly she nearly fainted on the spot. Her friend's expression grew sympathetic and encouraging. "Come in," she said gently. "Don't despair. He looks much better now that we've cleaned away some of the blood, and Adam will bring the doctor as quickly as he is able."

"Oh no, I—I—I'm no good in a sickroom," Georgiana stuttered, resisting her friend's tug toward the door. Mounds of red-stained linen were already piled up on the floor. The marquess lay motionless on the bed. She did not want to see another man die.

"Of course," said Kitty at once. "You've had a dreadful shock. Go lie down and I'll fetch you when he wakes."

When he wakes. When he opened his mouth and said he was most certainly not Lord Sterling, but Lord Westmorland, coldhearted destroyer of family homes. Georgiana jolted forward. "No!" She forced a nervous smile. "I should be there when"—*if*—"he wakes."

Still, her feet dragged as she went into the room. The scent of blood was strong and sharp. Kitty said a quiet word to the two maids, who scooped up the soiled linens and left, closing the door quietly.

"Are you sure he won't die?" asked Georgiana, then wished the words back.

"Well, no one can be certain, but I swear to you we shall fight desperately for him to live." The door opened and one of the maids brought in a basin of water, which she set down beside the bed. "Let's clean him up before the doctor arrives."

She had got herself into this mess, and she would have to cope with it. Georgiana forced her feet to take her to the side of the bed. She touched the marquess's hand, lying limply on the mattress. A heavy signet ring gleamed on his finger. Why hadn't the thieves stolen it? It must be valuable. It also had a W carved deep into the gold, which was unlike anything Sterling would wear. With a covert glance at

Kitty, Georgiana twisted it off his finger and slipped it into her pocket.

The next half hour was almost unreal. Together with one of the footmen, they stripped the injured man of all but his buckskin breeches, which was small consolation to Georgiana. Lucy, the maid, took the clothes away, leaving her and Kitty to finish washing the blood from his face and torso.

"They beat him all over," Georgiana murmured, her hand hovering just above a giant bruise blooming on the side of his rib cage. As long as she didn't look at his face, her instinctive sympathy for anyone in this plight could drown out the guilt at what she'd done.

"But he doesn't seem to have any broken bones." Kitty washed and dried his arm with a gentleness that made Georgiana's stomach knot.

"How can you tell when he's unconscious?" Carefully she cleaned away the crust of blood over a scrape on his swelling knuckles. It could be from falling on the road, but she suspected it was from punching one of the thieves. There had been at least two of them, and maybe more. Any man, even one as tall and strong as Westmorland, would have been overwhelmed.

Kitty put her hands on her hips and surveyed him. "Nothing is at a bad angle. There is no obscene swelling. I grant you we won't know for sure until he wakes and can tell the doctor what hurts—"

Georgiana shuddered at that prospect, and Kitty mistook the cause. She rushed around the bed and flung her arm around Georgiana's shoulders. "Don't lose heart."

"It's just—it's just so . . ." Georgiana found to her dismay that her throat was clogged with tears. Not so much for Westmorland—it seemed incredible that he wouldn't be his usual rude self in a few days—but from fright. The reality of what she'd done was growing larger and larger in her mind. The marquess had been badly beaten, which meant that even if he had no broken bones or fatal wounds, he wouldn't be able to travel for some time. She pictured him waking up and announcing that he now owned Osbourne House and they must all leave immediately.

No. No, he could not do that. She steadied herself, unconsciously gripping his hand tighter. She would not allow him to do that. When he woke up, he would be in pain, disoriented, vulnerable. She would persuade him that Kitty had saved his life, and in return he mustn't do anything to harm her. If he had taken Charles's deed, he must return it immediately. Surely even the Malicious Marquess couldn't be so evil—or so stupid—as to turn on his benefactress.

And if he were, well, she knew where all his bruises were. A few careless swings of her elbow would persuade him. Her nerves began to recover as she considered how she might turn this around. All she had to do was ensure she was present when he woke.

"No," she said to Kitty, her voice calmer. She returned the embrace. "I shan't give up hope." They exchanged hesitant smiles.

"You didn't tell me Lord Sterling was so handsome," said Kitty, her tone growing warmer.

Georgiana avoided her gaze, turning away to dab at the marquess's scraped knuckles as if it required her entire concentration. "Of course I did. Pooh, Kitty, did you think I would marry an ugly man?"

Kitty laughed. "Of course not! I always knew you would have your pick of gentlemen. I only meant that your description of him left out a great deal."

"Did it?" She affected surprise. "I'm sure I told you what he looks like . . ."

"Please don't take this amiss, but you didn't do him justice." Kitty gazed at the unconscious man before them in open appreciation. Georgiana looked, too, in spite of herself. The marquess was tall and broad-shouldered, and had more muscles than any rakish scoundrel had a right to. "I suppose he's handsome beyond words when he smiles and you can see his dimples."

Good Lord. Georgiana had no idea if he even had dimples; she'd never seen him smile, at least not in her direction. "As long as he wakes up and smiles again, I shan't care if there are dimples or not," she said, silently begging Sterling's pardon for giving his dimples to another man.

"Of course!" Kitty straightened the bedclothes. "Forgive me, I didn't mean to make light of it when he's so injured—"

"I know."

Thankfully a servant knocked, and Kitty hurried to the door. Georgiana looked darkly at the man on the bed and blew a loose strand of hair away from her face. She'd better get used to lying about him.

"Williams sent up Lord Sterling's effects," said Kitty, returning. "He didn't bring much. I had his saddlebags put into your room, so they would be out of the way."

"Oh, he travels very lightly," lied Georgiana without hesitation. "I expect he thought only to make a brief visit to surprise me." A wave of longing swamped her. What wouldn't she give for that lie to be true, for Sterling to be here now, not beaten but with his charming smile in place. *Just thought I'd come see how desperately you've been missing me*, he would say, his dimples showing as he kissed her hand.

"Of course." Kitty caught sight of her face. "Georgiana, go rest. I can sit with him until the doctor arrives."

"No!" Georgiana grabbed the cloth and made a show of soaking it in the basin. "I'll stay with him."

"You're covered in blood," her hostess pointed out quietly.

She shook her head, sponging at a streak of red on Westmorland's shoulder. "I don't care. I'll change when the doctor comes to examine him." Kitty hesitated, and Georgiana stripped off her blood-streaked riding jacket and flung it aside. "I'm fine," she said firmly.

"All right." Kitty touched her arm. "I'll be close at hand if you need me."

"Thank you, Kitty," Georgiana said with honest fervor. "For everything." *Especially for not questioning me too closely.*

"Of course." Stained jacket in hand, Kitty left, closing the door behind her.

The silence seemed deafening. Georgiana took a deep breath and made herself look full into the marquess's face for the first time since he'd hit the gravel drive outside. As wrong as it was to stare at his very attractive naked chest, it felt even worse to gaze right at him as she told lie after lie about him.

Someone had taken a few hurried swipes at his nose and mouth, but the rest of his features were still spotted and streaked with blood. She wet the cloth and gently finished cleaning his face. It didn't change anything but he looked a step farther from death. Suddenly she wanted all the blood gone. It was too much, too violent, too *red*.

His hair was drying in stiff, dark spikes. She brought over the basin and awkwardly slid it under his head. The water went crimson in an instant as his long hair fanned out in it. Gritting her teeth against the thought of her hands being covered in blood again, she scrubbed it as best she could, flinching every time her fingers brushed his scalp and felt another gash.

It was wrong to do something so unspeakably intimate for a man she didn't know. Westmorland himself would be the most appalled, if he ever knew that a silly, empty-headed girl like her had saved his life and cleaned him up. For a few minutes she contemplated that. His jaw would drop, she expected, and his eyes would narrow, and he would say something scathing and belittling—perhaps that she was rubbish at it, or that a lady ought to have left it to a servant.

That crushed any dark pleasure she might have had at the thought of him being in her debt. She couldn't leave this—this *disgusting* job to a servant because Westmorland might wake at any moment and start babbling that he owned this house and they would all have to leave. But it was scraping her nerves to be this near him, and she thought she'd scream in fright and fall unconscious on the floor if he suddenly opened his eyes and asked what the devil she was doing to him.

"You had better wake up humbled and deeply grateful for all this," she whispered to him as she combed her fingers through his wet hair. "Or else I shall seriously consider pitching you back into the road."

Her patient made no reply. He lay so very, very still, his face slack. It was unnerving. She had never seen him except at his cynical, elegant best, standing at the side of a ballroom, one fist on his hip, a glass of wine in hand, his hazel eyes roving the room in search of someone to mock. He was handsome—despite her dislike, even Georgiana couldn't deny that—but aloof, with none of Sterling's easy charm. That was what she found attractive in a man, she told herself: a man who could laugh at himself and not just at others. A man who wanted to be liked rather than feared. The Malicious Marquess did not care what others thought of him. He had his title and his fortune and his looks to make him feel superior to everyone else in the world.

But now he wasn't. Now he was helpless, dependent on her . . . and her ability to maintain the lies she'd told.

By the time the doctor arrived, evening had fallen. True to her word, Georgiana hadn't left his bedside. She'd sat in a daze, almost a stupor, afraid to take her eyes off him. It didn't matter. Westmorland lay motionless, only the slight rise and fall of his chest assuring her that he still lived. When she heard the clatter of hooves on the gravel drive outside, she gave a loud gasping sigh of relief.

The doctor's pronouncement was not much different from what she had expected. "Several hard knocks to the head," he said after a lengthy examination. "That's where most of the blood came from. Cuts on the head bleed quite persistently. He's been beaten about the body as well, but I discern no broken bones, only bruising."

"But he will recover?" demanded Georgiana.

He smiled. Kitty had already told him she was the injured man's fiancée. "He is hale and strong. I have high hopes."

"That's excellent news, Dr. Elton," said Kitty warmly.

"Even in the best circumstances he will take time to heal," cautioned the doctor. "He must be tended. If he develops a fever, he should be bled at once."

Georgiana's stomach turned over at the thought of more blood. "I shall tend him," she said quickly. "Kitty, would you send my dinner on a tray?"

Her friend's brow creased. "I know you are worried, but you should have a care for yourself. Dr. Elton is here and can tend him tonight. Come down to dinner."

"I want to be here." Kitty drew breath to argue and Georgiana lowered her voice. "If it were Charles, would you leave?"

"No," said Kitty at once, her face softening in understanding. "I will send a tray."

Georgiana felt a pang of remorse at manipulating her friend so cravenly. *It's for a good reason*, she told herself, *and I will sort out how to deal with the truth later.* And so Georgiana settled into her vigil, uneasily aware that she had dug herself a very deep, dark hole.

Chapter 6

•∞•

HE HAD AN itch.

There was nothing in life more irritating than an itch one could not scratch. This spot happened to be on his head, above his temple. He burned to scratch it even as his hands refused to move. Frustration made his muscles tighten and flex, but with no discernible response from his hands.

In fact, now that he thought about it, he could not actually feel his hands at all.

With monumental effort he pried open his eyes, and beheld a blur. Good God. What had happened to him? Was he blind as well as handless and paralyzed?

For the better part of an hour—in his estimation—he tried to bring his vision into focus. His eyes felt hot and sticky. *Because they've been closed for a long time*, he thought, and then wondered why, and how he knew that.

This, he realized, was no ordinary nap. Had he been drunk? This thought fell so easily into his mind, he thought it must be true—he was used to sleeping off drink. But he couldn't shake the thought that he really had been asleep for a very long time, which made him wonder what on earth he'd drunk.

And why he couldn't remember any of the revelry that ought to accompany a bender of this magnitude.

With another great effort he swept his gaze around the room. It was utterly unfamiliar—walls of pale green, a plain ceiling, some ordinary pictures . . . nothing felt right. Unsettled, he turned his head and almost screamed in pain as he looked right at the windows and the daylight hit his eyes like sharp needles.

There was a flurry of motion and noise on the other side of him. "My lord?" said a man's voice. "Are you awake?"

"No," he said. Moving his lips hurt; they were stiff and sore. On second thought, he didn't want to be awake. He closed his eyes against the blinding light.

"I beg you, wake a moment longer," said the man quickly. "Are you still in pain?"

Still. "Yes," he croaked, suddenly more aware of the aches that seemed to pulse from his bones. "Who are you?"

"Daniel Elton, Your Lordship, a doctor. Lady Winston sent for me when you were found."

Elton? Winston? He didn't know anyone by those names. Where was he? Why was he here? He ought to be . . .

The first real feeling of unease prickled his neck. *Where* ought he to be? He wasn't sure. This was not his bedroom, not his own house—he thought—so where was he?

"Lord Sterling . . . Lord Sterling," that man was saying, louder and louder. "Can you hear me?"

Yes. He nodded. *All too well. Please shut up.*

There was a flurry of more noise; the doctor's voice resumed, although he didn't pay attention. But then there was a new voice, hushed and shocked . . . a woman's voice. He forced up his eyelids again.

Things came into focus a bit better this time. Elton turned out to be an older fellow with bushy gray hair and spectacles on his long, large nose. He was beaming and leaning over the bed. "Ah, see, he's awake!" Elton turned and motioned with one arm. "Come, my lady."

And a young woman came into view. *Beautiful,* was his first thought. Golden-blond curls straggled out of the knot atop her head, and she gazed at him with wide green eyes. Her pink lips were parted in astonishment. Who was she?

As pleasant as it was to wake up to the sight of her, it was beginning to alarm him that he was surrounded by strangers.

"She must be a comforting sight," Elton went on jovially. "She has been at your bedside the entire time, Lord Sterling."

"No—" The woman bit her lip, and set down the tray in her hands. She came closer, although she looked half frightened to death. "How are you feeling, sir?"

"Not my finest," he said. God, he still sounded drunk. What had happened to him? "Where am I?"

"Why, at—" began the doctor.

"Dr. Elton!" He winced at her exclamation. She gentled her tone. "Would you be so kind as to allow us a moment alone? His Lordship must be tired and—and perhaps a trifle bewildered after his ordeal . . ."

What ordeal? He frowned, even though that caused the skin of his face to pull painfully.

"Of course, ma'am," said the doctor after a pause. "I shall speak to the cook about some broth for Lord Sterling."

"Yes, brilliant!" she said quickly and a bit loudly. Her green eyes flickered to him, then away again. It struck him that he must look dreadful. "Thank you."

"Wait," he said, trying and failing to raise his hand. "What happened?"

"You were waylaid by thieves," said the woman at once. "You suffered a terrible beating. I think you should stay calm and easy. There will be plenty of time to discuss it when you're more recovered."

He jerked in shock. "Thieves?"

"Yes, vicious ones." She turned again to the doctor, who was hovering at the foot of the bed. "Dr. Elton, the broth," she urged.

"Where?" he demanded. That explained the pounding in his head and the ache in his entire body, but why the devil had he been robbed? What had he been robbed of? Where the bloody blazes was he?

"Between here and Maryfield," said the doctor, ignoring the lady's attempts to prompt him toward the door. "You were struck repeatedly on the head. It may be some time before your brain recovers enough to remember it, if you ever do."

"What?"

"Shh," said the woman, touching his shoulder as he started trying to climb from the bed. "Please stay calm. Dr. Elton, fetch that broth!" There was a sharp tone of command in her last words.

"Tell me," he demanded, even though the weight of her hand was enough to hold him still. It felt like he'd tried to scale a mountain instead of merely sit up. "Where am I? Why? Who are you? I don't remember any of this!"

"You're at Osbourne House, my lord," said the doctor. "To visit your fiancée."

"Who?" he barked again.

The doctor blinked. "Lady Georgiana." He gestured at the woman. "Your fiancée."

He stared at her in shock. If asked, he would have sworn he'd never seen her before in his life.

She jabbed at the pillow. He sucked in his breath as a spasm shot through him. His head was not ready to move. "Dr. Elton, you have been telling me he will need beef broth when he wakes," she said forcefully. "Do fetch it at once!"

"Of course, ma'am. Rest, Lord Sterling," said the doctor again. "It will come back to you. But you should know she saved your life." The man gave him a smile clearly meant to be encouraging.

His brain felt like a boulder inside his head. He had a fiancée . . . whom he did not remember at all. He was at a house he'd never heard of . . . for reasons he couldn't remember. And the doctor kept calling him . . .

"Sterling," he said. At the door, his hand on the latch, the doctor paused. "Why do you keep saying that?"

For the first time, the doctor's smile faded. "Do you not know who that is?" The subtle change to his voice was deeply alarming.

Instead of replying he looked to the woman, who had been tugging the blankets into place but now stopped and raised her head to stare. Her perfect pink mouth formed a circle. Shocked.

"No," he said slowly.

The doctor adjusted his spectacles and came a step nearer. "No?"

"He's raving," she said in a rush. She put her hand on his forehead, nearly covering his eyes. Her palm was soft and cool against his skin—comforting. It also blocked some of the blazing sunlight. "Doctor, he really should rest!"

"But he doesn't remember his name." Now frowning, the doctor returned to the bedside. "Do you not recognize your fiancée, Lady Georgiana?"

He looked up at her, at her beautiful, fearful green eyes. "No," he said tensely.

"And do you not know your own name?"

"Of course I do," he said. "It's . . ."

"He's disoriented," said Lady Georgiana sharply. "Doctor, you are making him upset!" This time she took the doctor's arm and almost dragged him to the door, closing it behind him with a loud bang.

He lay still, staring at the ceiling, suddenly wishing to fall asleep again and not wake until his head and everything else around him reverted to normal. She had spoken over him, but it didn't hide the fact that he had no idea what he would have said to the doctor.

He didn't know his own name. There had been nothing on his lips, and if she hadn't leapt into the breach, it would have been obvious.

"There." She was back at the bedside, a bit breathless. "He's gone. He's been nattering about broth for two days, hopefully he won't come back without it. You must be starving . . ."

"Two days," he repeated. That was a long time, but it was actually somewhat reassuring. He'd clearly got a pounding; surely his brain would settle back into place in a few hours. "Have I been asleep for two days?"

She paused without meeting his eyes. "Three, actually. Do you truly remember nothing of what happened?"

That was less reassuring. He'd got a very *thorough* pounding, it seemed. "No."

She wet her lips and glanced at the door. "Nor where you are, or why you came here?"

"No." He attempted a smile but it hurt too much. "You'll tell me, won't you?"

She flinched. "What?"

"He said you're my fiancée. Is that true? I can't believe I wouldn't remember a lady like you."

Slowly she sank into the chair beside the bed. Her wide eyes were fixed on him, but her expression was inscrutable. "You don't remember me."

He studied every inch of her face. "Are we truly engaged?"

Crimson flooded her cheeks. She looked humiliated, and he felt bad at once.

"Sorry," he mumbled. "I . . . I can't seem to recall much of anything."

"Including your own name," she said again. "Not at all?"

"No." He paused. "The doctor called me Sterling— is that it? It doesn't feel right . . ."

"Sterling is a title," she said, her gaze veering away. "Viscount Sterling."

It struck no chord within him. Shouldn't it? Panic began to rise in his chest.

She hesitated, her fingers tapping nervously on

her knee. "Your given name is Robert," she said softly.

Something eased inside him; *that* felt right. Thank God he wasn't completely mad. "Yes," he said on a sigh. His eyes wouldn't stay open. Weakly he opened his hand to her. "I'm sorry . . ."

"Oh no! Don't be!" She took his hand, her fingers curling around his gently but with comforting firmness. He relaxed a little more. His mind felt oddly distant from his body. This ought to be more upsetting, but he had no strength for anger or fear. But she was here—Georgiana, the doctor called her. She had been tending him. The doctor even said she'd saved his life. She had stood over him protectively, and he sensed she wouldn't leave him. Bereft of any other lodestar, he used his last waking thought to grip her hand, and fell back into unconsciousness.

GEORGIANA SAT AS STIFF as wrought iron, Westmorland's fingers wrapped around hers. It wasn't enough that she had to strip him and bathe him, bracing herself for his caustic reaction when he woke. It wasn't enough that she had been forced to sit beside his bed for three straight days now, terrified that the moment she left would be the moment he woke and brought her edifice of half-truths and outright lies crashing down.

And, of course, he had. She'd only stepped into the corridor to have a quick word with Kitty, who had brought a tray of sandwiches and tea. She slipped back into the room just in time to hear Dr. Elton, who could not keep silent to save his life, tell

Westmorland that she'd been by his side the entire time. That she was his fiancée.

She had braced herself for a withering reply. Instead, Westmorland had stared at her blankly.

Then he said he had no idea who she was.

And before she could even decide whether to be relieved or piqued that he'd not paid her so much as a sliver of attention in all the times they'd met in London, it became clear that he didn't remember who *he* was.

Perhaps that was not as alarming as it seemed. Surely, she told herself, getting beaten as badly as he had would rattle anyone's brain. Once he slept some more, had something to eat, and was more recovered, he would wake up his old self—the sharp-tongued, arrogant Marquess of Westmorland, who inspired no pity and deserved to be taken down a peg or ten for his cruel intentions toward Kitty.

For three days Georgiana had planned all the scenarios in which she would tell him off properly. Mentally she had composed a list of sins to reproach him for, from rude comments about people at balls, to the immorality of gambling so recklessly, to the utter depravity of turning a family out of their home. In truth, she had begun to look forward to it.

She'd envisioned just how it would be: he, lying there furious and weakened, forced to listen as she righteously excoriated him for being a heartless scoundrel. She, of course, would extort his promise to leave Osbourne House and never come back. She would make him swear not to breathe a word of his true identity to Kitty, and she would badger him into writing a letter to Charles explaining that he'd had a change of heart and would forgive whatever debt had given him possession of Osbourne House.

It hadn't bothered her that he would probably be glaring at her with murder in his eyes as he wrote such a letter—sealed with the signet she'd taken from his hand and hidden in her room, of course. She had even planned how she would get him out of Osbourne House as quickly as possible: an invented crisis at his invented uncle's house in Somersetshire. She'd already composed the urgent letter in her mind, replete with floods and plagues of life-threatening illness. No one had ever accused Georgiana of lacking imagination.

Instead, though . . . he slept, clinging to her hand as if he needed her. When she tried to tug her fingers loose, his tightened even though he didn't wake.

She was still sitting there, her hand trapped in his, when Dr. Elton returned. "Ah, fallen back to sleep, has he?" He clucked his tongue, waving at the maid behind him to set down the tray with the broth.

Georgiana waited until Lucy had gone. "Is it normal for people to wake up not remembering?" she asked quietly.

"It is not unusual," said Dr. Elton. "He was beaten rather badly, and the bruising on his head indicates he took several hard blows there, which often causes considerable confusion."

Georgiana exhaled in relief.

"However . . ." the doctor went on slowly, "it is alarming that he did not recognize you or his own name. A man does not easily forget either of those things."

"But he'll remember eventually?" she pressed. "Perhaps the next time he wakes up?"

"Perhaps," said the doctor. "We must hope so."

He went and fussed with the curtains, leaving Georgiana staring at Westmorland in renewed terror. Her heart hammered and a chill ran over her arms. She had thought it would be terrible when Westmorland woke up and recognized her.

She hadn't thought of how much worse it might be if he woke up and actually fell for her lunatic, untrue story.

Chapter 7

THE NEXT TIME he woke it was dark. Cautiously he opened his eyes, and sighed in relief that the only light was from a lamp turned down low. Either due to the darkness or because he'd taken a long nap, he felt much better this time, and better able to ponder his surroundings.

It was too dark to see much in the unfamiliar room, but he could see *her*. Lady Georgiana was curled up sideways in an armchair right beside him, her cheek pillowed on one hand, fast asleep. Someone was snoring in the room, but he didn't think it was she.

His fiancée.

He stared at her, trying to draw even a slight memory from his still-fuzzy brain. She was a beauty, no question. But just as he could not recall coming to this house or where he'd come from, he couldn't remember meeting her, or courting her, or dancing with her, or kissing her, or asking her to marry him. Perhaps it was arranged.

No. He wouldn't have an arranged marriage.

That thought caught him off guard. It had been

strong and visceral. Well then. He wanted to marry her, and she must have wanted to marry him. The doctor said she'd been here for three days.

As he watched, her eyes opened. For a moment they regarded each other in silence. "Are you awake?" she whispered.

"I think so." He flexed his hands and shifted, trying to ease the stiffness in his neck.

She leapt out of her chair. "Don't hurt yourself!" She adjusted the pillows and helped him find a more comfortable position. "Better?"

"Yes." She smelled lovely, like oranges. He cleared his throat, liking the way she leaned over him. "Could you explain what happened?"

Her hands, tugging the blanket smooth, went still. She sank back onto the edge of her chair. "Do you still remember nothing?"

"I'm trying to." Especially regarding her.

She stared at him intently for another moment, then her shoulders sagged. "I don't know exactly what happened."

"Start with what you do know." He tried to smile. Damn, his lip must be split. It hurt like the devil.

She sucked in a deep breath and bent her head, plucking at something on her skirt. "I was out riding when we heard a disturbance on the road—"

"Before that," he interrupted. "Where are we? Is this your home?" He was sure—*sure*—it wasn't his.

"This is Osbourne House." She peeked at him through her lashes as though waiting for a response. "In Derbyshire." Another expectant look. He made a helpless gesture. Nothing was familiar. He supposed it should be; surely he would know all this about his fiancée.

She sighed and pressed her hands together in her lap. "The lady of the house, Lady Winston, is a dear friend of mine from school." She shot him a quick look again, as if checking for a flash of recognition, but the name meant nothing to him.

"She's had a baby and can't go to town this year, so I came to visit," she went on. "The countryside is lovely, and I was out for a ride, as I said, when we heard trouble. The groom went to see, and he found you in the road, unconscious, and the men who beat you were fleeing."

"How many?" he wanted to know.

"At least two, probably three. Adam didn't get a close look."

It had taken three men to bring him down. He felt a wholly unwarranted satisfaction at that. Idiot. They most certainly *had* taken him down, and beaten him to flinders as well. What did he have to be proud of in that?

"It was faster to bring you here than to the village," she was saying, "so we brought you to Osbourne House, where you've been ever since."

He frowned, as much as his face could bear. "Why would you think of the village, when you're here? How distant is the village?"

Her lips parted, and she blinked. "Oh—I—I did not recognize you at first. You were covered in blood . . ."

"Wasn't I coming to visit you?"

"Obviously," she said tartly. "But I was not expecting you and was very much astonished by your appearance!"

Ah. A surprise. He grinned. Yes, he liked that thought. "Do I do that often? Surprise you?"

"Constantly," she muttered, almost to herself.

That also pleased him. "The doctor said you saved me."

She rolled her eyes. "If anyone did, it was Adam, the groom."

"The doctor said you've been tending me ever since."

Her brows went up. "Do you want another nurse? I can wake the doctor, he's asleep on the sofa—"

"No!" He abandoned his attempts to tease some declaration of devotion out of her, and snagged her hand as she started to rise. "Please don't wake him." He struggled to shove himself upright. "I'd prefer you over anyone, but especially him. He talks far too much."

She had gone still the moment he took her hand. Now she gave a tiny snort of laughter. "You have no idea. You've been asleep, and haven't had to listen to him for three endless days."

He winced at the thought. "He can go home."

"Good luck persuading him of that, my lord."

Her hand felt very nice in his. He turned it over, touching the smooth skin of her wrist. "Are we always so formal?"

"Er . . . what?"

"With each other." Her skin was mesmerizing, like warm silk. "Georgiana."

She jumped, yanking her hand from his. "We— that is—yes, we are somewhat formal with each other. As is proper."

Proper. He frowned a little, not liking that word. "Very proper?" Surely he'd stolen a kiss by now. He must have made love to her hand, which was simply perfect.

"*Properly* proper," she said tightly.

"Could we stop?" He gave her a coaxing smile. "I am very injured, you know. It's extremely taxing to my brain."

Instead of smiling or agreeing at once, she went pale. "Stop?"

"Being so perfectly proper." His eyes were starting to grow heavy again. Damn it. There was still so much he needed to ask. "Do I call you Georgiana?"

Her lips parted. "You may," she squeaked.

Meaning he didn't already. It sounded like he'd needed that hard knock on the head. Well, now that he'd got one, he planned to take shameless advantage of it. "And you shall call me Robert." That name felt familiar, but still slightly off. "Rob," he tried, and felt better. "Yes, Rob."

She looked aghast. "That would be wrong!"

"To call your future husband by his name?" He forced his eyes open at that. "How so?"

"We—our engagement—well, it *is* only an engagement . . ."

"How long?"

She clamped her lips shut and glared at him.

"How long have we been engaged?" he pressed.

"Two years," she muttered. "Almost two and a half."

"Over two years?" Jolted, he struggled out of the pillows. Two bloody years of his life and memory, vanished. "Why so long?"

She leapt to push against his shoulder. "Don't hurt yourself!"

"Why?" he demanded again, even as he let her urge him back down. He was finding he liked the feel of her hands on him very much. He preferred to think about that instead of the rather alarming weakness in his muscles.

She scowled at the blankets she was tucking around him. "The settlements aren't done. My brother is being difficult."

Oh. He relaxed. Something dreary like that was the only possible reason he could be engaged to her for years and not run mad.

Because he found her very attractive. Hell, even her voice was beautiful. Why the devil would he remain formal and distant from her? Perhaps it had been her choice; perhaps she didn't want to marry him as much as he wanted to marry her?

The thought was unsettling. But if she'd said yes in the first place, it was a start, and if he'd been remiss in not winning her heart, at least that was something he could change.

"I'll fix that as soon as I get out of bed," he told her. "Difficult or not."

She blushed—he thought. It was hard to tell in the low light. "I'm sure there's no hurry now! Your health—"

"Two years is an unconscionably long time to leave a woman waiting. I'm sorry."

She looked up, all but gaping in astonishment. He nodded once, but his head was starting to ache again. His eyes fell closed, and he sighed in weariness.

"Rest," she said at once.

He groped for her hand. "Sorry," he mumbled. "I can't . . . stay awake."

"Don't try." After a moment, she clasped his hand in both of hers. He folded his arm, bringing her hand to his heart. He liked the feel of her hand in his, and it comforted him greatly to know, without anything being said, that she would be there when he woke.

At the moment, she was all he had.

GEORGIANA ESCAPED THE NEXT day into the gardens. She had to, for Westmorland had woken up in much stronger spirits than the previous day. He sat up to eat, and then said he wanted to bathe. Kitty told Angus, the senior footman, to help him, and sent Georgiana out of the house.

She hoped it would save her from running mad.

It had been five days since the marquess's very unfortunate appearance. He was no closer to recovering his memory, but his health was improving. Dr. Elton had pronounced him out of danger and gone home early that morning, which was a blessing of sorts. The man did talk entirely too much, although the marquess could quiet him with a piercing stare and a single word of command.

The marquess. She squeezed her eyes shut. She would have to stop thinking of him that way, because she had nearly slipped twice and said it aloud. It was strange enough to refer to him as Sterling, but he wanted her to call him Rob, or Robert, which was in fact his real given name.

By an unlucky stroke of fortune, Robert was also Sterling's name. Westmorland couldn't know that she had looked forward to calling Sterling Robert, in the privacy of their own home after they married. It wasn't fashionable, and Sterling had stared in surprise when she asked him, but Georgiana's friends were on such intimate terms with their husbands and she wanted the same. After all, he sometimes called her Georgie, which was surely even more familiar, and sounded like a little boy's name to boot.

But now Westmorland was coaxing her to call him Rob, while Sterling, her true and actual fiancé, had merely laughed and agreed that she could if she wished to. Westmorland was asking so hopefully she felt worse and worse avoiding it, even though it would only heap more anxiety on top of the rather enormous load she already carried.

Perhaps she had been mistaken. Perhaps he was not actually Lord Westmorland. This man was not at all like the arrogant, disdainful marquess she'd met in London, who stalked the *ton* like a bored panther in search of prey. She might be harboring a completely different fellow than she thought. The idea was almost cheerful, because she did not know what to do with a grateful, friendly, *charming* Westmorland.

Wouldn't that be a terrible joke on her? If he turned out to be some perfectly ordinary, decent gentleman who happened to resemble Lord Westmorland . . . very strongly . . . she would have lied and debased herself for no reason.

"Georgiana," called a voice behind her. "Where are you?"

She gave a guilty start. "Here!"

"Enjoying a bit of sun?" Kitty stopped beside her and turned up her face to the sky, breathing deeply. "You must be starved for it, after so many days inside."

Georgiana mustered a grim smile. She was trapped in that room by her own stupid actions. "There's nowhere else I would be."

Kitty touched her arm sympathetically, no doubt thinking her extremely devoted to the injured man. "I know. One can bear anything for the man you love. I would do no less for Charles."

Georgiana tried not to squirm.

"Speaking of Charles . . ." Kitty lowered her voice, and Georgiana tensed. "I received a letter from him just this morning. He has done as I feared, and wagered above his means. He did offer this house as his stake in a debauched card game with Lord Westmorland."

Oh Lord. Georgiana wondered if Kitty would shoot her as well, if she discovered the truth. "Is Charles coming home, then?" she asked, trying to act as if she hoped so, instead of dreading it with every fiber of her being.

"No." Kitty's face had settled into terrifyingly implacable lines as she watched some birds splash in the pool at the center of the garden. "He has other things to tend to in London. Mr. Jackson has sent him instructions." A slight, wry smile touched her lips. "And I believe he apprehends the alarm he has caused here, and wishes to wait out the storm elsewhere."

Thank goodness. "How like a man," Georgiana said lightly, "causing a tempest and then not wanting to suffer through it."

Kitty laughed. "How clever you are. It will serve you well when you and Lord Sterling are married. In fact, I've come to tell you he's asking for his own clothes. Lucy cleaned what she could, but his shirt was ruined beyond repair. Shall I send Angus to find his baggage and fetch a new one?"

Westmorland's saddlebags were in Georgiana's

own room, where any identifying marks or materials would be safely hidden from view. Since she'd not left the sickroom any more than necessary, they were still there, their secrets undisturbed.

"No, no," she said quickly. "I shall fetch one. Although I doubt very much Dr. Elton wants him to get out of bed, and what reason is there to get dressed when one can't stir from bed?"

Kitty smiled. "Oh my, you've got a lot to learn about men. The sicker Charles is, the more determined he is to rise from bed and go on as if nothing bothered him. A trifling cold, on the other hand, will reduce him to an invalid. I expect Lord Sterling is going a bit mad from being indoors for so long."

"He can barely stay awake for an hour at a time."

"Perhaps you should go speak to him," Kitty replied. "I heard him badgering Angus about procuring a Bath chair to wheel him outside."

As if Kitty would have such a thing standing around. Even without his memory, Westmorland was still arrogantly oblivious to others. Georgiana reminded herself that this was her cross to bear, and that she had fashioned it and loaded it upon her own shoulders. She steeled herself and turned toward the house. "I'll tell him," she vowed, and hoped Kitty took the edge in her voice for concern.

In her room, she couldn't find the saddlebags. For a moment her heart almost stopped; if Angus had come to fetch them, the marquess could even now be rifling through them, finding who-knew-what inside that would remind him of who he really was.

After a moment's frenzied searching, though, she located them under a table. Nadine, her maid, must have pushed them there out of her way.

Oh heavens. She had forgotten about Nadine, who knew perfectly well what Sterling looked like. Nadine hadn't been into the invalid's room—as a lady's maid, nursing was well beneath her—but if she ever saw him, she'd know at once that Georgiana had lied.

Georgiana covered her face with both hands. She'd have to make a bargain with Nadine to keep her from spoiling everything. This stupid lie she'd told was becoming more inconvenient by the moment.

She took a deep breath and let it out slowly. Enough of that bother; she'd deal with Nadine later. She undid the buckles on the saddlebags and dug inside, feeling at once squeamish and wickedly curious as she lifted out the marquess's possessions.

He hadn't brought much. Clothing, all decidedly wrinkled after being stuffed into the saddlebags. She set aside a clean shirt, then realized he would need other clothes, too. She stared fixedly at the wall for a moment, screwing up her nerve. *What an idiot you are*, she told herself silently. *Now you have to handle his undergarments.*

Telling herself they were just pieces of linen and silk, she added stockings and drawers to the pile. If only she'd told the truth, Angus would be doing this. In fact, he *could* do the rest; she dumped out all the clothing and set it aside. With a stealthy glance at the still-closed door, she turned her attention to the remaining contents.

A pistol, which he ought to have kept closer to hand. A small leather bag, embossed with a crest, that held shaving items. A rolled-up portfolio of writing implements and paper. A small penknife fell from it, and Georgiana retrieved it, mildly surprised. She hadn't thought Westmorland the letter-writing type, but he'd devoted precious space in his luggage to this. A journal was next, and although she didn't dare read it, she did slide out the document protruding from the cover. She unfolded it, and read enough to realize it was the deed to Osbourne House.

Her heart almost broke her ribs. He *had* come to throw them out, armed with the deed of possession. All her animosity, which had burned down to coals in the face of his serious injury, came roaring back to white-hot life. That *scoundrel*.

Well. She wasn't about to let him do it, not after she'd lied to her friend for him, nursed him when he was unconscious, and now had to play at being his loving fiancée. She took the deed and hid it under her stockings, where she'd already secreted his signet ring.

There was nothing else in the saddlebags. It was just enough for a few days, she thought. He must have been utterly confident in his ability to toss Kitty and her family out into the hedgerows.

Unless he had a carriage following with luggage.

She pictured a coach driving up and spilling out a half dozen of his arrogant, scandalous friends. They would demand to see him. He might recover his memory at the sight of them. Kitty might take down her gun and shoot them all, and then quite possibly turn the gun on *her*. Oh Lord, why hadn't she thought of that before?

"Do you need help, m'lady?" asked Nadine behind her.

Georgiana started violently and whirled around. "What do you mean, sneaking up on me like that?"

Nadine blinked. "I didn't sneak! Angus sent me to ask if you've found Lord Sterling's clothing yet."

"As you can see, I have." She scooped up the armload of clothing, minus the few things she'd set aside, and gave it to the maid. "Have this cleaned and pressed. It's in a dreadful state after being stuffed into saddlebags."

"Yes, m'lady." Nadine took it and disappeared.

Georgiana pressed her trembling fingertips to her temple. This was getting out of hand. She'd have to think what to do about Nadine. And about the deed. And about the possibility of Westmorland's friends showing up. And the chances his memory recovered. And, of course, the ultimate problem of how to disentangle herself from the mess she'd created.

It was enough to make her want to flee back to London and the close supervision of her chaperone Lady Sidlow. At the moment, she didn't feel competent to look after herself at all.

Chapter 8

SHE TAPPED AT the sickroom door, and opened it at a muffled call to enter. Then she stopped short, mouth hanging open. Westmorland was out of bed.

He was clinging to the bedpost, pale and shaky in a blue banyan, but his face lit with a smile of fierce triumph when he saw her. "Good morning, my dear."

"You cut his hair," she said stupidly, looking at Angus.

Westmorland ran one hand over his head. "It was a nightmare. Easier to cut it off."

Georgiana felt an odd sinking feeling in her chest. When his hair was long and scraped back from his face in a queue, it emphasized the hard lines of his jaw and nose. He looked predatory and cold with it long, like one of Lucifer's angels. Cut shorter, it fell over his brow with a slight wave and made him look younger and more approachable.

And merciful heavens, he was taller than she'd remembered.

With broader shoulders.

"Do you not like it?" he asked as she stood staring like an idiot.

She shook herself. It shouldn't matter if he cut his hair, got a pirate's hoop in one ear, or started wearing doublet and hose like Henry VIII. He was still the same, she told herself, hoping it was actually true. "It's different," she said vaguely. "And why are you out of bed? Dr. Elton—"

"Bother him." The marquess took a deep breath and flexed his hand, then released the bedpost, standing unsteadily but unaided. "I had to get up before I went mad."

As if he weren't enough trouble when confined to bed. She thrust the clothing she held at Angus. "They told me you wanted to get dressed, but I don't think you're well enough to get out of bed. You can barely stand without holding the bedpost."

"Probably not," Westmorland agreed.

"Please get back in bed, then, before you fall and injure yourself again."

His lips thinned. "I'm going mad," he repeated. "I can make it to the garden and sit there for a bit." Seeing her face, his mouth crooked. "Please, darling."

She looked to Angus, who carefully avoided her gaze. Everyone was deferring to her because they thought she was his future wife. "If you wish," she said with a huff, and left.

When the door opened again, he was shaved and fully dressed. He should have appeared more like the arrogant Malicious Marquess she knew from London, but instead he looked, if possible, less like that person than ever. He flashed her a tentative smile. "Look a bit better now?"

Even pale and still bruised from his ordeal, he looked much better. He was, she thought grudgingly, decidedly handsome. "You should be in bed," she said again, feeling peevish.

He grinned. "I'm dreadfully inconvenient, aren't I?"

You have no idea, she thought. "I don't think you ought to go outside."

"Just for a few minutes," he cajoled. One arm braced on the wall, he reached out and took her hand, bringing it to his lips. "Come with me, if you're worried. I promise to behave, Georgiana."

At that moment, Kitty came around the corner. At the sight of them, apparently in intimate conversation, she smiled broadly.

Caught, Georgiana smiled awkwardly and let Westmorland kiss her hand. It was a very sweet kiss, she had to admit; he held her fingers lightly and released them promptly. "How can I refuse when you ask so gallantly?"

"It's wonderful to see you on your feet again, Lord Sterling." Kitty joined them.

Something flickered across his face, but he replied politely. "Thank you, ma'am, for your hospitality. I do apologize for the trouble I've put everyone to. In fact, I was hoping to enjoy your gardens for a bit. I've always been happier out of doors than in."

Georgiana glanced at him from beneath her lashes. The marquess preferred the outdoors? How curious. She'd have sworn he was a creature of ballrooms and gaming hells, routinely sleeping the day away so he could prowl the city by night.

"Of course," Kitty was saying warmly. "Georgiana has long been the same! Let Angus assist you."

He hesitated. "Perhaps Lady Georgiana might lend me her arm."

"I'm sure she will," Kitty said with a laugh. "She's been quite devoted, you know!"

Georgiana wished Kitty would go back to rocking her baby or planning the menu or anything other than pushing her at Westmorland. *Robert*, she told herself. *Rob*. As much as it made her writhe to call him by name, it was much better than accidentally blurting out his real identity.

"Then we'd best be on our way," she said. "I don't like you up and walking around so soon, Rob, but I see you won't be argued out of it."

His brilliant hazel eyes lit up. He was eager to go, she realized. "I've won her over," he said with a wink at Kitty, who gave Georgiana an amused smile in reply.

She let him link his arm in hers. He shifted with the first step, leaning more heavily on her, and she stumbled under his weight.

"Perhaps Angus should come," Kitty began.

"I can make it." Rob drew himself up, although Georgiana felt the tremor that went through him. Without thinking, she wedged herself against his side. She did know the feeling of wanting to prove herself, and somehow his determination made her want to help him. Together they made their way toward the garden.

By the time they reached the bottom of the stairs, his arm was around her shoulders. By the time they reached the door, her arms were around his waist. She could feel the intense effort he was expending, without a whisper of complaint, and somehow that made it easier for her to offer him aid.

"Perhaps you were right," he said breathlessly,

dropping onto the garden bench with a heavy thump. "That was more arduous than expected."

"And now you shall have to make the same trip back in." She sat on the far end of the bench, trying to shake off the feeling of his body against hers. Her shoulder had fit precisely under his arm, and even after several days in bed, he was firm and solid all over.

"Not for at least half an hour, and it will be worth it." He raised his face to the sun and exhaled, eyes closed. "I had to get out of that room."

She sympathized with that. But when she glanced at him, the image of him sitting with his head back, eyes closed, rattled her composure. There were tawny highlights in his dark hair, and he looked so strong and peaceful, aside from the bruises. She concentrated on smoothing her skirt across her knees.

"It's driving me mad that I can't remember anything," he said. His eyes were still closed, but Georgiana flushed guiltily. "Tell me about you."

She looked longingly at the gate. What would everyone do if she just walked out, all the way into Maryfield, and took a place on the mail coach back to London? No sensible way out of her impossible predicament had come to her yet, and if he began asking questions . . .

"Georgiana?" She started. He was watching her with concern. "What is wrong?"

"Nothing," she said with a laugh she hoped was carefree. "Nothing at all!"

"Truly?" He slid a little closer, his expression somber but somehow mischievous at the same time. "I'm a terrible trial to you, I can see."

Not for the reasons you think. "Whatever makes you say that?"

"Hmm. The way I had to beg to come outside for a few minutes."

She whirled on him indignantly, and he laughed, his eyes dancing. "You *ought* to be inside," she said with a reluctant smile. "You know it, too. Don't put it all on me, being cruel and uncaring of your suffering."

"Cruel! Never." He caught up her hand and kissed the back before she knew he meant to do it. "And no one could call you uncaring after all you've done for me."

To protect herself from the consequences of her own lies. Uneasily, she tugged her hand from his.

"Were you frightened?" he asked after a moment.

"When you turned up half dead in the road, drenched in blood, and didn't wake for days? Of course."

He was quiet for a moment. "You're angry with me."

Another laugh, more forced this time. "Don't be ridiculous."

"I can tell," he said softly.

Georgiana drew breath to argue, then didn't bother.

"You've been conscientious and sensible as far as I've seen," he went on. "Even if this was shocking and upsetting, it seems unlikely you'd be angry at me for being robbed and attacked."

"Of course I wasn't," she protested. "You were not to blame for that!"

"That means you're upset for another reason," he went on. "Over something I did before. What was it?"

There was no way to answer that.

"Was I cold? Or thoughtless?" he pressed.

It was too much to ignore, this chance to be honest. "Yes," she burst out. "As a matter of fact, you *were*."

A frown creased his brow. "Was that why I was coming to see you? To make it up?"

"I don't know," she said, still truthfully. "I had no idea of your coming to visit at all."

"It must have been," he said, almost to himself. "Why else would I come into Derbyshire?"

She tensed, afraid he *would* remember why he'd come into Derbyshire. "You remembered that you like being outdoors," she said to divert him. "That's something."

"I remember how to walk, and how to dress myself as well," he said wryly. "It's a rather small something compared to all the rest. How did we meet?"

Georgiana clenched her teeth together behind her smile until her ears hurt. What to tell him? Thus far she had relied strongly on the truth—the truth of her romance with Sterling, that is. This time that wouldn't work, though; her family estate bordered that of Sterling's father, and they'd known each other since they were children. She'd been in love with him almost as long as she could remember. When he went down on one knee and asked her to marry him, it had seemed like something that was Meant To Be since the dawn of time itself.

She couldn't possibly tell Westmorland that, even if it didn't feel like one betrayal too many of Sterling.

"In London," she said evasively, falling back on a heavily edited version of the truth, as it pertained to the Marquess of Westmorland and herself. "Some ball or other. I don't really remember."

"Ah." He looked rueful. "I didn't make a good first impression."

"Not especially," she agreed.

A determined expression settled on his face. "Tell me. Spare me nothing. I hate feeling that there's something ugly between us, but without knowing what it is."

Oh Lord. Nervously she rubbed her palms on her skirt. Lies, lies, lies. "I don't want to. It's unpleasant."

"I expect it must have been," he said, giving her a look that was both penitent and coaxing. She almost smiled. "Did I step on your lapdog?"

She blinked in astonishment. "What? No."

"Did I spill champagne on your gown?"

"No!"

"Forget to request a dance?" He could make the most beguiling expression. Who would have thought it of the Malicious Marquess? "Whatever it was, I was an absolute idiot."

Her reluctant amusement withered and died. Would he say that if he remembered, as she did, that he had thought her vain and shallow at that long-ago ball? That he would have never thought of requesting a dance with a girl like her, let alone bring her champagne? "Don't let it trouble you," she said, looking away. "I don't."

"It will trouble me, but I'll stop asking." He laid his hand on top of hers. "You've a tender heart, my dear."

She didn't know what to say to that. She thought she was a coward and an idiot, and probably going mad as well. Every day she racked her brains for some way to cleave this knot, and somehow, every day it grew a little tighter instead—and it felt like it was around her neck.

"A soft head, more likely," she said, trying not to think about that too much. "Letting you come outside when you would be better in bed, resting and recovering."

He grinned, looking for all the world like a boy exulting in getting away with something. "I won you over."

"I couldn't let you stumble out here and fall flat on your face," she said tartly. "Seeing you lying bloody and insensible in the dirt once was enough, thank you."

"It is a performance I have no desire to repeat," he agreed. "Not even for the most beautiful nurse in the world."

She made herself laugh. "Kitty will be delighted to hear it! I must warn you, she's already married."

"You're going to keep me on my toes," he said in amusement. "I didn't mean Lady Winston, and you know it."

Georgiana widened her eyes and dipped, again, into truth. "Why should I think you meant me? You've never told me anything so flattering before."

"No!" He laughed, then stopped. "Is that true? That can't be true."

Oh, it is. Smiling brightly, she just shrugged.

"No," he said again, this time sounding genuinely shocked.

"It doesn't matter," she said quickly. It was unnerving that he was so appalled. If he'd kept laughing, it would have soothed the niggling worry inside her that he seemed quite different from the man she'd known in London—only from afar, but well enough to be entirely justified in her dislike of him.

"Of course it does!" He slid closer to her. "Do you think I don't find you beautiful?"

She flushed. "I'm sure I don't know . . ."

He reached out and turned her face toward him. "You're quite the loveliest woman I've ever seen in my life." His eyes were almost golden as he studied her face. "Even if you hadn't saved my life, I'd think so."

Georgiana had been told many times that she was lovely, pretty, even beautiful, as stunning as a princess and as fair as a summer's day. None of those compliments had ever left her speechless, as this one did.

"You . . . you got hit on the head," she said unsteadily. "Quite hard."

He smiled. His smile was crooked, she realized; one corner of his mouth went higher than the other, and his eyes crinkled unevenly, too. It made his handsome face even more endearing, and she realized with a bolt of alarm that she was coming to like Lord Westmorland. Or at least *this* Westmorland, who didn't remember that he thought her vain and shallow, who liked being outside, who found her beautiful.

"I didn't get hit so hard I went blind," he murmured.

"I didn't save your life," she said in reply, her wits scattered by his fascinated gaze. "Adam did."

"Really?" He leaned a little closer. "It wasn't Adam

who decided to bring me here, who washed all the blood from my smashed-in head, who sat by my bedside day and night."

"Well—of course not, he's a groom, he has responsibilities with the horses—"

"It wasn't Adam who helped me come outside, just because I wanted to, even though it was foolish to get out of bed so soon."

She smiled in spite of herself. "That's more like an accomplice than a savior."

His shoulders shook with a silent laugh. "I haven't seen Adam . . . at all, as far as I can remember. Which is not that far, I admit, but I *do* remember you've been there every time I opened my eyes."

"Of course," she said faintly. She had to be there, in case he woke up with his memory restored and reverted to his malicious former self. But all she could see right now was the way his eyes laughed at her, and the way he looked at her as if he were about to . . .

Kiss her.

"Of course I was there," she said in a rush, jerking bolt upright, privately terrified to realize she had been tilting toward him. She was definitely going mad. She did not want to kiss him, and she could not, under any circumstances, allow him to kiss her. "I can hardly expect Kitty's servants to sit up with you all night, can I? They've got work to do."

She busied herself with smoothing away nonexistent creases in her skirt, but she felt him retreat. His disappointment was palpable. "I appreciate it dearly nonetheless," he said, his once-teasing tone subdued. "Thank you."

You wouldn't thank me if you knew the truth. "Pooh," she said with a forced laugh. "You shouldn't thank me!"

"Perhaps not," he said with obvious reluctance.

She laughed again, but stopped as he pressed one hand to his temple. "Does your head hurt?"

"Not much more than usual." He squeezed his eyes closed. "Usual as it's been the last two days, at any rate."

She was on her feet at once. "That's it. You simply must go back inside."

"Perhaps it will be better in the shade," he mumbled. His head dipped, and he swayed on the bench, and with a horrified gasp she flung herself at him, holding him steady as she cried out for Angus.

"Much better already," came his muffled voice. His hands came to rest on her hips.

Georgiana blushed. To keep him from falling over, she'd thrown her arms around his shoulders, and was holding his face pressed up against her bosom. If she didn't feel his hands shaking as he held on to her—for support at least as much as . . . anything else—she would have let go, even if he toppled into the wisteria. But he was shaking and his breathing was labored, and when Angus came running, Rob didn't make a sound of protest at being half carried back into the house while Georgiana hurried ahead, throwing open doors along the way.

Only when he was back inside, paler and weaker by every measure, did she realize how ill he'd become. Angus barely managed to grab the basin before Rob leaned over the edge of the bed and wretched violently.

"I shouldn't have allowed that!" She grabbed a towel to dab his face clean as Angus took away the basin. "Such a mistake! Now you're ill again, and all for a few minutes of sunshine!"

"Not so little as that," he rasped. He sipped from the mug of tea she held to his lips, not protesting the laudanum she'd hastily added to it. "I felt like myself for a few minutes. That was worth it."

"And now you've frightened me half to death again." In despair she sat with a thump in the chair beside the bed. She had not expected to feel so responsible for him. Her hands were shaking and her heart was racing from fear that he would suffer a serious setback from a simple visit to the garden. A visit she could have prevented, and yet had not, because she let herself be swayed by the eagerness in his face.

Smiling faintly, he turned onto his back and draped one arm across his face. "I'm sorry for that, love, but it was still worth it. You're beautiful in the sunshine." And he fell asleep before she could recover from the shock of his words.

Georgiana gazed at him, completely at a loss for what to do. Nothing was going as planned—not that she had planned any of this at all, but things weren't even going as expected. Even without his memory, surely Westmorland ought to have remained the same person. Could someone's entire nature change from a blow to the head? Unthinkingly she leaned over him, looking for any sign that she had in fact made a mistake—that it was not Lord Westmorland but some other, kinder, more amiable man.

Not that she could let some other fellow kiss her, either.

Georgiana shuddered. She was drowning, in so far over her head she had no idea how to get out. Lady Sidlow had warned her that imagination was a dangerous thing in a girl, and she had always laughed. Who knew the countess would turn out to be right? How on earth had she ended up deceiving her dear friend Kitty and now contemplating betraying her one true love, Sterling? Because as bad as the lies were, a part of her had thrilled at hearing Rob say he found her beautiful—had reveled in the interest in his gaze—had wondered what it would be like if he did lean forward and kiss her. She'd never kissed anyone but Sterling.

And now this man—the Malicious Marquess, of all people—was making her wonder.

Her eyes drifted over his mouth. That was all she could see, with his arm still draped over his eyes. What would it be like to kiss him? She might have enough sense not to let it happen, but her brain kept thinking about it anyway. Sterling's kisses were soft and tender; the joy of them came from being held in his arms, even if only for brief moments. Lady Sidlow kept a close eye on her and she'd had just a handful of moments alone with Sterling when he could kiss her.

Kitty was far more lax as a chaperone. She'd left Georgiana alone for hours with her supposed fiancé—not that it was her duty to chaperone anyone, with a baby to care for and a house to run, and as ill as Rob had been, the chance of anything indecent happening must have seemed minuscule. And Georgiana, knowing he was not her fiancé at all, had expected that kissing the marquess would be the last thing on earth she would ever think of.

And look at her now, sitting by his bedside, staring at his mouth and wondering.

She told Angus to make His Lordship comfortable and fled.

SHE HAD APPROXIMATELY TWO minutes of peace before another ugly problem reared its head.

"Lucy told me it was Lord Sterling who got beat to a cinder and lost his mind," remarked Nadine.

Georgiana jumped. She'd barely closed the door of her own room, and had begun contemplating barricading it against the world. "Goodness, Nadine, you're startling me at every turn today!"

Nadine was about Georgiana's own age, and had been with her ever since Georgiana left school. Nadine was very good at arranging hair and needlework, and she had a bold, daring streak that proved invaluable. Every improper thing Georgiana wanted to do, Nadine was willing to aid and abet—for a modest price. Would Nadine purchase the latest Minerva Press novel or gossip paper on her way home from getting new stockings and laces? She would, for an extra sixpence. Would she hide that purchase from Lady Sidlow and agree to take any blame for its presence in the house? She would, for another sixpence. Would she smuggle letters, and buy naughty etchings, and lie for Georgiana when Georgiana had to sneak out? She always would— which was wonderful—but always for a price—which quickly grew expensive.

And now, obviously, she'd seen Lord Westmorland.

"I never guessed there were two Lord Sterlings in Britain," Nadine went on as she folded clothes. "One several inches taller than the other, with darker hair, and handkerchiefs monogrammed with a W—"

Georgiana came off the door. "Hush! Don't say another word!"

The maid blinked. "O' course not, m'lady. I expect you've got good reason to lie to Lady Winston, and tell her she's taken in Lord Sterling instead of someone else. Someone who, if I had to make a guess, was actually the horrible, hated Lord Wes—"

"Ten shillings," blurted Georgiana in a panic. "To keep it secret."

Nadine paused, then finished folding the handkerchiefs. "If you wish, m'lady."

"Thank you." Georgiana stalked past her, but inside she wilted. It was two months until she'd get more pin money. Her tightfisted brother Alistair regularly wondered how women managed to spend so much money, and he wouldn't advance her a farthing. And now she'd spent part of it covering up this stupid, idiotic lie for a man she didn't even like.

"But why did you, m'lady?" Nadine stowed the last of the clothing in the drawer and turned around. "I thought you despised Lord Wes—"

"*Please* do not say that name!" Georgiana moaned.

Nadine's eyebrows went up. "But you and Miss Hotchkiss agreed he was the very worst sort of gentleman and lower than the dirt on your shoe."

Georgiana flushed. Nadine had chaperoned on that carriage drive, when she'd been consoling Joanna Hotchkiss that Westmorland's cutting remarks weren't worth the tears and anguish Joanna was suffering over them. "He said some very unkind things about Miss Hotchkiss and I was attempting to cheer her."

"So you *don't* dislike the mar—?"

"Nadine!" Georgiana cried, half whisper, half shout. She glanced uneasily at the door, and lowered her voice even more. "For the next few days, he is Lord Sterling, and don't you dare breathe one word otherwise."

"No, ma'am," said Nadine, taken aback. "Of course I shan't. But how many more days? And what shall you do if Lord St—the *real* one decides to visit? Or even to write?"

Georgiana put her hands over her face. "I don't know. I only said he was . . . *you know* . . . to save his life. I feared Lady Winston would throw him out."

The maid looked dubious. "Surely even if he's rude and arrogant she wouldn't do that to one so injured."

Georgiana sighed. "Something happened between Sir Charles and . . ." Helplessly she waved one arm toward Rob's room. "It was dreadful, and Sir Charles warned Lady Winston not to let him in if he should arrive . . ."

She hesitated, not wanting to darken Kitty's name too much. Perhaps she'd been all wrong about Kitty's ruthless streak, and had been an idiot for no reason at all. *A bit late to think of that,* she thought. "Sir Charles believes the marquess might try to take possession of this house. I didn't know what Her Ladyship would do, and I said he was Sterling before I could think better of it."

"Would he really throw the family out?" Nadine gasped.

"Well . . ." Before he woke, Georgiana would have said with complete confidence that Westmorland was not only capable of such cruelty, but probably relished it. Now, she wasn't sure. "Most likely," she insisted, to herself as much as to Nadine. He'd brought the deed, after all.

Eyes wide with amazement, Nadine shook her head. "But m'lady . . . won't you be in awful trouble if anyone discovers the truth?"

Georgiana flinched as if she'd been struck. "I hope to get him away from here before Lady Winston or anyone else has cause to suspect who he really is."

The maid's brow wrinkled. "How do you plan to do that, with him not able to walk and not knowing who he is?"

I have no idea. "I'll work it out," she said with a confidence she did not remotely feel.

Chapter 9

GOING OUTSIDE HAD been worth it, but only by
a narrow margin. The headache that had begun
outside under the wisteria burgeoned into a long-
toothed, sharp-clawed monster. Georgiana urged
him to take more laudanum, and in misery he did.

He must have slept for a long while. When he woke
next, the room was as dark and still as a grave; he
sensed he was alone. His head felt somewhat better.
The Stygian darkness helped, though it also served
to make him feel utterly unmoored, lost at sea without a compass. Who was he? He had no idea, and was
beginning to think he didn't really want to know.

He'd never told his fiancée she was beautiful.
That might be one thing if she weren't, and saying
so would have been obviously empty flattery. But by
God's truth, she was—thick golden hair that curled
into glowing wisps around her neck, moss-green
eyes that could dance with merriment and darken
with concern, and a ripe pink mouth he thought
about kissing every time he saw her.

But her look of alarm as he leaned toward her
in the garden had stopped him; she did not share

his interest in kissing. Which meant that either he'd never kissed her, or she hadn't liked it when he did.

Ballocks. How had he thoroughly ruined things with the woman he would spend the rest of his life with? She refused to tell him, and, uneasily, Rob sensed it was yet another answer he wouldn't much like.

It bothered him intensely that he could remember nothing of their relationship, his courtship . . . or her feelings. Perhaps that was fair, as he clearly hadn't made any romantic declarations himself, but it meant he had no idea what she felt for him.

At times, he thought theirs must be a match of some affection, when she smiled and laughed at his teasing. She'd been so devoted since his injury; surely she cared for him. She *must*.

At other times, though, there was a yawning gulf between them, and he thought in frustration that it could have been the most businesslike of arranged unions between strangers.

That felt wrong, though. Surely she would tell him if her feelings were not engaged; why would she pretend to be a devoted fiancée? And if he cared so little for her, why had he come haring off into Derbyshire to make up whatever falling out they'd had?

The best explanation he could form was that their betrothal had been amiably arranged. If they'd been caught in a scandal and obliged to marry, they wouldn't have been engaged for over two years; they would have been standing in front of a vicar within a week. If the marriage were arranged, the settlements would have been sorted before the engagement was even announced. But if there were some affection, and the match was suitable, it might have been made for convenience . . .

Rob exhaled loudly in frustration, staring up into the dark. Georgiana should have had a dozen suitors. Was there something disreputable about her? About her family? She'd only mentioned her brother, and not in affectionate terms. Perhaps the rest of her family had died in some scandalous blaze of ignominy. Perhaps they were so scandalous they were still alive, gallivanting about Italy after leaving her to an indifferent brother's care.

The door opened, and Georgiana came in. He could tell by her scent and the way she picked her way quietly across the dark room. "I'm awake," he murmured, smiling.

"How do you feel?" Her cool hand rested on his forehead for a moment.

"Better." *Now that you're here*, he added silently.

"Is there anything I can do? Are you hungry?"

"No. Would you sit with me?" He tried to lighten his tone. "Dashed odd, lying alone in complete darkness. I woke and thought for a moment I'd died, and was already shut up in the coffin."

She gave a horrified gasp. "No! Never! How dreadful—"

"Imagine my relief when you walked in," he said quickly. "Quite worth the moment of dread."

"You have peculiar notions of worth, sir." He could hear her dress rustling, and then the scrape of a chair on the floor.

"Ah, because I said it was worth the headache to go outside?" He grinned. "It was."

"It was not worth it for me," she muttered.

"No, I see that." He turned toward her, even

though he couldn't see a blasted thing. "I'm a terrible burden on you."

"Stop saying that." She touched his hand, and instinctively he grasped it. "I've brought a compress for your head. May I put it on?"

"Please." And then he nearly moaned in relief as she draped a thick cloth over his eyes and forehead. It smelled of lavender and was cool and damp to the touch. And even better, she took his hand again once it was settled.

"Do you want more laudanum?"

"No," he said on a sigh. "This feels marvelous. Will you stay and talk to me?"

Her hand flinched in his. "It's probably better if you rest quietly . . ."

"I'm going quietly mad from quietly resting," he said a bit testily. "Please. Talk about the weather, I don't care."

She laughed. "That would send anyone into a stupor."

"Faster than laudanum," he agreed. "What did we talk of before?"

An ominous silence greeted this query.

Rob cursed himself but forged on. "I cannot remember anything of your interests. Horse racing? Theater? Politics?" Those all sounded appealing to him.

"Oh. Er . . . some?" The lilt of her voice made it sound uncertain. "Theater, and some politics—I know very little about it. Lady Sidlow tells me it's not something young ladies should tax their brains with and she refuses to take the political papers."

"Why not?" he exclaimed. "Many ladies care deeply about politics."

She gave a little snort of disgust. "And perhaps when I am married I shall be at liberty to care as well."

He was inordinately pleased that she referred to their marriage. "You shall be. Of course I'll allow it."

Another fraught silence. "Horse racing isn't my passion," she said hastily. "Although I did like the Ascot, the one time I attended. I envied the jockeys— what a thrill it must be to ride so fast! Sir Charles has a very fast gelding, and I shall miss him terribly when I go back to London."

"There's nowhere to ride all-out in London." Something fluttered at the back of his mind; there *was* a place that was ideal for riding all-out, across grassy fields and atop dunes overlooking the sea. He could almost feel the wind blowing his hair back, and the horse surging beneath him. Where was that?

"Nor permission to do it," she grumbled, unaware of the memory taunting him, just out of reach.

The glimmering memory faded, leaving him frustrated but also hopeful. Perhaps if he didn't think directly about it, it would become clearer in his mind. "Who is Lady Sidlow?"

"My long-suffering, shockingly overtaxed chaperone." She said it so wryly, he laughed, despite the danger that it might make his head rupture.

"Because you've no family."

She hesitated. "Yes, that's right. My brother engaged her to bring me out in London. She was a friend of my mother's, although for the life of me I cannot see how. She's quite stiff and pompous and is forever prosing on about how ramshackle and hoydenish I am."

"Never," he said loyally. "She sounds like the most dreadful old dragon." It struck him that he must have met this woman, during the years of their engagement. "I shudder to imagine what she thinks of me, if she finds you a hoyden."

Another long pause. "Pooh!" She laughed. "She looks forward to me being married and no longer her responsibility—I've no doubt she sighs and clucks her tongue in pity whenever she thinks of my husband."

"I feel tempted to send her a bouquet every year and expound at length on how happily married we are."

"Well," she said after another pregnant pause. "I think she would be enormously astonished if you did."

He grinned. "I like surprising people."

Her fingers twitched again. "I see that," she said softly.

Rob had a feeling he had been surprising her a great deal lately. Why was that? Had he changed so greatly as a result of being beaten on the head? Again he thought that he might not want to know what he had been like before.

There was a quiet knock at the door. Georgiana slipped her hand from his and went to answer it. Now used to the darkness, he could discern every footstep as she made her way around the furniture and opened the door. He heard the murmur of female voices, one older.

Georgiana returned to the bedside. Not only could he hear her, he could smell her perfume. "Are you able to receive visitors?" She tugged at the blankets, settling them around his shoulders. "Mother

Winston would like to pay her respects. It's her compress you're wearing on your head."

"By all means." He started to sit up but stopped as her hands landed on his shoulders.

"Stay where you are," she scolded. "Mother Winston knows how injured you are, and she does not stand on ceremony."

"Yes, ma'am." He ignored her commands until he heard her walk away, then pushed himself up on the pillows and listened intently.

"My dear Lord Sterling," said a new voice. Female, older, warm and rolling, not the crisp diction of a society lady. "What a pleasure to make your acquaintance."

"And yours, madam." He made a motion toward the compress covering his head. "I regret not being more able, but I understand I owe this absolutely lifesaving device to your ingenuity."

"Is it helping?" she cried in delight. "Oh, I do hope so. 'Tis an old recipe I've had since I was a new bride—although I am terribly sorry you needed it!"

"And very grateful I am," he said gravely. "I also believe my face is rather battered at the moment, and this spares me the humiliation of scaring anyone."

A muffled laugh caught his ear; Georgiana, he realized.

"Bosh," said the older lady stoutly. He could hear the smile in her voice. "You're a right handsome fellow, just as Lady Georgiana told us. The bruises will fade, my lord."

"If not, I may keep wearing it. Perhaps with slits cut to allow me to see, so I won't be dependent upon Georgiana to guide me around."

Mother Winston tittered like a girl. "I can see your charm suffered no damage!"

"Just my wits," he agreed. "Although I have hopes they may recover."

"Of course they will!" A soft hand patted his. "Such a strong, healthy fellow. You'll recover, I feel sure of it."

"With such a wise lady's assurance, now I feel certain of it as well."

"You'd better listen to *my* advice, too," put in Georgiana, "and not go charging outdoors again before you're better."

He grinned beneath the compress. "I shall try to be more patient," he said, adding quietly, "but it *was* worth it."

"Mama?" whispered yet another voice. "Is Lord Sterling awake?"

"Go away, Geneva," scolded the older lady at the same time Rob said, "Yes, indeed he is."

"May I come in?" asked the new voice eagerly. The door creaked, and Georgiana told her to push it closed. "I hope I'm not intruding," said the girl even as she hurried across the room.

Rob guessed that his appearance and injury had caused a significant amount of drama in the household. "A pleasure to make your acquaintance . . ."

"Miss Geneva Winston, sir," she said pertly. "And it is *my* pleasure to finally make yours, my lord."

The visitors stayed for a little while. He learned that Mother Winston was Geneva's mother, and mother-in-law to his hostess, Lady Winston. He heard about the infant Annabel, who owned the heart of everyone in the household. He learned Geneva would be making her debut in London next year, and he gallantly promised to dance with her at Almack's, even though he had deep suspicions that he never went to Almack's. He could go once, he told himself, to repay the Winstons for their hospitality.

After a while Mother Winston—the dowager baronetess, although she waved that aside and urged Rob to call her Mother Winston as well—excused herself. "I hope we shall see you at dinner soon, my lord," she added.

"I look forward to it most eagerly," he told her. She patted his hand very maternally and left, promising to send a fresh poultice whenever he felt in need of one.

"Must I go, too?" asked Geneva.

"No," said Georgiana in amusement. "By all means, stay and sit in the dark with us."

The girl gave a gusty sigh. "I wish you could read aloud, Georgiana, as you were doing before Lord Sterling's accident."

"What were you reading?" asked Rob, intrigued.

"*The Arabian Nights*." She cleared her throat. "Would you like to hear it, my dear?"

I like to hear your voice. He'd realized that as Mother Winston and Geneva talked. "Of course," he said.

"All right." She sounded a trifle surprised. "I'll fetch the book. I'll have to bring a lamp, too . . ."

He settled the poultice securely atop his eyes. "I am on guard against the light."

He listened to her leave, then lowered his voice to a conspiratorial whisper. "Miss Winston, tell me truly: How dreadful do I look?"

"Dreadful! Why, who said—oh," she said, understanding dawning. "You don't look terribly dreadful, sir, only bruised. Not nearly as bad as when you arrived."

"Yes, I gather it was quite a shock to everyone," he murmured. He would almost have preferred to hear that he looked horrible, to explain the anxiety in Georgiana's face every time she looked at him.

Geneva Winston was prattling on. "Oh, an incredible shock! Georgiana told us all about you, of course, but she'd only had the one letter—I shouldn't say so but my mother did wonder what had happened, because Georgiana wrote *you* a letter every week. But then you turned up—to surprise her! How romantic and delightful!—only so badly beaten we all thought you would surely die. Dr. Elton told Cook he'd never seen anyone lose that much blood and not be left an invalid at the very least. But I'm sure you're doing ever so much better than that," she added hastily, "and Georgiana seems determined to make you well just by her own force of will! She's so daring, you know, with such a strong spirit. I do admire her desperately, not just for that but she is so fashionable as well, of course—" She broke off laughing. "Of course you know that! I forget you haven't just met her, like I did. When she first arrived I thought she would be proud and elegant, because she's been in London for three years, but she's so lovely and charming—which of course you also know! My mother took to her immediately, and of course Kitty's been her friend since they were girls." Her voice turned a little envious. "I wish I had been sent to a school like Mrs. Upton's. I would have missed my family but when they talk of those days, it does sound so lovely, and it *is* very quiet here in Derbyshire. Nothing exciting ever happens here—until Georgiana came, that is, and then you showed up, which was *so* extraordinary—"

"Geneva," scolded Georgiana. "Are you gossiping? His Lordship needs rest and quiet."

Geneva gave a startled squeak. "I'm sorry!"

Rob raised one hand. "No, no harm in it. I believe it must be a good thing to hear someone else's voice, even as I lie here muffled like a mummy."

"It might be even better to hear uplifting and thoughtful things instead of gossip." Under the compress Rob grinned, picturing the stern look she must be giving Geneva.

"I'm sorry," said Geneva again, sounding cowed. "I'll be quiet now."

"If you want to hear the story, you'll have to be." Rob felt her hands adjusting the compress over his face, and her knuckles brushed his cheek. It was probably accidental, but he hoped not.

"We left off with the voyages of Sinbad the Sailor," said Georgiana. "Do you know the story, sir?" Without waiting for him to reply, she explained, "Sinbad sets off in search of adventure and riches as a young man, and faces the most incredible ordeals—shipwreck, buried alive, set upon by monsters—"

"Almost eaten by giant snakes!" put in Geneva eagerly. "But he comes away with pockets full of diamonds!"

"Precisely," said Georgiana with a laugh. "He seems to cheat death at every turn and come away with pockets full of diamonds or splendid gifts from some king or other."

"Well," said Rob, "if the giant snakes got him, it would be a rather disappointing tale."

Geneva giggled. "Not for the snakes," said Georgiana.

"No," he agreed in amusement, and she began to read. Rob settled back and listened, falling under the spell she wove.

Georgiana didn't just read; her voice rose and fell as the tenor of the story dictated. She spoke differently for each character: the caliph who sent Sinbad to a distant kingdom, the king who welcomed him there, the merchant who bought him as a slave after his ship was seized by corsairs. When she reached the part where Sinbad was set upon by a herd of vengeful elephants and feared imminent death, Geneva gave a little shriek. Even though he'd not been read to since he was a lad, Rob found himself enjoying it immensely.

When she reached the end of the tale, where the Princess Scheherezade began yet another story, Georgiana stopped. "That's all for now."

Geneva gave a sigh, half delight, half sadness. "Will you read more later?"

"Yes," she replied in amusement, "but not tonight."

With another gusty sigh, the girl got up and left. "It was lovely chatting to you, Lord Sterling!" she said on her way out.

"Is it evening already?" Rob asked in surprise when the door had closed behind her.

"Nearly dinnertime. Are you hungry?"

"A little. Will you dine with me?"

"I've taken almost every meal at this table since you arrived," said Georgiana with a laugh. "I'm not sure I know where the dining room is any longer."

Elation shot through him. She'd written to him

every week and not left his side since his injury; that argued for devotion and affection, even though he'd been cold and thoughtless, and written her only a single letter. Geneva's report had been a blow to his conscience. There seemed no question that he was terribly at fault, and must be the one to make amends.

Cautiously he lifted the cloth from his face, relieved that his head felt much better. Georgiana was marking her spot in the book. The lamplight made her hair shine like gold, and when she glanced up at him, her face was illuminated as if she had been painted by Rubens.

"Scheherezade was a clever minx," he said, mesmerized. "I've only heard the one tale and I would do anything to hear more." *From you.*

She wrinkled her nose. "She'd married a sultan who thought so little of women he married a new one every day. Cleverness was required if she wished to live."

"That does seem rather excessive. Much easier to marry only once."

She smiled but didn't meet his gaze. "Let me send for a tray. You've slept through so many meals . . ."

"It can wait. Come here a moment." He snagged her hand. "Let me tell you a story," he added.

She sat on the edge of the mattress. "What kind of story?"

"Lie back and listen." He gingerly moved to the far side of the bed and plumped up the pillows invitingly. Georgiana hesitated, then slowly swung her feet onto the bed and lay back.

God. She was in his bed—fully clothed, atop the blankets while he was beneath them, but still, she was in his bed, beside him. Her golden curls spilled across the pillow, and he made a fist to stop himself from touching them. Trustingly she clasped her hands at her waist and closed her eyes. "What story?"

Rob inhaled deeply. "About a man and a horse."

Her eyes opened. "What sort of horse?"

"Shh." He stroked her temple and she closed her eyes again. A stray wisp of her hair curled around his finger, and Rob went still. He had to clear his throat and gather his thoughts to avoid falling into a fascinated study of that tendril.

"The best horse in the world. Beautifully proportioned, strong and well-tempered, with a gait as smooth as silk and as fast as the wind. The sort of horse any man would want to ride.

"The man did not know this, of course. He fancied getting himself a horse, saw this one at Tattersall's, and thought it was a handsome creature. He sent his steward to buy it, and the steward brought it home to the stable, where everyone congratulated the man on acquiring such a beautiful animal.

"And yet, the fellow treated it like any other horse. He left the stable boys to groom it and exercise it. He took the horse to London with him, but he was busy in town and the horse was even more neglected there.

"One day, after many, many days of not riding his fine horse, he sent for it. The footman came back and said the horse had run off—burst the lead rope and disappeared into the fields and woods. Well, the man was indignant. Why had no one told him?

"No one could answer, not the footman or the steward or the head groom. Finally a kitchen maid, who had been fond of sneaking to the stables with carrots for the horse, piped up and said no one had told him because no one thought he would notice. He didn't ride the horse, nor care for it, nor even understand how excellent a horse it was."

Georgiana opened one eye and gave him a suspicious glance. Rob grinned and touched a finger to her lips before going on with the story. "This fellow fell into a fury over that. Not care for his horse! He'd provided feed and a warm stable, and what more did a horse need?

"Did he know the horse could do tricks, asked the kitchen maid bravely. Of course he didn't. Did he know the horse would let the stable cat lie upon his back? He'd never heard of such a thing. Did he know the horse had saved a groom's life by refusing to ride down a certain path, where the stream had overflowed its banks and washed away the road? He'd no idea.

"By now this fellow began to feel sorry for having lost this horse. Even worse, a terrible storm was brewing, and he couldn't leave any animal, let alone his fine, proud, clever horse, out in it. He sent for another—very inferior—mount and set out to find the missing horse. He looked far and wide, but when a bolt of lightning struck a tree in the wood, the horse he was riding bucked him off and bolted, leaving him lost in the dark, with a turned ankle as well."

"Why didn't he take a groom along with him?" she asked.

"We've already established that our hero isn't the brightest lad," he said. "That's not the point of the story."

"What is the point?" Her lips were curved into an enchanting little smile. He thought about kissing her, then thought about losing all the ground he'd gained, and refrained.

"I'm getting there." He settled his elbow on the pillow next to hers and propped his head on his hand. It gave him a perfect view of her face. Her eyelashes were a thick, dark fringe against her cheeks, and her eyebrows were perfect arches, darker gold than her hair.

He kept talking to prolong the moment. "Our chap, on foot and feeling like a complete idiot, trudged along before realizing he was utterly lost. No idea which way was home. He decided to take a rest, empty the water from his boots, and sort out what to do. Perhaps he didn't deserve that horse, and should content himself with another one.

"But he *had* liked that horse, even though he'd not been a good owner. What's more, the poor animal was lost in this wretched wood, exposed to the rain and lightning and at the mercy of any lions or bears who might be about."

"Lions and bears?" Her eyes flew open again. "In London?"

"They escaped from the menagerie," he said. She raised her brows and he made a stern face and shushing sound. "It was this fear that drove him onward. He had to know if the horse would like to come home with him, now that he knew to be more caring, or if the horse still wished to be free. He trudged onward for what felt like a year, until finally he heard hoofbeats. And there, through the trees . . . why yes! It was his very excellent horse, trotting toward him.

"The horse stopped well back from him, and

when he went to stroke its neck, the animal danced away. When he tried to mount it, it ran off again. Finally he stood still in despair, and simply held out his hand. And slowly the horse returned to him, and took the carrot he'd brought along as a token of his goodwill.

"Now the fellow started to learn. He followed the horse without trying to catch it, and the horse led him through the trees, away from a deep pit in the ground. The rain came down in torrents, and the horse guided him safely across the only bridge for miles. At long last they came in sight of the streets of London, and still the fellow let the horse guide him. Straight to his own house the horse led him."

"That is a very kind and clever horse," she murmured.

"Far more so than our man deserved," Rob agreed. "Soaked, exhausted, and limping badly on his turned ankle, the fellow went not into the house but to the mews. He left the door open, and opened the stall door, too. The horse, he knew, must be just as cold and wet and tired as he was, but still it waited outside, not trusting him yet. It would not come inside for the grooms or any of the stable lads.

"The fellow got some more carrots, and went back into the rain. The horse ate his carrots. When the man went back into the stable, the horse followed him, and allowed him to brush it. The man did not leave until he had brushed and curried the horse from head to tail. He covered it with a blanket and brought it a bucket of oats. He filled the water trough and turned fresh straw into the stall, and then—only then—did the horse allow him to stroke its neck and muzzle.

"After that the fellow was much more considerate of his horse. He exercised it each day, and groomed it himself. He sent it to the country every summer, and when he could not ride, he made certain someone would visit the animal and bring it a carrot or an apple. And the horse never ran away again, even when the stall door was left open, because now it was treated with the respect and care it deserved."

She opened her eyes during the last part and watched him. "That's an odd story. Where did you hear it?"

"An old woman told it to me as a young lad."

A smile hovered on her lips at this blatant lie. "Did she offer you some enchanted beans, too?"

Rob grinned and stroked his fingertips over her hand. "No. Just the tale."

Georgiana turned to face him. "Rob. Really. Am I supposed to be the horse in this story?"

"Of course not," he said indignantly. "You look nothing like a horse. Haven't even got four feet."

She rolled her eyes. "You know what I mean."

"I don't, actually." He touched her hand again, now that it lay on the pillow between them. "I don't remember."

Her brow wrinkled, and she bit her lip.

"I'm not asking you to tell me," he added. Gently he touched her cheek, letting his thumb drift over her lips. They were velvety soft, and the urge to lean forward was almost overwhelming. Just one kiss . . . after being betrothed two long years . . .

Don't be an idiot, he rebuked himself. *You dug this hole, and it won't be easy to climb out.*

"I suspect I don't want to know," he added. "Let the past stay past. All I want is a chance to start anew."

Her eyes were shadowed. "I'm not sure it's that simple . . ."

"Pretend we've only just met." He raised her hand to his lips and kissed her knuckles once, then again, letting his lips linger on her skin. Her pulse was warm and quick against his lips. "Enchanted to make your acquaintance, my lady."

A reluctant smile tugged at her lips. "And I yours, my lord."

He grinned, pressing her hand to his thumping heart. "That's a fine beginning."

And this time, he meant to make the most of it.

Chapter 10

꧁꧂

To Georgiana's immense relief, Rob did not ask to go outside again.

His head was much better, he declared, and he kept adding pillows behind his back until he was almost upright. He asked her to read more, as the light no longer bothered him, and she ended up spending one of the pleasantest days she'd had in Derbyshire in his room. Geneva brought in her embroidery to listen, Mother Winston brought another poultice—although Rob folded it over the top of his head instead of on his face—and even Kitty came by for a short visit, professing herself vastly relieved to see him feeling so well.

Rob continued to be charming and lighthearted. He didn't tell any more silly stories, but he offered commentary on the stories she read, which always sent Geneva, and often Georgiana as well, into gales of laughter. He did have dimples, she realized, deep ones on either side of his mouth that showed themselves every time he laughed. He looked ridiculous with the poultice on his head, and he seemed merely amused by it.

At times Georgiana almost convinced herself he was another man entirely. The Marquess of Westmorland, as she remembered him, was becoming more and more nebulous in her mind. Instead there was only Rob, who was not Sterling but neither was he really Westmorland.

She knew this state of affairs couldn't last, but she still had no idea how to unwind it.

Kitty intercepted her that evening after dinner. Yet again she had taken her meal on a tray in the sickroom with Rob. His appetite was returning, and he'd said that he meant to start dining with the family soon. Georgiana said she looked forward to that, even though she had become rather fond of dining alone with him.

"Can you spare a few minutes in the garden with me?" Kitty asked, looking tense.

"Of course." Georgiana followed her friend outside. It was twilight, and the thrushes were stirring in the bushes.

"I received this earlier today." Kitty thrust a letter at her and paced away, fists swinging at her sides. "I don't dare alarm Mother Winston and Geneva, but I shall scream if I don't talk to someone!"

Georgiana recognized the seal in the wax, and almost cast up her dinner into the wisteria. It was the Rowland crest—Rob's father. With a tremor in her hands, she unfolded it.

"The effrontery!" seethed Kitty. "That monster!"

Georgiana cleared her throat. It was a brief, polite letter from the Duchess of Rowland. She implied the marquess had set out for Osbourne House and ought to have arrived by now, and would Lady

Winston be so kind as to inform him that his valet, left with baggage at Macclesfield, had sprained his ankle and would be going ahead to Salmsbury Abbey, the Rowland seat. She added that if His Lordship required a man, she would send another as soon as possible.

"You know what this means, of course," went on Kitty grimly. "He *is* coming. He must have got distracted or delayed on the way, but Westmorland is indeed coming here. That beast!"

Resolutely Georgiana kept her eyes away from the windows above them, where Lord Westmorland—*Rob*, she reminded herself desperately—lay, unsuspecting and unsuspected. "Her Grace may be mistaken . . ."

Kitty opened her eyes wide in disbelief. "Did you not read it?" She snatched the note and pointed. "*I beg you will inform Westmorland*—see, she believes him to be here already!—and here—*if he should require a man to attend him, I shall send one posthaste*—where she suggests he means to stay a while!"

Georgiana could feel her nape burning. "Who knows what he told her, Kitty? Perhaps he merely wanted to put her off for some reason, and told her a story about coming here. I daresay he's not the sort to confide in his mother about . . . things like this," she finished weakly.

A week ago it had been much easier to presume Rob would coldly lie to his mother. Now it felt like a betrayal to say such things about him, even though they might well be true. The man she knew, Rob, was wholly unlike the Malicious Marquess she'd despised in London.

Kitty was shaking her head. "You're much too kind to him, Georgiana. No, mark my words, he'll arrive, sooner or later." She took back the note and folded it, her eyes glittering. "He shall be sorry when he does," she said with quiet venom.

Oh dear. "I really can't think why he would," Georgiana said desperately. "It's quite a distance from London. Most likely he would grow bored and find something more entertaining to do along the way. For all you know, he's holed up in a tavern somewhere between here and town, drinking himself stupid."

Kitty was not convinced. "Perhaps. I hope so." A thin wail drifted from the windows above them, Annabel waking and wanting to be fed. "I must go in. Don't tell Mother Winston or Geneva."

"Of course not," Georgiana murmured, her eyes still fixed on the letter Kitty was tapping against her skirt. "What will you reply to the duchess?"

"Hmm?" Kitty glanced at the letter as if surprised she still held it. "I already sent a reply that he is not here, and shall never be welcome here. Perhaps she'll do me the favor of warning him away."

Georgiana said nothing as Kitty strode into the house. She'd been an idiot not to expect this. A man like Rob could not disappear without causing concern. He had family and friends who would wonder where he was.

And in truth, this had gone on too long already. Every day his health was better. Every day the chances improved that his memory would come flooding back. Most likely it hadn't happened yet only because he was in wholly unfamiliar surroundings, without anything that might remind him of the truth.

And, of course, there were the lies she had told him to prevent that happening. The lies she had begun to . . . not to *believe*, of course, but she'd certainly stopped *hating* them. He was nothing like she'd thought he was, and she uneasily realized she had begun to relish being with him. His flirting was flattering. His humor was irresistible. His determination to make himself well again impressed her.

She had not forgotten herself, but she had been tempted—oh so very tempted. "Idiot," she whispered to herself. She was going to marry Sterling, and she was letting her head get turned by another man.

That letter was the bracing dose of reality she needed. She took a deep breath and gave herself a mental smack. Salmsbury Abbey must be rather near, if the duchess could send a manservant at once. He ought to go there, where he would be surrounded by people dear to him, in a place familiar to him. He would recover his memory and his health there, and she would go back to her life in London. She would even take that troublesome deed with her and quietly return it to Charles with a warning not to be so foolish again. This was for everyone's benefit—most especially Rob's.

The only question was how to get him away from Osbourne House, and how quickly she could manage it.

ROB RESTED HIS HEAD against the back of the wing-back chair. He'd felt well enough, and was so enormously tired of being in bed that he'd decided to sit there for a while and savor the fresh breeze through the window. But eavesdropping, he suspected, was some kind of sin, and he supposed the disquiet he felt was his just reward for having overheard bits of Georgiana's conversation with Lady Winston.

Lady Winston had been enraged. He couldn't make out most of what she'd said, but her tone of voice carried perfectly well. Those few words he'd caught, though . . . Westmorland. That name resonated inside him like the vibration of a plucked string. It felt dear to him, familiar . . . and right. He knew Westmorland, very well indeed if he'd had to guess. In fact, if he weren't Lord Sterling, he might have thought that *he* was Westmorland.

It brought no elation. Lady Winston's open contempt had put him on guard, and the wary nature of Georgiana's response made him recoil. Whoever Westmorland was—and the feeling that it was he felt like a rash rising on his skin—he was hated here. Rob did not want to be hated here, not by kind Lady Winston and exuberant Geneva and maternal Mother Winston, and most certainly not by Georgiana. He wanted her green eyes to light up with delight when she saw him. He wanted her to laugh at his jokes and fuss over him in concern when he felt unwell. He wanted her to lie beside him and hold his hand, even if she scoffed at his tall tales.

And most of all he wanted her to fall hopelessly in love with him and not break their betrothal.

That thought sent a chill through him. If he were, somehow, Westmorland, Georgiana might not actually be his fiancée. She was betrothed to Lord Sterling—which *must* be he, he argued in his mind. No, he most certainly was Lord Sterling. Georgiana had saved his life, cared for him while he was unconscious, and rarely been far from his side since. She smiled at him and read to him and laughed with him. Damn it, he *wanted* to be Lord Sterling.

But it wouldn't go away, that prickle in his mind elicited by the name Westmorland.

Chapter 11
❧☙

THE NEXT MORNING dawned bright and warm, another beautiful day, and on the off chance the Duchess of Rowland sent someone, Georgiana decided they should be far away and out of sight. It was time to get Rob away from Osbourne House, but she needed to work out how to do it without disclosing the truth.

Deep inside her heart, she also knew she was buying herself one more day with him. Her genuine desire to return Rob to his family—before Kitty discovered what she'd done—was complicated by her increasing reluctance to end the charade and never see him again.

"It's so fine out, I thought I might walk to the pond." She turned to Rob. "What do you think?"

"Brilliant idea," he said at once. He'd come downstairs that morning to eat at the table.

"Do you think you should?" asked Kitty in concern. "It's at least half a mile distant."

"It's flat ground, and an easy walk." Georgiana watched Rob as she spoke. "If you'd like to get away from the house for a bit."

He grinned, charmingly abashed. "You have read my mind. Not that I don't appreciate this house a great deal, Lady Winston," he added to their hostess. "But some fresh air would be very welcome."

Kitty smiled. "Of course. I should have known Georgiana would marry someone who likes the outdoors as much as she does. I'll send Angus with you."

"Oh, we can manage," Georgiana exclaimed. "There's no need for Angus to come." She had things to say to Rob and didn't need Angus listening in.

"It's a long walk, dear," put in Mother Winston, concerned. "Lord Sterling may not be strong enough yet . . ."

"Nonsense." Rob put his hand on the cane someone had located in the attics for him, and tapped it on the floor. "I feel better every day."

"Which is not the same as being equal to walking to the pond and back," murmured Kitty over her teacup, an amused smile lingering on her lips. "If you wish to go, by all means go. But do take Angus along, to carry the hamper if nothing else."

Georgiana gave in. "I'll be ready before it's packed. Send him along with it."

She told Lucy to have Cook pack a picnic hamper and located an old blanket, and they set out. Rob leaned on his cane, slow but steady in his gait. Georgiana watched with veiled apprehension. It took a very long time to make it through the garden, and she realized it would be even longer on the way back. It probably was too much to expect him to do this.

"Perhaps we *should* wait for Angus," she began, when he inhaled a little sharply.

"What? Not for my sake." Looking determined, he quickened his pace. "I despise being trapped in bed."

"I could tell," she said. "But I may have been too eager to escape the house."

There was a world of sympathy and understanding in his glance. "Quite rightly. Stuck inside all day, expected to entertain an invalid . . . It would drive anyone mad."

"No!" she protested with a startled laugh. "I didn't mean that."

"You didn't *say* that." He navigated his way down three shallow steps with a perceptible hiss of discomfort.

"It's not your fault you're an invalid," she exclaimed, "and I don't begrudge the entertainment." Strangely, she didn't, not now.

"And I am too shameless to refuse it." He winked at her before assuming a martyred expression. "Oh no, dear Georgiana, do go out and carry on living your life. Never mind me, lying here alone and unwell. I shall endure . . . and waste away a little more . . . of boredom and loneliness if not of my injuries . . ." His patently false tone, weak and thin, warbled off.

Georgiana snorted with laughter and flapped one hand at him.

Rob laughed. "I'm not that noble, my love. Surely you must know that."

As always, the endearment made her uneasy. Even more unnerving was the reason: she rather liked it. Sterling never said things like that to her. He paid her compliments, flowery flattery that sounded lovely but, she realized, not quite heartfelt. He might have said them to anyone. "I feel I've come to know you a vast deal better in the last few days than I did before," she said honestly.

Rob glanced quickly at her, but the brim of his hat concealed his expression. "Another benefit to being knocked on the head," was all he said.

She cleared her throat. "I don't suppose any memories have come back to you?"

His cane came down on a loose stone in the path and slipped, sending him stumbling forward as if he might fall. She gasped in alarm and dove forward to catch him, and ended up with his arm around her shoulders and her hands clutching his coat.

"Sorry," he said, breathing hard. "Blasted stone." He knocked it off the path with a flick of the cane.

"All steady?" She tried to laugh, but was too breathless. Her heart was racing and her hands—if they weren't still gripping him—would be shaking.

His arm around her tightened. "Thanks to you— again. You're always saving me."

Georgiana released him as if her palms burned. "Oh no! You don't need me."

Rob pushed up his hat and gave her a searing look. "Never say that." He raised his head and scanned the path ahead. "I expect you'll have to catch me a dozen more times today alone."

"Oh." Color flooded her face that she had been thinking . . . and he had meant something completely different. "This was a mistake, wasn't it?"

"On the contrary." He started forward again. "I'm looking forward to being caught."

Georgiana blushed with pleasure, then realized what she was doing and resolved to keep her mouth closed. She would take greater care to watch the path and warn him before he could stumble again. That, after all, was preferable to having to catch him in her arms every time his steps faltered. She snatched up the blanket she'd dropped and walked on.

They reached the end of the garden, where the landscape turned into a narrow track through the meadow. Beyond it lay a small wood, with the pond nestled in the middle. Georgiana had been there before; it was a very pleasant spot to sit and read, where she could take off her shoes and stockings and sit with her feet in the water watching dragonflies glide over the pond's surface in the sunlight. She adored this little pond of Kitty's, and before Rob's accident had been fond of walking out to it every few days.

Today, of course, it seemed a dozen miles away as Rob leaned on his cane more heavily with each step. When her eyes fell on a small cart, left by the side of the path, she gave a chirp of relief. "Here! Let's take this."

"To what purpose, precisely?" Rob pushed back his hat and wiped his forehead. His hair was damp with sweat. It was a very warm day, and she felt another pang of remorse for encouraging him to walk out in it.

She put the blanket on the back of the cart. It was a low cart, with staves forming open sides. It was the sort of cart a gardener might use in the garden, with two long handles and a single wheel at the front. "Sit on the front and I'll wheel you to the pond."

Rob looked at the cart incredulously, then at her. Georgiana took up the handles and pushed the cart back and forth in illustration.

"You can't really mean to push that all the way to the pond," he said.

She laughed. "Of course I can. Really, Rob, I'm not a helpless maiden."

"I never thought you were." He eyed the cart. "But neither am I. By all means push the cart, but I shall walk."

"Don't you trust me?" She grasped the handles and trundled the cart forward. "You're already limping. Or does it offend your sense of propriety?"

His frown vanished at that word. "Of course not."

"Then let's have a spot of fun," she said impishly.

He eyed the cart. "You'll tell me at once if your arms hurt. And you'll go slowly."

"Oh, you prefer to move sedately and gingerly?"

"When you're pushing the cart, yes." He put the cane up beside him.

"Too bad!" she cried, and leaned into it, driving the cart forward.

With a loud exclamation Rob seized the staves beside him for balance. He looked over his shoulder in alarm, but his face eased into a grin as she laughed. It was not hard work; the track sloped gently downhill and the wheel ran easily over the packed dirt. She charged forward, pleased with herself for having spared him the walk and thrilling to the challenge. She'd been cooped up far too long in the sickroom.

And then he caught the spirit of it, too. "I say, madam," he said over his shoulder, "your driving is rather dangerous."

"It's more exciting that way!" She ran the cart over an exposed rock in the path, giving him a bump. He threw up his arms in exaggerated upset, and gave a whoop. All the way to the pond he teased, and she responded by wheeling him from side to side wildly, almost dumping him over at one point and leaving him clinging to the staves.

By the time they reached the pond, both were red-faced from laughing. Georgiana stopped the cart in the clearing. "We're here," she said gaily, grabbing the blanket and unfurling it on the only clear patch of ground. Her heart pounded from the exercise and the feeling of freedom, away from the house.

"I see what you mean." Rob came up beside her. "Exceptional beauty."

"Isn't it?" She inhaled a deep, happy breath. "Well worth the trouble of getting here."

"Yes," he murmured, but when she glanced at him, he was watching her with open desire.

It sent a bolt of pleasure through her, hot and intense. She could almost feel the flush rising to her skin as her blood raced in undeniable excitement. This time there was no laughter or gratitude in his face, only pure attraction. He'd called her beautiful, but this was something else—not mere appreciation but passionate hunger. Sterling never looked at her that way . . .

With a start she looked away, yanking at the ribbons of her bonnet. "It's very warm out! Thank goodness for the shade . . ." She cast aside her bonnet, stripping off her gloves to toss them into the crown before sinking down onto the blanket.

He followed, lowering himself beside her and stretching out his leg with an audible exhale. Georgiana recognized the opportunity she'd been both seeking and dreading.

"Does your leg hurt terribly?"

He wiggled his boot from side to side. "No. I fear it may give out at any moment, but the pain is mild. Weakness more than aches." He tossed his hat behind him.

"I've been thinking," she said, as earnestly as possible, "that it might be better for your recovery if you went to London."

He went still. "Why?"

"There are doctors there."

"Charlatans and poisoners, mostly." He closed his eyes and braced his arms behind him, letting his head fall back so a ray of sun illuminated his face. "Dr. Elton says it's not broken and will strengthen as I walk on it."

"More than your leg was wounded," she reminded him. "And Dr. Elton is barely a step up from birthing calves. In fact I think he might do that, when help's needed . . ."

Rob grinned. "If farmers let him help with calving, that's high praise."

"But your *mind*," she protested, laughing nonetheless. "Farmers don't care as much for cows' minds, so Dr. Elton has no training in injuries to the head."

"I expect most doctors in London know just as little."

"Being back in town might help restore your memories," she persisted.

"Oh?"

He said it absently, as if he were only being polite, but Georgiana knew that was false. He wanted to regain his memory. It wouldn't match the stories she'd been telling him, but he didn't know that now. And that's why she had to persuade him. What if his mind would be permanently damaged if he didn't remember soon? She couldn't shake the fear that she was impeding his recovery, and the only way out was to get him away from Osbourne House.

"I think it will help immeasurably," she said with more confidence than she felt. "And what could it hurt? We can't stay here with Kitty forever."

He sat up. "Of course not. I didn't mean to suggest it. I just . . ." He hesitated, his brow creasing. "I feel no desire to go to London."

Her heart leapt into her throat. "Why not?"

Looking puzzled, he shook his head. "I just don't want to go." He turned to face her. "Could we go to your home?"

She shuddered involuntarily. "Not unless plague has infested every other house in England."

"That bad?" He edged closer. "Why?"

"My brother," she said with a short, humorless laugh.

"Yes, him." Rob stared off across the pond, the water glittering in the sun. "I have a few things to say to him."

Only the thought that Rob would never have reason to speak to Alistair kept her from recoiling in alarm. "Well, he wouldn't welcome us, and I'd rather go almost anywhere but there."

"Why?"

Georgiana didn't like talking about her brother, but somehow she found herself answering his question. "He's not . . . kind. And in fairness, we hardly know each other. He's twenty years older than I, and was raised as the heir, supreme above all others." She couldn't keep the scorn from her voice, remembering too late that Rob had probably been raised much the same way. He'd have been the Marquess of Westmorland from birth, or at least child-hood. Perhaps that explained his arrogant attitude.

Well—his arrogant attitude *before*.

"Needless to say, Alistair had little to do with me," she hurried on. "His mother died when he was at university and my father married my mother soon afterward." She paused. "I think he resented her, and our father for marrying again at all, and then of course I was wholly unwelcome in his world."

"He sounds a right prince," said Rob.

"I don't like him, either," she confessed. "The trouble is, my father named him my guardian." She rolled her eyes. "Papa always wanted us to get along. He thought Alistair would relent and regard me fondly. But I—" She stopped, realizing how much she'd said. "I don't know why I'm boring you with all these ancient grudges!"

"Not bored at all." She was grateful that his gaze was trained out over the pond and not on her. "How long have you been under his guardianship?"

"Oh, since I was seven, when my father died." She plucked a wildflower from the grass and twirled the stem between her fingers. "It hasn't been dread-ful. He sent me off to school when my mother died the following year, and left me there for ten years."

"Ten years!" His startled outburst made her smile.

"Ten *glorious* years," she replied. "I was very glad he did. He had to be persuaded—left to his own de-vices he would have sent me to an orphanage in-stead."

Rob made a sudden motion, quickly arrested. He gripped his hands together, but she saw his jaw flex. "That seems unduly harsh. Who persuaded him against it?"

"My father's estate manager. I think he threatened to quit his post, along with most of the house staff, if Alistair persisted in that course." She pulled her knees up under her chin and wrapped her arms around them. "My mother was beloved. She was kind and generous to everyone. After the way Alistair's mother treated people—" She bit her lip. "I shouldn't repeat gossip."

"I shan't tell. The woman's dead, in any event." He gave her a wink.

Georgiana grinned in guilty amazement. All her life she'd been told it was wicked to speak ill of her father's first wife, whose dour portrait in the library had frightened her as a child before her father had it removed to a little-used room. "By all reports she was a rather cold woman. Her marriage to Papa was arranged, and he only met her twice before the wedding. Papa never spoke of her, but Lady Sidlow says she was surely the reason Alistair is as he is— aloof and critical and focused solely on himself. When she died, Papa married my mother within two months."

"I trust he was happier."

Her lips curled in a wistful but still happy smile. "Very. I don't remember him well, but every memory I have is of him laughing, running races with me across the lawns or playing bowls with my mother. There was no doubt that he married her for love."

"Clever fellow," murmured Rob.

She flushed and changed the subject. "Why don't you want to go to London?"

His brow lowered and his eyes grew distant, as if he were thinking very hard. "I don't care for the people," he said at last.

People like her, she thought uneasily, thinking of the scornful things he'd said about her and Joanna Hotchkiss.

"Is London the only possibility?" he interrupted her thoughts. He ran one hand over his head, ruffling up his damp hair into unruly spikes. "I must be a terrible burden on Lady Winston."

"Oh, I'm sure she doesn't think so! But . . ." She plucked another flower. "But you seem so much better now, and I would hate to slow your recovery by mouldering away here when being somewhere else might help restore your mind."

He was quiet for several minutes. Georgiana, waiting anxiously for his response, began to review what she'd said. She felt like she was picking her way across a moor, feeling for every foothold and half certain each step would sink her. But she did think Rob would recover better somewhere else—not least because he would finally hear the truth—and she did want to help him—although she'd had that urge before and it had got her into this mess to begin with—

"What if nothing does?" he asked. "Restores my mind, I mean."

She flinched. "I'm sure something will!"

"But if it doesn't." He tilted his head to glance at her. "What would you do, if I never remember anything? Would it change things between us?"

It was a terrible question to ask. If she thought about that, that this charming, romantic, good-humored Rob might be the new Rob, forever, it might allow dangerous thoughts and feelings to flourish. Of course she would still have to tell him he was not Lord Sterling, but if she did, and he never reverted to the Malicious Marquess . . . Already she was struggling to remember why she disliked him and that she must get him back to his family and out of her hands as soon as possible.

But she could not tell him that, not today.

"No," she said softly. "Of course not."

What did one more lie matter, at this point?

Chapter 12

T HE TENSION EASED from his shoulders, and he took her hand, bringing it to his lips for a soft kiss. "Could we go to my home, then?"

"If—if you prefer," she said unsteadily. He still held her hand, his fingers strong and gentle. She gave her head a shake, but didn't pull free. "Yes, that might be ideal—even better than London." And it was. She'd sneaked into Kitty's library last night and verified that Salmsbury Abbey was some forty miles away.

Rob glanced at her, clearly startled by this easy agreement. "Is it near?"

"Not too far," she said, secretly crossing her fingers that she could manage to get him there.

"Where?" he demanded, his face sharp with interest.

"Ah . . ." She couldn't tell him where Sterling's actual home was, since it lay in distant Yorkshire, near her own family estate. Kitty knew that and would wonder if he said anything. But she couldn't actually describe where Rowland's seat was, either, for the same reason. "It's nearer than my home," she said. "And going there must be better for your health."

"Yes," he said slowly. "All right. We'll do that."

"Brilliant," she said, trying to hide her relief. "Let's go soon."

He shot another glance at her, as if sensing something was off, but she only smiled back and tried to pretend she was wholly pleased with the plan. Which she was. It was for the best. And the sooner it was done, the better.

"I don't know about you," he said, breaking into her thoughts again, "but I have a fiendish desire to wade in the pond."

She jerked in amazement. "You do?"

"May I not?" He grinned at her as he released her hand and yanked at one boot.

Blinking rapidly, Georgiana began to smile. On her own, she'd have gone swimming, not just wading. "Of course you may. And we shall."

They were up to their knees in the water when Angus appeared with the hamper. He waved and set it down. He'd brought a fishing pole, and Rob gave him leave to walk around to the deeper part of the pond and see if he could catch any fish for dinner. Angus grinned, clearly having hoped for this, and made his way out to a fallen tree that jutted over the water, where he could cast his line out of earshot but not out of sight.

It was, she reflected with some wistfulness, the perfect day. It was bliss to be outside after so many days shut up in a dim sickroom. The sun was warm, the water was cool, and mud squished agreeably between her toes. As she held up her skirts and followed a glittering water bug skimming along the water's surface, she felt the happiest she'd been in days.

And no small part of that was Rob. He bore no resemblance to the cold, polished marquess who'd inspired such fear and dislike in London. He rolled up his trouser legs, and collected a large handful of flat stones. When his attempts to skip the stones failed, he scowled at himself and let her show him how to do it. As she adjusted the angle of his wrist and gave advice, his mouth firmed into a line of concentration. His hair fell over his brow as he slung the stones, and her heart gave an unsteady thump at the fierce elation that blazed across his face when he got the knack of it, and then skipped a dozen more as if to prove he could.

"I knew I couldn't have forgotten that," he muttered, flexing his fingers as he sloshed out of the pond.

"What?" She'd come out of the water before he did and was seated on the blanket, wiggling her toes in the sun. "Is something wrong?"

"Wrong?" he scoffed, lowering himself to the ground beside her. "Absolutely nothing is wrong today, on this beautiful day, in this beautiful spot, with this beautiful woman beside me. This is perfection."

She couldn't stop smiling. Privately she agreed, although not for reasons she could tell him. "Your standards are very low. Perfection! After what you've been through?"

He grinned. "I survived. I still have all my limbs, and all my senses." He paused. "Well, I have most of my senses." Georgiana burst out laughing. "All in all, I can't be sorry for it happening."

"No!" she gasped. "Never say that!"

He twisted toward her, smiling. The sun turned the ends of his tousled hair to copper. Georgiana felt a flush of heat roll through her that had nothing to do with the sun. And she knew, as he slowly lowered his head, that he was going to kiss her . . . and she knew she should protest and not let it happen, but the breath seemed to have stopped in her chest and the view of his handsome face seemed to have mesmerized her into a state of breathless wonder.

One little kiss meant nothing, surely. Plenty of young ladies kissed more than one man before they got married. Some of them reveled in it, in fact, and considered it a vital part of choosing a husband. And she'd been so sure she was in love with Sterling, and would be forever, that it had never occurred to her before that she might be a little curious what it was like to kiss someone else . . .

But he didn't. He touched his lips lightly to her forehead. "I'm sorry," he breathed.

Her heart leapt into her throat. "What—for what?"

"For whatever went wrong between us," he murmured, his breath warming her temple. "Something I did but do not remember. Whatever it was, I'm sorry."

"No," she mumbled, her face scarlet.

He brushed a stray wisp of hair from her cheek, his fingers gentle. "Can you forgive me? Someone's already properly thrashed me for it."

"Rob!" Mortified, she still laughed a little. "Don't say that!"

He grinned. His fingertips traced feathery spirals on her cheek, over her jaw until she wanted to tip back her head and let him stroke her throat. "For all you know, they heard I needed a thrashing and decided to take up the cause."

"That is utterly ridiculous."

"No, no, it's only logical," he countered, still tracing those circles on her skin, his fingers skimming lazily over her collarbone. "Even if those particular fellows didn't know, some almighty power must have, and delivered me into their hands. I don't see how you can argue with divine justice."

"Divine—!" She gave up and laughed. "How can you say such things? It was terrible and terrifying and you're making jokes about it."

"It helps to endure it," he said with a philosophical nod, "if I believe I deserved it. Getting thrashed for cause—every lad understands that. You take the whipping and go on with yourself, chastened to some degree and certainly resolved never to commit any similar sin, or at least not get caught at it." He made a face. "The other sort of thrashing . . . that doesn't bear thinking about. Leads to grousing about ruinous luck, which no man wants to think he's got."

Georgiana could only stare, openmouthed, marveling at him. "You're different," she said on impulse. "Not like you were before."

"Better, I hope," he said with a devilish wink.

Without thinking Georgiana touched his jaw. She never would have thought the Marquess of Westmorland would make light of being beaten. Or of himself. Or apologize for . . . well, for anything, let alone for something he didn't even remember doing. He was like a different man.

Either that or she had completely misunderstood and misjudged him. Which was, she allowed with some fresh humility, entirely possible.

"I think so, yes," she whispered.

His hand covered hers, holding her fingers gently across his cheek. "Then it was all worth it." He closed his eyes and turned his head, pressing a kiss into her palm.

"You," she told him, "are a madman."

"Mmm." He smiled, still nuzzling her palm. "Quite likely." He opened one eye. "Do you like me that way?"

Her smile softened, growing wistful. "Yes," she murmured. *Very much.*

"That's good enough for me." Before she could react, he bent his head and brushed a kiss—lighter than a feather—on her mouth, then immediately released her. "Where did Angus put the hamper?"

Slowly Georgiana sat up, her heart throbbing and her lips tingling. She watched, dazed, as Rob retrieved the hamper and rummaged inside it. As if he had no idea he'd just upended her world.

She should not have let him kiss her. She shouldn't have let herself slide into such informality with him at all. But part of her—a wicked part that seemed to grow larger and stronger every day—liked it. That part of her didn't want to put an end to it, even though she knew she must.

Just . . . not today.

They devoured the hamper contents and went wading again. He took off his waistcoat and went into the pond in his shirtsleeves with his trousers rolled to his knees. Even though she'd helped strip and wash him when he was unconscious, it was wreaking havoc on her good sense to see his bare limbs.

When she discovered a swarm of tadpoles near

the reeds, she called him over in delight. He seemed just as charmed by the wriggling creatures as she was, and Georgiana thought yet again how odd it was to be standing barefoot in a pond with the Malicious Marquess, in his shirtsleeves with his hair ruffled into a glowing nimbus around his head. And as if to permanently banish her image of him as a languid, spiteful rake, Rob snapped off a reed nearby and tried to make it whistle, to no avail.

"That's terrible!" She made a face at him.

"I suppose this is another thing I've forgotten, but you can do," he shot back.

"You knew how to skip stones," she replied. "You're merely out of practice." Because he'd been prowling London ballrooms, slicing young ladies to shreds with one cutting word. Just as he would no doubt do again soon. Georgiana broke off her own reed to avoid thinking about that. She put it to her lips and blew, shocked when it produced a thin but clear whistle.

Rob stopped flattening his reed and gazed at her in astonishment.

"I didn't know that would happen!" she cried, laughing even as she backed away. "It was an accident!"

"It's completely unfair," he charged, sloshing after her. "You skip stones better than I, you whistle better than I—*accidentally*, even—and you drive the cart with more verve than any man—come here!"

"No!" Gasping now with laughter, she turned and tried to run, catching up her skirts higher. The pond was deeper than she'd thought, though, and her toes caught on an unseen underwater root. She would have pitched headfirst into the water if his arm hadn't gone around her waist and caught her, pulling her back against him.

"Completely unfair," he said again, his breath hot on her nape. "It's like the gods deliberately designed you to enchant and bewitch me . . ."

Her heart thundered, and she felt light-headed. He held her securely against him with one arm, his hand spread on her belly. He was so warm and strong, so comforting and exciting. His free hand skimmed up her arm to her shoulder, and his fingers caressed her cheek.

She felt like a criminal, conniving to steal affections she had no right to. "Enchantments . . . rarely end well," she said breathlessly.

"No?" He turned her to face him. The corner of his mouth tilted upward, and his hazel eyes darkened. "I think this one will. But either way, I'm willing to risk it . . ." He tipped up her chin, and Georgiana knew, with a mixture of alarm and exhilaration, that she wasn't going to stop him from kissing her . . .

"Ho there," called a voice. "Lady Georgiana! Lord Sterling!"

Rob froze, his lips less than an inch from hers.

Angus emerged from the trees, fishing pole on his shoulder and basket in his hand. With a mortified gasp, Georgiana twisted out of Rob's embrace. "Beggin' your pardon, my lord. I forgot, Lady Winston told me to inquire if you and Lady Georgiana plan to dine with the family. She worried you might take ill again, in the sun."

Rob's jaw flexed. "No, no one is ill. We'll be at dinner."

"Yes, m'lord. Shall I carry back the hamper?"

"Absolutely."

"And the blanket, please." Her face on fire, Georgiana splashed gracelessly out of the water. If not for the servant, Rob would have kissed her . . . might still be kissing her . . . might have kept kissing her as he carried her back to the blanket and gave in to the undeniable attraction sparking between them. And she would have let him—worse, she might have even *encouraged* him. She would have betrayed and dishonored herself and Sterling, all for a fleeting moment of pleasure.

And the worst part was, she felt more misery that it hadn't happened than that it *had* almost happened.

"We should return to the house," she said over her shoulder, avoiding looking directly at Rob as she reached for her stockings and boots. "It's gone quite late, and I shall have to change for dinner . . ."

He started to speak, hesitated, then glanced at Angus, who was packing up the hamper, blissfully unaware. "Of course," Rob said. He crushed a handful of reeds as he made his way out of the pond.

Angus gathered up the supplies and put them back into the gardener's cart. Georgiana insisted he help Rob get his boots back on, and then they all headed toward the house. Despite his load, Angus strode along briskly, and soon left them behind.

In truth, they lingered.

The taut moment in the pond, when he held her close and moved to kiss her, she must try to forget. She was taking him back to his family, and it would never happen again. Today would be her secret memory, her moment of daring, like an illicit love affair without the wickedness. It would never happen again.

She could not be sorry for it, though. It had been too much *fun*. And since today might well be the last time they had such fun together, she made a conscious effort to recapture the lighthearted air of earlier.

By the time they reached the garden again, Rob was leaning on her arm because he'd forgotten the cane by the pond. Georgiana made a show of pretending to pull him up the three shallow steps near the fountain, and he repaid her by pretending to stumble into her, catching her around the waist. She laughed, and he grinned, and his arm lingered around her as they made their way up the path toward the house.

"Thank you," he said as they strolled past the honeysuckle hedge. "For a brilliant day. Far better than any I can remember."

"All six of them?"

"Supreme among them," he agreed, laughing with her.

It made her heart give a happy leap. It would probably be the last time she pleased him so much, but for this moment it brought her joy. She hoped he truly had enjoyed the day, and that it would weigh in his mind in favor of forgiving her, or perhaps forgetting what she'd done.

They came within sight of the house, the topiary giving way to neat beds of roses and lilies. The late afternoon light slanted steeply across the gravel when Georgiana happened to glance toward the house and catch sight of a visitor, tall and fair. He must be leaving, for Adam held the bridle of his horse. The man had his back to them, checking his horse's girth, but some premonition warned her why he was here.

She almost stumbled over her own feet. All her logical decisions went straight out the window. This was not how she wanted Rob to learn she'd lied to him. It could be a terrible shock to his system, causing him to fall ill again, or everything might come flooding back to him at the sight of that fellow, and he'd erupt in fury at her.

Her choice was made in the space of a heartbeat. "Let's go this way," she said, pulling Rob down the path under the wisteria arbor. "The sun is so bright, I feel a bit light-headed."

"Should we sit for a moment?" He slowed down.

"No! No." She shook her head, still towing him toward the back of the house. "I want to go inside. As should you."

"Of course." The way he bowed to her wishes, and even pulled her shawl back up over her shoulder, made her feel awful.

A shout from the front of the house made her jump. Rob paused, looking over his shoulder. Heart battering her ribs, Georgiana looked, too, holding her breath.

The tall blond stranger was striding toward them.

"Oh my," she said, trying to keep her calm. "Please pardon me. I should speak to him. Do go inside, my dear . . ."

"Someone you know?" asked Rob, letting her push him toward the door.

She nodded vigorously. "I—he wants to speak to me—I'll go see. It must be a message from my brother, or Lady Sidlow! I'll just be a moment."

He threw up one hand in surrender. "Yes, ma'am." He went inside.

Georgiana whirled around and all but ran toward the angry visitor. As he drew near, her heart sank. This was no polite servant from the duchess; she feared she was facing Rob's brother instead. Oh Lord, she was in trouble now.

"Fetch that man back," he demanded without preamble, jerking his head toward the door Rob had gone through.

She purposely blocked the path and bobbed a quick curtsy. "Georgiana Lucas, sir. Delighted to make your acquaintance."

His blue eyes narrowed. "I am Major Lord Thomas Churchill-Gray," he said in icy tones. "I've come seeking my brother, Lord Westmorland, who Lady Winston quite recently assured me, without a shadow of a doubt, has not set foot on this property."

Georgiana wet her lips, trying not to look at the house, as if that might prevent anyone from observing this conversation. She lowered her voice. "Yes, she would say that—"

"What the devil is going on?" he interrupted in fury. "That was my brother walking with you!"

"If you want answers, be quiet and let me give them!" she snapped in exasperation. "This way." She stomped off out of sight of the windows, feeling him close at her heels.

When she spun around, he was right behind her, his arms folded. The set of his mouth and his eyes were just like Rob's, and he was as livid at her as she expected Rob to be when she finally told him the truth. *It'll be a good trial run*, she told herself in dark, nervous humor.

"Explain," he bit out.

"I will, if you keep your voice down!" She took a deep breath. "Yes, of course you already know your brother is here."

"Why the devil did Lady Winston say otherwise?"

"Because she doesn't know," Georgiana whispered, sparing an anxious glance toward the house. They were well away from it, but she felt as if every word and action must be as clear to every member of the household as if she and the major were on an illuminated stage. "It's a complicated story, but your brother was terribly injured and lost all memory of who he is."

"What?"

"Shh!" she hissed. "He would not have been welcome here if Lady Winston knew who he is. I told everyone he was someone else, and then he woke up not knowing that was all wrong, so now he believes he's someone else."

The major stared at her in disbelief. "Are you serious? No, you can't be—you're mad. West doesn't know who he is? He was terribly injured, yet I saw him walking arm in arm with you? What sort of idiot do you take me for?"

"One who can't listen very well, obviously," she retorted. "I am trying to explain. He was very, very ill. He's recovering, but his mind is still not well."

He was shaking his head. "This is the most ridiculous tale I've ever heard."

"But it's true!" She tried to calm her temper. "I suppose you've come to take him home?"

"I bloody well have," he growled. "Fetch him down immediately."

"No." She swallowed as his glare turned ferocious. "I think it would do him harm to have such a shock. Meet us tomorrow at the inn in Maryfield, and give me a chance to prepare him."

"Now," he said.

She threw up her hands. "No!"

"I'll go demand Lady Winston fetch him down."

Georgiana pictured it, and the shouting fury that would follow. "Don't be an idiot," she snapped. "What will you do? Haul him out of here like a wanted criminal? You've only got a horse, not a carriage. I swear to you, he *was* injured—beaten almost to death. He didn't wake for three entire days, and when he woke up he did not know his own name! A mere walk into the garden a few days ago made him violently ill, and he can barely walk without a cane! If you barge in and tell him he's someone else all of a sudden and drag him out of here, and his health suffers a reversal, I will tell *everyone* that *you* caused it because you hadn't the patience of a pig!"

His face had grown increasingly furious, but at the last, he suddenly grinned, and looked so much like Rob that Georgiana stopped with a pang.

"You're howling mad," he said, almost conversationally. "But otherwise harmless, I think. Very well. Tomorrow. I'll have the patience of a pig and await you—and my brother—at the Bull and Dog. But if you're not there," he added, in a tone more frightening for being so even and pleasant, "you'll never regret anything more."

She let out her breath in relief. "We'll be there."

"You'd better be," he promised, before striding to his waiting horse and riding off.

Rob stood inside the house, gripping the plain newel post of the back staircase and trying to calm his thundering pulse. Despite Georgiana's efforts, he'd seen that man around the corner of the house, that blond fellow with the furious expression and the familiar face. That was . . . that was his brother.

His skin seemed to be shrinking, pulling in too tightly around him until he wanted to twist and run away from the agony of it. He wiped his brow with a shaky hand. His head felt like an egg cracking open, as if seeing his brother had splintered the shell around his injured mind. Chunks of memory dropped heavily into place, few of them comforting and none of them welcome, not now.

He *was* the Marquess of Westmorland, the hated, reviled fellow who had come to Osbourne House intent on doing something—still not quite clear to him—vile.

Which meant he was not Lord Sterling.

And he was not Georgiana's fiancé.

She'd lied to him. Emotion boiled through him, and his hands tightened around the newel post in a death grip. Every sparkling glance, every gentle touch, every kindness had all been a lie. Fury rose up in his chest—what had she been up to? Was this some massive game to her, leading him along by pretending to care for him?

Except . . . she hadn't. She'd kept her distance, wary as a cat, until he coaxed her near. His fury was quickly subsumed by a wave of despair.

She was not his fiancée. She never had been.

Why would she lie and say she was?

"Sir?"

Rob jerked out of his tortured reverie to see Angus regarding him quizzically.

"Are you well, sir?" the manservant asked.

Rob swallowed hard. "Yes," he croaked. Without conscious thought he decided to continue as he was, and not let on that he knew so much more than he had only minutes ago.

"Shall I help you up?" asked Angus; kind, simple Angus who had no idea who he was.

Rob nodded once. He let the fellow haul him up the stairs, but said he could manage the rest on his own. He limped into the bedroom and closed the door, sagging against it.

Why had she lied? *Why why why* throbbed the question in his brain. He supposed it had something to do with Lady Winston's dislike. Beyond that, his fractured memory offered no answers.

But there were many lies she could have told to spare him Lady Winston's ire. She'd chosen the most lethal one. He closed his eyes and rubbed his fist across his chest. He was losing his heart to the woman, only to learn she'd kept something vital from him.

And the worst of it was, he still wanted her lies to be true.

Chapter 13

⧤⧨⧤⧨

Kitty agreed that they could take a drive the next day. Adam hitched up the coach and Georgiana told him to drive toward Maryfield. "We'll stop at the inn and take a respite," she said brightly, "before the drive back. His Lordship may need to rest." Rob grinned at that, and Georgiana smiled back, helpless to resist despite everything. She was going to miss this Rob. She rolled up the windows to let the breeze in and didn't object when he tugged her across the carriage to sit beside him.

She put off the inevitable as long as possible. Rob took off his hat and put his head out the window, declaring that he ought to have insisted they ride, even though he still leaned on the cane to walk. He teased her that they should make Adam ride inside while they sat up on the box together. He wanted to stop and see the spot where he'd been beaten, which Georgiana told him was ghoulish but they did it anyway.

Finally she could delay no longer. Major Churchill-Gray was waiting, and she couldn't send Rob in to see him unknowing and unprepared.

"I have to tell you something," she began when they were well along the way, almost to Maryfield. "Something which may be . . ." She hesitated. Horrifying? Comforting? Infuriating? She had no idea how he would react. The man she knew—*thought* she knew, after these several days with him—would probably be surprised but not angry. The Malicious Marquess, though, would be furious, and she still didn't know who was the true Rob. "Rather surprising."

"Good Lord. Ought I to apologize again?"

She flushed. "No, of course not."

"It sounds as though you're winding up a very grave speech. Whatever I did to make you so somber, I am sorry."

"You won't think so when you've heard what I have to say," she muttered.

"No?" He laid his hand over hers. "Give me a chance."

He was laughing now, but he was going to hate her. She drew a shallow, agonized breath and forged onward. "I haven't told you the full truth about yourself."

"I know," he replied. "You won't tell me what I did to hurt you."

If only that were all. "You won't care about that once I've told you the rest." Her fingers tapped nervously on her knee.

"I could guess," he offered as she hesitated. "Or play at charades."

"I didn't tell you your proper name," she blurted out.

The carriage rocked back and forth a few times.

Rob drew a deep breath. "Am I really Ebenezer?"

"What?" A burst of hysterical laughter escaped her throat. "No! You're Robert—"

"Thank God," he declared.

"—Churchill-Gray," she finished, her voice fading with each syllable. She braced herself for an explosion of shock and fury. "Marquess of Westmorland."

He turned his head to look at her for an endless, fraught moment. "What do you mean?"

"You're the Marquess of Westmorland," she repeated in a tiny voice. "Not Viscount Sterling."

"The hateful, despicable Lord Westmorland?"

Georgiana's face burned, despite his even tone. "What—how do you know?"

"I overheard bits of your conversation the other night with Lady Winston." He was still calm, but his eyes were watchful.

She wilted. "Oh. I thought . . . perhaps you had remembered . . ."

"No," he said after a moment. "Not really."

The carriage rocked in silence.

"I never set out to deceive you," she said, then stopped at his expression. "No, obviously I did. I don't know why I thought of it—so, so stupid on my part." She shook her head, picking furiously at a loose thread on her reticule. "I didn't think at all, I suppose. And then I didn't know how to tell you the truth."

"So why now?"

His tone was fraying her nerves like nothing else could have. Where was the shouting, the furious demands for an explanation? Not that she had a good one, but she had expected he would want it. "We're not just going on a drive. We're going to meet your brother in Maryfield."

"The fellow at the house yesterday," he murmured.

She cringed. So much for her sneaking abilities. "Yes. He's come looking for you. Your family is worried at your long absence, and you should be with them."

He gave her a long sideways look. "Is that right?"

"Of course! It will be best for your health, and hopefully you'll recover your memory completely there . . ."

He just looked at her, his expression unreadable. Georgiana felt a flood of guilt. "I'm so sorry," she said, taking his hand without thinking. "I did not intend for any of this to happen, and everything is my fault. I will never forgive myself if you suffer a relapse over the shock."

"Unless you mean to give me another beating about the head, I don't think I shall suffer a relapse." His hand turned over under her grip, and his fingers threaded between hers to clasp it fully. Her heart throbbed with relief and joy. "Then our engagement . . . ?"

She grimaced. "We are not engaged."

His thumb went over her knuckles. "Ah. A great pity, that. I quite liked that part."

Georgiana closed her eyes in mortification. Gently she eased her hand from his. "But I *am* engaged. To Lord Sterling."

"Ah," he said again after a pause. "He's a real fellow, then." She nodded once. "Have I got a fiancée, too?" he asked. "Another one?"

His voice had stayed carefully even and neutral, but she heard the subtle change. It stabbed at her heart. "I've no idea," she acknowledged. "I think not. We . . . we were not much acquainted in London, before . . . this."

He glanced at her sharply, but the horses were turning into the yard at the Bull and Dog. Georgiana wet her lips. "We're here," she said, pointlessly, and her hand reached for his again before she remembered herself and put it back in her lap. "Are you well enough to see him? His name is Thomas. If you are not, I will go speak to him and explain—"

"No," he said, his gaze on her hand. The carriage rocked to a halt. "I'll go."

His mind churned as they made their way inside the squat little inn. He had to duck beneath the lintel of the door, and almost choked on the cloud of tobacco smoke and pungent smell of cooked mutton. Georgiana asked a question of the landlady, hurtling past with a tankard of ale in each hand, and the woman directed them down a narrow passageway with a nod of her head.

Rob followed Georgiana, his gaze fixed on the crown of her bonnet. A stray golden wisp of hair had escaped to curl at the nape of her neck. Even though he'd known since last night that he wasn't really Lord Sterling, he couldn't shake his attraction to her. Overnight his temper had cooled, and he'd decided to see what she did next. He ought to be furious at her, and yet . . .

He still wanted to hold her hand and see her smile. When she apologized and looked as if she would cry, he only wanted to comfort her and assure her he was fine.

That wasn't entirely true, of course. He'd suffered

a hard blow; he'd thought she was his. Even if he'd been idiotic and caused a rift between them, he'd thought there must be *something* deeper connecting them, some affection or bond that kept her by his side. Something that would give him time to win her heart, this time forever.

But there was nothing.

Georgiana knocked at a door, and a moment later opened it. With one more anxious glance at him, she stepped inside and Rob followed. At the last second he reached for her, thinking to give assurance, and realized he'd been seeking it just as much when she seized his hand and sent his heart leaping.

At their entrance, the man who had been at Osbourne House the previous day rose. He was almost Rob's own height but with sandy hair and a trim mustache. Rob stopped abruptly, pelted by a sudden swarm of memories. A fair-haired boy shinning up a tree to retrieve a kite while Rob shouted instructions from below. A young man falling off a horse and cursing a blue streak while Rob bellowed with laughter. An officer grinning broadly and shaking hands all around, his new regimentals blazing scarlet in the sun.

"Tom," he said in a low voice.

"Yes." His brother drew near, shooting a dark glance at Georgiana. "You remember me?"

"I told him in the carriage," she retorted.

Rob pressed her hand, then released her. "A bit, I do," he acknowledged. "Just now."

"Lady Georgiana said you'd lost your memory." Tom said it evenly, but Rob heard the suspicion in the question.

"I did."

"He was seriously injured," she put in defensively. "He was struck very hard on the head, and the doctor said sometimes the mind is affected. Not long ago he was unconscious in bed, and now he's ever so much better . . ."

"Who did you tell him he was?" interrupted Tom.

Pale but undaunted, Georgiana replied, "I told Lady Winston he was my fiancé because I feared for his life."

Tom's brow went up in obvious cynicism. "Indeed. What an interesting choice you describe. How would his true name have cost him his life?"

Bright spots of pink flared in her cheeks. "Lady Winston would not have received Lord Westmorland graciously."

"Why not?" Rob asked swiftly.

She glanced at him, her face tragic, then immediately away. "I think that ought to wait. You and the major should have a chance to speak, to help restore your memory. I'll wait outside." Without looking at him again, Georgiana left, closing the door behind her.

For a moment the brothers just looked at each other. "Managing chit," said Tom, jerking his head toward the door.

Rob ran one hand over his head, wincing as he touched the still-healing gashes. "She took care of me."

"Yes, and made you her fiancé in the bargain. That's a clever way to snare a future duke."

Rob scowled, ignoring the pull of the scar at his temple. "I don't think that was her plan. She's got a fiancé, a real one. Who is Lord Sterling?"

"Sterling?" Tom repeated, then again incredulously. "Sterling? She's wedding that scoundrel? Ah,

I remember now. She's Wakefield's sister. Well, that explains a great deal."

"What?" Rob demanded. He glanced at the door, and lowered his voice. "Tell me."

"Explain first how you got into this mess. And sit down, man, you look like you might fall over."

Rob grimaced as he made his way to a chair, sinking into it with a sigh of relief and setting his cane aside. "I was attacked by highwaymen or thieves on the road, pounded hard about the head, and left for dead. She found me, took me to the Winston home, and has been caring for me ever since I woke up not knowing who or where I was."

Still frowning, Tom pulled another chair closer. "That's true, then? You did forget everything? I thought she must be lying."

"No, no, it was real," he said. "I gather the Winston family hates me—"

"Oh, they most certainly do," murmured Tom.

"Why?" Rob asked testily. "I believe Georgiana lied about my name to help me—but I don't know *why*." He hesitated. "Do you know what made me come into Derbyshire? I can't recall anything about it."

Tom leaned back in his chair. "You won the deed to Osbourne House from Charles Winston at the Vega Club. You don't recall it?"

Rob thought hard. It felt like there was a tattered cloth over his mind, some memories perfectly clear and others completely obscured. "No."

His brother gave a bark of laughter. "Drunk as a lord, from what I heard. Well, Winston spread tales you'd taken advantage of him and cheated him. Mother got wind of it and told you to clean up the scandal. Hobbes said you expected to spend a few days there and then continue on to Salmsbury."

Rob digested that in silence. He'd won the deed to the house. That would make Lady Winston despise him, if she feared he would turn her out of her home . . . although he was sure he wouldn't have. What would he do with a house in Derbyshire?

But if he hadn't come to claim the house, why was he here?

Tom was still talking. "You left Hobbes in Macclesfield and went on alone. Hobbes sprained his ankle and took himself off to Salmsbury. Mother sent word to let you know, in case you needed a man, and Lady Winston replied with a note saying that you'd never been to Osbourne House, nor were you welcome to cross its threshold alive."

"Right," Rob murmured, his thoughts racing. Perhaps Georgiana's fears had been justified. "Who is Sterling?"

Tom's lips quirked. "Like that, is it?"

Rob glared.

His brother's grin widened into an evil smirk. "Earl Pelham's heir. He's accounted a handsome bloke, charming and eligible. Very popular with the ladies—of all persuasions, from what I hear, and he very much enjoys them in turn. He's got a bit of a wild side, which I'm sure Lady Georgiana has never seen. Chaps like him always hide it. He'll be some competition if you mean to steal his fiancée."

Rob had some very rude thoughts about this Sterling fellow. "What now?"

Tom shrugged one shoulder. "Mother's been frantic with worry since she got Lady Winston's reply.

She sent me out in a lather, convinced that you'd already been murdered and buried in the garden. Quite relieved I am, not to have to dig you up, West."

He grinned a little at the name. It did feel good to have his own name back. "Quite relieved not to be interred."

"I'll get a carriage," his brother went on. "We can be at Salmsbury by nightfall."

He thought of Georgiana, sitting outside the room now, waiting for his response. She'd known his brother would tell him everything, in unsparing detail, revealing that she'd brazenly lied to everyone. And yet she'd driven over here with her hand in his, trying to comfort and reassure him.

He believed that Georgiana had not lied to humiliate or harm him. It was a ridiculous thing to do, but she had believed it necessary to secure Lady Winston's aid, and she was honestly sorry for it. She'd read to him and laughed with him and talked to him. And he couldn't bear the thought of hurting her.

"No," he said in reply to Tom's proposal. "Not just yet."

Chapter 14

❦❦❦

GEORGIANA SAT ON a narrow bench near the tap-room, feeling curiously distant from everything around her.

Rob was hearing, right now, all the truths she had kept from him. Major Churchill-Gray was filling in the gaps in his memory, restoring his family and friends to him. Rob must be enormously relieved, she thought wistfully. His frustration at not knowing had been palpable, and for his sake, she was glad he would wonder no longer.

What he would think of her after this conversation, she did not care to contemplate. No matter how she told herself she had acted from good intentions, it was indisputable that she had lied to him and prevented him from remembering sooner.

If she had kept him from reverting to his arrogant, rude ways . . . Well, she couldn't be sorry about that. It would happen soon enough. How would Sterling react if she'd told him such a lie? She squeezed shut her eyes as she thought of her fiancé for the first time all day. In just a week Rob had come to dominate her entire attention.

She took a deep breath and straightened her skirts. That was wrong. Rob was not her fiancé. This was the best possible solution, she told herself. Rob would become the Malicious Marquess again and she would go back to town, humbled and chastened by this misadventure. In fact, it would be easiest for everyone if Rob turned on her in fury, and gave her a scalding dressing-down before storming out of her life in disgust. Hopefully he would be gentlemanly enough not to spread stories in London, but she supposed she should be resigned and prepared for anything.

And if Sterling got wind of this and declared himself unwilling to marry her . . . Georgiana found that the thought didn't alarm her very much. Most likely because she was exhausted from trying to keep her stories straight, and numb from fighting off her growing attraction to Rob.

She pinched the bridge of her nose. How on earth had she made such a mess of her life, which had been rolling along so blissfully?

The door down the corridor opened, and she flinched. *Time to face judgment*, she told herself, and got to her feet.

"Georgiana." Rob gazed at her, that wavy thatch of dark hair flopping over his brow again. "Won't you come in?"

So your brother can help you strangle me? she thought, but still she nodded and went into the room. She noted that this time, Rob made no effort to touch her—in fact, he drew back a little as she passed him. Her heart twisted in sorrow, but she ignored it. Any part of her heart that yearned for Rob had better die a quick and fiery death.

"Lady Georgiana." The major pushed forward a chair. "Please, be seated."

"I'm very happy standing, thank you." She clasped her hands.

"I'm not." Rob lowered himself into the chair beside the one designated for her, his breath hissing between his teeth. Instinctively she started to reach out to help him, but stopped herself in time. Rob's hazel eyes flashed her way, and he made a small motion with his head toward the chair.

Reluctantly she took the seat. Her skirts brushed his boots, and she tried to twitch them away without anyone noticing.

"We're in a bit of a fix, it seems," said the major. Unlike the two of them, he did not sit, but stood leaning his elbows on the back of the opposite chair. "And we both wondered how you planned to get out of it."

Georgiana jerked. "I?"

The major nodded, his eyes never leaving her. "What's your plan?"

"Obviously I do not think that far ahead," she said under her breath. Rob made a sound that might have been a muffled snort of laughter. "What do you mean, sir?"

Smiling faintly, the major gestured from her to Rob. "You told Lady Winston that my brother is Lord Sterling. One presumes you don't wish to go back and tell her that no, you made a dreadful mistake, and he's really Westmorland."

Georgiana gave a tiny shake of her head. No, she hoped to be halfway across Britain before Kitty discovered that.

"One also presumes you did not intend to live there with him indefinitely."

"Of course not!"

He raised his brows. "Then what was your escape plan?"

She took a deep breath, then let it out. "None of this was planned—I spoke without thinking of anything other than his health."

"For which I am deeply grateful," put in Rob.

She managed a wan smile, still unable to look at him even though she could feel his eyes on her.

"My best idea was to persuade everyone that I should take him to London, to consult a doctor, and hope his mind recovered there. But I still hadn't worked out exactly how to tell anyone the truth." She lifted one shoulder in useless apology. "In short, Major, I cede to you, utterly and completely, all control of the situation. I've made a terrible mess, and it would be a relief if someone else sorted how to repair it. And besides, I suspect you've got a plan all worked out and I shall simply be run over if I try to interfere."

The major had a curious smile, one corner of his lips higher than the other, with a small lift in the middle. It was like Rob's smile, but on the major it looked more cunning than amused. "As a matter of fact, I do."

He explained it, answered her questions, and then stood, pulling loose the fastening at the collar of his coat. "All right then, off with you both. Lady Georgiana." He executed a crisp bow.

Dazed, she got to her feet and turned to go. Her reticule caught on the arm of the chair and she stumbled. Rob caught her with an arm around her waist. For the briefest moment she melted into his tall, strong figure. In just a few days she'd got so used to him, his crooked smile, his wicked humor, the way he looked at her . . .

And it was all a lie. He'd only looked at her that way because he thought they were engaged. Now he knew the truth . . . and quite possibly hated her for it.

She straightened with a murmured apology. Rob said nothing, but his hand lingered on her back until she made herself step away. Face burning, she went back into the hall. Rob followed, leaning on his cane again. Without a word he offered her his arm, and Georgiana took it.

Neither spoke until they were in the carriage, driving away from the Bull and Dog.

"How much have you remembered?" she finally asked.

"Not everything," he said slowly. "I've no memory of our meeting in London."

She flushed scarlet. "I daresay you never will remember that. It wasn't much of a meeting—more like an introduction in passing . . ."

"Yet I made quite an impression."

She bit her lip and said nothing.

He let out his breath. "I don't remember why I came to Osbourne House. My brother tells me I won the house in a wager."

Georgiana thought of the deed still hidden in her stocking drawer, and some of her spirit revived. "You did. You taunted Charles about turning it into a house of vice and demanded the deed from his solicitor. We all believed you meant to toss out Kitty and her family."

A deep frown settled on his face. "Why on earth would I do that? What would I want with a house in Derbyshire?"

"It's a lovely house!"

"A charming cottage," he said. "If I wanted to live in such a rustic spot, I would go to Salmsbury."

She snapped her mouth shut. "Then why did you take the deed?"

"Why did Charles Winston offer it to me?"

"Because he's an idiot when he drinks!" she shot back.

Rob gave a snort of laughter. "We all are, I suppose. But I don't want the house."

Some of her antipathy had returned. "How do you be sure of that if you don't remember why you came?"

His mouth tightened. "What did I do to make you think I would travel halfway across the country to toss a woman and baby out of their home?"

"You're *here*!" she cried in frustration.

Rob went still. He stared at her a moment, then turned to the window. "I don't want it," he repeated. "I must have come to give it back."

Georgiana glared at the passing scenery in misery. She wanted to believe him—she *did* believe him. Whether he'd meant to do that originally or not, she trusted what he said now.

And if he'd always intended to give it back . . . then she'd leapt to awful conclusions about him.

She pressed trembling fingertips to her brow, remembering how cold and disdainful he'd been in London. She had seen him and heard him several times, over two years, heap scorn and mockery on others. Surely she couldn't have been utterly wrong. Surely he must have changed as a result of his brush with death and the trauma of losing his memory.

Of course, that didn't pardon her own behavior.

They rode in silence for several minutes. Georgiana kept her hands tucked around her sides, remembering how he'd held her hand on the ride to the Bull and Dog, little more than an hour ago. *That's over and done with*, she told herself. *It'll be a miracle if he doesn't hate me after all this.*

"Have you really been engaged to Sterling for over two years?" he asked abruptly.

Georgiana bristled. "Yes."

"Why haven't you set a date?"

She kept her gaze fixed on things outside the window. She wanted to reply that it was none of his business, but that would feel like her biggest lie yet. "I told you the truth. My brother is difficult and he's dithering over the settlements. One month he'll agree to something, then the next month he says it was too generous and won't suit him after all."

"And Sterling puts up with that?"

"What can he do?" she exclaimed. "Alistair is . . . quarrelsome. If you argue with him, he'll retract what he already promised out of pique. He has to be persuaded and coaxed, and that takes time."

"And you're willing to wait all this time?" He cast a glance at her. "Sterling is willing to wait?"

Georgiana went rigid. "I fell in love with Sterling before I was ten years old. Everyone knew we were meant for each other—*everyone*. Our families are in favor, even Alistair, for all his grumblings. Of course, if Sterling finds out I told everyone you were he and treated you as my fiancé—" She stopped, not because she was terrified to think what Sterling would do, but because she was not terrified. Not of Sterling, at any rate. Not of him breaking their betrothal. Not even of him looking at her with disappointment or irritation, and asking how she could have been so foolish.

She couldn't look at Rob. She was too afraid it would show on her face, how dangerously her thoughts had turned.

"You shouldn't ask such questions," she said stiffly. "We're betrothed, and that's that."

Neither spoke again until the carriage turned into the lane toward Osbourne House.

Rob leaned forward to peer out the window. "Are you certain you can do this?"

He meant keep up the pretense. That was the escape Major Churchill-Gray had offered her: they were returning to Osbourne House for tonight, still pretending that Rob was Sterling, still her fiancé, still without his memory. She would tell Kitty that it was time for her to return to London, that she was taking Rob to town to consult as many doctors as it took to restore his mind. She would say they had discussed it on their drive today and decided it was best.

Tomorrow a travel chaise would come for them. They would meet the major at a nearby market town and travel together to Macclesfield, from whence Rob would go with his brother to Salmsbury Abbey, while Georgiana would continue with her maid to London. The major had promised to arrange for safe and comfortable travel for them.

He left it to her how and when she chose to tell Kitty the truth.

It had sounded very simple when he laid it out, and she had agreed with a sense of relief that someone had planned the exit for her, but now it hit her that these were her last hours with Rob.

She glanced at him. He was facing straight ahead, but after a moment turned to meet her gaze, his expression somber and a bit wistful. It blew away her tension and frustration. Today was the last time he would hold her hand or touch her cheek. Tomorrow was the last time they would sit beside each other. And then, after tomorrow, if she ever saw him again it would be from across a room, when they would be strangers again, by necessity and because they never should have been more.

All in all, the easiest part of the plan was tonight, still pretending that he was hers. She didn't want to waste it arguing.

"I can if you can," she said with a faltering smile of apology.

His mouth crooked. He took her hand and raised it to his cheek, his lips on the back of her wrist. A shudder of regret went through her.

He kept her hand in his until they reached the house. But she only realized later that he never answered her implicit question.

Chapter 15

Kitty accepted the news with a smile. Georgiana suspected she must have tired of having an invalid in the house, and Georgiana herself hadn't been a very engaging guest since Rob's arrival. Geneva exclaimed in disappointment for the blink of an eye, then lapsed into envious musings about the life in London she pictured Georgiana returning to. Mother Winston fussed, but only briefly, and declared that of course dear Sterling must have the best doctors. Georgiana told Nadine to pack her things and prepare to leave in the morning.

Rob was at his most charming that night. It made something inside her chest twist to see how he made Geneva laugh and Kitty smile. Mother Winston looked on fondly, tittering when Rob turned his gallantry upon her, too.

Georgiana tried to be cheerful as well, reminding herself that the stressful pretense was about to end and she could be herself again soon. Instead all she could think about was that this was the last evening she would be seated beside Rob, the last night he would turn to her with his rueful, crooked smile, the last chance for those casual touches he gave that each seemed to send a little shock to her heart.

"Well, my love," he said to her after dinner, "shall we take a turn in the garden?"

Another stupid lurch of her heart. "Are you sure?" she asked. "You're not too tired?" It had been a long day, and he'd been on his feet far more than he ought to have been. She was sure she wasn't imagining him to be a little paler, his mouth a little tighter, than usual.

"Never too tired to walk with you," he replied.

Georgiana smiled, even though the words were all for show. "Then of course we shall walk. Whatever you desire, my dear."

They made their way into the twilit garden. Georgiana hitched her shawl higher on her shoulders in the cool night air. Rob offered his arm.

She blinked at it. "There's no need," she whispered.

"For Lady Winston's sake," he replied as quietly. "And perhaps a bit for mine. I forgot the cane."

"Oh! Yes, of course." She knew she ought to have protested more, but she leapt at the chance to hold his arm again. And when she tucked her hand around his elbow, he pulled her close to his side as if he, too, didn't want to miss a moment of this particular last time.

They walked in silence until well out of earshot of the house. "You must be eager to go home," she finally said. The impending end hung over her like the approaching night, casting everything into melancholy shadow. "Your brother seems very keen to pry you from my wicked clutches."

She'd spoken lightly, but he didn't laugh.

"I suppose I can't blame him," she babbled on. "Of course he must be very suspicious of anyone who would do such a thing. Now that I think back on it, I don't even know why I did." She laughed, but stopped at once because it sounded hysterical to her ears. "No doubt you wonder the same thing."

They had come around a row of topiary and could no longer see the house. Rob stopped. "I do."

Georgiana sighed, her bravura draining away. "You deserve a full confession," she said softly. "Kitty . . ." She paused, wanting to be fair to her friend. "Charles sent her horrible, dire letters, about you and the deed to this house, claiming you'd tricked him out of it and meant to turn it into a house of sin. He raised everyone's fears that you were en route to throw the family into the hedge-rows, and told Kitty to bar the doors and windows and not to let you in under any circumstances."

He made a scornful noise.

"We didn't know," she hurried on, her face burning at the memory of how she had thrown fuel on Kitty's anger. "*I* didn't know how wrong that might have been. But the end result is that every person in the house braced for your arrival as they might have prepared for Bonaparte himself.

"I didn't recognize you when Adam and I first encountered the thieves. I hope you can believe me: I did *not*," she repeated emphatically. "Adam feared the thieves returning but I couldn't leave *anyone* to die in the road—you were almost dead already, and if we hadn't brought you here—" She stopped and calmed herself. "It wasn't until we reached the house that I saw your face clearly. Kitty . . ." Again she hesitated. "I don't know what Kitty would have done if I'd told her your proper name. She had sworn she would never admit you to her house— thinking you meant to evict her—and yet there you were, beaten and looking for all the world like you were on death's doorstep . . . I never thought she would *harm* you. But if she had refused to help, it would have been much the same thing." She raised her hands helplessly. "In the shock of the moment, covered with blood and fearful that you might die no matter what, I told her you were someone else."

"Why Sterling?" he asked quietly.

Georgiana flushed. "It was the only name that came to mind that I knew would assure her help. She might have guessed the truth otherwise, since Charles had put her on guard against your arrival. She's never met Sterling and wouldn't know."

"She'll know when she does meet him."

"I know," she said on a sigh. "I am not eagerly looking forward to it."

He stared out over the hills, no more than dark smudges against the indigo sky. "What would you have done if I woke up without having lost my memory?"

"Oh, I was prepared for that," she assured him. "I expected it, obviously, and had it all worked out. I would impress upon you—quite firmly—how generous it was for Kitty to take you in and save your life, and how unconscionable it would be for you to hold Charles to some stupid wager about the house. I knew exactly what your contrite letter of apology would say, as you declared no intention of putting a family out of their home."

"Did you?" He sounded amused, and, remembering how energized she'd been at the thought of telling him off, Georgiana also smiled.

"I was prepared to write it for you, actually."

He laughed.

"But you didn't know your own name when you woke," she went on, the moment of levity fading. "And Dr. Elton told you I was your fiancée before I could stop him or think of a better story. It all spiraled completely out of control in just a few minutes and then I . . . I was trapped."

"You played your part very well."

He said it mildly, but she felt it like an accusation. "I could not be cold or distant. Not only would Kitty have wondered, but you—" Her voice faltered. "You needed someone to support you. I cannot imagine how frightening it must have been to wake up with no idea of one's own name. How awful would it have been to be treated coldly or distantly by the person you believed to be your future wife? I hated pretending, and your questions—the ones I could not answer, about how we met and why we were not married yet—filled me with shame for what I was doing.

"But the alternative was to admit that you were injured and alone among people who disliked you intensely. What if it had compromised your recovery? I could never have forgiven myself for that. I—I judged it less wicked to keep silent, to be as helpful as I could manage to be, and when the moment came that you remembered yourself . . ." She bit her lip. "As long as you did not die, I told myself I would do my best and suffer the consequences later."

"Your best was magnificent," he said.

He took her hand. Neither wore gloves, and she inhaled at the warmth of his flesh on hers. How on earth had she got so used to this man in just a few days? She couldn't remember the last time Sterling had held her hand, yet every single touch from Rob seemed to be engraved on her memory.

For a moment he seemed at a loss for words. He turned her hand over and stroked the inside of her wrist, sending a faint tremor through her. Again she knew she should protest—no one from the house could see them and there was no reason for this— and again she did not. It was dark enough now that she couldn't see his face, only the shape of him, tall and strong. *The last time*, whispered a voice in her head.

They stared out at the night for a while, side by side, hand in hand. The sky was violet-black now, sparkling with stars winking into view as the last vestige of day faded behind them.

"I love to come out and look at the stars," she said softly. "You can see so many more of them than in London."

"It's beautiful here," he agreed. "There's nowhere else I'd rather have been an invalid."

"Please don't be an invalid anywhere." She shivered. "You did it so thoroughly this time, I hope you never try it again."

"Obviously we do not always get what we hope for," he said, sounding wryly amused. "Still, I could have been left senseless on the muddy bank of the Thames or on a Yorkshire moor. I'll take Derbyshire over that any day."

"I admire your genius for finding the bright side of your misadventure."

"Do you?" He chuckled and nudged her with his shoulder. "After all, you wouldn't have been likely to find me on a Yorkshire moor."

"Good heavens no." She shuddered. "Yorkshire's bleak and cold at the best of times, and the moors are the worst part."

She felt him turn to look at her. "Yorkshire's where you're from, isn't it?"

"A long time ago," she said. "I never go there now." She changed the subject away from that morbid place. "Have you remembered Salmsbury Abbey?"

"Yes," he said slowly. "It used to be a priory. Some ancestor pulled down half of it and rebuilt the rest into something more like a castle. It's within a few miles of the sea and one of the most beautiful places on earth."

She sighed wistfully. "How lovely it sounds."

"It is." He paused. "I think. My memory has not been reliable of late. I may be thinking of another place entirely, and find myself wandering the corridors in confusion."

Georgiana smiled. "You'll find out soon enough. But I'm sure it's just as you remember—and either way, it's home, isn't it?"

"Perhaps you ought to come along and see it with me. I may have a relapse if it's not as I think it is."

Her heart jumped even though it was impossible. Thankfully she was able to answer in jest. "I should be very disappointed in you if you relapse after all the effort I've put into getting you well again."

"I shall endeavor not to let you down," he said with the same mock gravity, and they both laughed. Overhead a shooting star whizzed silently across the black velvet night, causing Georgiana to point it out in delight. A nightingale called nearby, and something rustled in the grass to their left. If it must be their last night, at least it was a splendid one.

"Do you still want to marry Sterling?"

His voice made her start. His question made her flush, then go cold. "What?"

"You talk about him the way a girl might talk about her brother. It's been over two years since he asked you to marry him. He doesn't seem particularly anxious for the wedding, and—"

She pulled her hand out of his grip, and he fell silent for a moment before continuing. "You go tense every time his name is mentioned. I wondered if you feared his reaction when he hears about this."

"Oh." She flushed again. What a goose she was, thinking he meant something else, some other reason why she might not want to marry Sterling. "I'm rather hoping he never does."

"Is that likely?"

Georgiana sighed. Of course it wasn't. "I shall tell him what I told you—I meant well but spoke without thinking ahead. Obviously I shall have to apologize for using his name."

"Only for that?" he asked dryly. "Not for telling another man he was your fiancé? I just want to know if he's a jealous sort who might . . . react badly."

Was he? She didn't know. She'd never given Sterling cause to be jealous. "I don't think so," she murmured.

"Georgiana." He touched her cheek; her head had sunk during this depressing little conversation, and Rob waited until she raised her eyes, even though they could barely see each other. "If he does anything hurtful, will you tell me?"

And he would do . . . what? Even though the thought of Rob defending her brought a burst of warmth to her heart, she knew that would only make Sterling's upset worse—if he were in fact offended. Rob's remark, that she spoke of Sterling more like a brother than a lover, had struck a nerve. Coupled with the fact that she'd not heard from Sterling since a brief letter soon after she arrived, she tended to think he might not much care what she'd done in Derbyshire, nor be bothered to find out.

"I'm not worried," she told Rob. "But I am very grateful for your concern." With a faltering smile, she placed her hand over his on her cheek and pressed it.

He went very still. Instead of dropping his hand away, his fingers twitched, tightening on her jaw almost as if he meant to pull her to him. He cupped his other hand around her nape, his hold light but fraught with suggestion. The breath clogged in her lungs and her imagination took off. What if he kissed her? He knew who he was now, and who she was; there would be no excuse. What would she do? She could no longer pretend it was in service of protecting his health or keeping up her story.

A wicked thrill of anticipation went through her. After all, they were alone out here in the dark garden, alone for the last time, out of sight and hearing of the house. No one—no one but the two of them— would ever know . . . It might be the last chance . . .

"Promise you'll tell me if he's unpleasant."

"And what would you do?"

His thumb brushed her lower lip. "Something. Anything to keep him from hurting you."

She drew a shallow breath. "It—it won't be your concern then . . ."

His lips touched her brow, sending her heart leaping. "It will always be my concern."

"No . . ." She tried to force her thoughts back into order. Feeling his breath on her skin was making her want things she could not have and should not want. "I mean," she said unsteadily, "you needn't worry. He won't hurt me."

"He'd better not," Rob muttered. His fingertips traced her features as if he were memorizing them. "What will happen when we meet again in London?"

Georgiana could barely think. Her skin might be glowing from the heat sparked by his touch. "A civil greeting, I hope."

"Will you pretend we're strangers?"

We won't be strangers, whispered her heart. *Never.*

"I don't think I can manage it," he added in a low voice. "Pretending I don't know you."

Something prickled inside her—something hot and hopeful and dangerous. It was sharp enough to frighten her, and blow away some of the haze of longing that seemed to enfold her. "I'm sure once you're back amongst your friends there it won't be that difficult," she said, trying to quiet the tumult inside her. "It's not as though we met very often."

He raised his head. "Why not?"

She shifted uncomfortably, then decided to just say it. It would be easier if he snapped back to his usual disdainful manner. "Your circles and mine don't overlap. My friends like fashion and gossip, shopping in Bond Street and eating ices at Gunther's. Your friends are rakes who never dance, gamble all night, and are generally too wild and daring to notice a girl like me."

He was quiet. "But I *have* noticed you now."

For one wicked moment, in spite of herself, she imagined him noticing her in London. He'd always been a lethally attractive creature, but now he was mesmerizing, with his tousled hair and wicked grin and mischievous air. She pictured him approaching her at a ball, sweeping her into his arms and around the room. She imagined him coming to call, setting Lady Sidlow—and all the neighbors—aflutter. She imagined walking in the park with him, her arm in his, him smiling down at her, pulling her against him under cover of an arbor much like this one and bending his head down to hers . . .

With a start she realized where her thoughts were leading. God save her—she wanted him to kiss her, and call on her, and do many more things only a husband or a lover should do. She had walked right up to the precipice of disaster, and had only caught herself at the last moment.

"I'm sure it will fade," she said in a rush. "Your friends will remind you that young ladies like me are frivolous and vain, little prick-teasers who prance about trying to trap hapless gentlemen into marriage. She-devils in expensive gowns, only appeased by a steady offering of new jewels and ridiculous bonnets. A cross between a hangman and a Siren, the sort of creature you'd rather be flogged than dance with. That's what you said about me once. I know you don't remember," she added quickly as he drew audible breath to protest. "I don't hold it against you." She couldn't any longer, not now.

"But you should know . . . I don't expect there will be a problem in London," she went on. "The more you remember, the less you'll care about me, and soon this will be simply something terrible, and a bit farcical, that happened to you. It will all fade once you've recovered. And I do hope for your complete recovery, you know—entirely. Please believe that much."

"Georgiana," he began, but she had to say her piece and escape, before any of those wicked thoughts in her head actually slipped out.

"Rob. My lord." She clasped her hands around his wrists, gently removing his hands from her. Her shoulders and neck felt cold without his touch, and she shivered in the night air. "This has been the most incredible chain of mischance and misfortune and bad judgment—all mine, on the last," she hastily said, lest he think she blamed him. "The less said about any of it, the better, I suspect. After tomorrow . . . after tomorrow we shan't have any reason to know each other, and that is probably for the best." He made a sharp motion, reaching for her again, and Georgiana leapt backward, already in retreat. "We should go back to the house. Your brother will be expecting us early tomorrow."

Without waiting for a reply, she turned and hurried back to the house. He did not follow, nor did he stop her. And Georgiana wished she didn't wonder, all the way through the garden, what she would have done if he had.

Chapter 16

Sunlight streamed through the windows the next morning. It should have been dark and gloomy, to match his mood, and Rob threw off the blankets rather grimly.

Georgiana came downstairs in her traveling clothes, and mentioned more than once over breakfast that they hoped to make a start soon. Lady Winston wished them Godspeed on the journey, and Geneva begged Georgiana to send her some fashion periodicals when she reached London. Rob recognized that he was the only person not anxious for them to leave, so he ate his breakfast in silence.

The travel chaise was waiting by the time they finished eating, their luggage loaded in the boot. Georgiana's maid, Nadine, a round-faced girl with brown skin, climbed up with the driver, a small blessing he appreciated. Then Georgiana was hugging her hostess good-bye and stepping into the carriage. Rob said his thanks as well, adding a silent promise as Lady Winston wished him a full recovery and good health: *I will not forget this.* Whatever he had done to make the Winstons hate him, he would make up for it.

They drove off with cheery waves out the window, Geneva wagging her handkerchief. Georgiana waved for a long time, then finally fell back against the seat opposite him with a sigh.

"Glad it's over?" he asked.

"Aren't you?" she asked in astonishment.

No, he thought with a pang.

"I've been faint with fear I'd say the wrong thing, and cause a row with Kitty, or a setback for you, or even get us both thrown out of the house. Now I can breathe easily again," Georgiana continued.

"Well." He smiled wryly. "Breathing easily is good."

She laughed, and he couldn't help laughing, too.

The inn where they were to meet Tom was seven miles away. That left him barely two hours alone with Georgiana, and he did not know how to spend it. His brief moment of fury at her deception had dissipated in the face of her heartfelt apology, and the realization that she really meant to leave and not see him again.

Last night, he had wrestled with that. He ought to be pleased. She'd been lying to him from the start, and there was a chance she still was. Had he really said those dreadful things about her? He had no memory of it, but it did feel uncomfortably familiar. His friends would say things like that. If he *had* said that, she was perfectly justified in hating him, and he would be well rid of her as well.

Instead he could think only of her cool hands on his feverish skin, of her voice reading *The Arabian*

Nights in six different accents, of her eyes growing dark with desire when he caught her in the pond. Had she only been acting then? Or did she feel the same potent attraction he did?

In spite of everything, he wanted that part to be real.

"There are some things I must return to you." Unaware of his turmoil, she opened her reticule and dug inside, producing a thick gold ring, engraved with a W. "It's very distinctive."

He slid it back onto his finger and closed his fist. It fit perfectly and felt right. "When did you take it?"

She blushed. "When everyone was in uproar at the beginning. I hid it in my stocking drawer."

At the beginning, when she'd stripped off his clothing and tended his wounds. "You're practically a spy."

She rolled her eyes, but with a smile that made his stomach tighten. "Do you think? I'm sure I'd be found out and hanged at once if I tried any real spying." She turned back to her reticule and took out a folded paper. "And there is this."

He had a suspicion he knew what it was, and a quick read of the first few lines confirmed it. "Why are you giving it to me? You could give it to Lady Winston and put her mind at ease."

She gazed at the document, then lifted her seagreen eyes to his. "I took it from you, and I should give it back to you." She lifted one shoulder and turned to look out the window, not quite hiding the color in her cheeks. "I trust you to do the right thing with it."

She obviously had not trusted him to do the right

thing earlier. Rob slid it inside his jacket, not interested in discussing the deed. "Come sit by me."

She blinked, startled. She'd taken the backward-facing seat before he could.

He moved over and patted the seat next to him. "It's wretched to travel backward."

"Oh! Yes, it is." She switched seats without another word of protest. He caught a whiff of her perfume as she arranged her skirts, and he inhaled greedily. "Thank you," she said with a warm glance at him.

"I didn't want you to cast up your accounts on my boots," he replied. "There's been far too much illness between us already."

She nodded fervently, and he grinned. Let nothing grim or unpleasant sully this last hour with her to himself.

"In the interest of that, then . . ." She tugged loose the ribbon on her bonnet and tossed it onto the opposite seat. Without hesitation Rob threw his own hat to join it, and she laughed in surprise. Encouraged, he stretched out his legs and even propped his left foot on the opposite seat. Georgiana scrunched up her nose, still smiling, and put up her own feet. Her leather half boots looked dainty and delicate next to his.

"Are you eager to return to London?" he asked.

"All things considered, yes." She heaved a sigh. "Even to Lady Sidlow."

"Even her?" He clapped one hand to his heart as if in shock.

Georgiana laughed. "She thinks I'm very headstrong and silly, and she would prefer I have no fun at all. I don't think the woman knows how to smile, Rob."

The name struck him in the heart. "Who on earth put someone like that in charge of you?"

"Alistair," she said. "I used to think he looked for the dullest person who would take the post, to put me in my place. But she was a friend of my mother's—or so I've been told, for I cannot square her temperament with what I remember of Mama's—and despite all her scoldings and declarations that she's at the end of her tether with me, she refuses to give her notice."

"Georgiana," he drawled in amusement, "have you tried to drive the woman off?"

"A little," she admitted impishly.

Rob snorted with laughter.

"Clearly I failed in my every attempt," she went on, enjoying herself now. "Even when I ran off she wouldn't leave. It's very unsporting of her, actually."

"You ran off?" he asked in astonishment.

She nodded, her golden curls bobbing around her neck. With this sparkle in her eyes and a pink flush in her cheeks, Georgiana Lucas was enchanting. For the first time Rob grasped what a strain she'd been under. All the uncertain glances, all the nervous looks, all her hesitation had completely vanished. Even the way she moved exhibited relief, as if a great weight had rolled off her.

He supposed it had, or rather was about to—that weight being his presence.

"I did," she said rather proudly. "One of my dearest friends, Eliza, left her husband. Not that he didn't deserve it, but Eliza loved him so desperately before that, and when she wrote to me that she was leaving him, of course I had to go to her! I did take another friend," she added. "I suppose that's what saved me. Sophie brought her husband, and his title cured all Lady Sidlow's anxieties." Her brow furrowed. "Perhaps, in hindsight, I ought not to have done that. If I'd gone to Kings Langley by myself, it might have given her such an apoplexy she *would* have given notice . . ."

"Who is Sophie's husband?" Rob was entertained beyond belief—and just a touch dismayed. A whole week he'd had with her and only now, for the last hour, was he seeing this side of her. He'd found her previous manner appealing. If she'd been this carefree the entire time . . .

"The Duke of Ware," she said. "He's not as stuffy as he seems."

"Ah."

"Do you know him?" She gave him a curious glance. "Do you remember—?"

"Not Ware," he said thoughtfully. "I know his brother slightly. I think."

"Lord Philip," said Georgiana with a sigh. "Such a scapegrace! I used to tease Sophie that she should set her cap for him, but she fell in love with Ware instead."

"Sophie . . ." he said slowly, memory stirring. "Sophie Campbell?"

"I thought you might know her!" Georgiana beamed. "She played at the Vega Club. You're a member there, aren't you?"

Rob frowned. "Yes." He remembered the club, just as he remembered Mrs. Campbell, the youngest, most attractive woman who'd ever tossed the dice there. He'd never sat at a table with her, because she played too low. But there was something else about the club that niggled at the edge of his memory . . .

Georgiana's demeanor had darkened. "If you ever see Charles Winston there, please promise me—that is, I hope you won't play against him. He must be horribly incompetent."

Rob smiled briefly, the nagging memory slipping away before he could grasp it. "Never again will I trade cards with Charles Winston. I hope he's learned that lesson as well, since one of us really ought to remember it."

She laughed behind her hand, and Rob rested his head on the back cushion and watched her, wishing the trip could last another year.

Sadly it did not. They reached the King's Arms and found Tom waiting. Once he had joined them in the carriage, there was no chance of talking about anything other than The Plan, as Rob had begun to think of it.

He was less and less enamored of Tom's plan to separate him from Georgiana—which, he suspected, was his brother's primary goal—while Georgiana seemed genuinely anxious that he recover his memory by returning to familiar surroundings. While Tom quizzed her about every particular of his time at Osbourne House, Rob mostly stared out the opposite window, having realized that gave him the best covert view of her. The play of emotions over her face as she answered Tom's questions made him maudlin, and angry, and wistful.

Damn it all, he didn't want to go back to Salmsbury Abbey yet. He didn't want to leave Georgiana at the inn and drive off with Tom; more the other way round, he thought, listening to Tom pick apart some minor inconsistency in Georgiana's story and feeling his temper stir.

"Leave it," he finally snapped.

"This story is gaping with holes." His brother shot a black look at Georgiana. "Sir Walter Scott himself would be taken aback by the leaps of logic and flights of fancy."

She flushed. "I suppose you'd have done a better job of it, without even a moment to prepare."

"I suppose I would've," he shot back.

"What a terrible pity you weren't there, when you might have been useful for a change," she exclaimed.

"Stop," said Rob testily, glaring at his brother.

Georgiana flinched and lowered her head. "I'm sorry."

"Not you," he murmured. Tom made a childish face and turned to face the window. Rob wished his brother would get out of the carriage and ride his horse, but he had to settle for silence. Not only did Tom finally hold his tongue, so did Georgiana. A heavy, taut air seemed to fill the carriage and suppress all conversation.

By the time they reached the inn where they would spend the night before going their separate ways, Rob had discarded no less than a dozen ideas for how to delay. He could go to London, too. He had a house there; he'd remembered it, near Green Park. Then he could call on Georgiana and see her at balls and parties. She was still engaged to someone else, but perhaps, if he had some time . . . He wanted to ask her if she'd be glad to see him in London. He wanted to ask if he could begin again, as himself, and see if she found that man more to her liking than the old Westmorland.

Not to mention, more to her liking than Lord Sterling.

But there was never a moment to speak to her. Tom had made the arrangements, all too well; the innkeeper had two large rooms waiting when they arrived, and Georgiana hurried up to hers with her maid trailing behind. Rob decided he'd try at dinner, but again Tom maneuvered to prevent any conversation by ignoring every hint that he ought to step outside or at least withdraw to the corner of the private parlor for a few minutes.

And then, with startling suddenness, it was over. The servants had cleared the dishes and brought a bottle of port. Georgiana rose from the table. "It's been a very tiring day. I would like to retire."

"Of course," said Tom with a bow. "Godspeed on your travels to London."

"Thank you. Have a pleasant journey, Major." She turned her clear green eyes to Rob. "I wish you all the best, sir. I hope everything will be as it once was, with you."

The servants were still going in and out of the room. She was trying to be discreet. Rob nodded. "I could write to you," he heard himself say. "And let you know how I'm getting on."

Her eyes brightened, but Tom cleared his throat loudly, and the light faded. She gave a muted smile. "I'm sure I'll hear. And it might be best . . . well, not to write."

He nodded. Right. "Good night," he said formally.

She curtsied. "Good-bye, my lords." And she was gone.

"Make a clean break," said Tom after the door closed behind her. "It's for the best."

Rob twisted the stopper off the bottle of port and flung it at his brother, eliciting a yelp of outrage from Tom.

There was a clean break, all right. It went straight through his heart.

Chapter 17

GEORGIANA TRUDGED UP the stairs, trying not to think of how she should have ignored Major Churchill-Gray in that last moment and told Rob that she would be delighted to have one letter from him. It would have been a very short and simple letter, of course, she told herself. She would wonder about him, as was only natural, and even a few lines would put her mind at ease . . .

And yet, it was absolutely not her business. The major was right to remind her that this was the end, if she were lucky, and inviting any letters would only be asking for trouble.

She closed the door of her room, inexpressibly tired and numb. Nadine had prepared the room but was still down in the kitchen, having her own dinner. In the distance a church bell tolled the hour mournfully: *Gone, gone, gone,* it seemed to say. *Go, go, go.* Go where? To London? Or go to Rob and . . . what? She squeezed her eyes shut and exhaled a shuddering sigh. She was going back to London. Rob was going home. It was for the best.

The knock on the door made her jump. She had

barely opened the latch when Rob pushed it open and stepped in, sweeping it closed behind him. With one motion he caught her to him, sending her heart leaping with joy. When he lowered his head and kissed her, an electric shock went through her, and she wrapped her arms around him and kissed him back, desperately, longingly, without thinking of anything beyond that moment.

His hand cupped the back of her head. She sighed into his mouth as his fingers tangled in her hair. He made a smothered moan and rained frantic kisses across her brow and down her throat before capturing her lips once more. His arm swept around her waist and pulled her against him until she could feel every beat of his heart.

And something inside her seemed to swell and ache for more, as if she'd just been jolted to life from a deep stupor. Her heart beat like a bird's wing against her ribs. His tongue teased hers, and a shiver of surrender went down her spine as she opened for him. This was what she had feared and craved, all at once, and she never wanted it to end.

He tore his mouth from hers and clutched her to him so tightly she felt his ragged breath vibrate through her. "Don't go," he whispered urgently. "Please don't leave." He kissed her again, and she almost swooned into it. *No,* she wanted to say; *I don't want to leave you.* She pushed her fingers into his hair and held on, pulling him closer and kissing him back with every fiber of her being.

"Georgiana," he breathed, his arms trembling around her. "Come to Salmsbury with me."

For a moment the floor seemed to buckle under her feet. She pressed her face into his neck and breathed deeply, and for one wild, mad moment, she let herself imagine it—hiding away with Rob, *this* Rob, charming and devilish, who made her laugh, who cared for her thoughts and feelings, who kissed her like a man in love . . .

"I don't want to leave you. Come with me," he said again, his voice low and coaxing, as if he knew she was wavering and needed only the slightest push to say yes. "We'll work out what to do about Sterling."

Sterling. The name landed like a blow of an executioner's axe. That was not the push she had needed.

Heartsick, she pulled away. "I can't," she said in a stifled voice.

"You can't marry him," he said—pleaded. "Not now."

"You want me to jilt Sterling." It was frightening how close she'd been to doing just that. She had given Sterling her promise and here she was in another man's arms. Georgiana turned away and wrapped her arms around her waist to keep her heart from bursting.

The silence that followed hurt her ears.

"He doesn't deserve that," she added softly. A tear trickled down her cheek and she dashed it away. "I can't go with you, Rob."

"Georgiana—"

"We don't know each other," she interrupted, to herself as much as to him. "This is a lingering madness, from pretending we were engaged. A few days apart and it will all seem like a fever dream, something that would never happen if we were ourselves . . ."

"No," he said, so low she barely heard. "It isn't. Not for me."

"But you don't *know* that," she retorted. "You can't! And I—" Her voice wavered. "I can't do that to Sterling." It was unnerving that she had to keep reminding herself that *Sterling* would be the injured party, that she was doing this for *Sterling's* sake—Sterling, whose face she could not recall at the moment.

"You kissed me back."

She had, and God help her but she wanted to do it again. If she turned around now, if she saw his face, she would probably throw herself back into his arms and let him kiss away every sensible thought in her brain, and persuade her to go with him. Resolutely she kept her back to him, even though he was so close behind her she could feel the heat of his body. "It can't happen again," she whispered. "Good-bye, Rob."

An agonizing moment later, he moved. His fingertips brushed her shoulder, but she shuddered, scalded by his touch, and his hand fell away. Then the door opened and closed, and he was gone.

ROB SLUMPED AGAINST THE wall in the corridor, his leg aching again. It hadn't hurt at all when he'd thrown caution to the wind and run after her. At that moment, he would have hobbled through a blazing furnace on two broken legs to see Georgiana again, to kiss her just once more.

And that kiss . . . She'd wrapped herself around him and kissed him back with her heart and soul in her mouth, and he'd almost combusted on the spot. Forget what had happened before. In that one delirious kiss he'd seen his future: she was meant for him and he was meant for her, not for show or pretense but forever.

Instead he was standing unsteadily on a bad leg, still burning for Georgiana at the same time he felt cold to the center of his bones.

He limped toward his room. Tom intercepted him at the top of the stairs, port bottle in hand. "What did you do?"

Rob ignored his brother. He let himself into the spacious room they were sharing and made his way to the small writing table under the eaves, where he collapsed into the chair with a thump. Digging his fist into the throbbing muscle of his thigh, he rummaged in his valise until he found the folded paper she'd given him in the carriage.

"What's that?" Tom, ever the busybody, peered over his shoulder.

"The deed to Osbourne House." He took out a sheet of paper and his writing utensils, and began preparing a quill.

Tom gave a low whistle. "The fair Georgiana had it all this time?"

"Tom," said Rob evenly, "do be quiet."

His brother raised his brows. "You knew she was engaged."

I thought she was engaged to me. "Yes."

"I told you Sterling would be some competition."

She kissed me back. "It's not your concern."

"Wakefield is a very dodgy fellow," Tom said, ignoring his silent commands to stop talking. "You ought to think twice before getting twisted up with that one or his sister."

He could hardly think of anything but getting twisted up with Georgiana. "Tom."

"The best way to smooth over this entire debacle is to maintain a wide distance from the lady," his idiot brother went on, coldly and callously to Rob's ears. "If Sterling does hear of it and won't have her after all, you don't want to be caught up in the scandal."

"Shut it," snarled Rob. "Keep your bloody stupid advice to yourself!"

After a startled moment, his brother heaved a sigh. He poured a glass of port and thumped it down on the desk. "You know it's a bloody stupid idea. You don't need me telling you that."

Rob gave a harder-than-necessary pull on the penknife and split the quill in half. With a curse he flung it aside and got a new one. Tom retired to the far side of the room, still arguing under his breath and drinking his own glass of port. Rob ignored him and uncapped his ink.

There was only one thing he could do for Georgiana now, and he did it, though it gave him no pleasure. Then he drank the port and went to bed, and tried to forget the golden-haired temptress with laughing green eyes down the hall, and how soon she might be another man's wife.

Chapter 18

❧❧❧

THE JOURNEY BACK to London took the better part of three days, most of which passed without a word spoken. Nadine seemed to know there was nothing to say, and thankfully held her tongue. Georgiana caught the girl's dark eyes on her from time to time, and knew Nadine wondered what had happened.

"Are you all right, m'lady?" the maid finally asked as they reached the outskirts of London.

"Perfectly," Georgiana murmured, her cheek resting against the window of the travel chaise Major Churchill-Gray had hired. Normally she almost hung out the window, eagerly watching the spectacle of town unspooling past their carriage. Today she saw nothing beyond the glass.

"I expect I'm not to mention Lord Westmorland," Nadine went on.

Georgiana flinched. "Please don't."

"He did seem a decent gentleman," Nadine said after a moment. "Are you certain he's all bad and hateful? Angus said—"

Georgiana made a violent motion, and quickly stopped. Angus would have seen Rob holding her, almost kissing her, in the pond. He would have seen her captivated and enthralled by Rob. "No, he's not hateful. But it's still a secret. Best not to speak of him at all."

"No, m'lady," murmured Nadine. She twisted a handkerchief, the linen stark against her dark fingers. "But if Lady Sidlow were to ask me, what should I say? She'll turn me off if she catches me in a lie."

Georgiana raised her head. "You've lied in the past."

Nadine's lips compressed. "About buying Minerva Press novels and gossip sheets, which Lady Sidlow reads herself. She wouldn't kick up over that. But you spending hours alone in a gentleman's bedroom . . . She'd be upset."

Georgiana barely even noticed the tidbit that Lady Sidlow read the same sensational novels she did. "I won't let her turn you off," she told the maid. "Please don't mention anything about . . . him. Say you don't know or don't remember what I did." She sighed. "If Lady Sidlow grows suspicious, I'll be in far worse trouble than you."

"She can't sack *you*," muttered Nadine.

"I won't let her. If I must, I'll confess it was my doing alone," Georgiana promised. "But it would be enormously helpful if you never mentioned anything, either."

The maid's face eased. "Thank you, m'lady. I don't want to be sent back to Yorkshire."

Georgiana shuddered. She'd lie, steal, and cheat to avoid being sent home to her brother's house, and if Lady Sidlow gave notice in a fit of outrage, that's where she would end up. "Nor do I."

Lady Sidlow was not in a good temper when they reached Cavendish Square. "What do you mean, rushing around the country?" she scolded as footmen carried in Georgiana's trunks and Nadine went to prepare a bath, after the long, dusty journey. "I thought you were to stay in Derbyshire another fortnight at least!"

"I was ready to return sooner." Georgiana took off her bonnet. "One might think you didn't want me back."

Lady Sidlow's mouth pursed up. She was forever finding fault with everything Georgiana said and did—too exuberant, too energetic, too wild. She had always been so, but ever since Georgiana had sneaked out to find Eliza a few months ago, there had been a permanent cloud over Lady Sidlow's chaperonage. She was far more suspicious and less tolerant of anything impulsive or high-spirited, and Georgiana had counted escaping her company as one of the most prized benefits of marriage. She'd jumped at Kitty's invitation to Derbyshire for a respite.

"You'd better learn a more modest and compliant demeanor before you are married, Georgiana. This forward way of speaking and behaving will not endear you to Lord Sterling."

That was the exact wrong topic to mention. Georgiana paused in the doorway of the morning room, and turned back. "Lady Sidlow, I begin to think 'modest and compliant' means 'silent and subservient' to you. If that is the case, I must tell you it will never happen."

Lady Sidlow's nostrils flared. She had quite a prominent nose, and Georgiana was sure the woman knew how dramatic this expression looked. "And will Lord Sterling approve of that?"

Sterling again. The unfairness of having to change her manner to suit Sterling's preferences combined with Georgiana's guilt over the last fortnight with Rob to push her temper to the boiling point.

"Well, it won't be a surprise to him," she said defiantly. Lady Sidlow's jaw dropped. "Sterling has known me since I was six years old! I have always been this way. It doesn't seem to have shocked him thus far."

Lady Sidlow clucked in disapproval. "What men find charming in a girl, they find less so in a wife. Lord Wakefield directed me to see you were prepared for marriage. I would be remiss if I didn't warn you to mend your ways before you give your husband a disgust of you."

Then he can find another fiancée. It was on the tip of her tongue; she very nearly said it aloud. And that, more than Lady Sidlow's words, stopped Georgiana's outrage cold.

"If you no longer wish to undertake the challenge of advising me, I will write to my brother and ask him to find a new chaperone," she said.

It was a low blow. First, by reminding Lady Sidlow, a widowed countess whose spendthrift husband had left her very little, that she was barely more than a paid companion. Second, because Lady Sidlow was extremely well compensated and would never relinquish the position before she had to, no matter her threats to resign the post. Georgiana knew her brother paid for not only this house in fashionable Cavendish Square with its full complement of servants, but also the carriage and all Lady Sidlow's bills, from the furrier to the modiste. Georgiana had once overheard Lady Sidlow tell a friend of hers that she wouldn't have taken the post but that Wakefield begged her to take Georgiana off his hands. Georgiana knew the truth was that Lady Sidlow had approached Wakefield, playing on her friendship with Georgiana's late mother, and asked for the position to spare herself having to beg her late husband's nephew for an income.

Georgiana had known all this for years. She had always felt at least a sliver of sympathy for her chaperone, and she had never put any of it in the older woman's face. But Lady Sidlow had never managed to strike so precisely at her most vulnerable point before, and Georgiana felt her composure and restraint running very thin.

Lady Sidlow inhaled deeply. "That is not necessary. I was only trying to help, but I see my advice is not wanted. I beg your pardon." She swept out of the room, leaving Georgiana deflated.

She was not overly fond of Lady Sidlow, but she did not hate her. It was rude to have spoken to her that way, and Georgiana was instantly sorry. Glumly she pulled off her gloves, collected her bonnet, and went upstairs, her feet heavy.

It was not a long trip to Salmsbury Abbey, but it felt like a thousand miles to Rob. Partly that was due to his brother, who wedged himself into the carriage opposite him. Rob was incredibly tired of Tom watching him as if afraid he would have a nervous outburst at any moment.

Georgiana had been gone when they came downstairs that morning. The innkeeper told him she'd been up early, hoping to get a start on the long trip. "Cheery and gracious, she was," he told Rob. "Ever so apologetic to the poor lads who were to go with them, yawning as they put the horses to harness. She asked for an extra hamper of food, just for them."

She would do that. He could just picture her bright smile, charming everyone into setting out an hour sooner than planned and taking every effort to make it up to them. And she'd done it because she wanted to be gone before he woke, to prevent any awkward meeting after that kiss.

He had lain awake half the night thinking about that kiss. Perhaps he ought not to have done it; he knew she was engaged to Sterling, and Georgiana was intensely loyal. But then he thought how he would feel if he'd never risked it, and knew he'd do it all over again. If he never saw her again—or if the next time he saw her she was Lady Sterling . . . at least he would know he had tried.

They reached Salmsbury in the late afternoon, when the sunlight took on a particular golden hue. Tom, who had finally got the hint and gone quiet for the last part of the trip, sat up. "They'll be expecting us. I sent word to Mother yesterday."

Rob put his face to the window and watched as they rolled down the gentle slope toward the house. Salmsbury was home, where he and his brothers had grown up running wild in the fields and thickets. The weathered gray stone house, as sprawling as any castle, came in sight, and he heaved a silent sigh. He remembered it, yet with a strange feeling of detachment.

It would help if he could stop thinking about how he'd asked Georgiana to come with him, and how she might have been sitting where Tom was, her green eyes wide with interest and her hand comfortingly in his. He could have covered any lapses in his still-sluggish memory by letting her ask the questions and hearing the answers.

The carriage stopped at the side entrance, where the family usually went in. Tom jumped down and stood waiting, but Rob steadfastly ignored his implicit assistance. He climbed down gingerly, leaning on the cane. As the servants hurried forward to fetch the luggage, a woman came around the corner of the house, a large basket over one arm. She stopped cold at the sight of them. Her basket fell to the ground, spilling its burden of flowers. Beside him, Tom raised one hand in greeting and took a step backward.

"Don't leave," Rob said without thinking. He wasn't ready for this, not alone, not yet.

"Just clearing her path," murmured his brother.

The woman broke into a run, clutching up her skirts indecently high in both hands. As she ran, her wide-brimmed hat blew off, although she didn't seem to notice. Her blond hair shone in the sunlight, and more memories trickled through his brain.

Barely a step away, just short of slamming into him, she stopped, hands outstretched. Tears welled in her anxious eyes. "West," she said, her voice breaking. "*Rob*. Are you—are you well?"

"Better now," he said. "Mother."

Her face convulsed and she flung her arms around him. Rob returned her embrace and buried his face in her hair and remembered—lilacs. His mother had always smelled of lilacs. As a boy he had helped her pick the flowers in the spring to perfume her soaps and pomades. He remembered walking in the gardens, holding her hand, resting his head on her lap as they sat on a bench.

"You're home at last." She released him and unabashedly wiped at her eyes. Silently Tom offered a handkerchief, and she took it with a little laugh. "I feared—and then I *hoped*—and there was no word—and you, Thomas, you *found* him. You wonderful boy!" She threw herself at Tom, who goodnaturedly let himself be embraced and kissed on the cheek. He rolled his eyes at Rob over her shoulder, but Rob couldn't say anything. His chest felt tight as memories spilled through his stupid damaged head.

His mother dabbed her eyes again. "Have you seen your father?"

"We've barely stepped down from the carriage," Tom said. "Is he in the house?"

"Yes, somewhere. Agnes!" the duchess called to the servant behind her. "Fetch His Grace immediately!" The woman curtsied and ran off.

"What happened?" She turned to him again, her face softening with concern. "Tom said nothing except that he found you in good health."

"I wrote a letter!" said Tom in outraged tones. "A long one!"

"Barely a page and almost devoid of information," his mother shot back. "You're forgiven now, naturally, but I've been beside myself wondering what happened."

Rob managed a smile. "It's a long story, Mother."

"Of course," she said at once, "and you're tired from your journey. Come see your father."

They went inside, and more memories trickled into his brain. The banister they'd slid down. The suits of armor they'd tried on. The polished marble floor that had proved as slick as a frozen pond, once Will spilled a bucket of soapy water on it.

A tall, broad-chested man appeared at the top of the stairs. "Rowland," called the duchess, "Thomas found him."

Rob looked up in time to see the blaze of joy that flashed across his father's face before the duke stormed down the stairs and gripped his arms. "By God," he said softly, studying Rob's face. "We feared for you, lad."

He smiled. "I heard."

The duke laughed, turning to thump Tom on the back. "Well done, Tom, well done! I knew you would run him to ground." He wheeled back to Rob. "What the blazes happened? You disappeared without a trace and your mother worried about murderers and press gangs."

"He's tired," said the duchess. "We'll discuss it over dinner."

The duke scowled but threw up his hands. "All right! You rousted me from my study, then tell me I've got to wait to hear the tale." He glanced at Tom. "You know, eh?"

Tom wore a faintly smug grin. "I know some."

"Well, come tell me that bit so I'm prepared at dinner." Rowland looked at Rob again. They were the same height, so Rob could see the genuine concern and relief in his father's eyes. "Good to have you home, son," he said gruffly.

"Thank you, sir," he replied.

The duke nodded. "Have you told Will?"

The duchess's hand flew to her throat. "No! Someone must go fetch him—he's taken out the gray gelding, I believe."

"I'll send someone to find him," said Tom.

"Thank you, dear." The duchess smiled at him, then clasped Rob's hand once more. "Your room is ready. Rest as long as you like, dear. Oh, thank God you're home!"

He promised he would, and his mother hurried off to find the housekeeper, calling back that he must want a bath and that she would tell Cook to send up his favorite refreshments. The duke's secretary was lingering on the stairs, and Rowland grumbled about not being able to welcome his own son home without being pestered by the fellow, but went back up the stairs after extracting a promise to hear all at dinner.

Rob and Tom were left alone in the soaring main hall. "Welcome home," said Tom wryly.

"It's good to be back." Rob did not add that he'd rather have been with Georgiana, wherever she was now.

As if hearing his thoughts, Tom cocked one brow. "I suppose we're not going to make mention of Lady Georgiana's fanciful stories."

His mother must know her. The year Rob reached his twenty-fifth birthday, his mother had seemed to memorize, virtually overnight, a catalog of every unmarried young woman above the age of fifteen in Britain. She would say, at random times, that she longed to see all four of her sons happily married. They had all disappointed her thus far.

"No," he said to his brother. "You're not to mention her name."

Tom snorted. "Not to mention—?"

"No," he cut in again. "If anyone tells Mother about Georgiana, I shall do it."

Tom's brow arched. "And will you?"

At some point. Rob had no idea how or when, but he thought his brain would burst if he never spoke to anyone about her. "Not your business."

His brother's other brow went up. "No? I think it's quite a tale. I might dine out for a fortnight on it, now that I think about it. The week West thought he was someone else—and relished it!"

"Don't you have a regiment missing you?" Rob made his way toward the stairs.

"Compassionate leave." Tom dogged his footsteps. "To search for the body of my late brother, tragically murdered by footpads. Or, perhaps, assassinated and resurrected by a scheming minx."

"Have some compassion on your resurrected brother, and go back to the army."

"Don't fancy it just yet. Lingering concern for your health and all that."

Rob made a rude gesture and hoisted himself up the stairs one painful step at a time. His leg had got stiff in the carriage and now felt weaker than ever. He should be delighted to be home but instead he felt . . .

Trapped.

Chapter 19

LONDON, ONCE THE center of the world, seemed tiresome and dreary to Georgiana. Lady Sidlow clung to her grudge for several frosty days, but Georgiana didn't have the spirit to be annoyed. Dutifully she went on calls with Lady Sidlow, and sat in the drawing room when they had callers in Cavendish Square. Normally she chafed at the company Lady Sidlow preferred, and tried to get out of it. Now she had nowhere else she preferred to be, so there was no reason to protest.

Finally Lady Sidlow remarked on it. "You're very quiet and out of sorts lately. You barely said a word to Lady Capet."

Georgiana had never liked Lady Capet, whose gossip always had a malicious tilt. "I had nothing of interest to say. I thought it best to refrain from proving it aloud."

Instead of being pleased by this, Lady Sidlow stiffened. "Don't be impertinent, Georgiana."

Georgiana sighed and rolled her eyes, sipping more of her stone-cold tea.

"There!" Her chaperone seized on the gesture.

"That is precisely what I mean! You are too obvious with your disdain, young lady."

"It wasn't disdain," she said. "Nor was it impertinence. How many times have you told me to hold my tongue if I have nothing clever or thoughtful to say?"

Lady Sidlow rose, her feathers well and truly ruffled. "I daresay you're set in your ways by now, despite my best efforts."

Yes. Georgiana's head bobbed slightly. *Very set.*

"I cannot say I'll be sorry to let Lord Sterling take charge of you," continued Lady Sidlow. "Perhaps he can make you see reason and sense. You give in to your feelings too much. A lady is more dignified and restrained. She does not show her disdain or impertinence; she projects a composed and gracious manner at all times. Did they teach you nothing at that school?"

Georgiana shot an annoyed look at the woman but the words spurred her thoughts. She'd been at school for ten years, from the time her mother died until she was eighteen. Alistair had wanted rid of her so desperately that he'd suggested sending her to an orphanage, before his steward had prevailed upon him to reconsider how that would look, an earl's daughter in an orphanage.

But at school, she'd made friends who were closer than sisters. In her gloomy mood, she hadn't even thought of going to one of them.

"Yes," she said slowly, setting down her teacup. "Mrs. Upton taught me a great deal." She got to her feet. "I'm going to Alwyn House."

Lady Sidlow's look of displeasure melted away at the mention of the home of the Duke and Duchess of Ware. It was only a few miles outside London. "Yes," she said warmly, "that's a wonderful idea."

Georgiana remembered Lady Sidlow's tirades when she had wanted to visit her friend before her marriage, when Sophie was supporting herself at the gaming tables and building a modest fortune of her own without help from anyone. *Then* Lady Sidlow had carried on about the unsuitability of their friendship, the impropriety of young ladies visiting each other without chaperones, the vaguely indecent and nefarious things she was sure Sophie was enticing Georgiana into doing. Since Sophie was the most levelheaded person she knew, Georgiana had ignored most of this.

All Sophie had to do was marry a duke, though, for Lady Sidlow's objections to go up in smoke. *Now* Lady Sidlow smiled benevolently upon the friendship and always allowed Georgiana to visit. Georgiana thought it terribly amusing that Sophie had turned so decidedly from being a terrible influence to being the best influence in the space of one marriage ceremony.

"I may spend the night," Georgiana said. Once she told Sophie what brought her, her friend would insist she stay.

"Of course!" All approval now, Lady Sidlow nodded in agreement.

Georgiana told Nadine to pack a valise and gave her the night free. It was a fine day, the roads were dry, and it took only an hour to reach Alwyn House, the duke's chateaulike house in the English countryside.

Sophie was delighted, if astonished, to see her. "I thought you were in Derbyshire!"

"I was." Georgiana smiled brightly, hoping not to give everything away yet. "I came back."

Sophie's eyes narrowed. "Why?"

Georgiana waved one hand. "The pleasures of town. You know I can't bear to be away from it. Have I come at a horribly bad time?" The last time she'd gone to Chiswick unannounced, the duke and Sophie were newly married and Georgiana strongly suspected she'd interrupted a romantic moment.

Sophie smiled. "No. Is something the matter?"

Georgiana drew a deep breath. "We're going to need tea. Vast quantities of tea."

Even to her dearest friend, it was a difficult story to tell. She trusted Sophie more than any other person in the world, but certain parts still made her squirm to say them aloud. Once or twice Georgiana thought she detected a faint smile hovering over Sophie's mouth, but when accused, the duchess protested that she was not laughing.

"I'm not," she insisted. "It's not a laughing matter."

"No," Georgiana groaned. "It's like a farce that ends in tragedy."

Sophie sipped her tea. "*Tragedy* is an interesting word."

Georgiana flushed. "I shouldn't have said that. It all came out well, didn't it? Rob—Westmorland, I mean—has recovered his memory and gone home to his family. He'll be vastly more comfortable there, and soon return entirely to himself."

"His reprehensible self?" murmured Sophie.

Georgiana seized on it. "Yes! Doesn't it seem likely?"

Sophie put up one hand. "I've no idea. I only ever knew the man by repute."

"But wasn't he awful?" pressed Georgiana, as if it would make her feel better to think of Rob reverting to the Malicious Marquess.

"I never thought he was worse than any other wealthy gentleman." Sophie tilted her head thoughtfully. "A bit rakish, but no scandalous love affairs. And quite good for a gambler, for I don't recall him losing badly."

"Would that he had," Georgiana muttered. If Rob had lost to Charles instead of the other way 'round, none of this would have happened.

"Do you want him to be reprehensible?" asked Sophie.

Georgiana flushed. "I think he will be, that's all."

"Because you want to hate him again."

"No—well . . ." Georgiana stared into her tea. She didn't want to hate Rob. But neither did she want to miss him or wonder how he was, or yearn for a letter from him to arrive out of the blue. Nothing about Rob should matter to her now. "Of course I don't want to hate him, I just . . . would prefer him to be unlikeable."

"And why is that?"

Her friend's gentle question was like a needle to the building pressure of guilt and longing and she didn't even know what else. She cast an anguished glance at the door and lowered her voice. "Swear you will never tell anyone. Not even Eliza."

Sophie's eyes widened at this embargo on telling their mutual friend. "I swear."

"I *liked* him," Georgiana said in misery. "As he was. As he woke. He thought I was his fiancée, and he was warm, and kind, and charming, and he flirted with me constantly, and he—he—he was not at all the way I thought he was. And then he kissed me, the night we parted, and asked me to go with him instead of to London. He—he all but proposed that I elope with him and desert Sterling, and, Sophie—*I thought about it*." The last came out in a tearful whisper, although no one but the duchess could possibly hear.

Sophie leaned forward. "Why do you think you did?"

"I don't know!"

"No?" Sophie cocked her head. "Not even a guess?"

This was not helping. Georgiana drew a deep breath. "I love Sterling."

"I never said you didn't." Sophie's gaze didn't waver. "But you've been in love with him since you were a child. I heard your raptures about him at Mrs. Upton's, year after year after year. Dear Sterling, who was so charming, so amusing, so daring and handsome and dazzling as well. But Georgiana . . ." She hesitated. "You were never much exposed to any other gentlemen, were you?"

Georgiana's mouth dropped open in outrage. "I've met dozens of gentlemen since I came to London! Handsome, charming, witty ones!"

"But not many before Sterling, and by the time you met those other men you knew you were taken. You accepted Sterling's proposal your first Season in London, so you never had cause to look twice at another man."

"Nor desire!" she retorted, her heart beating wildly. It had been true, it had . . . but now she wasn't sure.

Sophie lifted one shoulder. "I'm not calling you inconstant—quite the opposite! You've been so loyal to your childhood love that you've never once questioned it, or him. You loved him, and therefore he must be wonderful. You made Sterling perfect, in your mind."

"I did not!" Georgiana practically threw her teacup back on the table. "You're not being fair!"

"Nor were you, to Sterling," said Sophie with a speaking look. "He is a flesh and blood man, with faults like any other. I can't help but think that you finally had reason to look at another man, not merely as someone to while away a dance with, but as a suitor—even as a lover. And even if it was only a pretense, I'm not surprised it made you wonder."

"Oh," said Georgiana as the light dawned. "It was just the novelty of spending time with another gentleman, you mean?" That almost sounded exculpatory. It might have happened with any fellow, and wasn't about Rob himself. Novelty would wear off, and she would settle back into her devotion to Sterling.

"Well," said Sophie hesitantly, "not precisely. I meant . . . you never imagined marrying anyone but Sterling. Of course it would be novel to think of anyone else, but . . . it is rather telling that you fell so quickly into considering *eloping* with someone else."

Georgiana shot to her feet, knocking into the tea table and giving the dishes a rattle. "I told him no!"

"Of course you did," Sophie replied. "You're too sensible to do otherwise. But Georgiana . . . in the space of a fortnight you found Westmorland appealing enough that you *thought* about it. It's been over two years since Sterling proposed, and there's still no wedding date set. And you seemed to accept that without complaint." Sophie bit her lip, looking up at her. "Do you think that's a sign—?"

"No," said Georgiana before Sophie could say it. "It's a sign I went mad for a few days. I'm better now."

Her friend fiddled with her teacup, then set it down and got to her feet. "You're like a sister to me, you know. I will support you whatever you decide."

"I've already decided! I decided years ago!"

Sophie took her hands. "And if that will bring you true happiness and joy, you should marry Sterling. But if you have any doubts . . . you should not. Marriage is forever. It's best to be sure before you enter it."

Georgiana stared at her, panic fluttering in her breast. "You think I made a mistake." About Sterling or about Rob, she wasn't sure—or perhaps it was the same thing.

"No," said Sophie at once. "I do not know. But I want *you* to be certain you aren't making one." She said it so simply, Georgiana felt a prickle of tears.

Not because Sophie was standing by her, and had been neither horrified nor disappointed by her confession. Not because Sophie had said some truly terrible things to her. No, it was because . . .

"I'm just not sure," she whispered.

Chapter 20

THE DAYS DRAGGED at Salmsbury Abbey.

The duchess seemed bent on reliving any and every memory he had. In the evenings she made all of them sit in the drawing room and reminisce. Sometimes it was surprisingly pleasant—Rob found himself grinning in shamefaced recollection as Will recounted the time Rob and Tom had convinced him and George, the youngest brother, that there was Viking treasure buried on the seashore, several miles from the house. The two little boys set off on their ponies, only to get lost and not return home before dark.

"We took quite a thrashing for that," said Tom as the duke tried to hide his chuckles. "I couldn't sit for a week."

"You earned it," exclaimed Will. He was three years younger than Tom but taller and whip-thin. His face was browned and his hair lightened from hours working with the horses, his only passion in life. "We could have died!"

"Died," scoffed Tom. "We only wanted rid of you

for a few hours. I'm the one who told Mother where you'd gone."

"Because I made you," murmured Rob. He did remember that, the creeping, uncomfortable knowledge that he'd be responsible if anything happened to his younger brothers.

"I'm the one who nearly died," exclaimed their mother, "of fright! If George hadn't taken a lantern—"

"He wanted to press on for the shore even when it began raining," scoffed Will.

"*Years* off my life," said the duchess firmly.

"It's a fair miracle we survived all four of them," said the duke. "We should have had a girl or two who would play the pianoforte and do watercolors and not want to be a knight in a joust."

"That was Tom," said Will at once.

"Oh? I remember all three of you following my suggestion," drawled Tom.

"I hope you have more compassion on your wives, when you marry," put in their mother.

Will and Tom went silent, exchanging uneasy glances. Rob felt his mood sink at this mention of wives and, by extension, fiancées and betrothals. His brothers were horrified at the mention of those things, ready to flee the room. He wasn't, not when he pictured Georgiana.

It must be a sign, as Tom had said, that he had gone slightly mad. His brain was still jumbled. He'd been weak and might have felt the same for any woman who'd been kind to him.

That thought made no difference to the ache around his heart.

After dinner he went outside. It was a clear night, cooler than in Derbyshire. He raised his face to the sky and wondered if Georgiana went out to look at the stars in London.

Footsteps crunched along the path, coming to a stop just behind him. Rob didn't turn. From the silence, he guessed it was one of his brothers instead of either parent.

"Still got an ache in your head?" asked Tom after several minutes.

"Not really," Rob said. It wasn't his head plaguing him now.

"Hmm." Tom took a step forward. "Any other aches?"

Rob spun the cane under his palm in silent acknowledgment of his sore leg. He didn't know how to describe what *was* bothering him.

"I've half a mind to take some mates into Derbyshire and track down the fellows who thrashed you."

"Have you? It's been weeks. Anyone who knew of it has probably forgotten."

"No," said Tom thoughtfully. "I doubt they'd forget pounding a man half to death so soon."

Rob shrugged. "Obviously I remember nothing of it and cannot help."

"A bit odd, don't you think, that they took nothing? Thieves usually get right to the robbery."

He'd thought of that, too, but had been in no condition to do anything about it. "Perhaps Georgiana and her groom gave them a fright before they could."

"Did they?" muttered Tom. "I wonder."

"What, Tom?" Rob snarled. "What do you wonder?"

"Nothing about Lady Georgiana," said Tom quickly, backing up at his tone. "I'm persuaded her part was no more nor less than she told us. I only wonder about the thieves."

Rob shifted his weight on the cane. His leg was aching again. "It's possible they stole something I don't remember having, you know."

"Hobbes said you took almost nothing," Tom pointed out. "They didn't steal your boots, your horse, the deed in your saddlebag, or your signet ring."

Rob's hand closed into a fist at mention of the ring. Georgiana had taken it off his finger to conceal his identity. She'd hidden it to keep him safe, and she'd given it back to him with the deed. *I trust you to do the right thing*, whispered her voice in memory.

"It was idle curiosity, that's all," said his brother after a moment. "It seems a very striking coincidence that you were waylaid on the way to a house you'd won from someone who seemed very keen to prevent you setting foot in it."

"So Charles Winston set them on me?" He glanced at his brother. "That's what you're thinking?"

Tom shrugged. "He doesn't seem to be the brightest fellow. He might come up with a cork-brained plan like that."

Rob blew out a breath. Was Charles Winston behind it? Did he even care? If he hadn't been beaten, after all, he might have ridden up to Osbourne House and been arrogant and cold. Georgiana would have continued hating him. He would have gained a house he didn't want, and missed out on discovering her . . .

"What did you know of Georgiana before all this?"

"I told you to forget about her," began his brother, aggrieved.

Rob rapped the cane into his shins, taking mean pleasure from Tom's hiss of indignation. "That's not the question I asked."

"I don't think I ought to answer!"

Rob glanced at him, and whatever was in his face made his brother throw up his hands in surrender.

"So be it!" Tom shook his head in disgust. "She hasn't got many connections besides her brother, the Earl of Wakefield, whom no one likes. He's a misanthrope, thoroughly unpleasant and unwelcome. Otherwise she's a typical girl on the marriage mart, as far as I know, vain and frivolous, the sort who giggles and gossips behind her fan and throws tantrums for a new bonnet. But she's been engaged to Viscount Sterling since she made her debut, so no one's spent much time thinking about her."

He meant no men had spent time thinking about Georgiana because she was as good as married.

To Sterling, the undeserving lout.

"Thank you," Rob said, choosing to ignore the aspersions Tom had cast upon Georgiana herself.

"Put her out of your head," his brother said. "She's marrying someone else. You'll make yourself mad if you keep tormenting yourself with some bizarre fantasy that she meant anything she said to you."

Rob turned and limped back into the house. Blessedly Tom did not follow, and inside he met his father.

"There you are," exclaimed the duke with pleasure. "I've hardly been able to get a word with you. Care for a drink?"

"Yes, sir."

They went into the duke's study, and Rowland closed the door. He poured two glasses of port and handed Rob one before dropping into a chair. "How's your mind really?"

Rob stared into his drink. "Perfectly well."

Rowland snorted. "Is it! A fortnight missing, Tom has to track you down to prevent your mother calling out the constabulary, tales of head injuries and lost memory, and now everything is perfectly well?"

"Near enough," murmured Rob.

His father shot him a look, but he let it go. He rested one booted foot on the opposite knee and balanced his glass on the instep. "Your mother worried she'd sent you to your death, scolding you about that deed. Winston, was it?" Rob nodded, and the duke went on. "It seemed very unlike you, to take a man's house and home. What went on that night?"

It made his head ache, trying to remember. "Heathercote planned it."

"Hmm." The duke sipped his port. "Is it one of Beresford's harebrained schemes?"

Lord Beresford was Heathercote's uncle. Rob's frown deepened as more memories blossomed in his head, some as sharp as cut crystal but most cloudy and dark. "What do you mean?"

Rowland was watching him thoughtfully. "I always thought Beresford was putting Heathercote up to some very questionable activities, and that you might be involved in them."

He was. He and Heathercote . . . Yes, he'd forgotten about that. But even now, it felt like a large black boulder sat in front of him, blocking most of it from his view. Not only did it make his head hurt to try to move that boulder, Rob instinctively felt that he didn't really want to remember what he'd been up to in London.

"I don't quite know," he said slowly.

The duke grunted. "Be wary, lad. Beresford's got his heart in the right place, but he has no strategy or sense. Once his mind fixes on something, he pursues it at all costs, sometimes past reason or sanity. A bad plan is a bad plan, even if in service of a noble goal. Don't let him tempt you into some bit of stupidity."

Troubled, Rob nodded.

"As much as I might have wished to separate you from that rascal Heathercote, though, I didn't wish this upon you." Rowland finished his drink and set the glass on the desk. "Are you certain you're well? Tom hinted you had quite the adventure in Derbyshire."

Tom should keep his bloody mouth closed, thought Rob in aggravation. "Quite certain," he snapped.

"Aside from the cane, the scar on your forehead, and the melancholy expression you get whenever you think no one's looking." Rob glanced at him sharply, and his father nodded sagely. "*Something's* troubling you, and it's clearly not any business with Beresford. You don't have to tell me, if it's none of my concern, but don't try to persuade me all is well."

Rob swirled his port and debated. He'd not said a word about Georgiana to anyone, not while Tom was heaping scorn on her name at every turn, but his father hadn't Tom's hot temper or rash judgment. And after all these days he was desperate to tell someone about her. "In strict confidence?"

"If you wish," replied the duke, unperturbed.

Rob jerked his head yes. "There was a lady at Osbourne House."

When he paused for a long moment, the duke clasped his hands behind his head. "A fetching one, I suppose."

"Yes." Rob cleared his throat. "She cared for me when I was ill."

"Very kind of her," remarked Rowland.

Rob hesitated again, then decided to tell everything. "In confidence . . . she saved my life. Not only did she startle off the thieves who were making every effort to beat me to death, she took me back to the house and persuaded them to help me."

"Why did they need any persuading?" The duke's tone was carefully neutral, but Rob grimaced anyway.

"The owner of the house, who lost it to me in that card game, wrote to his wife that I was coming to throw her off the property and turn it into a brothel." He pressed one fist against his temple. "I have no memory of saying that, let alone what I intended by going into Derbyshire with the deed. But needless to say, the lady of the house was not anticipating my arrival with eager delight."

"Hmph," was his father's only comment.

"So Georgiana told them I was her fiancé, thinking that would move them to kindness. And it did," he added quickly. "They were very good to me."

"Because they thought you were someone else." The duke reached for the decanter and poured himself more port. "There's a lesson in that, if you ask me."

No doubt. Rob nodded once.

They sat in silence for a while. Rob finished his

drink and carried on with his story. "She didn't have to help me, but she did, and now I can't stop thinking about her."

"Were you one of the people she told this story to, about you being her fiancé?"

His blood warmed at the memory. "Yes."

His father cocked his head. "And you liked it, didn't you? Not knowing it was a lie."

He had. He did. "It wasn't entirely a lie. She *has* got a fiancé. It's just . . . not I."

"And there's the rub," murmured the duke.

"I don't want her to marry him."

"No?" Rowland leaned forward. "Why not?"

Rob raised his head and met his father's mild gaze. Rowland was no fool; he'd always known when his sons were lying or troubled. Rob was sure his feelings were written all over his face, to his father's knowing eyes.

"You hardly know the girl," the duke reminded him.

I know enough. He might not know everything about Georgiana—not things that Sterling, the bloody scoundrel, probably did—but he wanted to. He knew her heart. He knew he would never forgive himself if he sat around and did nothing while she married Sterling, always wondering if she'd done it out of loyalty or some misplaced duty. At the very least he had to see her again, and see if she felt anything for him like what he felt for her. If she didn't . . . he could accept that, somehow.

But if she *did* . . .

"I'll fix that," Rob said, the decision reached without conscious consideration. "I'm leaving for London in the morning."

Rowland's brow arched. "Are you, now? To what purpose?"

"To see if she might want to know me better," he said. "My real self."

"Indeed? And what will you tell your mother, who will rail at me to prevent you racing off and ruining your newfound health?"

His mouth curled. *Obviously I do not think that far ahead*, echoed Georgiana's voice in his mind. He understood that feeling now. "That's why I told you, so you can explain to her why I'm gone when she wakes."

Rowland scoffed. "A dirty trick, lad!"

Rob acknowledged it with a wave of one hand. "Do you think I'm mad?" he asked on impulse.

The duke didn't reply for a moment. Rob glanced up to see him staring moodily into the fire. "I was about your age when I met a girl," Rowland finally replied. "The most beautiful girl I'd ever seen, with wit and spirit and more dash than any other five girls put together. I turned myself inside out trying to get her to notice me, and then made a fool of myself when she did. Nothing anyone said could have diverted me as long as she kept encouraging me. Are you mad? I'd say so, merely because I recognize the symptoms, having been afflicted by them myself." He glanced up. "It came out rather well for me, although your mother still thinks I make a fool of myself sometimes."

"Then that's all right, isn't it?" Rob exclaimed in relief.

"If you're lucky," grumbled Rowland. He slapped one hand on his knee. "Go, then, and see if you've caught the same happy madness I did. I hope this lady is pining for you just as badly as you are for her."

Rob grinned. "I hope so, too. But I mean to find out."

Chapter 21

Two days after her visit to Sophie, Sterling came to call.

Lady Sidlow herself announced him, sweeping into Georgiana's room with a slight frown on her face. "Still not ready! My dear, what are you about, lying in half the day? Lord Sterling has come. Unfashionably early, of course—the manners of that young man—but that's neither here nor there, you mustn't keep him waiting. Hurry, Nadine," she snapped at the maid, who was pinning Georgiana's hair into place.

Sterling. Georgiana's heart jumped into her throat, but not for any good reason. It wasn't eager anticipation, but something much more like dread spilling through her. Her visit to Sophie had done nothing to set her mind at ease, nor to answer the questions lingering in the back of her mind. She was sure her guilt and doubt would be stamped upon her face.

That thought brought on another surge of self-reproach that she was dreading seeing him. The best way to forget all about Rob was to spend as much time as possible with Sterling, and remember why she'd been in love with him for most of her life.

"And do put on a more flattering dress, Georgiana. You've looked wretchedly pale lately," added Lady Sidlow as she sailed out the door.

"Will you be changing your dress?" asked Nadine in the silence.

Georgiana stared at her reflection. Did she look pale? It was surely not the fault of the dress, and would hardly be fixed by changing clothes. "I can't think of what Lady Sidlow means for me to wear, so no, I shan't change."

"As you say, ma'am," mumbled Nadine around the hairpins she'd stuck in her mouth. "Pinch your cheeks. Her Ladyship'll relent a bit if it looks like you did something."

Georgiana rolled her eyes. Surely it was more important not to keep Sterling waiting. Once she saw him, things would settle back into the way they'd been before, and she wouldn't need to pinch her cheeks.

When Nadine was done with her hair, Georgiana rose and went downstairs, her steps slowing as she approached the drawing room door, and her nerves suddenly tightened. There was the rumble of Sterling's voice, so familiar and yet also strange, after all these weeks. It had been over two months since she saw him last, she realized, and for one frightening moment she couldn't quite recall what he looked like.

With a quick motion she opened the door and went in. Sterling came to his feet, his face alight with sly laughter. He delighted in teasing Lady Sidlow, who endured it with frigid politeness. Sterling,

Georgiana remembered, was very fond of teasing, and he was so clever it almost always made her laugh.

"There she is," he said, coming toward her. "I've missed you, darling."

Even though she had known him for years, and had thought his likeness indelibly etched on her memory, today it seemed her mind was playing tricks on her. He was shorter than she remembered. His hair was lighter brown. His eyes were brighter green. It was disorienting, even more so when she realized with a start that she had somehow expected him to look more like Rob.

Do not think of Rob.

She smiled and took his outstretched hand. "I didn't expect you today, Sterling."

He laughed. "No, I thought to surprise you! I hope I haven't caught you off guard or unprepared."

She'd been back in London almost a week. "A little," she said. "I haven't seen you for weeks! You might have surprised me on the day of a ball, when I would have dressed with more care."

He smiled. "Did you not take care today? I wouldn't notice—you look even lovelier than I remembered. It's been an eternity since I laid eyes on you." He bowed and kissed her hand, and for a moment the familiar affection shot through her. "Letters are a poor excuse for seeing you."

That reminded her that he'd written her only once in the weeks she'd been away. Georgiana snuffed that thought. "I'm delighted to see you again, too."

He led her to the sofa and took the chair opposite. Lady Sidlow rang for tea, which Mary trundled in almost at once. The countess always presided over

Sterling's visits with a stony expression, as if she found this part of being a chaperone tedious beyond bearing. Georgiana had often wondered why, but today she looked at Sterling's face, relaxed in amusement, and realized that Lady Sidlow did not like him.

Sterling, it must be admitted, did not like Lady Sidlow, either. In private he called her stuffy and prickly, and usually Georgiana agreed. Today, as usual, he turned in his chair, angling himself toward Georgiana and putting his shoulder to the countess. "I trust you had a pleasant visit to Derbyshire," he said as she served the tea. "A school friend, wasn't it?"

"Yes. My friend Kitty, now Lady Winston, and her new baby."

"Oh yes, a baby," said Sterling, with the air of someone just remembering something. "How charming. I trust she's well."

She'd told Sterling at least five times that she was going to visit Kitty because of the baby. She'd written to him of the baby as well. She'd written to him almost every week, until Rob landed in her life and commanded her entire attention. She was just now noticing that, along with only sending her one letter in that time, he didn't seem unduly concerned that *her* letters to him had stopped some time ago.

Of course, Sterling was busy here in town and it wasn't a significant point. He'd never been a reliable correspondent. She hurried on. "Yes. She has a beautiful daughter named Annabel." She hesitated, then asked, before she could think better of it, "I don't suppose you saw Sir Charles here in London?"

Sterling coughed a bit over his tea. "Who? Charles

Winston? Yes, of course I saw him. The usual haunts, you know."

"The Vega Club?"

He grinned at her over the rim of his cup. She'd long been fascinated by the Vega Club, where Sophie had once been a member. It always sounded unbearably illicit and thrilling to her. Sterling knew she liked a bit of excitement, and he'd never reproved her for it. It was one of the things she loved about him. "Might have been."

"Then perhaps you heard about his wager." She told herself she was asking for Kitty's sake, and nothing to do with Rob. She was done with Rob.

"Georgiana," said Lady Sidlow sternly. "This is not a suitable topic of conversation for a young lady."

Sterling's eyes danced. It always amused him to provoke Lady Sidlow. "I did," he agreed. "Beastly thing."

Lady Sidlow inhaled loudly, but she did not scold Sterling. She never did, even though she always made clear her disapproval.

"What did you hear?" Georgiana asked. "We received such a tale from Charles, in his letters."

Lady Sidlow clucked under her breath. Georgiana ignored this, too.

"Ah . . ." Sterling glanced at the chaperone. She glared but said nothing. His devilish grin reappeared. "Well, one doesn't like to gossip . . . but it *was* a bit of a scandal. Winston and some mates of his got caught up with Westmorland and Heathercote and that lot, and came out much the worse for it. Westmorland took the deed to the house without so much as a blink of his eye, not even when Winston appealed to his decency and mercy." Sterling looked vaguely contemptuous. "Cold fellow, West-morland."

Georgiana instinctively bristled at that descrip-tion of Rob, but bit it back. She wanted information, not an argument, and she wasn't supposed to know Rob anyway. She widened her eyes in affected dis-may. "That's what Charles told Kitty! Although . . . why did Charles risk the deed to his house?"

"Things happen at Vega's," said Sterling. "West-morland wouldn't give Winston the chance to win it back, then disappeared from London and hasn't shown his face since. Damned scoundrel."

She prayed her face wasn't flushed. "Yes, perhaps. Still, I'm astonished at Charles, and wonder how he wound up a wronged party."

Her fiancé's brows went up. "What's that?"

"Wagering the deed to one's home is a very stu-pid thing to do," she replied. "I'd have been furious with him if he'd been my husband."

"Oh, quite," said Sterling with a laugh. "To be perfectly frank, Winston ought not to have sat down with them—Heathercote's a devil at cards. Still, once he did, he had to make a wager."

"Why?"

Sterling cleared his throat. "I believe he'd lost a rather large amount. The only way to right his ship was to make a bold play."

"Because he was already losing badly, he ought to risk even more?" Georgiana could only imagine what Sophie, who always played the odds, would say about that. "Isn't that utter madness?"

He smiled indulgently. "It's complicated, darling. Not something you need to worry about."

"But I can't help it," she exclaimed. "My dear friend Kitty spent several weeks in absolute despair that her husband had lost their house! Of course I want to know."

He darted another glance at Lady Sidlow, who sat in stony displeasure. "And I'm telling you—against my better judgment," he added, despite no evidence of reluctance or hesitation. "I don't know why you're upset about it."

"Charles lost the deed to their home!"

Sterling waved it away. "He'll come about. If Westmorland is any sort of gentleman, he'll allow Winston the chance to win it back."

"But what if Charles doesn't win?"

For the first time a shade of annoyance flickered over his face. "Then perhaps he deserves to lose the house."

"What?" Georgiana exclaimed. "What about Kitty and their child? Sterling, you can't approve of that. Surely you wouldn't do such a thing?"

Sterling paused, startled. "Of course not. I wouldn't let that lot get the better of me—they're a sharp bunch, Heathercote and Westmorland. Winston was a fool, but don't you see, this is his best chance to come about."

Georgiana threw up her hands irritably. "I'm afraid I don't. Charles lost the deed to his home, and therefore he must wager more and more until he wins. But what if he never does? You said Heathercote and Westmorland are devils at cards. Charles might just keep losing until he's got nothing left. Yet you think that is his best chance to come out whole. Is that right?"

Sterling shrugged. "It's a matter of honor, my dear."

"Well, if that is gentlemen's honor, I'm very glad not to be a gentleman," she declared, sitting back in her chair.

He burst out laughing. "And I am twice as glad you're not! You're the perfect lady; why would you want to be a man?"

"I would never wager my house, if I were."

Still chuckling, he made a motion of surrender. "I'm sure you would not."

He took his leave soon after, promising to come again soon now that she was back in London. Mary came to clear away the tea tray, and Georgiana sat in discontented silence. Sterling thought Charles Winston should keep gambling with Rob and his friends, even though they were far better at it, because that would be the only honorable way for Charles to regain possession of Osbourne House. For the first time she wondered at her fiancé's perception and judgment.

"I know you do not welcome my advice, Georgiana," said Lady Sidlow, breaking into her thoughts. "But you are asking for trouble."

She tried not to roll her eyes. "I know—gambling is not appropriate for ladies, nor is talking about gambling."

"Of course it is not," said her chaperone. "But I refer more to pushing Lord Sterling to tell you things men generally don't tell ladies."

Lady Sidlow was forever telling her that she was wrong, and Georgiana was forever chafing at it—even when she knew her chaperone was right, and she'd stretched some bound of propriety too far. Today, though, there seemed more to it.

"Why don't you like Sterling?" she asked on impulse.

Lady Sidlow froze. "It is not my place to have an opinion about Lord Sterling."

"But you don't."

The older woman hesitated. For a moment, something like doubt flashed across her face—an expression Georgiana had never seen before. "Lord Wakefield was very clear about my duties. He approves of Lord Sterling, and that is all that matters."

She should let it go. Lady Sidlow was starchy and prim and Georgiana had spent two years dreaming of being free of her fussy oversight. But that flicker of doubt, and her own turbulent thoughts about Sterling and Rob, pushed her to ask. "I know," she said. "But I am asking, one woman to another, why you don't like Sterling."

Lady Sidlow's lips parted in surprise. She stared for a moment, then clasped her hands in her lap. "Very well. I will tell you, on the clear understanding that I am not trying to contravene your brother's wishes. It is only my opinion, and I am well aware it carries no weight with anyone but myself."

Georgiana nodded, too interested in the answer to be taken aback by the lengthy warning.

"Lord Sterling is very confident of your affection. He takes it for granted, to my eyes, and as a result he does not treasure it. You've known him for quite some time."

"Since we were children," she said. "My father was great friends with his."

"I know," said Lady Sidlow, startling her. "Your mother, not as much."

"Really?" This was all new to Georgiana, whose mother had died when she was eight. She'd heard all the tales about her father and Earl Pelham, Sterling's father, and thought her mother must have been just as fond of the Pelham family.

"She was always gracious and polite," admonished Lady Sidlow, "but no, she was not friendly with the earl and his wife."

"I never knew that . . ."

"I don't suppose anyone wanted you to," said Lady Sidlow in a gentler tone. "Certainly not she! I never met a kinder lady than your mother. Always willing to forgive a slight, always compassionate to those worse off than she, always ready to think the best of people. She never said a word against any Pelham while your father was alive, because he and Pelham were bosom mates. But in the little things, one could tell she did not share his affection."

Georgiana was speechless. Yes, she had always heard that Lady Sidlow and her mother were friends—even distant cousins, actually—but this was the first time the countess had spoken of her, except to scold Georgiana for being a sad tribute to the late Lady Wakefield's memory.

"She was my kindest friend," went on Lady Sidlow. Her voice had grown tender and fond, as Georgiana had never heard it. "I would tell her she ought not to hide her feelings so, and she would laugh and tell me it was better to think too highly of people than unfairly ill. Perhaps she was right. I was never able to adopt such kindness myself." She sighed.

"Your mother wanted so much for you to find someone who would treasure you."

"And you believe Sterling does not?" asked Georgiana slowly.

Her chaperone's mouth pursed. "He is very handsome and charming and I don't doubt that he is very well aware of both qualities. I would only caution you that even devils can be handsome and charming."

Having fallen into a rather somber mood, Georgiana was so startled by that warning that she burst out incredulously, "Sterling? *Sterling*, a devil?"

Lady Sidlow's face reverted to the austere, slightly offended expression she'd worn throughout Sterling's visit. She got to her feet and said in chilly tones, "Of course, it is your decision. Your brother has given his approval, and that is all that matters."

"Lady Sidlow, wait," said Georgiana, contrite. "I ought not to have laughed. I was so astonished, though—Sterling, a devil! Surely that goes too far."

The woman's gaze turned almost pitying. "I know, my dear. You don't think it possible. Perhaps he isn't. But I've had a wider experience of men than you, and I can only say I would counsel my own daughter not to be so hasty." And with that, she left in a swish of silk skirts.

ROB REACHED LONDON AT dusk, after a punishing journey undertaken without regard for cost or convenience. Tom, who had insisted on coming along, never missed a chance to point out how uncomfortable this made the trip, even though Rob offered, and then threatened, to toss him out of the travel chaise without stopping. If he hadn't needed his brother's help, Rob thought he might have thrown him out of the chaise anyway, but his valet was still indisposed and had remained behind.

But now he was back in town, dusty and sore but hopeful. At Salmsbury he'd been in an odd state of paralysis, unable to forget Georgiana but also unsure that they had any future. No matter what he felt, no matter what he thought he'd sensed in that one wild, passionate kiss, he did not know what *she* wanted. And he felt that until he knew, one way or another, he would be stuck in suspense, wondering.

"Welcome to London, my lord," said Bigby as Rob shed his coat and hat in the hall. "I shall have a room prepared for the major."

"Excellent," said Tom.

"He's not staying," said Rob with a dark look at his brother.

Tom adopted a wounded look. "After I saved your life! Where would you have me stay?"

"Berkeley Square," said Rob, referring to their parents' house. "Or see if George will offer you a spot on his floor." Their youngest brother, an aspiring artist, had rooms somewhere by the river. "And you did not save my life."

Tom grumbled and glared. "You'll never notice I'm here."

"I'd better not. One word, and you're gone." Tom knew what he meant, and he acknowledged it with a mocking salute before climbing the stairs behind the footman carrying his luggage.

Rob turned to his butler. "Hobbes has a severely turned ankle and remains at Salmsbury. I'll need a man to attend me."

Bigby bowed. "Of course."

"What invitations have arrived?"

Bigby blinked. Rob had never, *ever* asked about invitations before. "I—I am not certain, my lord. You were away from town . . ." Rob raised his brows. Bigby bowed. "I will locate them, sir."

Rob nodded. He had no possible excuse to call upon Georgiana. He would have to "happen" to cross her path, and even if it meant attending every tedious society event and causing a storm of gossip, he meant to do just that. "Send them all upstairs."

Chapter 22

THE ARRIVAL IN London of a bachelor as eligible as the Marquess of Westmorland was noticed. Lady Sidlow read it from her favorite gossip sheet at breakfast.

"'To the delight of many an unmarried lady, the Marquess of W was present at the opera on Tuesday evening'—Georgiana, do be careful, you'll chip the china," scolded Lady Sidlow.

"I'm sorry," she babbled, blotting up the tea that had splashed onto the table when she dropped her spoon into it. "I didn't mean to interrupt."

Her chaperone gave her a curious look, peering over the spectacles she wore to read. "What gave you such a start? You're not usually clumsy."

"I was woolgathering," she said quickly. Her heart had taken a giant leap at the sound of Rob's name, and her hands still shook.

"Indeed," murmured Lady Sidlow. She turned back to her paper, but did not read anything else aloud.

Georgiana ate her toast in silence, her mind galloping along and leaping like a horse over hedges.

Rob was back in London. Why? He ought to be at Salmsbury Abbey recovering from his injuries.

Unless, of course, he had. After several days at his parents' home, he must have regained his memory in full, come back to all his senses and feelings, and returned to take up his rakish life again. She felt a sharp sting of regret for several minutes, then realized what she was doing.

She might think she knew Rob, but she most assuredly did not know Lord Westmorland. What he did mattered little—*nothing*—to her. He could come to London or go to Scotland or sail to China, and it did not matter to her. She should be glad he was his old self, because then there would be very little chance of them meeting ever again.

STILL, THE COLBOURNES' BALL a few days later made her unreasonably tense. It was late in the year for society events elegant enough to tempt a bored marquess, but the Colbourne ball would be one of them. The gossip papers, obviously starved for material these days, had mentioned his presence at several fashionable affairs, and Georgiana walked into the ballroom braced for anything.

Several of her friends were at the ball, and there was a flurry of conversation about him—eligible, handsome marquesses being rather rare—but no sign of the man himself.

Thankfully.

"I was having such a splendid time tonight, until that news," murmured Joanna Hotchkiss behind her fan. "Dreadful man."

Georgiana flinched. "It hardly matters to either of us where he goes."

Joanna sighed. "Perhaps. But I can't help despising him."

"Oh, Joanna!" Georgiana tried to laugh. "Don't waste your thoughts on him."

Her friend turned to her in disbelief. "He and Lord Heathercote told Lord Marlow I'm a vapid little leech."

"I doubt Lord Marlow remembers."

"But they all laughed!" Joanna whispered angrily. "And who knows who else he told? Mr. Parker-Pierce asked me to dance three times before that, and then never again afterward."

Georgiana's head began to hurt. She didn't want to defend Rob any more than she wanted to think of him being so spiteful. "Prove them wrong by being kind and gracious, and no one will remember it."

Joanna sighed. "Perhaps you're right. But it's so hard to forget! Mr. Parker-Pierce was charming. I hoped he'd call on me." Her chin wobbled. "If he listens to Lords Heathercote or Westmorland, he never will."

Georgiana felt a pang of sympathy. Joanna's family was respectable and wealthy, but she was neither a great beauty nor brilliantly clever. She was kind and warm, but shy, with a great fondness for animals and books. She didn't have a raft of suitors to ease the sting of cruel sobriquets. "You have friends who will stand by you, no matter what anyone else may say. And if Mr. Parker-Pierce is so stupid as to listen to no-account scoundrels like Lord Heathercote, you don't want him to court you anyway. He would have proved himself utterly unworthy of you."

Joanna's face dissolved in gratitude. "Dear Georgiana. I don't know what I would do without you. No one else would have said that to me."

"And that is why we love her so," said an amused voice behind them.

Georgiana swung around to see her fiancé. "Sterling," she said in surprise. "I didn't expect you to be here tonight."

He laughed, making a very gallant bow. "A last-minute decision, and a very happy one for me. I hope you've not promised all your dances?"

She smiled. "Of course not." She hadn't felt much like dancing of late, but hopefully that would change now that he was here. She bid Joanna farewell and took his hand.

"What dreadful terror have you saved Miss Hotchkiss from?" he asked as they took their places for the country dance.

She waved one hand. "Malicious gossip—or rather, her fear of it."

"An endless battle, I presume."

She blinked at his amused and dismissive tone. Joanna's fear might be a bit overwrought, but it was grounded in very real fact. "What do you mean?"

He leaned toward her and lowered his voice. "You know perfectly well. She's got that nervous disposition that always twitches and jumps in fear of what other people are saying about her."

"She's sweet!" protested Georgiana.

"I never said she wasn't," returned Sterling. "Merely that I expect she requires a great deal of assurance and comfort." He sighed. "Pity her future husband. He'll never know a moment's peace."

Georgiana frowned. The dance began, and she moved through the steps automatically. Sterling

didn't mean to be unkind, and yet . . . his words
rankled. One of her dearest and oldest friends, Eliza
Cross, was shy and quiet—not unlike Joanna. Eliza's
father was enormously wealthy though of very low
birth. He'd long hoped Eliza would make a splendid match, and had spared no expense bringing her
out, but Georgiana knew just how miserable Eliza
had been during the one Season she'd had in town.
All ladies were not the same; some were vivacious
and charming, drawing in gentlemen regardless of
their fortune or birth. Others were shy and with-
drawn, and had no suitors . . . regardless of their
fortune or birth.

"Joanna will make someone a wonderful wife,"
she told Sterling when they joined hands again in
the dance.

"Who? Oh, no doubt," he said absently, nodding
at someone in the crowd.

"It's not fair to say she constantly needs assurance," she argued. "You know as well as I that any
silly, stupid rumor can cause people to drop an acquaintance. She's kind and loyal, but she hasn't got
the sort of social position that can shrug at cruel
gossip."

"Then she ought not to strive so hard to be part
of society," he said in surprise. "Darling, you know
the *ton* can be vicious. Anyone who can't weather
their storms ought to find a placid country squire
and settle in Hertfordshire."

The dance separated them again. Georgiana
seethed with discontent. Was he right? Would Joanna be happier if she abandoned the fashionable,
but sometimes snobby, *ton*? Eliza had hated it, but
now Eliza was the Countess of Hastings; she was

no longer snubbed, and she no longer said she hated London. A little confidence, and the support of her husband and his family, had made a vast difference. Not in Eliza herself—she was still much as she had been before—but in the *ton*'s reception of her.

Now that Georgiana thought of it, Sterling had never cared to meet Eliza until she became a countess. At the time she had thought more of Eliza's shyness and dread of London, but now she realized Sterling had never once asked to be introduced to her friend. The same was true of Sophie. Only after her marriage had Sterling gone to make her acquaintance.

"That is too harsh," she told Sterling when they came back together. "To say anyone who can't thrive among the most haughty members of the *ton* ought to surrender and scuttle off to Hertfordshire. By that accounting only the most fortunate few would remain, and we both know they would turn on each other eventually."

His brows shot up. "What's caused this? You haven't been the object of some stupid rumor, have you?"

"What would you do if I had been?" She raised her chin. "If people began whispering that I was a simpleton, or had no sense, or no style?"

"They never would!" he exclaimed in astonishment.

"But if they did." She wet her lips. "If people looked askance at you, and wondered why you were marrying me, would you leap to my defense, or would you begin to wonder yourself?"

Pique flashed across his face. "What's got into you tonight? I've never heard so much philosophical nonsense from you. Are you outraged over what

I said about Miss Hotchkiss? I humbly apologize, my dear."

He was only sorry that she pursued the matter. He didn't really see what she meant, or why she was troubled on Joanna's behalf. Georgiana said nothing, turning to her next partner in the dance and trying not to let her turmoil show. Quite against her will, she wondered what Rob would say if she asked him the same thing.

No. It did not matter one bit what Rob thought or would say. This was about her and Sterling and whether she still wanted to marry him.

That thought caught her utterly off guard, and nearly made her trip over her own feet. She couldn't even remember when she hadn't wanted to marry Sterling. It had simply *been* for so long . . . but this might be the first time she actually pictured their future life together.

Georgiana knew she was one of the fortunate people. She had an illustrious name and had been left a very respectable fortune by her parents. She knew she was attractive as well, and she was neither shy nor awkward with others. She had been excited to come to London, thrilled by the adventure of it, delighted by the glittering world of the *ton*. And she had, for lack of a better word, thrived.

But she had also been an orphan for most of her life. She knew what it felt like to be alone and uncertain of where she belonged. When Alistair sent her off to Mrs. Upton's Academy for Young Ladies at the age of eight, she had been entirely alone. The other girls weren't impressed by her name, her father's title, or her wealth, for they all came from similarly elite families. Georgiana had learned that being kind and amusing and loyal made her a much-desired friend. Her instincts had been honed over ten years there, not only into the graceful deportment Mrs. Upton taught, but also into keen awareness of everyone else's perception of her.

Sterling, unsurprisingly, was less mindful. Not only was he a man—and a handsome, clever one at that—he was heir to an earl. There was nothing to mock about Sterling. He was used to leading society, not chasing it.

The same could all be said of Rob, of course. She herself had called him malicious and arrogant.

She closed her eyes and inhaled deeply. She was *not* comparing Sterling to Rob, who had surely recovered his former antipathy for society misses like herself. This was about wondering what it would be like to be Sterling's wife in reality, not in the watercolor vignette of their future she had composed in her mind.

The dance ended and Sterling gave her his arm again. "Will you walk with me?" she asked on impulse.

"Of course, my dear." He made a motion with one hand, and Georgiana saw a mate of his grimace in disappointment.

"Am I keeping you from something?"

"Bristow can wait," he said easily. "He's not half so lovely as you are."

They strolled around the room, and Georgiana caught Lady Sidlow watching. She lifted one hand in acknowledgment, and Georgiana let Sterling lead her into the next room. It was much cooler and quieter, with servants bustling past and the occasional guest coming or going to the retiring room.

"Are you upset?" Sterling asked. "You seemed so earlier, and I don't know why."

She sighed. "It's nothing." The minute she said it, she cringed. If she couldn't speak honestly to him about this, what would their marriage be like? "I was annoyed that you brushed aside my concern for Miss Hotchkiss."

"Annoyed!" He was amused again. "I apologized already."

"I know." She took a deep breath. "What do you picture our life like, when we are married?"

"Ah." Real interest warmed his tone. He stopped walking and pulled her closer. "I picture that a great deal, in exquisite detail, darling."

"Do you?" She put her hands against his chest, stopping him when he would have leaned down to kiss her. "Why have we been engaged for over two years, then?"

His eyebrows went up. "Pining for our marriage? So am I. Let me show you how much . . ." Again he tried to kiss her, and she turned her face away.

"Why, Sterling?" she asked, her heart throbbing painfully. "If you're so eager for it to happen, why haven't we set a date?"

He released her. When she glanced at him, his playful air had fled, and there was a thin puzzled line between his brows. "You know why. Your brother is impossible to deal with. Even my father's solicitor wants to tear out his hair over the settlement negotiations."

"Yes, but if you were eager, surely something could have been agreed by now."

"Something," he scoffed. "I don't see the need to give in to Wakefield's every caprice." He frowned at her. "What's got into you tonight? Why are you attacking me when your own brother is the one who's delayed and hampered everything?"

She bit her lip. Perhaps it was all Alistair's fault, and there was nothing Sterling could do. She wanted to believe it. She almost *did* believe it.

And yet . . . Was it too much to wish for some sign of impatience or eagerness from her bridegroom? Was it too much to wish he would call on her more often, or write letters when she was away, or show any sign of devotion while Alistair made them wait? Perhaps the wedding was out of Sterling's control, but affection was not. She was slowly realizing that she had been content to adore Sterling, and he had been content to be adored. Shouldn't there be more, between a couple about to be married until death did them part?

"What's he done?" she asked directly. "Why haven't you been able to persuade him?"

Sterling's mouth dropped open in shock. "What—are you—*Georgiana*," he said indignantly. "You are not yourself tonight, you're clearly overwrought and hysterical."

"I think you don't really want to marry me," she said softly. "Or at least, not in the near future."

His eyes flashed, and for a moment she thought he would turn and walk away. His jaw flexed, and then he swept out one arm. "Very well. You wish to have a row. Let's not make a scene, too, shall we?" He indicated a door a short distance away.

As she turned to enter it, she caught sight of someone watching them from the ballroom doorway, arms folded and head tilted quizzically. Lord

Bristow. And from the corner of her eye, she saw Sterling motion to him to wait.

Right. He'd come tonight to see Bristow, and had been surprised to see her, too.

Sterling followed her into the small parlor and closed the door behind them. "What are you going on about?" he demanded.

"We've been engaged for over two years," she pointed out. "And there's no wedding date in sight. I'm not the only one who thinks you're hesitant." He threw up his hands, looking disgusted. "Why did you ask me to marry you?"

He jerked in surprise. "You know why! It's been settled between our families forever—"

"Not settled, obviously," she said.

More and more irked, he waved it away. "Your father wished it, just as mine does."

"And that's why?" she pressed. "Because our fathers wanted to unite our families?" Her father had died when she was seven and Sterling twelve; at best one could say he might have thought it a lovely idea.

"You wanted it as well," he exclaimed.

Georgiana's heart hit her breastbone. "But *you* didn't," she whispered. "Not as much."

"Of course I did," he said, his tone softening and becoming more coaxing, as if realizing the blow he'd landed. "Of course I do!" He took her hands. "Marriage is a complicated thing, darling. You only have one chance to settle the terms. I'm pushing for the best settlement for us—for you. For our future, and our children."

It dawned on her what he was saying. "My father

set out my dowry very explicitly. You know exactly what it is, as does Alistair. You want more, don't you?"

His expression answered for him. Sterling dropped her hands and stepped back. "You've been so different since you returned from Derbyshire. Did something happen there?"

She supposed he would hear about Rob eventually. Sooner or later Kitty, or Geneva, would mention him, and it would get back to Sterling that he'd allegedly been knocked about the head in Derbyshire and lost his memory for a while. Even Georgiana's fertile imagination had failed to concoct a plausible explanation for that story, and finally she'd given up. Perhaps it was because she'd had a sense, ever since Rob had asked her if she really wanted to marry Sterling, that it would come to this.

"I had a lot of time to think in Derbyshire," she said, lifting her chin. "About us, and our engagement, and why it's lasted so long."

He sighed. "I see. And you want a house and baby of your own, like Kitty. Is that it?"

"No. I didn't think about that at all." She swallowed her irritation. "But I finally wondered why neither of us felt any urgency. *Neither* of us," she repeated. "I acknowledge my own lack."

For the first time he looked wary. "Wakefield . . ."

"I can't help but think that if we were desperately in love, we would have found a way to be married by now. Perhaps with a smaller settlement. But neither of us ever even suggested it."

"That's not how things are done," he said with a disbelieving laugh. "Do you want to elope, like a common strumpet?"

Like Rob had asked her to do. She closed her mind to that. "No. But we hardly see each other. I was in Derbyshire for six weeks and received only one letter from you the entire time. I was back in London a full week before you called on me. Tonight you came to see Lord Bristow, not me. I daresay you didn't even know I'd be here."

He was genuinely amazed. "Did you have some vision of us living in each other's pockets, never out of sight?"

"No," she said. "But I would like more than an occasional visit or dance when our paths happen to cross."

For a moment he stared at the floor, his hands on his hips. Georgiana had the sudden thought that he was thinking very hard what to say. "You're right," he said at last, calmer than before—almost too calm. "There is a reason Wakefield and I haven't come to terms. There is a piece of land, bordering my father's estate. My father always believed your father meant for you to have it. You know what great friends they were. It should be your birthright, darling, and I want you to have it—for our son, if you don't care for it."

Of course there was a piece of land. "So you've been arguing with him for two years over a property?" She exhaled, at once humiliated and vindicated. "He won't give it, you know."

"We're negotiating—"

"Because getting that land is more important than getting me," she finished.

Sterling's eyes nearly popped from his face. "No! Of course I want you!"

"All right," she said steadily, even though her

pulse was so frantic she ought to be shaking where she stood. "Kiss me."

"What?" Sterling looked astounded.

"If you want me, not that bit of land, you must want to kiss me. Don't you?"

For answer, he stepped forward and hauled her into his arms. His mouth crashed down on hers, and for one taut moment, she waited, hoping . . . But no burst of delight hit her; no flush of pleasure made her blood race, certainly nothing like the way it had when Rob—

She stepped back. Sterling stared at her, his eyes wide in surprise.

But not, she thought, because she'd broken off the kiss.

"You know what I'm going to say," she whispered, her lips numb. "You felt it, too. Or rather—you didn't feel anything."

He blinked rapidly. "That's nonsense. We've known each other our whole lives—"

"Which doesn't mean we are suited to marry." Her eyes felt hot, and she could feel tears prickling behind her lids. "I don't blame you. I admitted I also never pressed Alistair to conclude the settlements. I don't know that he would have heeded me, but I never even tried. I—I began to wonder why that was, and in the end I realized it's because we're not actually in love with each other."

"I do love you," he said swiftly. "How can you say I don't?"

"And I love you," she said, fighting back the wobble in her voice. "But . . . more like a brother, I think. Or as a dear friend. Not as a husband."

This time the silence felt as sharp as a razor. Sterling straightened his shoulders, his face devoid of expression. "Georgiana, be careful what you say. If this is a ploy to push me into a hasty wedding, it won't work."

"Hasty!" She gulped down a burst of wild laughter. "The fact that you could call it *hasty* after more than two years says everything about your feelings." She shook her head. "I am not trying to manipulate you. I am not hysterical. I am trying to tell you . . . that I don't think we shall suit each other as husband and wife."

"What?" Sterling demanded, as if he couldn't believe his ears. "*What?*"

Georgiana swallowed hard, and cast the die. "I release you from our betrothal."

For a moment she thought he would burst out in anger; his face grew dark and his eyes flashed. But then he mastered himself. His expression grew stony, and he gave a sharp, formal bow. "I see. If that is your desire, I withdraw my offer of marriage." He turned on his heel and left the room.

Georgiana gasped, and then gasped again. Her stays seemed to be strangling her. She staggered to a nearby table and braced her hands, only beginning to comprehend what she'd just done.

She'd first declared her intention to marry Sterling when she was eight, after he mended her kite and helped her fly it. She'd repeated it every year after, when he sent her amusing little drawings while she was at school. She'd told Alistair, her governess, Mrs. Upton, her friends, virtually everyone she knew that she was going to marry him someday. And when he proposed to her, almost three years ago, she'd told *him*, joyfully, that she would marry him.

And now . . . she wouldn't.

She lowered herself into a chair and laid her head on the table, welcoming the hard, cold marble against her forehead. Part of her mourned his loss, and part of her felt a tidal wave of relief. That ought to reassure her she'd done the right thing, but at the moment it was all too overwhelming.

"Georgiana?" The door creaked. "Lady Sidlow bade me find you . . ."

She sat up and swiped at her eyes, which were dry despite being burning hot. "Yes, I'm here."

Joanna Hotchkiss came into the room. "I saw Lord Sterling leave." As she drew closer she gasped. "Are you well? You look upset . . ."

"No." Georgiana rose and smoothed down her skirts. She would have to tell Lady Sidlow, and Alistair, and everyone else, that she was no longer engaged. They would learn eventually; Sterling would tell people, even if she didn't. He might well be out in the drawing room telling everyone at this moment.

Tonight, now, it was too raw for her to say aloud.

She mustered a smile for Joanna. "Yes, Sterling has gone. I needed a moment alone with my thoughts, and now I—I wish to go home. It's too warm in there. Would you send someone to fetch Lady Sidlow, please?"

Joanna nodded. "Of course. I wish I could go home, too. Millicent Harlow is prosing on and on about her new fiancé. Another decent gentleman, taken." She heaved a sigh that was only half in jest.

Georgiana wondered what everyone would say when they learned Sterling was free. She wondered if any of her friends would try to catch his eye. "Then go home. Do as will make you happiest."

Joanna blinked in surprise. "Perhaps I shall."

"So should we all," Georgiana replied on a sigh, wondering what, in her case, that might possibly be.

Chapter 23

ஒ~ல

It rained for two days after the scene with Sterling, and Georgiana was glad for it.

Rain meant there was no chance of walking in the park, or going for a drive. It was a cold, heavy rain as well, and that ruled out a shopping trip or an evening out. Even Lady Sidlow was content to stay at home and write letters by the fire, which left Georgiana some space to contemplate the enormity of what she'd done.

She was not sorry. The first day she had felt so odd, and wondered if Sterling would come to call, to argue or plead with her or even to scold her, but he did not. When she unthinkingly said something about it, Lady Sidlow was astonished. "He was here a few days ago," she said in surprise. "Were you expecting him to call again so soon?"

No one expected him. He came barely once a week, sometimes not for a fortnight or more. Georgiana was just now realizing how little attention her own fiancé had paid her, and how accepted that had become.

But she had to tell someone, so she wrote a long

letter to Eliza. She wrote a slightly shorter one to Sophie, who would probably not be as surprised, and then a very, very short one to Alistair. Putting the words on paper was quite difficult; it reminded her of the years and years she had spent adoring Sterling and telling everyone how much she adored him.

But by the time she finished the brief note to her brother, she felt at once exhausted and peaceful. It had been comforting to explain everything, and despite the emotional toll it took, she had never started to doubt herself. When the three letters were sealed and ready to send, she went to tell Lady Sidlow.

The woman was struck speechless. "Why?" was all she could gasp.

"Partly for the reason you yourself told me the other day." Georgiana was intensely glad she had written the letters first. She had shed a few tears over the first two, but in the third letter she had dried her emotions to dust. "I have great affection for Sterling, but not of the sort that a woman should have for her husband."

"My goodness," said Lady Sidlow faintly. "And over that, you broke it off with him?"

Georgiana frowned. "Is that not enough? Sterling deserves a wife who will adore him, and I would like a husband who is . . ." She stopped, unable to think of a phrase other than *passionately in love with me*.

"My goodness," said Lady Sidlow again. She put down her cup of tea. "I hope—that is, I would be mortified if my words the other day caused you to have unreasonable expectations, my dear . . ."

"Unreasonable?" Georgiana exclaimed. "You said you thought Sterling took my affection for granted. You suggested he didn't truly love me!"

"Yes, but I didn't think you would take it to heart!" The chaperone's face was pink. "You never take anything I say seriously, and I did warn you it was only my opinion—"

"Yes," said Georgiana softly. "And I realized you were right."

"My dear." Lady Sidlow moved to the edge of her chair and reached for her hand, almost anxiously. "In no way did I wish to disrupt your engagement."

"No? What *did* you wish?" This was interesting, Georgiana thought. She would have sworn Lady Sidlow would be pleased, perhaps even gloat at being right. The woman looked almost worried, though.

"I wished . . . I hoped you would be more on guard, and not give your love so freely. I hoped you would insist he change his behavior and become more . . ." She hesitated.

"Faithful? I know he's been to visit loose women," said Georgiana frankly. "Is that what you mean?"

Lady Sidlow jerked in horror. "Please do not speak of things like that!"

"Well, it doesn't matter now. He is free to do entirely as he pleases now."

Lady Sidlow closed her eyes, and appeared to be struggling for words. "Have you told Lord Wakefield yet?"

She nodded. "I've written the letter to him already."

The older woman sighed. "I suppose we cannot keep it from him."

"Why would I?" she asked in surprise. "He must know. If I don't tell him, Sterling will."

"No, no, of course we must tell him." Lady Sidlow reached for the teapot and filled her cup. She took a long sip, and seemed somewhat restored by it. "I don't suppose this decision was taken because another gentleman has caught your eye?"

For some inexplicable reason she thought of Rob. "Of course not!"

Lady Sidlow's eyebrows went up at her vehemence. "Very well! It wouldn't be a crime if you had. I only wondered if I should expect any gentlemen to call."

Georgiana calmed down. "Not to my knowledge." Inwardly she cursed herself for still thinking of Rob. It did not help to know he was back in London, and attending social events at an alarming pace. Why couldn't he have stayed in Lancashire for another month or so? She'd suffered enough anxiety this summer to last an entire year.

"Well." Lady Sidlow set down her empty cup. "We shall have to remedy that, then."

"WHERE DO WE SEEK our pleasures tonight?" asked Tom, rubbing his hands together.

Rob finished tying his cravat and took the pin from Jacobs, who was standing in for Hobbes. He stabbed it into his neckcloth. "I am attending the theater. What do you plan to do?"

"The theater as well, of course."

"I thought you disliked theater." Jacobs held up his jacket for him to don. "When I went last week you had no interest." Rob took his gloves from the manservant and walked out of the dressing room.

For several days now Rob had gone everywhere: the opera, the theater, a soiree, even a ball. Tom had gone with him most of the time, although once he assured himself Georgiana wasn't there, he'd generally taken himself off. Rob was ready to punch his brother in the face to get rid of him.

Tom trailed down the stairs behind him. "I'm allowed to change my mind. I didn't care to see that production."

"And you have a fiendish interest in tonight's?"

"I might. What is it?"

Rob glared at him and took his hat and coat from the butler. "Good night, Tom."

His brother only laughed and followed him out the door. "If you decide to be more genial, I might be persuaded to share some intelligence I received."

Rob paused with one foot on the carriage step. "What intelligence?"

Tom put up his hands at the query. "Nothing about any lady. About a man."

Rob stepped into the carriage and waved one hand wearily at the other seat. "Who?"

He fully expected his brother to name Charles Winston or Frederick Forester. Perhaps even something related to the fellows who'd beaten him. Instead Tom smirked and said, "Robert Pelham, Viscount Sterling."

"All right," Rob said after a long pause. "What is it?"

"He lost a good sum at the Vega Club last night. I heard he was in a foul temper, drinking heavily and playing recklessly."

Another reason to dislike Sterling. "Fool," said Rob coolly.

"What makes it noteworthy," went on Tom, as if Rob hadn't spoken, "is that it's apparently very out of character for him. So much so, someone asked in jest if his mistress had turned him off, and Sterling's response was to hurl a wineglass at the fellow." Tom paused. "Again, not his usual manner."

Rob said nothing and looked out the window. It was too much to hope Sterling's *fiancée* had turned him out.

Wasn't it?

The last few weeks had taught Rob some humbling lessons. He'd realized how cold and arrogant he'd been toward people. He was uncomfortably certain he'd let himself get drawn into a rather idiotic plot to spy on Forester. Soon after his injury, he'd told Georgiana that perhaps he deserved to be beaten; he hadn't been serious then, but as time went on he began to think it might have been the truth. He didn't want to go back to the way he was before, when he'd been cruelly dismissive of girls like Georgiana, when he could callously take Charles Winston's deed, when he was amused by the misfortunes and failings of others.

Still, he could not stop himself hoping that Sterling had indeed been jilted.

The Theatre Royal was staging a benefit performance tonight. At the Colbournes' ball, Rob had gleaned that it would be quite the event, especially given the limited society in town at this time of year. Therefore it wasn't entirely a surprise to walk into the crowded lobby and spot Georgiana almost at once.

He still wasn't ready for it; he all but stopped in his tracks. Her hair was up in a loose, shining mass of curls, with tendrils teasing her neck. She wore a dress of shimmering blue, with silver spangles that glittered in the candlelight when she moved. She was talking to another young lady and gesturing with one hand, causing the other lady to laugh behind her fan. She was smiling. She was *dazzling*.

Beside him, Tom let out a sigh. "There is something about her," he admitted. "She does look rather fine tonight."

"If you come within five feet of me again this evening, I shall throttle you." Rob tugged at his gloves and spotted a woman he knew. "Lady Baldwin, good evening, ma'am!"

Lady Baldwin was a friend of their mother. As hoped, Tom fled at the sight of her. She was only too pleased to take Rob around and introduce him to anybody and everybody nearby. Georgiana was still speaking to her friend, her back to most of the room. They were three feet away when she finally turned and looked right at him, and Rob braced himself for a negative reaction—

And instead felt the air leave the room. Her green eyes went wide at the sight of him, and for a moment joy suffused her face. A moment later it turned to alarm, which was in turn quickly replaced by a polite mask, but he held on to that joy. She was glad to see him; she just didn't know what might come of it.

Lady Baldwin must have noticed. "Here is a young lady who may amuse you," she murmured to him. "Lady Georgiana, may I present to you the Marquess of Westmorland? Sir, this is Lady Georgiana Lucas."

Her fingers were in his again. He bowed, and caught a whiff of her scent again. "Enchanted to make your acquaintance, my lady." Her green eyes flew up to meet his gaze, and he winked.

Color flooded her face. She curtsied, and he heard her breathless murmur: "And I yours, my lord."

"Are you looking forward to the performance?" Lady Baldwin was too near for him to say anything else. "Ought to start rather soon."

Georgiana swallowed. "I—I suppose. Are you as well, my lord?"

He gazed at her. "Yes, Lady Georgiana, I am tremendously delighted to be here tonight."

An older woman sailed up beside Georgiana, her nose practically twitching with interest. Lady Baldwin introduced her, and Rob bowed very properly to the Countess Sidlow. Georgiana had called her long-suffering and stuffy, and Rob could see why. Her nose was like the beak of a hawk and she had piercing blue eyes, which seemed to size him up from head to toe. They exchanged banal conversation for a few minutes before Lady Baldwin asked Lady Sidlow a question, and he managed to lean close enough to whisper to Georgiana.

"Meet me in half an hour in the saloon upstairs."

Her eyes went wide, and he just had time to add a quiet, "Please," before Lady Baldwin turned and spoke to him. Rob replied absently, watching Georgiana from the corner of his eye. She hesitated a long moment, then finally gave a tiny nod. Lady Baldwin led him away to meet any number of other people who were neither interesting nor remembered, and he began counting the minutes until he could speak to Georgiana again.

Chapter 24

❧❧❧

GEORGIANA DID NOT hear a word of the play, even though it was a rare treat to be at the theater. Lady Sidlow considered it idle entertainment and generally refused to attend. But tonight, Georgiana could only perch anxiously on the edge of her chair and agonize over what to do.

Part of her longed to leap up and run to the saloon. The sight of Rob in the lobby, so unexpected and—she finally admitted—so *longed* for, had made her heart soar with delight, as he looked at her with the same faint, crooked smile she had come to adore sitting by Kitty's pond in Derbyshire. He was even more staggeringly attractive than she remembered, but with—seemingly—all the warmth and humor he'd displayed during their brief acquaintance.

The other part of her was terrified to go, afraid that she had overreacted to the sight of him. She had no idea why he'd come back to London, nor why he wanted to see her. Her own words from the inn at Macclesfield echoed in her mind, just as true and valid as they'd been that night: *We don't know each other, not really.*

Of course, she'd also thought her attraction to him would fade once they went their separate ways. Out of sight would become out of mind. That had not happened, and she'd had very little success convincing herself that he must have reverted to his old unlikeable, arrogant self. She had preferred to imagine Lord Westmorland as a distinct person from Rob, who could remain forever charming and amusing and half in love with her.

Her breath shuddered in her chest. She was probably more than half in love with him.

There was no clock in sight. She changed her mind half a dozen times, and then finally decided to do it and be done with it. Unclenching her hands, she slipped from her seat and murmured something to Lady Sidlow about the retiring room, and bolted from the box.

Barely breathing, fearful her chaperone would follow, she hurried through the rotunda. No one was about, even when she reached the saloon. She hesitated, and then Rob stepped out from behind one of the ornate columns, and something inside her seemed to burst wide open. He was devastatingly handsome in evening clothes, once again the polished and elegant marquess, but it was the wild elation in his face that sent her forward.

They stopped a few paces apart. "It's good to see you again," he said.

She managed a tremulous smile. "And you." They both spoke quietly, the vaulted ceiling amplifying every sound. "I cannot stay long. My chaperone will miss me."

"Right." He swept out his hand, and she fell in step beside him. "I only had one question," he said as they walked through the large, empty saloon. "It's been plaguing me since Macclesfield, when Tom spoilt my idea of writing to you."

"I did wonder how you were," she said quickly. "I—I'm glad to see you're much better."

"Mostly," he said wryly. "Don't think I ought to recover everything about the way I was. But since I could not write to you—"

"You could have," she put in, unable to stop herself. "I would have been very glad to get a letter."

"You would?" He grinned, his eyes lighting up just the way she remembered. "Well, I didn't know that, so I thought I'd come back to London and see if I might call on you—"

A journey of four days, she thought with a tremor of delight. Merely to see her.

"As . . . friendly acquaintances," he finished. "I haven't forgotten your engagement—"

Georgiana's mouth dropped open. He didn't know.

"And I understand there are rules . . ." He grimaced. "Never paid much attention to them before, and now, when it would be useful to know—"

"Rob." She stopped and wet her lips again. "I should tell you . . ."

He straightened, drawing back. "If you'd rather I not, I understand—"

"I broke off with Sterling," she interrupted.

Rob went still. "What?"

Her face grew hot. "You were right. Neither of us was very eager to marry, and finally I realized I don't love him. Not as he deserves his wife to love him."

"You broke it off," he echoed.

"Yes." She summoned a tentative smile, trying to

hide the trembling in her hands. She would have broken with Sterling no matter what, but she could not deny that some small part of her heart nursed a vivid fantasy of Rob turning to her with his eyes dark and hungry, whispering what he'd said in Macclesfield: *Come with me . . .*

"Well," he said. "That does change things." And before she could say another word, he seized her hand and pulled her around the corner into an arched recess. There he stopped so suddenly she collided with him, and his arm went around her waist. "You're not going to marry him," he rasped, wrapping his free hand around her nape.

She shook her head, already pulling him closer.

"Thank God," he muttered, and then he kissed her, just as desperately as he had in Macclesfield. And Georgiana flung herself against him and kissed him back. There was no need to wait and hope for a spark; it shot through her at the first touch of his hand, setting her every nerve ablaze with sensation. Her toes curled and her heart leapt and she might have forgotten to breathe.

By the time the kiss ended, her world had gone up in smoke. At last she admitted she was one of those impulsive, wanton creatures who would throw away their reputation for a moment of pleasure. Before, she had been mindful of the rules; Sterling had never urged any serious impropriety, and she would have been shocked if he had.

Tonight she didn't spare a moment's thought for her reputation. The notorious Marquess of Westmorland kissed her, in the grand saloon of the Theatre Royal where anyone might see, and she was only sorry it couldn't last forever.

"I'll call on you tomorrow," he whispered, his lips still skimming hers. "You'll be home?"

Dizzily, she nodded. Her hands were under his jacket, and she wanted to rest her cheek against his chest to savor the rapid thump of his heart.

"Georgiana." He nudged up her chin and pressed another lingering kiss on her mouth. "I missed you."

A tiny smile crossed her lips, then grew and grew until she had to laugh. "And I you. Obviously," she added, finally remembering where they were and sending a chagrined glance past his shoulder. She slid her hands out of his jacket and smoothed a lapel back into place. "I must go."

"I know." One last swift kiss. "Until tomorrow."

Georgiana smiled at him, then stepped out of the recess, head held high, and walked away. She could feel her pulse like a jolt inside her, and that charge still seemed to be tingling along her skin. At the moment, she could have sung and danced as enthusiastically as anyone on the stage.

She did not hear a single word of the play that entire evening.

ROB LEFT THE THEATER before he started punching holes in the walls in exultation. She wasn't marrying that scoundrel Sterling, and she'd kissed him passionately enough to melt his brain. What a bloody brilliant decision, coming back to London.

Tom loped up beside him. "Did you cause an uproar?"

Rob stopped and faced his brother. "I want to marry that girl. You can either offer your congratulations or go back to Lancashire."

Tom's eyes popped. "Marry her? Ballocks! You

knew her for a week, and you were out of your head!"

Rob nodded once. "I'll tell Bigby to pack your things."

"Wait!" His brother scrambled after him. "What the devil? You can't spring that on a fellow and walk away."

"Oh, I can." Rob kept walking.

"West!" Tom caught his arm, swinging him around to a stop. "You can't really mean to . . ." He gestured with one hand.

"Why not?"

Tom gaped. "You know why!"

"Because I ought to make some dull society marriage?" He raised one brow skeptically. "Or because you don't want to marry and can't comprehend anyone else wanting to?"

"She's engaged to Sterling," hissed Tom.

Rob grinned jubilantly. "She threw him over. Explains his discontent at Vega's, don't you think?"

Tom scowled. "She threw him over for you?"

"Since it happened several days ago, no." But he sincerely hoped he'd been part of her reason.

His brother was not appeased. "I don't like it."

"No," Rob corrected. "You don't like *her*. Which is stupid of you, and irrelevant to me." On impulse he added, "Come with me tomorrow when I call on her."

Tom recoiled in horror before a grim resignation settled on his face. "I suppose I'll have to."

Rob lifted one shoulder. "It makes no difference to me. But I think she'll improve on you."

"Ho there! West!" The shout made them both turn. A passing carriage had stopped in the street, and a man hung out the window, waving one arm enthusiastically. "God's blood, man, you've been gone an age!"

"Friends of yours?" murmured Tom.

"Marlow," said Rob reluctantly, lifting one hand in reply. "And Heathercote." Heath put his head out the other window and doffed his hat with a sly expression.

"Come on, come on." Marlow had half fallen out of the carriage and jogged across the street. He slung an arm around Rob's neck. "We're for Vega's. Come along!"

Rob hesitated. He'd avoided the Vega Club since returning to town.

"Another Churchill," said Marlow, blinking at Tom. "Welcome to come."

"You must be Tom," drawled Heath, strolling across the street. "I've met George, and been assured William avoids town."

Tom acknowledged it with a slight bow. "Lord Heathercote."

Heath grinned. "My reputation precedes me! Come, lads, we could be sharing a bottle instead of standing in the street." He cocked one brow meaningfully as he turned back to the carriage. "We're to meet Forester and Sackville, too."

"Glad you're back, West," added Marlow. "It's been desolate without you. Heath's even let a new fellow take your place at Vega's."

"Right." Rob did not want to go to Vega's. Not only had all the trouble with Charles Winston begun there, Heath was after him to rejoin their fast set, gambling until dawn and drinking themselves blue. He still couldn't completely remember what the business with Forester was. It was probably better if Heath did replace him.

But as he started to shrug off Marlow's arm, his friend added, "You'll like him. Capital bloke, name of Sterling."

"Viscount Sterling?" repeated Tom with a sideways look at Rob.

"Aye." Heath shouted from the carriage for them to hurry along, and Marlow made a rude gesture in reply. "You're coming, of course?"

He should go home. He meant to remain the man Georgiana liked, and not slide back into the arrogant, rakish ways that had made her hate him. But he was undeniably curious about Sterling, after thinking he *was* Sterling and then hating the man sight unseen, and somehow he let himself get towed into the carriage, Tom at his shoulder, and carried off to the Vega Club.

Chapter 25

⤜⤛⧫⤚⤝

GEORGIANA TOOK GREAT care when dressing the following morning. She wore her finest day dress and told Nadine to put up her hair in soft ringlets and braids instead of the usual simple knot for morning. Breakfast seemed to last an eternity, and she jumped every time a horse paused outside. Finally she was able to station herself in the drawing room, conveniently near the windows overlooking the street, with a book open in her lap.

"Are you expecting someone?" Lady Sidlow swept into the room.

"Sophie has returned to town," Georgiana told her. "I hope she might call." It was all true. She would even be pleased to see her friend.

The countess sat, clearly torn between suspicion that Georgiana wasn't telling her something, and the happy prospect of a duchess visiting. "You went very recently to Chiswick."

"That was before Sterling." It was shocking how easily, how carelessly the name fell from her lips.

Her chaperone coughed. "Yes. Ahem. I suppose

we ought to wait to hear from Wakefield before letting it be widely known your engagement is at an end—"

"Why?" Georgiana swung away from the window. "I shan't change my mind."

"As your guardian, it is his right to approve your marriage," said her chaperone.

"But he does not get to choose whom I marry."

Lady Sidlow pursed her lips. "Let us hope he agrees."

Frowning, Georgiana was about to ask about that when the butler opened the door. "My lady, the Marquess of Westmorland and Major Lord Thomas Churchill-Gray have come to call."

Lady Sidlow's mouth dropped open. Georgiana fought down the urge to leap from her chair in eager elation.

"Who?" asked the countess blankly.

The butler repeated the names. Georgiana tried to look artless. "We are at home, are we not?"

Slowly Lady Sidlow turned her head to fix an amazed stare on her. "Yes, Higgins, we are," she said to the butler. He bowed and left, and Lady Sidlow lowered her voice. "What did you do?"

"Lady Baldwin introduced me to the marquess last night," she replied. "You were there."

Lady Sidlow waved that aside. "Lady Baldwin ought to have known better. But why would he call? Did he say something to you?"

Yes. He'd said he missed her. Georgiana's heart quivered at the memory.

Lady Sidlow was still fretting. "And everyone still believes you are betrothed to Lord Sterling, and therefore almost married. It would be improper for another gentleman to call upon you. Whatever can he mean by it?"

Georgiana tossed aside her book. "By all means, ask him."

"Really, Georgiana, do not be smart with me," snapped her chaperone. "What can you have done to attract the interest of a man like Westmorland? Despite his recent attendance at a few parties, he's a shocking rogue. Even if he is looking for a wife, are you sure you want to encourage the attentions of a man like that?"

There were footsteps on the stairs. Georgiana's heart was beating so hard she barely heard Lady Sidlow's words. "I thought you were sorry I hadn't set my cap for someone more illustrious than Sterling. You used to cluck sadly over all the noble gentlemen like Westmorland I'd ignored."

"I never named him! Someone more respectable and less—" She pressed her lips together. "But why is he calling on you?"

There were voices in the corridor. Georgiana rose to her feet, her palms suddenly damp. "We'll find out," she managed to say to Lady Sidlow's last anxious question.

Higgins opened the door. "Lord Westmorland and Major Churchill-Gray, madam."

She ducked her head and curtsied, only to give a gasp when she looked up and saw them. It was Rob, but no longer polished and elegant. His eyes were bloodshot, and his lip was swollen. His brother, sporting an incredible black eye and a grim expression, looked no better.

"Lady Sidlow." Rob bowed. "Lady Georgiana." His eyes met hers, wryly apologetic.

"Won't you sit down, my lords?" Lady Sidlow was obviously trying to decide what to do, not wanting to offend a marquess but also not approving of their appearance. She rang the bell and crisply said, "Tea," when Mary popped into the room a moment later.

Slowly Georgiana took her seat, feeling just as thrown as her chaperone. Last night he had been polished and perfect, the Rob she remembered from Derbyshire, and today he looked like he'd come out the loser in a fight. "How kind of you to call, sir," she said cautiously.

He gave her one of his crooked little smiles. "'Tis my pleasure. Thank you for receiving me." *Like this*, his eyes seemed to say.

"It was a delight to make your acquaintance last evening, sir," said Lady Sidlow. "Forgive us for being taken by surprise by your visit today."

"The fault is mine," he told her. "I did not think to pay calls today, but then . . ." His gaze slid toward Georgiana for a moment. "It seemed too fine a day to stay inside."

"Of course," Lady Sidlow murmured. An awkward moment of silence. "Have you returned to town for the duration? Gentlemen are scarce in London these days, with the excellent weather making the country so appealing."

"I do fancy the outdoors," he agreed. "We were recently in Lancashire, at our parents' home, where one might be pardoned for wishing to live outdoors."

"Ah." Real pleasure finally warmed the countess's voice. Georgiana could guess why; Rob might be a shocking rogue, but the Duke and Duchess of Rowland were entirely different. During the Season, the duchess's parties were the envy of the entire *ton*. Not that Georgiana had ever been invited to one of the Rowland routs, but Lady Sidlow had often expressed hope that her friendship with Sophie, Duchess of Ware, might lead to more elite invitations like that. "Her Grace your mother is such an admirable lady. So thoughtful and gracious."

"She is," Rob replied. "I have recently resolved to keep her guidance more in mind."

Lady Sidlow shot Georgiana a startled look. "I'm sure it will bring great credit to you, sir."

"No doubt she hopes so." He hesitated, his mouth tight. Georgiana noticed his hand was in a fist on his knee, and suddenly she realized he was in pain.

"I also prefer the outdoors," she said brightly. "Not that I've been to Lancashire, but I did spend the most delightful month in Derbyshire, which is surely the most beautiful countryside in all of England. I've not set foot outside yet today, and I wonder if perhaps we could take a turn about the square? The clouds threaten rain later, and I should hate to miss the sunshine."

Rob fairly beamed gratitude at her. "I would be delighted to escort you, Lady Georgiana."

"Splendid!" She jumped to her feet as Mary brought in the tea tray.

"Just a moment," protested Lady Sidlow, but Georgiana wasn't about to be deterred.

"You can see the entire square from this window. We'll just take one turn. I'm simply perishing for some fresh air!" She left, Rob on her heels. Behind her, she heard Tom say something to Lady Sidlow, but she kept going, down the stairs, tying on her bonnet at speed and almost flying out the door.

On the steps she paused. Rob stepped out behind her, setting his hat on his head. Once they were seen in public together, the gossip would start, and it would be incendiary. She had not told anyone except Sophie and Eliza that her engagement was over. Walking out with another man, let alone a man as notorious as Rob, would set every tongue in London wagging . . .

But then she saw the cane he leaned on again, and her concern over gossip vanished. He hadn't had that in the drawing room, but must have retrieved it from Higgins. "Are you hurt?" she asked anxiously.

He limped down the steps and offered his arm. "Not when I look at you."

Her heart fluttered. "An obvious lie, but a flattering one." She took his arm and they crossed the street.

The green at the heart of Cavendish Square was a small one, with a path around it and an iron fence enclosing the whole thing. Only a few trees impeded Lady Sidlow's view from the drawing room windows, and when Georgiana stole a peek over her shoulder, she saw the woman watching from there.

Let her. There would be nothing scandalous to see.

Probably.

Sadly.

"Are we being watched?" Rob murmured.

"Without doubt." Georgiana paused to give a cheery wave. "She likes to keep an eye on everything and everyone. She made certain to take the large room at the front for hers as well, leaving me to the back." She smiled impishly. "Which only put the joke on her, as that makes it far easier to sneak out, let me tell you!"

Rob laughed. "Well worth it."

"Where is your brother?" The major hadn't followed them.

"Doing penance," said Rob as they reached the path. It would take a quarter hour, at a sluggish stroll, to circumnavigate the whole thing.

Georgiana blinked. "For what?"

"A multitude of sins. He started the fight that caused this." He motioned at his face.

She gasped. "No! Why?"

"I don't know."

Georgiana stopped in alarm. "You don't remember? Is your memory still suffering?"

"No," he said with a flick of one hand. "I meant that God alone knows why Tom was in a fighting mood." His voice fell to a low growl. "I remember last night very well."

She blushed at the heat in his gaze. She had relived the way they fell on each other, and everything that kiss suggested, all night long. "Do you, my lord?"

Eyes fixed on her, he nodded. "I remember that you're no longer engaged to Lord Sterling. I didn't dream that, did I?"

She had to clear her throat. "No," she whispered.

His mouth crooked wickedly as his gaze dropped to her mouth. "Good."

They started walking again. Now Georgiana was intensely aware of his arm under her hand, of his shoulder next to hers, of the warmth and strength and smell of him and how much she had missed him. Her fingers twitched on his arm. She didn't know what she would have done if he hadn't returned. Quite likely something mad and scandalous, because she hadn't been able to forget him, or convince herself he was nothing to her.

"Do you have any regrets?" he asked, breaking into her thoughts.

She opened her mouth, then paused. "About breaking off with Sterling? Or about kissing you last night?"

"Either."

"No," she said at once. "It was the only thing I could do."

"Oh?" he murmured with a sly glance.

Georgiana blushed. "I meant Sterling. Every time I thought of being his wife, I felt more and more certain it would be a terrible mistake. It was better to end it before we found ourselves trapped."

"It is far better to avoid mistakes like that," he agreed. "And kissing me . . . ?"

"You kissed me," she pointed out.

A faint smile hovered about his lips. "I did. I've thought of almost nothing but kissing you since we parted." Pleasure spilled through her, so intense she shivered. "Curse me for a sinner, but I came back to London to see if you might have felt the same."

"Oh." She was so distracted by the memory of his mouth on hers she could hardly speak. "I'm sure that's not a sin."

"Don't be so certain," he said with a low, wicked laugh. "I've never been known for my saintliness."

He stopped and turned to her, placing his free hand over hers where it gripped his sleeve. "But this time I'll try. I want to call on you. May I?"

Yes, she wanted to cry. She licked her lips. "Why, my lord?"

Now his expression turned rueful. "I didn't represent myself well before—or perhaps I did, but that was my old self. I do think that blow to the head changed something in me, or perhaps just knocked some sense into place." He lifted one shoulder. "But either way, I would like a chance to become acquainted with each other, and see if you like me more than the old Westmorland."

"Oh." That sounded rather tame, after what her unruly imagination had been anticipating. "Well—yes, I suppose that would be fine. We don't really know each other, after all . . ."

He stopped her babbling with a fingertip to her lips. "I know a great deal about you," he said softly. "Deeply loyal to your friends, and conscious of not wanting to hurt them. Considerate, even to the memory of a dead woman you never knew. Kind and compassionate enough to risk your friendship with Lady Winston to help a stranger you disliked. Determined in the face of obstacles. Inventive and fiendishly clever. Fond of racing and splashing in a pond but still the most beautiful woman in any room. You read adventure stories, with different voices." He paused as she gaped at him. "And you kissed me like you wanted to run off with me."

I do, whispered a voice in her head. "Then I suppose you'd better come to call," she said, trying to remain poised. "Since we can't run off with each other."

"Not yet," he murmured, his eyes gleaming.

She started. "That almost sounds like you propose we elope."

"Does it?" He leaned closer, as if they shared a secret. "What would you say if I did propose that?"

Oh Lord. She would say yes, fool that she was. After spending most of her life expecting to marry Sterling, here she was, ready to run off with a man she'd known less than a month. What had got into her? "I would say that would be very scandalous," she said, only a slight tremor in her voice. "Most people still believe I'm engaged to Sterling."

As soon as she said his name, she wanted to cringe. The intimate air vanished, and the playfulness faded from Rob's face. "Do they?"

"Because I had to inform my brother first," she blurted out. "I sent him a letter the day after I broke off the engagement, but he's a prickly sort, and if he heard it from someone else, I don't know what he would do." She forced a grim smile. "I wasn't afraid of Sterling, but my brother is a different matter."

A frown touched his brow, then disappeared. "You don't need to be afraid of him."

You don't know Alistair, Georgiana thought. "I've told my dearest friends and Lady Sidlow. I'm not trying to keep it secret, or nursing some hope of reconciliation."

"Is Sterling?"

She frowned. Why had she brought up Sterling? "He shouldn't."

Rob's shoulders relaxed. "Ah. He certainly didn't mention it last night."

"No, he—he what?" she demanded, thrown. "When did you see Sterling?"

"We met at the Vega Club last night." Rob resumed walking.

Apprehension clutched at her, for no good reason. "What did he say?"

"Nothing much," replied Rob vaguely. "He didn't correct someone who mentioned it." He shot a glance at her, some of his mischief returning. "Tom mentioned it, more than once."

Georgiana wished the earth would swallow her. "Your brother tweaked him about me?" she asked weakly.

"Tom just tweaked him," Rob corrected. "No one said your name. Tom was trying to stir up trouble."

"Was Sterling angry?"

For answer, Rob just grinned and tapped his jaw—right near his split lip, she realized. Her eyes rounded. Had Sterling punched him? It seemed incredible, and yet—Rob had been very concerned that Sterling might not take it well—

They had circled the green. The figure of Lady Sidlow was still visible in the drawing room windows, and Georgiana raised one hand in acknowledgment as Rob led her back across the street.

"What happened last night?" she whispered.

"Ah, it's much too thorny a tale to relate now. I shall have to come visit again. The story would be worthy of Scheherezade herself, and I must rehearse my performance of it, to match yours." He winked.

She couldn't help smiling, and then Higgins was opening the door, his face impassive. Rob escorted her up the stairs, where the major sat with Lady Sidlow over the remains of tea. After a few banal pleasantries, Rob and his brother took their leave, and Georgiana sank onto the sofa, feeling as if she must be glowing with happiness.

She had not been mistaken in him. Whoever he had been, the Rob she had known, and fallen half in love with, was the same man who had come to visit today. He couldn't stop thinking about her—about kissing her. He wanted to know if she would run off with him. He was straying dangerously close to the silly romantic dreams that had plagued her since they parted, and she was having a hard time keeping calm about that.

"Georgiana," said Lady Sidlow, breaking into her thoughts, "does Lord Westmorland mean to court you?"

She couldn't keep her expression neutral. *What would you say if I did propose we elope?* "I think he might."

"My goodness." The woman sounded dazed. She poured herself another cup of tea and drank half of it in one gulp. "I did not know you had ever met His Lordship before last night."

"Oh." She flushed. "I believe we were introduced once or twice. Last Season, perhaps."

"Indeed." Her chaperone eyed her suspiciously. "It seems strange he would decide to call based on two introductions. You seemed very familiar with him in the square just now."

Georgiana made a vague noise neither agreeing nor protesting. "Are you suggesting I ought to turn him away? Is he that improper and scandalous?"

Lady Sidlow's mouth compressed and her eyes narrowed. "He has a rather scandalous reputation, but he is extremely eligible . . . I suppose, if he has honorable intentions, I cannot counsel you to refuse him. Yet."

I've never been known for my saintliness, but this time I'll try. A fever-flush of exhilaration warmed Georgiana. It would take a lot more than Lady Sidlow's counsel to make her turn away Rob now.

"Did you have a pleasant conversation with Major Churchill-Gray?" she asked to divert her chaperone.

"Yes," Lady Sidlow admitted. "He seemed determined to sing his brother's praises, as if we might see both of them again, and often."

"Well." Georgiana cleared her throat, unbearably pleased that it was true. "Perhaps we shall."

Chapter 26

꧁꧂

"YOU'RE GOING TO get us arrested," muttered Tom.

"Doubt it." Rob swung down from the saddle of his horse and handed the reins to his brother. "But if you're afraid . . ."

"Not a bit." Tom snatched the reins. He already held the lead rope of the third horse, a spirited mare who wanted to run. She pranced impatiently from side to side, and Rob paused to run his hand down her neck. She butted her nose into his shoulder, and he obliged by handing over a carrot from his pocket.

"Go on, then," growled Tom, staring straight ahead. "Before I get marked a horse thief."

Rob made a rude gesture as he strode away, around the corner and down Mortimer Street. He ducked into the stable yard and let himself through the wooden gate into the garden of Georgiana's house, still dark and silent.

She'd said her room was at the back, where it was easy to sneak out. Rob meant to be respectable, but that bit of knowledge was too enticing to ignore. Respectable meant a sedate walk in the park, a cup of cold tea, a dance now and then. That wasn't enough for him, and he thought Georgiana craved more excitement, too. He bent and scooped up some gravel, then counted the windows and threw one pebble.

It plinked off the glass, loud in the quiet. A dog barked somewhere, making him start, but he threw another pebble, and then a third.

Just as he was starting to count the windows again, afraid he'd chosen the wrong one, a face appeared. There was just enough light for him to make out her astonished expression as she opened the window.

"What are you doing?" she whispered.

He grinned. Her hair was down, and her nightdress had slid off one shoulder. What he wouldn't give to climb up that drainpipe and crawl through the window . . . "Come ride with me."

"It's dark!"

"Best time to ride flat-out." He opened his arms. "Will you?"

She stared, then she smiled, then she nodded. The window slid quietly shut, and he retreated to the shadows to wait.

When she finally slipped from the back of the house, his heart took a leap. She wore a riding habit, but her hair swung down her back in a long braid. "What are you doing here?" she whispered as she reached him, still buttoning her jacket.

In reply he cupped her face in one hand and kissed her. Her arms went around his neck and he lifted her against him, inhaling the scent of her hair and skin as he ravished her mouth. "Good morning," he breathed.

"A very good morning to you, too." Her head fell back as he nipped at her earlobe. "How did you know—?"

"You said your room was at the back, where it was easier to sneak out." He winked. "Seemed a shame to let that go to waste."

Her eyes sparkled. "It is. But where are the horses?"

"This way." Her hand in his, he led the way through the stable yard and back into Mortimer Street. The clopping of hooves led them around the corner, where Tom was walking the horses up and down. He handed over the mare's rope without a word.

"This is Artemis." He checked the mare's girth. "She likes to run."

"She's beautiful," Georgiana said on a moan of delight. She stroked Artemis's soft nose before letting Rob toss her into the saddle. "Whose is she?"

"My mother's. Damned good luck she left the horse in London."

"Will your mother be upset that I rode her?"

Rob snorted, adjusting her stirrup. "Not a bit. Artemis needs the exercise, if anything." He took hold of her boot and nestled it into the stirrup. His hand lingered around her ankle. "You don't mind, do you?"

She grinned. "You know I don't."

"Are we ready?" asked Tom curtly. "I've already had to speak to one constable, wondering why I'm out before dawn with three horses."

"By all means, return to your bed." Rob unhooked the lead from Artemis's bridle and took his own horse's reins and mounted. "I don't need your help any longer."

Tom made a face, but he fell in line behind Georgiana as they started off. There was virtually no traffic in the streets, and it took no time at all to reach the park. It had been a long time since Rob had been up and about so early, rather than so late. Normally when he saw dawn it was at the end of a night he barely remembered. Today, though, he didn't want to miss a moment.

The sky was the color of slate by the time they reached Piccadilly. Rob turned into Green Park and nudged his horse into a canter. Behind him Georgiana gave an exclamation of glee, and followed suit. He supposed Tom kept up as well, but he didn't care either way.

They skirted the basin and followed the path. Normally one couldn't ride this way in Green Park, but today it was deserted. They kept up the easy pace until they reached Hyde Park corner, where they had to cross the road. Aside from a few carts bound for market, they might have been the only people in the world.

He drew up his horse and let her come up beside him. "How is she?"

"She's a dream to ride!" Georgiana leaned forward to pat the horse's neck. Artemis tossed her head and jangled her bridle.

Rob looked out into the expanse of the park, silent and still, a thin miasma of fog hovering above the grass. "Shall we run?"

Her eyes lit up. "Can we?"

He winked. There was no one about to say they couldn't. "Race you to the Ring."

For answer, she touched her heel to Artemis's side. With a joyful snort the horse shot forward, taking off at last. Georgiana's whoop of excitement made him smile, and Rob sent his own horse after her.

He didn't want to lose, but he did like watching

her ride. Heedless of decorum, she almost lay across the horse's back, her blond braid bouncing on her back in time with the beat of Artemis's hooves. Her skirts fluttered up, revealing her boots and stockings. And when she glanced back to see how close he was, her face was alight with joy and determination. Her hat flew off, but she didn't stop.

They veered north, following the path around the Serpentine toward the Ring, the enclosure where carriages could make elegant turns to display their occupants. It was deserted now, of course, the balustrade spindly in foggy solitude.

He beat her by half a length. "Unfair!" she cried even as she laughed. "Your horse is taller!"

"Fair! I even gave you a head start," he declared, circling his horse back around to fall in beside her.

Georgiana stuck out her tongue at him. "Don't you dare say that ever again. I don't want a head start."

"All the better to appreciate your form, my dear."

She gave him a coyly flirtatious glance, and stroked Artemis's heaving neck again. "You were splendid," she crooned. "We'll take him next time."

His heart leapt at that casual phrase. By God, he wanted there to be a thousand next times. He'd forgotten how exhilarating it was to fly across the park on Bethel, his long-legged gelding. Doing it with Georgiana was ten times better.

Georgiana raised her head. "Have we lost the major again?"

There was no sign of Tom. Rob had asked his brother's help in carrying off this escapade, but made sure to mention that once in the park, Tom should feel at liberty to take himself off for a bite of breakfast or back to bed, as he desired. To his credit, Tom had been an able accomplice—especially now, leaving him alone with Georgiana.

"He's out there somewhere." He glanced at her. "Are you worried for propriety without him?"

"No, but I would hate to leave him to wander lost and alone, vulnerable to thieves and brigands."

Rob scoffed. "Tom? Pity the thieves and brigands who try to lay hands on him. He could use a good thrashing, though."

She laughed. "That's the way of it?" Rob gave a mock salute in acknowledgment. "I never know," she remarked. "About siblings."

Ah. "Tom and I get on well most of the time," he explained. "Always have. We were the oldest two. Will and George are a few years younger, and they had their antics while Tom and I had ours." He grinned, remembering the tales dredged up from memory recently. "Tom always had more spirit for adventure. I was the more responsible party."

"You?" Georgiana exclaimed incredulously.

"Of course I was," he retorted with some indignity. "Relative to Tom, that is."

She was still laughing. "The pair of you must have been a threat to all peace and serenity!"

Rob grinned proudly. "We were. Not any longer, of course. All quite respectable and proper now—"

"Sneaking out to ride across the park before dawn," she murmured.

"It's not illegal," he said, unruffled. "And if no one sees, how can it shock anyone?"

"And fighting at the Vega Club," she added.

Rob raised one finger. "That was also Tom's fault."

"So you said." They had circled around and now turned to head up the path that led back to the Serpentine. "Why? You promised a rollicking good story."

"So I did." He shifted in the saddle and cleared his throat. "Once upon a time there were two brothers, both handsome and proud, not to mention bold, clever fellows."

"Did either of them lose a horse?" she asked slyly.

Rob frowned at her. "No. Why would you think that? I said these were *clever* fellows."

"Ah, right. Go on." An enchanting smile lingered on her lips.

"The elder brother—the much handsomer, cleverer one, by the by—had led a sometimes wild life, but had recently sworn a vow to be more circumspect. The younger, though, was hotheaded and unable to control either his temper or his tongue. Together they went out one evening, and were subsequently invited to a notorious club. The elder brother did not much wish to go, but he was persuaded—"

"Against his better judgment? That does not sound very clever to me."

"He was cleverer *than his brother*," Rob explained patiently. "Really, all these interruptions are destroying the drama of my tale."

She gasped in pretend outrage, but spoiled it by laughing at the same time. "What drama? This story is taking a donkey's age to tell!"

He stopped his horse. "Come here." Eyebrows raised in impertinent glee, she rode closer. Rob reached out and grabbed the pommel of her saddle, pulling Artemis closer until he could lean forward and kiss Georgiana. "Will that keep you quiet for a moment?" he whispered, his lips still brushing hers.

"No," she whispered back, seizing his cravat and pulling him back for a longer kiss. His hand shifted from the pommel to her knee, stroking upward as her mouth opened under his.

By the time he lifted his head, his heart thumped wildly and he didn't know how he was still astride his horse. She smiled up at him, her mouth pink and tempting, her hair coming loose in golden tendrils around her face, and her green eyes smoldering. That, more than anything, almost made him lose his seat and slide right off Bethel's back.

He had suspected he was falling in love with her even before he kissed her in Macclesfield. The suspicion had grown stronger when he realized he needed to rush to London to stop her from marrying Sterling. Now he knew beyond all doubt, because the answer he wanted was shining in her eyes.

As his father had predicted, he was mad—but it would work out, because she loved him back.

"What is the end of the story?" she asked, breathless and flushed.

It took him a moment to remember the story. "Ah—right. Well, they went to a club, got a bit foxed, and fell into a fight with some prickly fellows." He made a face. "A bit stupid of them, really. The important thing to remember is that it was entirely Tom's fault."

Georgiana's peals of laughter made him want to laugh, too. "This is a terrible story! You're not explaining anything!"

"You really want to know how Tom annoyed Sterling to the point of blows?"

She sobered at the name. "No. No—I didn't mean to pry, it was only in fun—"

Rob stopped his horse and jumped down. "Come here." She bit her lip but put her hands on his shoulders and let him lift her off her horse. He wrapped both sets of reins around his fist and cupped her nape to hold her attention. "I'm not trying to conceal it. I only hope you don't decide I'm a terrible idiot after I tell you."

She put her hand to his jaw. "I hate that you got hurt again. You don't seem concerned by it, but you *have* shown a rather astonishing lack of concern before, for injuries that were far worse . . ."

His eyes closed under her touch. As her fingers wandered over his face, he wanted to growl with satisfaction.

"Did Sterling do this?"

Rob opened his eyes. Her fingertips were like silk against his lip. "A mate of his."

She winced. "Lord Bristow, I suppose."

He shrugged. "Tom was being provoking, despite my strong advice to him to be quiet. He truly was begging to be hit. So Sterling obliged, and when I tried to drag my brother out of there, another bloke took a swing at me." He tested the swelling with his tongue. It was better today, but still annoyed him; if he hadn't had his arms full of cursing, flailing Tom, he wouldn't have been caught off guard by Sterling's red-faced friend.

"Tom provoked him about me," she said in a low voice.

He caught a stray wisp of her golden hair around his finger. "He didn't quite trust that your betrothal was over. He spoke, very loudly, about how he thought engaged men ought to behave—not that Tom would know, being mortally terrified of all things related to marriage—and Sterling gave him a black eye for his trouble."

Her lips parted and she looked stricken. Rob was tired of discussing his brother and her former fiancé. "I told you Tom is an idiot."

"And this will only give him another reason to despise me." She put her face in her hands.

"Georgiana." Oh Christ. He hadn't meant to make her cry. Rob dropped the reins and put his hands on her shoulders. "Tom deserved what he got," he assured her. "*I* almost hit him! He got himself punched because he was piqued at me for saying—" In the nick of time he stopped short of saying he'd told his brother he meant to marry her. He ought to propose before telling anyone else.

She looked up at him, her eyes wet. "This is the most incredible farce," she said, her lips quivering. "We're worse than Drury Lane." With enormous relief, Rob realized she was laughing.

"I know it shouldn't be amusing," she went on, her voice beginning to break. "But it's the most ridiculous thing I've ever heard of!" And she burst into laughter, so hard she leaned into him and clutched his coat. Rob gathered her close and laughed with her.

"I wish Tom didn't distrust me so," she said when she'd calmed down. She dabbed her eyes with a handkerchief Rob fished out of his pocket. "He has every right to, though. I did lie to everyone."

"That's not why Tom is so suspicious." Rob grinned.

"He thought you'd done it to snag yourself a marquess."

"What rubbish!" she said witheringly. "I didn't even *like* you—" She stopped short, her face pink.

"No, and yet you saved my life," he said.

Georgiana went still. "I had to," she said softly. "I saw my father die." A spasm flitted across her face. "I couldn't bear to see *anyone* else suffer that—"

"No," he cut her off, pulling her tightly to him. "It was an act of matchless grace and kindness."

"Even the lies?" Her voice was muffled against his coat, but he heard the waver.

Rob smiled. "Especially the lies. Those were the best part."

Her shoulders shook in a reluctant laugh. She stepped back and dabbed her eyes with the handkerchief again.

"Thankfully Papa wasn't beaten," she said, staring across the misty grass. "It was an inflammation of his lungs. He coughed up so much blood, and every breath made him convulse . . ."

"My God. I'm sorry," said Rob swiftly. She'd been a young child. "How dreadful."

"I wasn't supposed to be there. He'd fallen ill a few days earlier, and seemed in no danger until that last day. My mother sent me to bed but I sneaked back in . . . It was *horrible*. I couldn't wish that on anyone, not even someone I hated. No one deserves that fate, to choke on their own blood and die in lonely misery." She inhaled a ragged breath. "So I panicked and told an enormous lie, because speaking the truth felt like the greater sin at that moment."

He put his lips to her temple, and she wrapped her arms around his waist. Her hair smelled of orange water, and for a moment he wished the sun would never rise.

When she lifted her head, he brushed his thumb over her cheek, dashing away the tracks of moisture. "I hope I would have the nerve to do the same," he told her. "Because I'm dashed happy you lied to Kitty, and lied to me, and gave Tom what-for when he tried to spoil it all with the truth—"

She gave a shaky laugh. "First this ride, now telling me lying was the right thing to do . . . You're a terrible influence!"

"No one will ever tell you otherwise, my lady," he said with a wink. "Does being a bad influence ruin your opinion of me?"

She lowered her gaze but he saw her pleased smile. "No."

The horses had wandered a few yards away to snatch a bite of grass. There was still no sign of Tom or anyone else. The sky was a pale pink now, warning of the impending dawn, when he would have to take her home and they would once more be bound by the rules of propriety. For this stolen moment, though, he had her to himself, and he reveled in it.

Arm in arm, they strolled along the Serpentine. The water was still and smooth, reflecting the sky above as it bloomed with shades of pink and gold. Georgiana's head rested against his shoulder. "This is mad, you know. Mad—but wonderful."

"It's the best time to ride all-out."

She smiled. "You remembered."

Rob's arm tightened around her. He remembered everything she'd said to him, every smile she gave him, every shocked glance that turned to impish delight. He wanted to be with her until there were so many memories his head couldn't hold them all.

"I wish we could do it again," she added wistfully.

"We certainly will," he assured her. "At Salmsbury, we can ride for miles, all the way to the sea."

"But will Artemis be there?"

Rob grinned. "The stables at Salmsbury are even better. My brother Will has been in charge of the horses since he was twenty—my parents couldn't keep him out if they padlocked the stable doors. He'll raise a fine mare for you, like Artemis but taller, so you can win without a head start."

Her eyes widened. "That will take years!"

"The first few years," he countered, "of the rest of our lives together."

One brow went up. "You're assuming my answer, sir . . ."

"No, I'm *hopeful* of your answer." He tipped up her chin. "Am I wrong to be hopeful?"

Her arms were around his neck. "No," she whispered, and went up on her toes to kiss him.

They had to go soon. The sky was growing brighter by the minute, and soon other early riders would be in the park. But when Georgiana clung to him, as eager to kiss him as he was to kiss her, his mind emptied of every sensible, logical thought, and he gave himself up to the pleasure of holding—and being held by—the woman he was falling deeper in love with every minute.

With urgent fingers he unbuttoned her riding jacket. She arched against him, sighing into his mouth as his hand slid around her breast. His heart banged into his lungs; she wasn't wearing a corset.

He could feel her flesh beneath the linen of her shirt, the nipple plump and firm against his palm. Yet another happy benefit to surprising her before dawn, when her maid was still abed.

Her head fell back and she gave a long, shuddering sigh as he rolled his thumb over that nipple in fascination. Her fingers dug into his shoulders as he played with her, marveling at her, tormenting both of them. She whispered his name, her voice hoarse with longing. The breath roared in his ears. He wanted to taste her—he wanted to lay her down and make love to her—he wanted to feel her mouth and hands on him. He wanted to hear her laugh as she straddled him and he wanted to see her eyes grow dark and excited when she came . . .

Tom, with his usual poor timing, turned up then, trotting along the path toward them. At least he had sense enough to do it loudly. Georgiana gave a startled squeak and ducked out of Rob's arms, hastily doing up her buttons. Rob turned his back to his brother, both to press one last kiss to the nape of her neck and to adjust his trousers. His blood still ran hot and fast, and he stepped away to fuss over the horses.

"It's nearly dawn," Tom called. "I thought you wanted Lady Georgiana to be home by now."

"I should be." Georgiana, beautifully flushed, smoothed down her refastened jacket. "And I must find my hat." She made a face. "Lady Sidlow will suspect something if I lose it."

Without a word Tom produced the hat from the back of his saddle. Georgiana's lips parted in surprise, but when she walked forward to take it, she took his hand as well as the hat.

"Thank you, Major," she said. "I hope you can forgive me for lying about your brother's name."

Tom looked at her for a long minute. "I daresay it was the sort of lark he'd have relished, were he in his right mind."

"Damned right," muttered Rob, busy adjusting the saddle girths again.

Georgiana lowered her voice, but he could still hear her. "Nevertheless, I would like your forgiveness. My actions caused you great distress, and I am sorry for that."

Rob peeked over Bethel's back. Tom sat on his horse, one fist on his hip, staring down at Georgiana with an odd little twist to his lips. Her head was tilted back as she waited for his reply. In the glowing light of impending dawn, her hair shone like gold. Her face was patient, sincere, waiting for the reply.

Finally Tom jerked his head. "You have it, my lady." He met Rob's gaze. "And not simply to stay in West's good graces," he added wryly. "I suppose one should never judge too harshly the well-meant actions of another, particularly those taken in urgent moments."

Her smile was glorious. She was truly relieved, Rob realized. "Thank you, sir. I hope we can get on better from now."

"I'm sure we shall." Tom looked toward Rob again. "Do you need help with that girth? I came to tell you it's half five. Her maid will discover her gone soon."

Georgiana snorted even as she hurried to Artemis's side. "Nadine won't open my door before eight at the earliest. She likes to take her breakfast leisurely." She grinned. "And this morning I certainly shan't mind!"

They rode the long way around the Serpentine, taking one last chance at a gallop. This time Georgiana folded herself low over Artemis's back and urged the horse on, and won the race by a nose. She let out a whoop and threw her hat, which Rob had to circle around to fetch for her again.

"Well done," said Tom, grinning at last.

"Thank you, sir, it was my very great pleasure beating you both." She bowed her head, flourishing the hat before setting it back on her head.

"I have one question," Tom went on. "Now that we're friends and all." Rob growled, and Tom flapped one hand at him. "How did Lady Winston take it when you told her what happened?"

Georgiana went pink. "Oh. Right. Well, I've been writing a letter to her. It's taken some time, you know, because it's not easy to explain."

"How are you getting on?" asked Rob.

"So far, I've written, *Dear Kitty, I hope you and everyone at Osbourne House are well, especially little Annabel.*" She paused. "That's all. It's a work in progress."

Rob coughed to keep from laughing. Tom didn't bother hiding his amusement. Georgiana gave him a gaze brimming with rueful humor. "I know. It's dreadful." She heaved a sigh. "I suppose we're all trying to come up with good stories to explain ourselves."

"You could claim a sudden failing of your eyesight," suggested Tom.

"I'd have to have gone deaf as well, not to recognize the difference in their voices," she replied wryly.

"Which might become very convenient, when next we meet and she rings a peal over me . . ."

"I doubt she will," remarked Rob.

"Oh, she will," said Georgiana with morbid certainty. "Kitty will be furious. I dread what she'll think of me, let alone what she'll *say*. And Geneva, and Mother Winston—"

"I'm not going to take their house," he pointed out. "Seems an end to the whole business, doesn't it?"

Her brow wrinkled in puzzlement. "I suppose, but still . . . She and I have been friends for years, she'll want to know why I told her such a tale."

Rob just winked at her, and said no more. They had reached Oxford Street, which was far busier than it had been before—and fortunately so, for it gave them cover to ride faster. By the time they reached Cavendish Square, the tips of the roofs above them were gilded with the first rays of sunlight.

Rob jumped off his horse and she almost leapt into his arms. Leaving the horses to Tom, they hurried down Mortimer Street, just as they had hurried out over an hour ago. After checking for any witnesses, Rob eased open the garden door. Then he paused, cupping her cheek. "Until later," he whispered, and gave her one last searing kiss.

"Not much later, I hope," was her breathless reply. She winked at him, her eyes sparkling, and then she slipped into the garden and out of his sight.

No, it would not be, he promised silently. Not if he could help it. With a jaunty step, he headed back to his brother and the horses, plotting his next move.

Chapter 27

❦❧

THERE WAS A small, silly smile permanently affixed to her face for the entire day. A stunning bouquet arrived, graceful red roses with sprigs of myrtle and hawthorn and a card signed only with a sweeping W, which made Lady Sidlow clap one hand to her heart in shock. Georgiana put them in her bedroom, next to the window where he'd thrown gravel to wake her. She wondered if he might do it again, but the next morning all was quiet.

Until, that is, Lady Sidlow burst into the room.

"Get dressed," she said in a tense, worried voice. "Lord Wakefield is coming."

"What?" Still in her dressing gown, Georgiana blinked out of her happy contemplation of the bouquet. "Today?"

"Within the hour."

Ice formed around her heart. In the mirror she met Nadine's gaze, as horrified as her own. "How can he? I sent my letter only a few days ago!" It was a week's journey to London from Wakefield Manor.

"He did not explain in his note, but he is here

in town and coming this morning, so make haste, Georgiana!"

It was true. Georgiana had barely scrambled into her clothes and pinned up her hair before a carriage stopped before the house. It had been so long since she'd seen her brother, she'd almost forgotten what he was like.

As a child she had thought Alistair was always angry about something. His face, in her memory, was set in a perpetual scowl, his pale blue eyes burning bright and his dark hair standing up as if he'd pulled at it in fury. She was glad he hadn't lived at Wakefield Manor with them. Georgiana once overheard Mama tell a visiting friend that Alistair's mother had been a cold, silent woman, and it wasn't Alistair's fault he was so distant. Her friend had clucked and said he was wrong in the head, which earned her a gentle rebuke from Mama, who always thought the best of everyone.

But young Georgiana had privately agreed with the visitor. There was something about Alistair that frightened her.

When she finished her schooling at Mrs. Upton's, she'd had to go home to Wakefield Manor for a short while, but Alistair had barely been there. Her only vivid memory was of him snapping at her to be silent at the dinner table. Fortunately he'd engaged Lady Sidlow within a month and they set out for London, where she'd been ever since.

Today he strode into the drawing room, almost visibly crackling with anger. His dark hair was now cropped short and he was thinner than she remembered, with deep grooves between his brows and around his mouth. He still dressed in severe dark colors, though, and his blue eyes still burned with fury.

Georgiana's instinctive word of polite greeting melted away, and she glanced nervously at Lady Sidlow. That formidable woman stood as straight as an iron pike, her hands clasped at her waist and no trace of expression on her face. "Good morning, my lord," said the chaperone, dipping a deep curtsy.

"What the devil is this?" He held up a folded letter—her letter, Georgiana realized.

"I wrote to you, sir," said Lady Sidlow quickly. "Dare I—?"

"Be quiet," he snarled at her. His attention veered back to Georgiana. "What the devil is this?" he repeated, each word bitten off.

"I have ended my engagement to Lord Sterling," she said, lifting her chin to keep it from sinking to her chest under his angry regard.

Glaring furiously, Wakefield closed his hand into a fist around the letter and threw it at her. Georgiana flinched as it bounced off her cheek. "What made you do something so stupid?"

She *had* explained it in her letter. "Lord Sterling and I do not suit."

"Oh?" His eyebrows shot up. "You don't suit! How, pray, do you know this? You no longer blush when he smiles at you? He doesn't send you enough vapid love poems?"

"He barely comes to see me," she retorted, her temper roused. "He almost never writes—letters *or* love poems—and even when I do see him, he's always on his way to meet his friends. He doesn't care for me—"

"What's that got to do with marriage?" interrupted Alistair.

"It's what I want in marriage! And you do not have the right to tell me whom I shall marry!"

His face darkened. "Leave us, Lady Sidlow."

The woman hesitated, sending an anxious glance at Georgiana. "Sir—"

He turned and gave her such a look, she made a hasty curtsy and left the room.

"I will ask again," said Alistair in a cold, eerily calm voice. "What made you break off with Sterling?"

It was unnerving to be alone with him. He was only a few inches taller than she, but seemed so much larger. "I no longer love him as I should to marry him."

He closed his eyes in patent fury.

"In honesty I did not think you were much in favor of the match yourself," Georgiana went on, in as calm a tone as she could manage. "It's been over two years since we announced our engagement and no date was ever set for the wedding. Sterling said the settlements were dragging on forever, and he finally admitted he was pressing you to hand over a piece of property along with my dowry. I thought—"

"Don't, Georgiana," he snapped. "It's never pretty when a woman tries to think."

Her face burned. "I don't want to marry him."

He put his hands on his hips and shook his head, his lip curled.

"I thought you'd be relieved," she couldn't resist adding. "Now he won't badger you over the settlements."

He slapped her. Georgiana recoiled in shock, one hand flying to her cheek. For a long moment they stared at each other, Georgiana with a mixture of alarm and revulsion, he with pure contempt.

"You're supposed to marry Sterling," he said, low and cold. "Now you think you're going to throw that aside for some girlish fit about love?"

"What do you mean, *supposed* to marry Sterling?" she asked warily.

His smile was twisted. "It's all I've heard for several years! How pleased Father would be with the match, how strongly Pelham approved, how big a fool you made of yourself mooning after him. So I gave Sterling my blessing, and he's the only one I plan to approve. You can make it up with him, or wait until you're twenty-five." He turned on his heel and headed for the door.

"What?" she cried after a moment's shock. "Why?"

He whirled and came at her so rapidly she stumbled backward until she hit a nearby chair. "You heard me," Alistair said ominously. "Our father made me your guardian until you either marry or reach the age of twenty-five."

"What if I want to marry someone else?" she demanded in renewed outrage.

He shrugged. "Who would have you without a dowry?" Her mouth dropped open in outrage, but he slashed one hand before she could protest. "Yes, Father set it aside. But it's under my control. Without my approval the funds won't be paid. So there is your choice, Georgiana. Make up to Sterling, or resign yourself to being a spinster for three more years." He looked her up and down. "I daresay you're used to it by now."

He turned to leave again, and Georgiana bit back a fiery retort. But at the door, Alistair stopped once more. "If you're to be a spinster, you might as well come home to Yorkshire. There's no need to pay London rents if it's all going to waste."

Georgiana stood tense with fury, her breath vibrating through her as his footsteps rang on the stairs. He was a monster. The door below closed, and she seized a pillow from the sofa and flung it at the drawing room door, almost striking Lady Sidlow as that lady hurried back in.

"My dear, what did he say?"

"He said I must marry Sterling," she said through tight lips. "Or go home to Yorkshire and marry no one until I'm twenty-five."

Lady Sidlow looked sick. "Dear heavens. I never dreamed he would demand *that*!"

The dark thought crossed Georgiana's mind that Lady Sidlow would lose her plum post if Georgiana went home to Yorkshire, but then the emphasis sank in. "Why?" The chaperone sank into a chair, handkerchief at her lips. "Why, Lady Sidlow?" Georgiana demanded, ready to scream it if she had to ask a third time.

"I . . . I do not know," faltered the older woman. "I have heard tidbits of gossip—only hints, mind you—that Lord Wakefield . . ."

Georgiana leaned over her. "Tell me," she ordered. "I want to hear everything."

The chaperone glanced up with a frown, but Georgiana's expression must have dissuaded her. "All right," she said in a low voice. "Close the door."

Georgiana almost ran to do so, then back to the chair beside her chaperone.

"This is *rumor*," stressed the woman. "I cannot vouchsafe any of it is truth. But there are whispers."

"About what?"

"After you ended your engagement, I spoke to Lady Capet—in *strictest* confidence, of course. She has heard whispers that your brother has encountered some financial difficulties. I made my own inquiries, and discovered he has not paid several of your bills. Unfortunately, I have some acquaintance with this, and fear it portends deeper trouble. The—the first sign of insolvency is delaying the payment of bills." She avoided Georgiana's gaze. "It was that way with my husband, Lord Sidlow—delay payment, then argue over the bill, then refuse to pay at all. Only when the milliner refuses more credit does a family discover what's happening."

"If he's not paying the bills," Georgiana said slowly, "does that mean he can't pay my dowry?" Her father had left that money for her, but she wouldn't put it past Alistair to hold tight to it if his own funds ran low.

Lady Sidlow bit her lip. "I do not know. But it does not bode well."

No, it did not. She digested that in silence.

"I won't go," she declared. "To Yorkshire. I won't go, not to live with him." Just the thought made her skin crawl.

"Quite right, my dear." Lady Sidlow was still very pale. "But what will you do?"

"He can't forbid me to marry anyone else."

"No," agreed the chaperone. "You are legally of age and can marry without his permission. But . . . it may be true that he can tie up your dowry."

Georgiana nodded grimly. Of course Alistair

would be able to keep from her the dowry her father had explicitly left her. Just as Charles Winston could wager away the house that had been in Kitty's family for decades, because it became his when she married him. Sterling's remarks about gentlemen being driven to do stupid things because of their honor ran through her head again, and she wondered why on earth men were allowed to be in charge of anything.

"I'm not going to Yorkshire," she repeated, returning to the main point. "And I shall marry whomever I choose."

Lady Sidlow darted a wary glance at her. "Please do not say you have some scandalous plan in mind."

She gave the woman a disbelieving look. "Scandalous! After Alistair said he would drag me back to Yorkshire and keep me there for three years if I didn't marry Sterling? What could I possibly do that's worse than that?"

"Yes," acknowledged Lady Sidlow after a moment. "Perhaps this calls for something scandalous."

Georgiana gave a decisive nod. "I think so, too."

ROB STAYED IN THAT night. Tom wanted to go to Vega's, but Rob had no desire to return there after the melee that had caused him to turn his ankle and given him a split lip, just when he'd finally recovered from the beating in Derbyshire.

"What will you do?" wondered his brother.

Rob shrugged. "Read a book, perhaps." He'd told Bigby to locate a copy of *The Arabian Nights*. Not only did he want to look up the story Georgiana had read aloud in Maryfield, he wanted to read the others.

Tom shook his head, but took himself off. Rob prowled the house for several minutes. He'd sent Georgiana flowers the previous day, and judged he could call again tomorrow. As he had often done before, he thought the rules of the *ton* were idiotic, but now he was willing to bow to them. For the first time in his life, he didn't want to make a hash of this.

In his dressing room he sank into the chair at the desk. What would he do with himself if he weren't out gambling and drinking all night? Heath had tried to prod him about the Forester business, whatever it was, and was still irked that Rob had put him off.

Rob's gaze fell on the desk. He hadn't thought to look through his own things in a bid to restore his memory.

As he opened drawers, it was as though he watched himself from a distance. There were bills, a ledger, a slim stack of letters. The handwriting on some sparked faces in his mind; that was his mother's hand, this one his aunt's. He remembered she had written to wish him a happy Christmas, and to relate a story about her pack of Pomeranians. A faint smile touched his face. As a boy he'd run with her dogs up and down the hills of Salmsbury.

He kept searching, memories filling in the gaps in his mind like sand pouring into a bucket of rocks. Some were tiny, inconsequential things, others more significant. But finally, in a leather portfolio, he found the letters that cast illumination on Heath's plans for Forester.

He was still reading when the door knocker sounded distantly. He thought it must be Tom, but the butler had a very odd look on his face when he came.

"There is a woman to see you, my lord." Bigby's face spasmed. "A young woman."

Without a word, Rob leapt from his chair and rushed downstairs. His instinct was borne out when the cloaked figure in his hall peered out from under her hood with familiar green eyes that had been haunting his dreams.

"You may go, Bigby," he said to the butler at his heels. He ushered Georgiana into the morning room and shut the door behind them.

As soon as he turned back to her, she flung herself into his arms. He caught her tight against him, lifting her off her feet as she kissed him.

"A good evening to you, too, Lady Georgiana," he murmured when it ended. A bloody *brilliant* evening, to him.

She smiled, betraying a tremor of her lips. "Was that presumptuous?"

"The kind of presumption I hope to see more of," he told her, levity dissolving into concern as a tear slid down her cheek. "What's the matter?" She appeared healthy and whole, but she wouldn't have come to him like this on a whim.

"My brother has come to town."

I'm not afraid of Sterling, but my brother is a different matter. Rob tensed. "What did he do?"

"I wrote to him that I had broken my engagement." Another tear slid down her face and she dashed it away with an impatient motion. "He said I must marry Sterling or go home with him to Yorkshire."

"The devil you must," he growled.

"I refuse to do either!" Her eyes flashed; she was enraged, not despondent. "But Lady Sidlow believes he can tie up my dowry funds, and he says he won't pay for the house in London any longer."

Rob's frown deepened. "Why does he want you to marry Sterling?"

"I don't know." She looked up at him with a determined gaze. Her tears were gone. "But I was hoping you would help me outwit him."

He clasped her hand and pressed it to his heart. "My lady, I am yours to command, from now until the end of time."

She smiled. Then she laughed. Rob grinned, and this time was ready to catch her when she threw her arms around his neck. "I love you," she whispered, and kissed him.

It felt like a vital spark of life being breathed into his soul. He kissed her back, winding his arms around her waist and holding her against him. She went up on her toes, clinging to him, and opened her mouth under his.

God help him. This must be what the poets meant about sunshine in one's soul and a fever in one's blood. He wanted time to stop, to let him savor this moment, and he wanted it to run at double pace, because he couldn't get enough of her in the normal seconds and minutes and hours of a day.

He kissed her eyes, her jaw, her temple, before devouring her mouth again. Her hands ran over his shoulders greedily, and his skin fairly burned to feel her touch. Her body arched against his, wrenching an almost feral growl from his throat.

"Right," he rasped, tearing his mouth from hers while he had the strength to do it. "We'll deal with

Wakefield. But you . . . you should go home before I forget that I'm trying to be a gentleman."

She pressed her forehead to his and curled her fingers into the hair at the nape of his neck. "I don't want to go home."

The rogue inside him stirred. Rob made one last effort to be noble. "Why not?"

Her hand drifted over his chest. "Because I want to stay with you."

The rogue was winning. "For how long?" he whispered.

"How long will you want me?" Her eyes were dark, ocean-deep with desire, glinting with a hint of mischief.

"For the rest of my life," he answered at once. "Georgiana Lucas, I want to marry you. Don't stay now if you don't want the same."

She laughed, her color high. "Will we elope?"

"Perhaps, perhaps not, but it will be a *very* short engagement."

"That would suit me perfectly, Lord Westmorland." She smiled shyly. "I accept your offer of marriage."

The rogue roared in triumph. "Are you certain?" Rob asked, hardly breathing. "Very, very certain?"

She smiled, her eyes glowing. "Absolutely certain."

Chapter 28

❧❧❧❧

GEORGIANA HAD HOPED for this ever since she sneaked out of the house in Cavendish Square and climbed into the hackney Nadine had fetched. Nadine was as eager as Georgiana to avoid being sent back to Wakefield Manor and had been a willing conspirator.

She suspected Lady Sidlow might have guessed what she was up to, but that lady had been conspicuously absent from view all evening. Georgiana thought the revelations about her husband, and her fears about Alistair, had sapped Lady Sidlow's sense of propriety, or perhaps her will to enforce it.

Not that it mattered; no one could have stopped her from coming to Rob tonight.

And he, wonderful he, had taken her inside without a whiff of shock, and listened to her concerns. He promised to help her, even before she told him her plan, and even though one of her previous plans had involved lying to him. He grinned as if he relished embarking on some mad scheme with her, and when he kissed her she thought her chest might burst.

Georgiana knew, in a way she'd never known before, that he was the one for her. Sterling had amused her and pleased her; they'd both been content for her to worship him. Rob consumed and enthralled her, and the fascination she felt for him was reflected in his face as he looked at her.

"Do you know," she said between kisses, "I undressed you once before?" She untied his cravat as she spoke.

"Did you? I don't remember it." He watched her with searing eyes.

"Pay more attention this time," she murmured, working loose the buttons on his waistcoat.

He laughed low in his throat. "I mean to. Come with me, love. Let's do this properly, not on the sofa where Tom might walk in."

"Your brother is here?" She caught up her skirt and hurried with him, hand in hand.

"On sufferance only." He led her up the stairs. It was a lovely house, Georgiana belatedly noticed, finer than her house in Cavendish Square and far more elegant than she'd have expected from a bachelor. The floor was a checkerboard of black and white marble, and a chandelier glittered above the curve of the graceful winding stairs. And it was Arlington Street, one of the most exclusive in London. Rakes and rogues did not live here, but government ministers, people who intrigued and kept secrets. She studied her new fiancé thoughtfully, beginning to believe there was far more to him than she knew.

He threw open a door and led her through a large dressing room into a bedroom. He released her to fetch a lamp from the dressing room, and then closed the door.

They were alone. The bed loomed behind her, shadowed promise of the pleasures to come. Her fingers tingled and her pulse raced. Rob's hands came to cup her jaw softly. "My darling," he whispered. "My love. Are you really here, or is this another fever dream of mine?" He kissed her before she could reply.

She gulped for air as his mouth moved over her skin. "I'm real," she managed to gasp. "And I'm yours."

That crooked grin crossed his face. "No, it's entirely the other way around. I've been yours since I opened my eyes in Osbourne House and Dr. Elton said I was." This time his kiss was even more intoxicating than the last, deep and hot and so long she thought she would expire from it. He flooded her senses and swamped her brain until she heard nothing but his rough, hungry murmurs, felt nothing but the scorching touch of his hands, and saw nothing but him, as drunk on desire as she felt.

"If you're going to undress me again," he whispered, sliding open the first few buttons on her pelisse, "you'd best work quickly."

Her stomach leapt. As girls, she and Sophie and Eliza had been intensely curious to know about making love. Other girls at Mrs. Upton's Academy, girls with mothers and cousins and older sisters, had passed on scraps of information gleaned from their married relations. Sophie, who learned cards and dice from the stable hands, picked up bits of the male view. When her friends married, Georgiana had demanded they tell her everything, for good or for ill, and they had obliged. Lady Sidlow's lips had never uttered a syllable on the topic, but Georgiana was not unaware of what she was doing.

Still . . . it was more marvelous than she'd ever expected. For all that she'd adored Sterling, never once had she wanted to peel off his shirt, as she did to Rob's, so impatiently she heard the rip of cloth. She had never imagined touching his bare chest and belly the way she did Rob's, greedily, marveling at the unexpected beauty of the male body. She had never dreamed that she would feel feverish and wild, wanting to tear off her own clothes and feel his warm golden skin against hers, but tonight she could think of nothing else.

While she had been absorbed in studying every firm inch of his skin, he had got her pelisse off and unbuttoned her dress. "I want to strip you bare," he said, his voice a taut thread of sound. "I want to see you and pleasure you and lose myself in you . . . God, Georgiana, I don't trust myself with you."

She pulled her arms free of the dress, the stupid thing, and let it fall to the floor around her. "I do," she whispered. "I trust you completely. And I came here hoping you would make love to me."

His throat worked. His eyes burned. "Do you know—do you understand—?"

A smile crossed her lips. "Yes," she said softly, running her fingers down his belly. "I know what I'm asking."

In reply he swung her into his arms and carried her to the bed. With one hand he flipped back the blankets and laid her down, taking care to prop her up on the pillows. He even added more until she laughed. "I feel like Scheherezade in her palace."

He braced one arm against the bedpost. "And so you should, my captivating princess." His scorching gaze wandered over her in potent appreciation.

Instinctively she stretched her arms overhead, arching her back and curling her toes into the softness of the linens.

"I haven't got any more fanciful stories to tell you," she murmured.

"You don't need to," he said in a low voice. "You've already beguiled me completely. From now on, we'll create our own wild adventures together, and someday you can tell our children about their scoundrel father getting carried away by a roc, or chased by angry elephants . . ."

She couldn't help laughing. "Shall I have to rescue you again?"

"I count on it." A wicked smile lingering on his lips, he climbed onto the bed, his knees straddling her hips. He pulled loose the ribbon of her chemise. She barely breathed as he loosened it and drew it gently away from her. "My God, you're beautiful," he murmured, his fingertips tracing a path of heat down her chest. His eyes flashed to hers for a moment before he reverently cupped his fingers around her breast, and Georgiana lost her last thread of thought.

His hands and mouth moved over her until she couldn't tell which way was up. He seemed bent on kissing every inch of her, rolling down her stockings with maddening slowness before smoothing his hands, hot and strong and sure, over the skin he'd just kissed.

And then, when he spread her thighs, he found the source of her aching hunger. She nearly screamed at the first touch, and then she could barely breathe as his hand settled over her, his fingers teasing her, inside her, wringing her entire body into a taut, shivering mess until she simply disintegrated.

Dimly she knew she had started sobbing, begging him, reaching for him, wanting him closer. It seemed as though she might burst without his body anchoring her. He resisted, his wicked mouth blazing a path over her hipbones, her stomach, her breastbone, lavishing attention on each breast before reaching her mouth. His tongue tangled with hers and his weight settled over her. Unabashedly she threw her arms around him and curled her legs around his.

He pushed himself up on one arm and hiked her knees around his waist. He stroked her once more between her legs, sending another delicious shudder through her. "With this act," he said, moving against her, "I take thee to my wife." Georgiana inhaled as he pressed inside her. That hot, throbbing feeling turned sharp, exquisitely sensitive and full. He pushed forward until she had to widen her legs and his hips were tight against hers. "With my body, I thee worship," he went on in a guttural whisper. He pulled back, and she reached for him with an inarticulate protest. As she pulled him to her for a desperate kiss, he surged forward and she rose to meet him on pure primal instinct.

It was a kiss without end. His free hand wandered up and down, cupping her breast, stroking her stomach, smoothing the hair from her neck so he could cradle her skull in his palm. The blood seemed to be singing in her veins, warming her from the inside out with joy. She held on to him and rose to meet his every thrust, reveling in the joining of their bodies.

He tore his mouth away and rested his forehead against hers. His eyes closed and his face pulled tight in a grimace, and then he reared up above her, his arm shaking this time. "I want to feel you climax." His eyes glittered beneath half-lowered lids, and he smoothed that free hand down her stomach. "Spread your legs wide," he growled.

Twined around him, Georgiana could barely understand what he meant. He was still inside her, still on top of her, and even though she felt that primitive pulse in her blood, she had no idea what he meant to do now.

Rob reached around his back and unhooked her leg, spreading it to the side. He licked his thumb and trailed his fingertips down her belly, making her shudder. "Like this," he breathed, and he touched her.

Georgiana sucked in so hard she almost saw stars; her back bowed and her hands fisted in the linens as he stroked her, delicately, firmly, relentlessly. He'd given her a climax, she thought she knew what it was, but this was harder, brighter, hotter—

It made her shake. She forced open her eyes and watched the fierce smile on Rob's face dissolve into something like rapture. He moved against her once more and went still, his arms taut as iron.

She had no idea how much time passed. When she opened her eyes again his head hung down, his dark hair damp with sweat. His chest heaved, and she saw with some alarm marks on his chest and arms. Just as she realized that *she* must have left those marks, scoring him with her fingernails, he raised his head and looked at her. "Till death do us part," he said in a ragged voice.

Georgiana managed a shaky laugh. "I think you left out some lines."

His lips curved into a lazy, sensual smile. "I'll get

it right next time." He lowered himself to kiss her, then rolled them both over. She had no protest; her muscles had melted, and she could have lain there forever, listening to his heart.

At some point he sat up and drew the blanket over them, settling onto his back. She stretched out against his side, thrilling when his arm tightened, pulling her closer. He was beautiful, and he was hers. In wonder she ran one hand over his chest, slowing at the ridges of scars.

Her brain, against her wishes, kept remembering images of how battered he'd been. "I'm glad this healed," she whispered, touching the spots where he'd been bruised and bloody.

"Entirely due to the high quality of devoted care I received, no doubt."

"I wasn't sure you would survive it." She gave a sharp shake of her head. "Everywhere I looked, there was blood . . ."

He canted his head to see her face. "And still you stayed."

"What choice did I have?" She wiggled one shoulder. "I'd already told Kitty you were my fiancé, and I was terrified you'd wake and tell her you were not, and also, by the by, you were the new owner of Osbourne House and would she please pack up and leave?"

"That would have been a very rude thing to do."

In spite of herself, she smiled. "Appallingly! You were deeply in her debt, merely for the amount of laundry created."

A silent laugh rumbled through him. "So practical!"

"Of course! I was stained red from top to bottom."

"You could have told Angus to do it."

She made a face of indignation. "I was supposedly violently in love with you. I could hardly hide in my room and let someone else wash you clean."

"Well now." Interest warmed his tone. "Violently in love?"

"I am now," she said, swirling her fingertips over his abdomen and marveling at the flex of muscle beneath his skin.

"Thank God. And you were the one who stripped all that bloody clothing off?"

"Yes—"

"And tenderly bathed my naked body?"

"*Rob*," she said, blushing and laughing. "You weren't quite naked . . ."

He rolled over on top of her. "Did you like what you saw?"

"Yes." She tried to school her expression into stern lines, but the heat in his gaze scattered her thoughts. "You're devastatingly attractive."

He kissed the tip of her nose. "For a week I had no idea what I looked like. But I did know I was a fortunate bloke, to be engaged to a girl as kind and beautiful as you."

"Did you really?" A hesitant smile of delight tugged at her lips.

He nodded. "I thought so at once, and then realized every day after that beauty was only the most trifling of your charms."

She looped her arms around his neck as joy bloomed inside her. "Perhaps you've not quite recovered from that blow to the head yet . . ."

He grinned and turned onto his back again. "Getting beaten on the head was quite possibly the best thing that ever happened to me, since it led to you here beside me." His arm pulled her closer.

Georgiana rested her cheek on his shoulder. His skin was vitally warm and intriguing, smooth and firm; she couldn't stop touching him. The idle play of his fingers down her back made her shiver and burn at the same time, and she thought they'd have to run off to Gretna Green, because the thought of waiting three weeks for the banns to be read would be unbearable.

"Why," asked Rob in a deceptively drowsy voice, "does your brother insist you marry Sterling?"

Alistair. Alistair, whose cruelty had driven her to throw propriety out the window and come here. She wasn't sorry for that, but her fury at her brother began to revive. "I don't know."

"Is he close friends with Sterling?" Rob asked. "Political allies? In debt to him? Why is he so set on Sterling?"

Georgiana shook her head in response to each query. "He said it was all he'd heard about, that I'd made a fool of myself mooning after Sterling, and that he only meant to give his blessing to Sterling. It's true I did make a cake of myself over him," she added softly, "but there's no affection or alliance between Alistair and Sterling, nor Sterling's father, Lord Pelham. I think he wants to punish me."

Rob lifted his head. "Punish you for what?"

Georgiana's hand, resting on his chest, closed into a fist. "I—I think he hates me." Rob scowled. "I told you Alistair was not fond of me, and wanted to send me to an orphanage. He once called me a bunter's cuckoo. My mother was not a lady, as Alistair's mother had been. Mama was a local squire's daughter and her marriage did not change her friendships or habits. She still dined with the vicar and local families, and played with village children. She was kind and cordial to everyone, no matter their rank, and Alistair is the opposite."

Rob covered her fist with his own hand until her fingers relaxed. "What has that got to do with you?"

She nibbled on her lip. "Alistair of course inherited almost everything when my father died, but Papa left me twelve thousand pounds for my dowry, with other funds to be used for my schooling and maintenance. I don't think Alistair was pleased about that, because none of it came from my mother. Her marriage portion was quite small."

"Was that why he dragged out negotiations with Sterling?"

"Sterling said there is a bit of land . . ." She frowned. "He said my father wanted me to have it, but Papa could have put that in his will and he did not. Naturally Alistair is refusing to give more than Papa specified, which Sterling must have known all along. But Alistair said he would withhold even my dowry if I married without his permission. He can't do that, can he? I'm of age, and the money is to be mine outright when I reach twenty-five."

Rob's fingers were tracing circles on hers. "If the funds were left in his care, God knows what he might have done with them."

She sat bolt upright. "He stole it?"

"Perhaps." Rob folded his arms behind his head, a sharp, thoughtful expression on his face.

"I refuse to let him steal my inheritance," she exclaimed. "I could file a suit!"

He didn't say anything. A deep frown had settled

on his face as he stared up at the dark canopy above them.

"Twelve thousand is a large dowry." He glanced at her. "You're quite an heiress—as if you weren't priceless already on your own merit. Why did Sterling press for land?"

She opened her mouth, then closed it. "He said my father had told his father I should have it. If Papa had wanted me to have that property, surely he would have put it in his will."

Rob was nodding. "Precisely. I'll wager there's more to the story than that."

"You mean . . ." Her voice faltered. "Sterling lied?"

He looked at her. "Why would he do that?"

She stared. He waited, brows raised expectantly. "Because he didn't really want to marry me? Because Alistair was lying to him? Because there was another reason he didn't tell me? I don't know."

His lips quirked ruefully. "You knew Sterling forever. He might have guessed you would accept him if he proposed."

Blushing, she nodded once. *Everyone* had known she loved Sterling, including the man himself.

"If he didn't want to marry you, he wouldn't have asked. He knew you would accept. Did your brother not give his consent quickly or easily?"

She frowned. "No. He agreed at once."

"Then you're left with the third option: there is something else." He pulled her down on top of him and kissed her brow until her frown faded. "And I thank God there was, because it gave me a chance to know you."

Slowly she smiled. "So I should thank them for arguing over it for two years?"

"Bloody right you should," he said with feeling. "I intend to."

She laughed, and he kissed her again. Georgiana spread her hands on his chest until he rolled them both over, his weight bearing her down into the mattress. Her legs parted, hooking around his without conscious thought. Her breathing hitched as he moved, thick and hard again, against her.

Rob tore his mouth from hers. "It's growing late. I should take you home before Lady Sidlow notices you're gone."

"I think she knows I left." She snuggled deeper into the pillows and ran one finger down his chest. "And if she doesn't . . . Well, then there's no reason to hurry back. I really don't think another hour will matter much."

His brows went up and his mouth crooked in that devilish way that made her heart race. "Is that so, my lady? Then we'd best make very good use of it."

Chapter 29

THE NEXT NIGHT was Lady Demont's annual Lammas night masquerade. Rob prowled the assembly rooms until he spotted Heathercote.

"Good evening."

His friend gave him a cool glance. "West. Fancy seeing you here."

Rob smiled ruefully. He'd been avoiding Heath since the Vega Club. "Care to take a walk? I've an apology to make."

Heath didn't reply for a moment, then unfolded himself from his languid pose and followed.

"I've remembered what our plan was with Forester," Rob said as they strolled through the rooms.

Heath turned on him in fury. "Remembered? Did you bloody forget it, West?"

Rob lowered his voice. "I did, actually. Got coshed on the head in Derbyshire, and it drove some things out entirely."

Heath's anger melted into incredulity. "What?"

Rob waved it away. "I've recovered, obviously, and it came back to me, what we are trying to do."

He gave his friend a piercing look. "Has this got any chance of working?"

"Of course it has." Rob raised a brow and Heath scowled. "As much as anything. My uncle—"

"My father's not too keen on his plans. He advised me to drop the whole business."

"No!" Heath sounded appalled. "Not when we've made such progress!"

"Have we?" Rob paused to take two glasses of wine from a servant. They'd found a quiet corner at last. "What progress? And to what ultimate end?"

This he had not been able to decipher from his papers, nor remember. Perhaps there never had been an answer. At the prompting of Lord Beresford, Heath's uncle, the two of them had undertaken to corrupt and bankrupt Frederick Forester, who had inherited his father's shipping company two years ago. The elder Forester had been cagey and ruthless, and quietly violating British law. The trouble was that Beresford's every attempt to exact justice fizzed out, despite voluminous evidence of guilt; he suspected old Mr. Forester had paid off and courted enough ministers and officials to impede any investigation. Rob suspected catching the man in a crime had become an idée fixe for Lord Beresford after years of being frustrated at it.

Freddie Forester, though, hadn't his father's cold-blooded drive. He had a taste for wild living and was drawn to aristocratic friends, the more rakish the better. The Marquess of Westmorland and Viscount Heathercote barely had to invite him once for the fellow to become a permanent fixture at their revelries.

Rob had no doubt he and Heath could have managed the corrupting and bankrupting. What he didn't know, in his newfound maturity, was what that would accomplish. Was Forester going to confess his crimes if they beggared him?

Heath glanced around uneasily. "What don't you remember?"

Rob also lowered his voice. "What are we to achieve?"

Heath raised his glass. "To put him out of business, ideally," he murmured under cover of sipping. "If nothing can be proved about his cargoes, the only option is to scuttle his whole enterprise."

"Heath, is this a reasonable plan?"

His friend glared. "It's working."

"How?"

"Forester's had to bring in investors to stay afloat."

"So his business is still carrying on." Rob sighed. "Isn't this better suited to the Royal Navy?"

"The navy is powerless. Give it more time," argued Heath.

"Perhaps." He decided to be diplomatic. "What do you know about the Earl of Wakefield?"

"A nasty piece of work." Heath finished his wine and set down the glass. "So we're still on Forester?"

Rob lifted one shoulder. "Tell me more about Wakefield. In confidence, of course."

Heath blew out a breath. "Suspicious, but greedy. The sort of man who wants to be the most powerful in any room. Doesn't like opposition, always thinks his view is the only valid one, and so on. My uncle doesn't like him—actually, no one likes him, as far as I know. A cold, abrasive fellow. Why?"

"He's crossed someone I know. If you hear any-thing about him, let me know." Heath nodded. "And Heath . . . don't mention my interest, will you?"

Heath raised one brow. "Not a word."

GEORGIANA WAS ASTONISHED HOW simple it was to persuade Lady Sidlow that they should attend Lady Demont's masquerade.

"I don't suppose it matters now," said the chaper-one morosely as they entered the assembly rooms, the windows and doors open to admit the warm summer air.

Georgiana wondered if she meant attending a masquerade, attending one at the public assembly rooms, or leaving the house at all. When she'd re-turned to Cavendish Square mere minutes before dawn, only Nadine had been waiting, sleepily, to let her slip back in, even though Lady Sidlow had the hearing of a hawk. Not one word of suspicion or reproof had come over breakfast, either. It was as if Lady Sidlow's will to scold had been broken.

The masquerade wasn't as risqué as it sounded. No one wore fancy dress, and the most potent drink was wine, which Grace Parker-Welby swore was wa-tered. Georgiana didn't mind; she always relished the chance to see some of her friends of slightly lower rank, like Grace, and dance with more élan than usual.

Tonight, though, she was on a mission, and af-ter an hour of chatting to friends, she spotted her quarry.

Sterling leaned in a doorway between salons, a glass dangling from his fingers. He looked flushed and brooding, and for a moment she felt a faint spark of appreciation. He was very handsome, and she'd loved him for so long.

After a few minutes she caught his eye. He went still, alert and startled. She gave a tiny smile and cocked her head questioningly. He nodded once, and walked off. Georgiana excused herself from Grace and the other young ladies, and followed.

She glimpsed Rob in the crowd, but resolutely looked away. They had decided, before he brought her home that morning, that their engagement should remain a secret for now. Neither had a solution to the Wakefield problem, but Georgiana had realized there was one way to discover more without too much trouble: her former fiancé.

Sterling disappeared down a long corridor, finally turning into a room. She made sure to compose herself before following. The small parlor was quiet and dim after the masquerade, even more so when Sterling closed the door behind her.

"Sterling." She managed a small smile. "Good evening."

"Georgiana." He took her hand, bringing it to his lips for a tender kiss. "It's good to see you."

She tugged free as gently as she could. "I hope you're well."

"Now that you're here, I am." He smiled at her, as warmly as he'd used to do.

Too late she realized what her actions might have implied. He thought she'd changed her mind. Georgiana eased back a step, hoping she hadn't made a dreadful mistake. "You've not told anyone our engagement is over," she blurted out. "I heard there was a scene at the Vega Club."

His smile faded. "Who told you that?"

"You know how rumor spreads," she said evasively. "So it's true, then?"

Sterling gazed at her. "Yes, I've not told anyone. It's not too late to reconsider."

She bit her lip. "Perhaps not, but I haven't changed my mind. I would never have done such a thing in the first place if I weren't entirely certain it was the right thing for both of us."

His eyes closed and he sighed, pacing away from her before swinging back. "Then why did you smile at me earlier? I've not heard anyone else speak of it, so you've not told people, either."

"I wanted to speak to you—"

"We were engaged to be *married*," he said with some despair, "till death did us part. Everything was splendid until you told me, all of a sudden, it wasn't. I loved you." He shook his head in confounded despair. "Now you want to talk?"

"It wasn't sudden," she said softly. "Not for me. I think you knew it, too, if you search your heart. I never wanted to hurt you. But Sterling . . . we would have been miserable. We might not have realized it for a year or more, but we would have. We were too comfortable apart, too happy spending all our time with others. And when we were together, our relationship was more like brother and sister."

He cocked one brow. "I never thought of you as a sister."

"Sooner or later one of us would have met someone who made us regret our marriage. Someday, you'll be very glad I did this."

"So that's it?" He put his hands on his hips and managed to look put out. "You've met someone else."

Georgiana pressed her lips closed. "My decision had nothing to do with anyone but you and me."

His jaw jutted out, and he nodded. "What did you want to discuss, then, if not resuming our engagement?"

"Alistair."

Sterling jerked. "Why?"

She was sure she didn't imagine his sudden tension. "Why could you and he not reach an agreement in the course of two years, if you wanted to marry me, your father approved, and Alistair knew my father would have approved?"

His gaze veered away. "He's not an easy fellow. Damned harsh negotiator." He gave a mirthless huff. "And I was a foolish one. If I'd just given way to his demands, we could have been married by now."

Thank goodness you didn't, thought Georgiana with a faint flush, remembering Rob's words the night before. When they were naked in his bed, marveling at how Alistair's obstinacy and Sterling's desire for a piece of land had given them the chance to fall in love with each other. "What did he demand?" she asked, instead of thanking him.

Sterling's eyes flitted to the door. "It changed. One month he'd want to pay the dowry in installments, the next month he'd offer it at once, but with more restrictions. Half in trust for children, things like that."

"Installments," she repeated, thinking of Lady Sidlow's confidence about the bills. "He's done something with my funds, hasn't he?"

This time there was no mistaking Sterling's discomfort. He retreated a step and looked away from her. "You shouldn't pry into it."

Georgiana let out an angry breath. So Lady Sidlow had been right—Alistair was short of funds, and he'd dipped into her inheritance. She followed Sterling, putting her hand on his arm when he would have backed away again. "He's trying to steal from me, isn't he? He would have cheated me—and you. Pretending to negotiate over that bit of land or how the dowry would be paid when he was really stalling. Tell me, Sterling," she insisted. "Please. For our lifelong affection for each other, for the friendship our fathers had, *please*."

He stared away from her, a muscle in his jaw flexing. "He invested it. Or perhaps he invested his own funds and lost them, then drew on yours to make up the loss, I don't know. He refused to agree to terms for so long, we almost came to blows before he admitted what he'd done. A trading venture, out of Liverpool. He dangled the prospect of that land in exchange for my waiting until the ships make enough trade runs to repay his capital—or *your* capital, I suppose. If he were to withdraw the investment now, he would take a large loss."

"Merchant trade?" Her brow wrinkled. That didn't sound like Alistair, who was contemptuous of anyone in trade. "It sounds quite risky. What if the ships sink?"

Sterling shrugged. "The cargo was insured. I had his word he would make the land your dowry if he lost the investment or couldn't redeem it. And I would have been content with that," he added quickly. "I *did* want to marry you. Land or money, either would have been sufficient."

"What company?" she asked.

Sterling blinked. "Why—?"

"I think I deserve to know where he invested my inheritance."

"Forester and Philips, I believe," Sterling said, with patent reluctance. "I know nothing about it except that he expects a handsome return."

"Thank you for telling me."

"What made you talk to him about it?" Sterling seemed to shake off his melancholy and grow more curious. "Every time I mentioned asking your opinion of something, he would snarl at me that he didn't care what you thought, nor should I."

A dull flush of anger rose in her chest. "He would say that," she muttered. "He's come to town. I did write to him, about ending our betrothal, but he arrived far too quickly. He must have been on his way when my letter found him."

"Yes." Sterling grimaced. "He told me he was coming—not pleased with something related to his investment, I gather. I've been avoiding him, to be perfectly honest." This smile was more like him, slyly charming. "After our last conversation, I rather thought I didn't have to subject myself to his tirades any longer."

She nodded solemnly. "Quite right. You're welcome."

"Thank you," he said without missing a beat. "Marvelous gift."

Georgiana laughed. Sterling grinned. "I wish you great happiness," she said on impulse, putting out her hand.

"I wanted it to be with you." He looked at her hand, then took it. "But I see it won't be. I wish the same to you, Georgie." He kissed her knuckles and released her.

"Find someone who's mad about you," she said, her voice wavering.

"As I trust you'll do, too, my dear." He gave her a wry smile, and left.

She stayed where she was, beginning to seethe over her brother again. Alistair, that despicable cretin, scorning her as too stupid and inconsequential to voice any opinion about her own marriage, while he *stole* her money and sank it into some foolish, risky venture. She would not give in to him; she would file suit in every court in England to get her inheritance from him until he was forced to hand it over, and she would demand an apology with it . . .

A sound behind her startled her out of her thoughts. She whirled around to see Rob, a fingertip to his lips as he gently closed the door. "I thought we weren't going to meet in public," she whispered as he crossed the room in two strides.

"We weren't," he said, cupping her face in his hands, "until I saw you follow Sterling in here." His mouth descended on hers, sinfully hot and hungry. Georgiana needed no prodding to kiss him back, until her head was spinning and her blood seemed to sizzle in her veins.

"There," he said softly. "That's what I needed."

"Did you doubt me?"

He grinned, resting his cheek against her temple. "Not a bit. I needed to know if you still made that entrancing little sigh when I kiss you."

Georgiana smiled, content to linger a moment. Wrapped in his arms, her head against his chest, she couldn't be angry even at Alistair. "Always."

He made a sound in his throat of fervent approval. "Why were you talking to Sterling? Was he unpleasant?"

"Hmm? Not at all." She raised her head to face him. "I asked him about my brother, and why the settlements had dragged on for so long. I thought he must know, or at least suspect. Alistair invested my dowry and then had to put Sterling off because he'd take a loss if he must pull the funds out soon. Sterling agreed to the delay on the condition he get a prime piece of land, bordering his family's estate." She paused. "Sterling kept that from me. He knew perfectly well why Alistair wouldn't come to terms, and he never told me. He waved it aside as Alistair being difficult, nothing for me to worry over and certainly nothing to be done about it."

"He's clearly not worthy of you," murmured Rob. "Where did Wakefield invest your funds?"

"Forester and Philips," she recited. "Sterling said it's a merchant in Liverpool. Twelve thousand pounds seems a very large investment, doesn't it?"

Rob's face had gone blank, then turned grim. "It does. And in that firm, it's a risky one as well."

"Why?"

"They trade in slaves."

Chapter 30

GEORGIANA RECOILED A step. "What? No, that's illegal—"

"Only if they get arrested. Until then it's very lucrative."

"And immoral!" she burst out. "Do you mean it? How do you know what that firm does? How do you *know*?"

"Shh." He glanced at the door. They were alone, but Georgiana had been gone a long time; someone might come looking for her at any moment. "This isn't the place to explain, but I do know that firm, and have very good reason to think they traffic in slaves—quite against the law," he added as she opened her mouth again. "But that doesn't stop some merchants and captains."

Georgiana felt sick. "He invested my inheritance in slaving?" Shaking her head, she backed away. "I know he's cold and callous but that's beyond bearing—"

Footsteps hurried past in the corridor outside, making them both freeze. Rob exhaled in relief as the person rushed by without pausing. "We have to meet somewhere else. It's not a brief story."

"I'll come to you again tonight," she said, but he shook his head.

"You shouldn't. Is there a friend who might help?"

She brightened. "Sophie! I trust her completely."

"Let me know the day and time and I'll be there." He caught her chin and pressed a quick kiss on her mouth. "I can't wait to do that without hiding away," he whispered, his lips lingering on hers.

Her own lips tingled. She smiled at him. "We don't need to keep it secret . . ."

"For now, let's." He kissed her once more. "Go back to the masquerade. Have your maid send the note via penny post so no one will see her at my house."

She nodded and slipped out the door after checking the corridor to be certain it was empty. She hurried back to the main rooms, turning over Rob's words in her mind.

Two days later, Rob approached Ware House from the mews behind it. A servant let him in and ushered him to a drawing room. Georgiana leapt to her feet at his entrance and ran to take his hand. She didn't throw herself into his arms, but as she smiled up at him, Rob thought she might have taken hold of his heart.

"Come meet Sophie." She led him to meet her friend, the duchess, a dark-haired woman with sharp eyes and a warm smile.

"We've met before," he said. "I daresay you may not remember, Your Grace—"

She laughed. "At the Vega Club! I do recall."

Kindly she said no more as they sat down. Rob knew he'd been rather notorious at the Vega Club, especially recently, and felt a prickle of remorse for some of his escapades.

The duchess poured him a cup of tea, and Georgiana moved to the edge of her seat. "What do you know about that company? And why?" she asked directly. "I've told Sophie everything I know and I shan't keep anything from her."

Rob grinned. "I supposed as much." He paused, getting his thoughts in line. "Forester and Philips is owned by the Forester family. Until recently the head was Mr. Henry Forester, a wily old devil whose only care was hoarding his fortune. He did excel at it, becoming one of the wealthiest merchants in Liverpool. But there is considerable evidence that he made that fortune in the slave trade."

"As repugnant as that is, it was perfectly legal until the last decade," said the duchess. "Ware procured a copy of the act to be certain. The Royal Navy patrols the seas to prevent it now."

Rob nodded. "Right. But it *is* illegal now, and Forester is still at it. The Royal Navy can't stop everyone. Even if they did, the consequences aren't harsh enough to deter Forester. Some within this government are still staunch supporters of slave trading and do everything they can to defend and protect those who skirt the act."

Georgiana put down her teacup and saucer with a loud clink. Her face was white.

"Nearly two years ago, Henry Forester died," Rob went on with the story. "His son Frederick inherited. Freddie's not like his father. He aspires to be a rakish rogue about town, and is a regular at the Vega Club. But he still owns the company, and they still sail in violation of the Slave Trade Act.

"A gentleman I'd rather not name is determined to put a stop to it. He's been aware of Forester and Philips for several years now, and has volumes of proof—reports of ships carrying manacles, fully outfitted for carrying human cargo. Captains with multiple flags and sets of papers, choosing which ones to show depending on whose treaty affords them more protection."

Georgiana's eyes were tightly closed, and her hands were in fists in her lap.

The duchess glanced at her in concern. "Are you well?" she asked gently.

Her eyes flew open. "Yes. Horrified, but I'm not about to faint, Sophie." Her friend smiled as she turned to Rob. "Why do you know all this?"

He cleared his throat, realizing how callous he was about to sound but unwilling to lie to her. "The gentleman who wishes to stop this activity has been frustrated in every attempt to hold Forester and Philips to account. He suspects Forester cultivated allies in Parliament—not that some of them don't support slave trading on their own—and may have offered shares in his company to align their interests with his. So this gentleman resorted to less direct methods in the hopes of stopping Forester. He . . . ah, he proposed that Lord Heathercote and I draw Mr. Forester into a rather debauched style of living and prod him to ruin at the gaming tables."

"That's it?" asked Georgiana after an expectant moment. "That's the plan?"

Rob shrugged. "Such as it was."

"Is it working?" The duchess looked doubtful.

"Heathercote claims it is. He says Forester has lost enough that he's had to recruit more investors."

"Like Alistair," said Georgiana softly.

Rob shook his head. "Freddie Forester wasn't in charge until his father died. If Alistair invested two years ago, it was with Henry Forester."

"Either way, he's profiting from slavery."

"With the funds he stole from me," murmured Georgiana.

Rob felt compelled to say, "Wakefield may not have known, explicitly, about the slave trading. Many companies don't speak of it; they engage in other trade and quietly run slaves as well."

"No, I expect he knew full well." Georgiana's eyes flashed. "You know my maid Nadine?"

"Yes." He remembered her, a dark-skinned young woman. He'd been grateful to her for riding with the driver when they left Osbourne House.

"Her grandparents were slaves on a sugar-cane plantation in Antigua owned by Alistair's grandfather—his mother's father. The plantation was part of her dowry, and had been in her family for decades. It—it included over three hundred slaves from Africa. My father sold the property after she died, and my mother urged him to free all the slaves held there. My mother's father was a Methodist and an abolitionist, and she persuaded my father that it was immoral. I don't remember any of this," she added. "I was an infant. But Nadine and her mother, among many others, came to Wakefield Manor as servants. A number of the freed people were in service there, when I was a child."

Rob let out his breath silently. God almighty. He

ought to have discovered that about Wakefield on his own.

"I told you Alistair hated my mother and me. I'm sure he blamed her for the loss of his *property*"—she spat out the word—"and I'm sure he saw my dowry as money that should have been his. So you see why I believe Alistair would invest in this—why he would put *my* inheritance into it. He would think it was his due."

"Does he still have freed people employed at Wakefield Manor?" Sophie asked. "How does he treat them?"

Georgiana hesitated. "I've barely spent a month there since I was eight years old. Nadine was sent to a neighboring family to be trained under that lady's maid, and only returned when I left Mrs. Upton's. I believe that after my father died, Mama pensioned off several of the servants—perhaps to protect them from Alistair." She bit her lip. "If you'd asked me before, I would have said that was the end of the matter. But it's not, is it? Even if Papa sold the plantation and freed his slaves, the new owner probably brought in more, purchased from people like Mr. Forester. The servants Mama wasn't able to pension off or find new situations for were left to Alistair's mercy. And I well know he has none."

They sat in silence for a moment. Rob was ashamed of his own rather cavalier approach to his role in this. He'd seen the pamphlet detailing the vicious treatment of both sailors and captives on board slave ships; he knew about the *Zong*, whose captain had cold-bloodedly flung a hundred living captives overboard to drown. He knew slavery was inhumane and barbarous.

But he'd not taken any action until offered an opportunity to be daring, at little inconvenience to himself. His family had never owned West Indies plantations, and the matter had never really touched him. The slave trade was illegal now. Like Georgiana, he'd thought it was settled.

"Your plan is mad, but it might work," said Georgiana at last. She looked at Rob. "Was Forester by any chance at the table the night you gambled with Charles Winston?"

He shifted in his seat uncomfortably. "Yes." He still hadn't told her what he'd done with that deed. "Not that I intended to win his house. He insisted on wagering it."

At last she laughed. "Of all the strange beginnings!"

Rob couldn't help grinning ruefully. He knew what she meant. If he'd not been trying to beggar Forester, they wouldn't have played so high that night, causing Winston to stake his deed, leading to Rob's impulsive jaunt into Derbyshire and the beating that changed his life. It wasn't remotely what he'd had in mind, but it was precisely what he'd needed.

"This plan is too uncertain," Georgiana continued, tapping one finger thoughtfully against her chin. "Even when Forester loses a great deal, he simply finds more investors and carries on."

Rob mentally totted up the sums he'd taken from Forester. It was a considerable amount—but as Georgiana noted, the man always had time to retrench and was still in business. "You're right," he said slowly. "To bankrupt him beyond saving, it must be done in one blow."

"How many people are involved?"

"Only Heathercote and I. The gentleman urging us on didn't want it to be widely known, for fear someone would give away the game."

"Well, that's up in smoke," said Georgiana under her breath. "I want to help."

"As do I," chimed in the duchess. "If you plan to ruin him at Vega's, I may be of some assistance."

Rob felt compelled to protest. "Thank you, Your Grace, but I did not intend to draw you into this."

"I'm not doing it for you," she said with a raised brow before turning to Georgiana. "If we succeed, it will also harm Wakefield. He will lose his investment—*your* inheritance. Even if you file a suit, if he's short of funds you may never have a dowry."

Georgiana's chin set. "Better that than Alistair use it for a vile purpose."

The duchess reached out, and Georgiana clasped her hand. For a moment the women exchanged such a look of determination, Rob was startled.

"Very well," he said, thinking quickly. "If we fill a table with conspirators and entice Forester to play deep, our chances improve. If we all play in concert—"

"And keep him playing long past prudence," put in the duchess. "You must swindle him without remorse."

"We can deal a devastating defeat." He began ticking off fingers. "Heathercote, I, Your Grace . . ."

"And I," declared Georgiana.

"Can you play loo?" asked the duchess with a dubious look.

"Of course!"

"Better than you could at Mrs. Upton's?"

Georgiana made a face at her friend, but her air of resolve didn't falter. "I can learn."

Chapter 31

"Do you really want to do this?" Sophie asked for the fifth time as they walked up the steps of the Vega Club.

"Absolutely," said Georgiana through the smile fixed on her lips. "It's worth a try. Do you think it's idiotic?"

"Either that, or brilliant, I can't quite decide. Good evening, Mr. Forbes," Sophie said to the man who opened the door at their approach but blinked in astonishment at the sight of them.

"Mrs. Campbell—I mean, Your Grace." The fellow bobbed his head hastily.

"Is Mr. Dashwood in?"

"Ah, madam, he requires an appointment," said Mr. Forbes apologetically. "And you're no longer a member."

"I was hoping he might make an exception. Would you be so kind as to ask him?"

Mr. Forbes glanced at Georgiana, who gave him a polite nod. "On what matter?"

"A desperately important one." Sophie glanced at

Georgiana. "It involves this lady, which is why I've brought her."

The man glanced at her again. "You know the rules, Your Grace. Send a note and make an appointment."

"No," said Sophie firmly. "We'll wait for him to have a moment free."

He sighed. "He won't see you." But he turned and disappeared through a door off to the side.

"That is the manager," whispered Sophie. "Another useful ally."

"He doesn't seem to be on our side," she replied.

They waited only a few minutes, though, before the manager returned. "This way." He held the door open, and Georgiana followed Sophie through.

Mr. Dashwood was a tall, lean fellow with a sharply angular face. One could tell by looking at him that he was not a gentleman, even though he was exquisitely dressed.

"Mr. Dashwood," said Sophie warmly. "Thank you for seeing me."

"Of course, Your Grace." His expression betrayed nothing as he bowed. "Forbes said it was a desperately important matter that brings you."

"I would like to be readmitted to the club," said Sophie. "And to bring my friend as my guest."

"One thing I do not do," said Dashwood, "is admit single ladies."

"I'm engaged," said Georgiana quickly, wondering how he knew she was unmarried. "To a member of the club."

"When you are married, you shall be welcome to apply for membership. Good day, Your Grace, my lady." He looked at the door in dismissal.

Georgiana took a fortifying breath. "Mr. Dashwood, please reconsider. We need to ruin someone."

His brow quirked, but no other sign of emotion crossed his face. "Not in my club."

"No? You limit what members are permitted to wager?"

"In some instances." He glanced at Sophie. "I trust you remember that."

Georgiana was interested to see a spot of color bloom in her friend's cheek. "I do, and this is nothing in that line."

"Perhaps I should have said, we wish to *try* to ruin someone," Georgiana amended. "There is every chance we may fail. If that happens, we'll accept the consequences and not trouble you any longer."

He sighed. "Everyone here is trying to ruin someone. They don't usually announce it to me beforehand, however. Why are you here?"

Georgiana moved to the edge of her seat. "To beg, if necessary. The person we're after . . . There aren't many ways women can confront a man and triumph over him in this way, and your club is one of the few places in London where the sexes are admitted on equal terms. All I ask is one night only, as a visitor."

He gave a tiny shake of his head.

"He is a criminal, but the government cannot or will not bring him to justice," she said in increasing desperation. "If he suffers a large loss, he'll no longer be able to flout the law. Mr. Dashwood, he's trading in *slaves*—illegally and immorally, but there is no way to touch him other than this. He comes here with his filthy fortune, using the Vega Club to support his vile business and his evil self. The only way to stop him is to bankrupt him. Please, sir."

For a long moment Mr. Dashwood stared at her, his face hard and inscrutable. "Very well," he said abruptly. His expression had not changed. "You may have one night. Your Grace, I will readmit you for one month. Shall I extend the same to His Grace?"

"Yes," said Sophie, looking just as astonished as Georgiana felt at this sudden approval. "Thank you."

"Don't thank me." He opened the door in dismissal. "Aim well, and don't miss," he added as they walked past him.

"What did he mean?" Georgiana whispered as they hurried down the corridor toward the club lobby.

"He means that if we try to strike down Forester, we must succeed."

"Of course we must!"

"Yes," said Sophie, "but it won't be simple. You know that, Georgiana?"

She thought of her brother, with his fury-bright eyes and stony heart. She remembered the silence of his servants, black and white, and the vague air of menace that shrouded Wakefield Manor. She thought of her inheritance, money left for her comfort and subsistence by her kind and loving papa, being used to snatch girls like Nadine from their homes and sell them into the living hell of slavery. Forester deserved to be ruined for his role, but Georgiana hoped it was deeply damaging to Alistair as well. "I know," she said soberly, "but it's worth the risk."

They returned to Ware House. Lady Sidlow had

given permission for her to spend a week there, Nadine in tow. Georgiana suspected the woman had sunk into a melancholy, after Alistair's visit, but there was nothing she could do about that now.

A few questions had elicited the information that her brother intended to remain in town only a fortnight more, if that long. Selfishly, Georgiana wanted him to learn of his investment's loss while in London. She wanted to see his face when he realized all was lost, that he still owed her twelve thousand pounds, and she burned to tell him she would be filing a suit to claim it, even if she must hound him for the next twenty years.

In the salon, Sophie set up a table with cards for practice. Rob came, slipping in through the servants' entrance every time, and Lord Philip Lindeville, Sophie's brother-in-law, joined them. He was assigned the role of Forester in their rehearsals.

"You always make me the villain," he lamented to Sophie.

"It's because you're a better player than Jack," she returned, naming her husband the duke, who was known to disapprove of gambling. She was shuffling the cards, sending them flying from one hand to the other. Georgiana was entranced. She'd known her friend supported herself at the gaming tables, but she'd not seen her at it since Sophie's last year at Mrs. Upton's, some six years ago.

Lord Philip laughed. "I'm *much* better than Jack!"

Georgiana knew how to play loo, of course, but she'd never played unlimited loo, where the amount at stake could quickly spiral into enormous sums. If a player failed to take a single trick in a hand, he got loo'd—forced to pay the pot an amount equal to the sum already in the pot. The amounts climbed with dizzying speed.

"I always avoided loo," confided Sophie, "but if you want to stick someone with a staggering loss at cards, this is the way to do it."

Rob, despite a generally careless demeanor while playing, won well over half of the time. Sophie won most of the rest, and Lord Philip managed to take a few pots as well. "I'd like to make clear that I am not trying very hard," he would announce as Rob won yet another round, causing Sophie to snort with laughter.

Georgiana was far out of her depth. She enjoyed cards but she didn't have Sophie's head for numbers, or Rob's instinct for the game. She thought she could beat Lord Philip from time to time, because he sometimes played carelessly, but deep down she knew she would have to leave the actual playing to her friends. It galled her that someone else would have to ruin Forester, and thus Alistair, but she reminded herself that the important point was that it happen, and who played the final, triumphant card did not matter.

The Duke of Ware came in at some point, watching in silence. Sophie told him their latest ideas, since he knew the gist of it already.

"Yes," he said when she had finished. "I understand the difficulties. Nevertheless . . . is this the only way?"

Sophie put down her cards. "No, but it is the cleverest and quickest."

Her husband nodded, his chin in his hand. "Except for the chance you'll lose. If you lose, and he wins . . ."

Georgiana wet her lips. "We'll have made it even more possible for him to support that abominable business."

The duke looked at her with sympathy in his blue eyes. "Yes."

"Well then," said Sophie firmly, "we must not lose. I believe we can fill the table sufficiently that, between us, we shall manage it. Lord Westmorland is exceedingly good at loo."

The duke glanced at Rob, and Georgiana thought it was not a happy glance. "That may be, but others . . ." His eyes traveled to her. ". . . are not as experienced."

She sighed. If the duke could tell in a few minutes, it would be obvious to anyone. "That is fair. I—I have been thinking that I ought to leave the play to the rest of you." She laid down her cards, hating to ask this of her friends but knowing she wasn't going to help by insisting she play. "I'm not very good."

"Nonsense," said Rob. "You'll be good enough."

The duke glanced at him again. "Dashwood has a low tolerance for suspicious play. If Georgiana joins the table, a novice gambler against cardsharps, he'll listen to Forester's inevitable charges that something isn't right."

Sophie looked at her in dismay, but Georgiana shook her head. "He's right. It's more important to do this right than to insist I do it myself."

"I'll fill out the table," said Rob. "Fellows who will play high and recklessly."

"Right, then." Lord Philip got up and stretched. "I need some tea to continue my false villainy." Sophie laughed and rose as well, ringing for the maid.

Rob leaned toward Georgiana. "Don't let Ware bully you out of it," he said softly.

She shook her head. "He hasn't. I can't hold a candle to Sophie, let alone to you." She gave him a mock look of amazement. "It's a bit alarming how good you are at this . . ."

He grinned, reaching out to run his fingertips over the back of her hand. "A man of many talents, my love."

She laughed. "Well do I know it!"

"And the sooner we conclude this trouble with Wakefield and Forester, the sooner I may demonstrate the more delightful of them," he added in a wicked growl.

Georgiana blushed even as her heart jumped in anticipation. "I can't wait."

Chapter 32

THE LARGEST TABLE at Vega's sat eight players. Aside from himself and Forester, Rob needed to fill six chairs with conspirators. He couldn't risk an idiot like Charles Winston spoiling things.

Heath would play, of course; not only was it his mission in the first place, the man could count cards after a whole bottle of whisky. The Duchess of Ware took another seat, and Lord Philip had agreed to play. He said he was well-practiced at losing to Rob and could carry on with no trouble at all. Marlow and Sackville were reliable, as well as customary members of Rob's set. Ware's words about raising Forester's suspicions were sobering, and Rob didn't want to risk that.

Telling Heath was a delicate business. His friend was furious that Rob had told so many other people, but came around as Rob pointed out all the ways this plan was far more formidable than the original.

"I suppose it doesn't really matter who does it," Heath finally said. "If the duchess will help, I can't say no."

The final member was a bit surprising to Rob.

Neither he nor Heath could name a truly suitable candidate, until Tom came in as he and Heath were plotting. "I'll play," he volunteered after hearing a bit of their dilemma.

Rob raised his brows. After the sunrise ride with Georgiana, Tom had mostly given up dogging his heels. Rob wasn't sure if this marked his brother's approval, or if Tom had simply found more pleasurable pursuits, loosed in London from his regimental restraint. "Finally done being a jealous nursemaid?"

His brother grinned. "Once you turned into a sentimental bore, yes."

"What's that?" Heath wanted to know.

Rob waved it away. He had stuck to Forester and the fault in their original plan, leaving out Georgiana. "Tom's running his mouth. We need to make certain Forester will attend . . ."

The night was fixed for two days hence. Rob arrived after ten along with Heath, Marlow, and Sackville, who were all fully informed and carrying on as they usually did. Wanting a clear head, Rob had drunk far less than usual, and was slightly taken aback by how loud they were. Heath had arranged to let Forester know of their plans, and Tom and Philip were to meet them at Vega's. The duchess would arrive last of all, when Forester was already hooked.

Things went wrong almost from the start. Heath boldly commandeered the table, chasing away a few fellows dicing there. This time Forbes didn't say a word. Rob thought perhaps he had been put on guard to expect something. Georgiana and the duchess had visited the club to reopen the duchess's membership, and Georgiana had told Dashwood what they wanted to do. None of them was cheating, and yet it made him very conscious that the club owner knew they were playing with coordinated, cold-blooded intent to ruin another member.

Tom arrived on time, taking a bow as Marlow whistled in appreciation at the lurid yellowish-purple remnants of the black eye he'd got at Vega's several days earlier. A few members, sensing high stakes, prowled about eagerly, but Heath repelled them with a ruthless mixture of mockery and arrogance, earning him a few scowls. Rob watched as they stalked off in high dudgeon; it was for their own good, poor fools. Let them ask Charles Winston.

"I say, Marlow, shall I join you?"

Startled, Rob looked up into the smug face of Lord Sterling. Sure of his welcome, he had already pulled out a chair before Rob managed to kick Heath's foot. "Not tonight, Sterling," barked Heath.

"Yes, we've limited it to honest fellows tonight," drawled Tom. "Sorry, old chap."

Sterling glared at Tom, who replied by blowing a thin stream of smoke from the cigar he'd just lit in Sterling's direction. "Forgive me, Marlow. I didn't notice your companions. I shall seek more congenial company."

"Aye, and tell the waiter to bring us another bottle of port while you're there," added Rob carelessly, unable to resist pricking the fellow's pride a bit. Sterling gave him a poisonous glare and strode off.

Rob didn't care. Georgiana would be here soon, and the last thing they needed was a scene. He had a feeling Sterling would take umbrage at her presence.

"Good evening, gentlemen!" Freddie Forester appeared, rubbing his hands in anticipation. "I trust you've all come with ready money to lose."

They laughed. Tom offered him a cigar, which Forester took with pleasure. Rob caught sight of Philip Lindeville, making his way toward them. The duchess was to arrive on his heels. Rob signaled to the dealer to shuffle.

And then a slim, dark figure stopped behind one of the two vacant seats. Forester shot to his feet. "Lord Wakefield!" Turning to the table he almost puffed out his chest with pride. "Your pardon, gentlemen. Wakefield is one of my business associates."

Rob studied Georgiana's brother with covert interest. Wakefield was a spare fellow of about medium height, his clothing as somber as a judge's, dark hair cropped close to his scalp. He had a long, pointed nose and a small mouth, and pale blue eyes that seemed to be made of ice.

"Ballocks," whispered Heath beside him. "Jack Ketch has come to Vega's."

On the other side of him, Marlow snorted into his wine at the reference to the hangman. Rob's lip curled as well. It was an apt description.

Wakefield's chilly gaze veered to Marlow, then back. "I want a word, Forester."

"Of course," declared Forester heartily, "but we're about to play a few hands."

Damn. First Sterling, now Wakefield. Rob tried not to react to the stirring of alarm that Georgiana would be walking in with no idea either of them was there. Heath was looking sideways at him for guidance; Tom was silent, focused wholly on Wakefield.

"I do not wish to wait all night," Wakefield said in a slow, furious voice to Forester. "If you please, sir . . ."

"I say," said Philip, finally reaching the table. "Shall I join you, Heath?" He looked Wakefield up and down. "Pardon me, old fellow." He pulled out a chair and dropped into it.

"As you can see, Wakefield," said Forester, obviously loath to relinquish his seat, "the play shall be excellent. I know you fancy cards. Join us!"

Bloody hell. "If he doesn't want to play," drawled Rob, "let him go, Forester. Don't plague a man."

But instead of leaving, Wakefield turned toward him with a curiously hostile stare. Rob stared back boldly, almost insolently, but inside he seethed at the thought of that man having Georgiana—or anyone—in his power. He was here to ruin Forester for principle, but he wouldn't have minded thrashing Wakefield just for sport.

And then Wakefield pulled out the chair beside Forester and sat.

GEORGIANA'S NERVES WERE WOUND tight with anticipation and anxiety.

On one hand, she would see the vaunted gaming room at the most infamous gambling establishment in London. Under normal circumstances she'd never be let through the doors, and even if she applied as a married woman, she wasn't sure she'd have the audacity to go.

On the other hand, it would not be a pleasure visit. She had great confidence in Sophie and Rob, but she was under no illusion that success was certain. Cards were fickle things, as Sophie had often told her, and a bad run of hands could lead to the exact opposite result from the one they wanted.

"Thank you for doing this, Sophie," she said.

In the dim carriage, her friend smiled. "Of course! How many times did you divert Mrs. Upton when I was sneaking back in from dicing in the stables?"

She had to laugh. That had been Sophie's only pin money at school. "I wonder how much she ever believed."

"You told her once you'd felt a tremor in the earth, and wondered if a volcano might be forming in Watley," said Sophie dryly. "I can't believe she let you finish the tale."

Georgiana laughed. "That was one of my better ideas. Of course, then I had to endure a lecture on volcanoes . . ."

"It's a miracle she didn't toss us out."

"Now we're top graduates of her academy," she said, causing her friend to burst into laughter.

"Oh, Georgiana," Sophie gasped, wiping her eyes. "I've missed you so."

"And I you." She grinned. "If we survive tonight, it will be our greatest caper yet."

They had reached the club. Georgiana jumped down first, but Sophie caught her breath as she stepped out. "Are you all right?" whispered Georgiana, eyes on the elegant, unremarkable facade of the club.

"Just a twinge," Sophie whispered back, pressing one hand to her side with a wince. "I—I'm with child."

Georgiana whirled to gape at her, but Sophie put a finger to her lips. "Don't say a word," she said firmly. "Yes, Jack knows. No, he didn't stop me from coming tonight. Yes, I will be absolutely fine. Shall we go in?"

"Well—all right," said Georgiana, disconcerted.

She'd seen the lobby in daylight, but at night the club glittered. Crystal chandeliers with dozens of candles illuminated the room, ringed by potted palms at strategic intervals. The guests were as elegantly dressed as they would be at any ball, although the men far outnumbered the ladies. She couldn't stop herself from craning her neck to see as much as possible, knowing it might be her only opportunity.

Sophie strolled through the club, speaking to several people who exclaimed to see her there again. She introduced Georgiana as her special guest, with Mr. Dashwood's permission. It was rather overwhelming, but also a magnificent joke, in a way. Gentlemen who knew her from more respectable venues gazed at her in shock, and the few ladies looked scandalized—an odd look on a woman playing faro, Georgiana thought. Still, for a moment, she couldn't resist enjoying it.

It wasn't until they reached the far end of the room that she spotted Rob. He sat at a large oval table with a green felted top. She recognized Lord Philip across from him, and Viscount Heathercote beside him.

"Georgiana!" She almost leapt from her skin at the sound of her name, and then blanched as she recognized the speaker.

"Sterling," she said as brightly as she could manage. "How lovely to see you." She held out her hand.

He stared incredulously. "What are you doing here?"

"I came with Sophie, as you see."

Sterling flushed, and jerked his head in Sophie's direction. "Your Grace. May I have a word with Lady Georgiana?"

Sophie looked to her. "Of course," Georgiana said quickly, adding to her friend in an undertone, "I'll just be a moment."

Sterling took her hand and hurried her away, into a sheltered area behind some potted palms. "What are you doing here?"

"I told you, I'm with Sophie. Tonight only." She looked around with real interest. "I've long wondered about the famous Vega Club."

"What is *she* doing here? She's not a member now."

"She is! She requested a renewed membership and Mr. Dashwood granted it."

He ran his hand over his head. "Georgiana. I know you better than that."

She raised her brows. "Do you? Then you know I won't be deterred by your fit of hysteria."

"That is not what this is," he whispered furiously. "You're an unmarried lady!"

"I assure you, unmarried ladies can withstand the same sights as unmarried gentlemen. And in any event, you have no right to tell me what to do." She slid her hand free of his grasp.

Sterling expelled a frustrated breath. "Very well. I shall warn you that someone who does have that right is here"—Georgiana started, thinking he had guessed about Rob—"and he looks in an ill temper," Sterling finished grimly. "I saw Wakefield arrive not long ago."

Her heart thudded. "I didn't know he was a member . . ."

Sterling flipped one hand. "I doubt it. He's probably here as a guest. But if he sees you, Georgiana—"

He'd send her and Nadine home to Yorkshire, probably this very night. She'd sworn to Nadine that wouldn't happen. She swallowed her alarm; Nadine was safe at Ware House, and she had friends here to prevent him doing anything to her. "Thank you for telling me."

He gazed at her with concern. "I don't like this. Whatever you're up to, you're playing with fire."

Yes. But she did not intend for it to consume anyone other than Alistair and Mr. Forester. "I know," she told Sterling. "And I'm not afraid."

ROB WAS RELIEVED WHEN the Duchess of Ware arrived, but only for a moment; contrary to plan, Georgiana was not with her. Her eyes met his for the barest moment, and then she spoke to Philip. She didn't seem alarmed, so he told himself to relax.

She inserted herself into the game beautifully. Philip wagered high and lost in the next hand, and she teased him lightly. Philip made a face and said he wasn't doing so badly. Then he lost again. Philip made a show of mourning his small number of markers before rising. "I'm out, chaps." He made a show of offering her his chair. "Would you care to take my place, Your Grace?"

She took the seat with a smile. "Your best play of the night, Lindeville," Marlow said to Philip, as Georgiana appeared at last.

She came to stand silently behind the duchess, but Wakefield caught sight of her and went white with unmistakable fury. Rob tensed to intervene, but Georgiana was poised. "Good evening, sir," she told him, dipping a polite curtsy.

"Bless my soul," said Sackville in an awed voice. "This evening improves by leaps and bounds! Good evening, Lady Georgiana."

"If only you'd come sooner," exclaimed Philip with a neat bow. "My luck surely would have turned."

"Such beauty might prove more of a distraction than anything," said Forester with an ingratiating smile. Rob fought back a scowl at the way the man's eyes moved over her.

Tom stubbed out his cigar. "The last thing you need is distraction, Forester. And if you mean to keep playing, Wakefield, sit down."

The earl had risen, his hands flat on the table. His glare at Georgiana was positively murderous. "Females," he said through his teeth, "do not belong in a gaming establishment."

"Goodness," said the duchess lightly. "One might think the gentlemen are frightened of losing to a woman, if they want us excluded."

Wakefield's eyelid twitched. Philip laughed. "Is that it, Wakefield? I'll take your place if you're upset. She's a better player than most of you lot."

Slowly the man sank back down, to Rob's disappointment. As much as he would have enjoyed ruining Wakefield, too, it was better to have control of the table. "Deal," snarled Wakefield.

Rob opened with a high ante. The duchess quirked a brow and made a smart comment, but she played along with him, and then everyone else had to as well. Marlow lost and paid the pot with a string of curses he abruptly choked back, looking at the duchess.

"That's the trouble with letting women play," muttered Wakefield.

She smiled. "I assure you, I've heard all those words and survived the experience."

"Nevertheless," he said acidly, "a man cannot speak them in the presence of a lady. What sort of club is this?"

"She's been a member here longer than you have," said Philip. "Ah—I beg your pardon, sir, you're not a member, are you?"

Wakefield went rigid. He started to rise. "Insolent little . . ."

"Is there a problem?" Mr. Dashwood had appeared, as silent as a ghost. He turned to Wakefield. "Have you a complaint, my lord?"

A vein throbbed in the earl's forehead. "Women gambling with men is appalling. One bad hand and we'll be treated to a case of hysteria and tears."

"I doubt it. Of course, you are welcome at the hazard table. I do not believe any ladies are playing there at the moment."

Again Rob hoped he would go, but again Wakefield kept his seat, scowling furiously at his cards.

"Very good, sir." Dashwood nodded to the dealer to proceed.

The pot grew by leaps and bounds. Rob made sure to lose one round to drive the pot higher. Wakefield lost, then Forester. Marlow staved off a loss only because he held the top trump in a hand of worthless cards. The depressed basin in the center of the table filled with markers. With every hand, Rob saw Georgiana's face. Her eyes were wide and anxious as she watched. Once when Rob glanced at her, the Duke of Ware was beside her, silent and watchful.

Because most people at the table were playing in concert, they made Forester lose again. His eyes darted from the pot to his markers, and Rob realized Forester had lost more than he had. Forester had to pay the pot, and if he folded he would lose everything he'd put in. That was how loo ruined men; once they had risked too much, their only hope was to stay in and pray their luck turned.

"Problem, Forester?" Heath asked.

The man cleared his throat. "Er—yes. I . . . I seem in need of more markers."

Heath made a noise of impatience. "Go on, then. Sackville, note how much he's lost, he can pay up tomorrow. Lindeville, do you still want to play?"

Forester yanked his gaze from the pot, brimming with his markers, to Philip. "I'm not bowing out!"

Sackville snorted. "No more markers, no more cards. We're not a charitable institution."

"I'll get more!" Forester insisted. "I—I have to request credit, but I'm not bowing out."

"Then pay the pot," said Rob. "Just not with a property deed," he added, causing guffaws from Marlow and Sackville, who'd seen him win Winston's deed but been treated to a highly fictional account of his trip into Derbyshire.

Forester took the bait. His face brightened. "I'll stake shares of my company."

Rob's heart leapt. Beside him, Heath tensed in excitement. Lord Wakefield growled something to Forester, who waved it away as he beckoned a waiter to bring paper and pen.

"Shares," said Rob dubiously. "What are those worth?"

"One hundred shares will amply cover my debt to the pot."

"What sort of company is it?" asked Tom with a frown. "Can't spend your shares at Tattersall's, after all."

Flushed with triumph now, Forester signed his name to the promissory note and added it to the pot. "A shipping company, my lord. Very profitable. I'll redeem them, of course." Wakefield glowered at him, and Rob suspected the earl knew it would be with investor funds.

But now . . . now they had him, and his company. Forester took up his next hand with renewed spirits, laughing and ordering another bottle of port. Rob laughed with the rest, and opened the next round with an ante of five thousand pounds, the highest of the night. *Keep him playing past prudence*, the duchess had said. He could do that. And now that he'd got used to it, Forester added more shares to the pot.

After the next round, though, the duchess put one hand to her mouth, looking distinctly queasy. Ware bent down. "Are you well, my dear?"

"Yes." She cleared her throat and took a tiny sip of her drink. "Perfectly."

The duke frowned. He muttered something to his brother, who hurried away. They played on, but a few minutes later the duchess put her head in her hands.

"Sophie," said the duke under his breath.

She looked up, as pale as milk and her eyes glassy. "Yes—I—perhaps I need some fresh air," she said unsteadily as her husband helped her to her feet. "Gentlemen, please excuse me . . ."

"Are you bowing out?" asked Heath. A large stack of markers stood before her.

The duchess looked at Georgiana in apology. She was a strong player, and had helped push the games in the direction they wanted. Rob took a drink of wine to cover his unease. Damn. Where had Philip gone? He was nothing to the duchess, but he knew what they were attempting and they needed another player . . .

"I'll play," Georgiana blurted out in the silence.

Wakefield all but erupted from his seat. "You will not! Close your mouth and remember your place!"

"Lord Wakefield," said Dashwood in a quiet but steely voice. The table fell silent. "She is a guest for tonight, with as much right to play as you have. Has anyone any objection to her participation?"

Wakefield glared at Georgiana as if he'd like to strangle her.

"Not I," said Tom.

"Not I," Heath echoed, his glance flickering toward Rob, who didn't dare say anything.

Forester shrugged. Wakefield stood angrily for a moment, but then sank into his chair, his expression malevolent.

Mr. Dashwood circled the table. "Go on, Carter. I'll take this one."

To Rob's shock the club owner took the dealer's seat himself. Heath glanced at him in worry. Rob didn't know whether to abandon the plan for the night, or plow onward. He'd never seen Dashwood participate in play. Was he displeased?

Dashwood took up the cards, which seemed to come alive in his long-fingered hands. "Are you in, my lady?"

Rob glanced at Georgiana. Wide-eyed, she gave a tiny nod. "Yes."

Georgiana took the seat, and Dashwood dealt.

GOOD HEAVENS ABOVE, WHAT had she done?

Georgiana could barely breathe past the furious pounding of her heart. Sophie had planned to do this, Sophie who could track every card in a deck and who knew the odds of every play. But now Sophie was ill, being led out by her husband, and Georgiana would have to do it.

"What are trumps?" she asked, more to get over her nerves than anything else.

Rob's eyes met hers. "Hearts."

She nodded and took up her cards. They were decent, and with some relief she played the hand well.

She didn't know how long they played. Her knuckles grew stiff from gripping her cards. *Don't lose*, she kept repeating inside her head. She didn't have to win, but she didn't want to lose. Miraculously her cards continued to fall, if not brilliantly, then at least well enough. She was quick to fold if they didn't.

"This will be the final deal," announced Mr. Dashwood at last.

"No," Forester exclaimed, staring at the overflowing pot with frantic eyes. "Not yet!" It would be split equally among the players according to how many tricks they took. Alistair had also lost recently, and only a handful of markers remained at his place, but Forester had staked hundreds of shares in his company.

"It will be, sir," replied the owner, implacable. "The house closes at four o'clock." He shuffled the cards another time and dealt.

Georgiana was going to fold. So far she'd managed not to lose, but neither had she won. The pot was obscenely large. Her head ached from the strain of trying to keep up, and her bodice was damp with nervous perspiration. *Take the cards and fold*, she told herself. Let Rob or Heath or anyone else finish off Forester. The man had scribbled several notes for shares, and those slips of paper in the mound of markers gleamed white with the promise of his ruin.

But when Georgiana took up her cards, she almost choked. It was the best hand she'd had all night—the best hand she'd held in her life. Hardly breathing, she stared at the cards until they blurred.

And when her turn came, instead of folding, she played the ace of diamonds, and held her breath until the trick went to her. The next round, she won with the ten of hearts, to her astonishment. Lord Marlow gave a low whistle and joked about lady luck. Forester hunched over his cards, his breathing audible to all. A hard line creased Alistair's forehead.

The next round fell to her queen of hearts. Forester went pasty pale, as he'd had the jack. She played the king in the next hand, stealing a trick from Rob, who'd played the ace of spades. He muttered to Heathercote, sounding disgruntled, but when she glanced at him, he winked.

It was the final hand. Georgiana looked at the last card in her hand: Pam, the jack of clubs. The top trump card in loo, the card that beat all the others. She laid it down without a word when it was her turn. If anyone else spoke, she couldn't hear it over the roaring in her ears.

She'd won the entire pot.

Chapter 33

꧁ ꧂

"I'LL BE DAMNED," murmured Tom.

"Well done, ma'am," cried Marlow, pounding the table.

Forester shot to his feet, gripping the edge of the table as he surveyed the cards. He looked dazed, but fury was bubbling through. "No," he said thickly. "*No! That's—that's—she cheated!*"

The table fell silent. Mr. Dashwood rose, wearing the same bland expression he'd worn all night. "Have a care, Mr. Forester. Do not make accusations you cannot prove."

"Of course there was fraud." Wakefield came to Forester's defense. His burning eyes jumped from the pot to the club owner to Georgiana. "She's not a gambler. She ought not to be at the tables in the first place. For a girl to beat all these practiced gamblers?" His scornful gaze raked the table. "Something's afoot."

Heathercote scoffed. "Which is she? An inexperienced girl, or a cheat so skilled none of us saw her do it?"

"Anyone watching her face could see that she

wasn't cheating. I knew she had a high hand the moment she picked up her cards. You've fallen prey to beginner's luck," added Tom.

"No," Forester insisted. "She had to cheat!"

Mr. Dashwood clasped his hands behind him. "How, sir?" Forester blinked at him. "Are you accusing me?" prompted the owner in a terrifyingly soft voice.

Wakefield snorted. "Perhaps he is. What sort of establishment do you operate?"

Mr. Dashwood gazed at him. Forester jerked out of his daze. "No! No, of course I'm not accusing you, Mr. Dashwood . . . I just . . ." His gaze went to the pot, this time with despair, before he turned to Georgiana. "My lady, surely you will have some compassion. I became overheated in the moment, and wagered rashly. I trust you'll be good enough to give me time to redeem my notes . . ."

"Don't be a fool." Wakefield's disdainful glance took in his business partner and his sister. "She's going to give them back."

Rob laughed. "Give it back? This wasn't a ladies' tea, Wakefield. *I* wouldn't give them back, and I don't think you'd ask it of me."

"No one made Forester wager those chits," said Heath in scorn. "He insisted."

"Be a man," muttered Marlow.

Wakefield's eyes narrowed at Rob. "You called on her the other day, Westmorland. Without my permission. Whatever your hopes there, they are futile." He turned to Georgiana. "She is under my guardianship, and I am removing her from this cursed club."

Georgiana shot to her feet. "No." She kept her attention on her brother, but over his shoulder she could see Rob and his brother, frozen in identical positions half out of their seats, poised to come to her aid. Her heart swelled to see them, ready but waiting for her. "I am not going with you," she told Alistair. "Not tonight, not *ever*. I am of age, and I can live where I choose, and receive the callers I choose." She glimpsed the pot again, and added, "And I'm *keeping* what I won tonight."

He stepped insultingly close. "You're not," he whispered. "Was this display meant to annoy me? I don't appreciate it." He shook his head. "Come. You've humiliated yourself and me enough."

"You've humiliated yourself," she replied. "And your investment, which you came to London to safeguard, was just wagered away by Mr. Forester. You did invest in his company, didn't you? With my funds, I believe. I've retained a solicitor to investigate." Alistair's face contorted and he made a threatening motion before he checked himself, but not before she flinched. Vibrating with anger, Georgiana glanced at Mr. Dashwood. "You require members to pay their debts, don't you?"

"I do," he said evenly. "Mr. Forester, transfer the shares to Lady Georgiana on the morrow or lose your membership."

Forester looked positively green. "Of course," he whispered.

Dashwood nodded once. "Lord Wakefield, if you lay a hand on a female guest at my club, I'll see you thrown out and delivered to gaol." He glanced at Georgiana, and she almost thought he winked at her. "Well played, my lady. Good evening."

"I've a carriage waiting for you, Lord Wakefield," said Mr. Forbes, the burly manager. White-lipped,

Alistair brushed past her. She didn't hear what he said in a low growl; she could barely hear anything.

She started when Rob took her hand. "Did we—was it enough?"

"Enough?" His eyes danced. "Not only is there close to eighty thousand pounds in the pot, there are hundreds of shares of Forester and Philips. My darling, you may own the company."

"Which means . . ." She could barely speak.

He nodded. "You can close it down."

Lord Heathercote came around the table and bowed to her, sweeping her limp hand to his lips. "A bravura performance, ma'am," he said grandly. "I'm quite tempted to fall to one knee and beg for your hand." He glanced slyly at Rob. "Perhaps another day. But I applaud you for your excellent play."

She gave a shaky laugh and caught sight of Sterling, watching her from a few yards away, leaning against a table with his arms folded. Sobered, she walked to face him.

He regarded her quizzically. "Impressive."

She flushed. "Thank you for telling me Alistair had invested my money with that vile man. Do you know what his company does?"

He sighed. "I've heard rumors. But *you*." He shook his head. "Have you nothing to tell me?"

She blinked. "What?"

Sterling glanced over her shoulder at Rob. "Charles Winston lost his deed to Westmorland, the deed to the house you were visiting at the time. Westmorland then disappeared from town, and Winston worried he'd gone into Derbyshire to see the house, but then it seemed he hadn't. Westmorland did, however, turn up in London not long after you came back, earlier than expected, along with his brother, who was curiously belligerent about our betrothal. Tonight I learned Westmorland called on you the other day, and when Wakefield tried to refuse him a few minutes ago, you told your brother off as I've never seen before. I'm not the brightest chap but I'm not an idiot." He gave her a wry look. "Have you *nothing* to tell me?"

She fidgeted, then gave in. "Perhaps something. Lord Westmorland did come to Kitty's house, but he was beaten and left in the road to die. I—I nursed him back to health."

Sterling shook his head. "You couldn't leave him to rot in the road, could you?"

"No."

He looked at Rob again. "I should call him out."

"Don't you dare!" she exclaimed. "If you want to call out someone, it should be me. But Sterling . . . he's not why I broke off our engagement. I hope you can believe me, because it's true."

"I still don't like the fellow," he muttered, then heaved a sigh. "I wish you great joy, even with a rogue like Westmorland."

Her smile was wide with relief. "Thank you, Sterling."

He bowed his head and walked off.

Rob came up beside her. "He took it well."

"I knew he would." She turned to him. "And now I feel completely free, since I've won back my inheritance—"

"Several times over," he murmured.

"—and Lord Heathercote has got Forester in a vise. Sterling knows about you, and I've told off my brother." She sighed. "Now what shall I do? I've lost my longtime fiancé, my house in London, my home in Yorkshire—not that I wanted to return—and everyone will think me a cardsharp."

"I think your best choice is to start anew. A new home, a new name, a new fiancé . . ." He cupped her face in his hands, despite her surprised gasp; most of the members had left, but the club was not empty, even though it was coming on to five o'clock in the morning. Three employees were still tallying the pot from their game. "Marry me, my love?"

"Yes," she managed to say before he kissed her, ignoring a few whistles from his friends, loitering at a discreet distance.

"Tomorrow?" he asked between kisses.

She goggled at him. "So soon?"

Rob smoothed his thumb over her cheek. "I knew the first time I kissed you, in Macclesfield, that you were the only woman for me. Tomorrow is not soon; it's been *weeks*. Will you be scandalous with me once more?"

She blushed, but couldn't help smiling. "Always."

Chapter 34

Six weeks later
Salmsbury Abbey
Lancashire

"THE RULES," ROB explained, "are simple. You must follow the path across the fields. There is a low stone wall, which you can jump or ride around, as you please. On the far side of that lie fallow fields. Ride directly west across them until you reach the large oak tree on the crest of the rise. Circle the tree on your left." He paused. "You may not pass it on the right."

"Why not?" Georgiana asked in surprise.

"It's a stupid rule," scoffed William Churchill-Gray. "Designed to help him win." He grinned at Georgiana. "West *hates* losing. He'll seize every last inch of advantage he can find."

Rob loudly disputed Will's charge as Georgiana laughed. Oh how she loved seeing him with his family—who were now her family, too.

When he'd suggested they come to Salmsbury to be married, she had been a little nervous; surely his family must have no good opinion of her. But as usual, he'd talked her into it, telling tales of his mother's longing to see him happily married, and of the beauty of Salmsbury Abbey, and how his father had urged him to go to London and see if she cared for him.

It must also be admitted that Georgiana was not sorry to leave town, at least for a while. Reports of her incredible triumph at loo had made her somewhat notorious. She was accustomed to being spoken of, but not gossiped about. Lady Sidlow declared that marriage to a marquess would soon scour away all stain, which was probably true, but in the meantime, Georgiana preferred not to face the stares and whispers every night.

And the Rowland family had welcomed her with open arms, especially the duchess, who pronounced herself delighted beyond measure to have a daughter at last. The duke sized her up with a long stare, then kissed her forehead and called Rob a damned fortunate madman—something Rob refused to explain but swore was a mark of approval. She would have loved Rob if his family had been cold and indifferent, but to be taken into the heart of this warm, boisterous family only made her fall in love with all of them.

Especially Will, who led out a mare with a pink ribbon and a sprig of dried lilac on her bridle, and said she was Georgiana's wedding gift from him. She was gray with a white nose and could run like the wind. Georgiana adored her at first sight and named her Athena. They had gone riding every day since, but today Rob had promised to show her the finest place to race horses in the world, across the fields of Salmsbury to the dunes of the Irish Sea.

When Rob and Will had finally agreed on a course and rules, they rode. Will had convinced her that riding sidesaddle was slowing her down, so today she was astride, with royal-blue breeches under her loose skirt—and he was right, she could go faster. Athena streaked along the fields, over the crest and toward the sea, and Georgiana couldn't resist letting out a shriek of pure joy. Even when Will thundered past to win the race, nothing dimmed her mood.

They returned to the house when the clouds blew away and the sun grew hot and bright. Will remained in the stable with the horses, and Rob put his arm around her to stroll back to the house. "I ought to take you on a wedding trip."

She smiled. "This has been better. Lancashire is new to me, remember." She'd sent one final letter to Alistair informing him that she was wedding Rob, and had received a terse response from his solicitor, explaining that there would be a delay in paying her dowry funds. After that Rob put everything into the solicitor's hands. Georgiana had a feeling she'd never hear from her brother again.

A servant was waiting for Rob. "From Lord Beresford, my lord."

Georgiana raised her brows as Rob took the letter. "I thought you were done with Beresford."

He shrugged. "Only with his mad schemes. He was pleased with how Heath and I took on Forester, though, so I asked if he might commend me to someone in the Home Office, for more respectable pursuits. Forester's not the only merchant violating the Slave Trade Act, and I'd like to put more of them out of business. Hopefully I can make myself useful in some way that doesn't require drinking and gaming all night."

"No, *I* shall require your attention all night," she told him, tugging at the lapel of his jacket.

"You already command it, morning, noon, and night." He kissed her. "I'll see you later."

Georgiana beamed at him. "You shall."

Her husband grinned and strode off, already opening Beresford's letter. Her heart fluttered. How gloriously, and unexpectedly, her rash decision to lie and call him her fiancé had turned out. He wasn't the rogue everyone called him; he was a prince, and he was hers.

Teatime only brought more proof that she'd been right about Rob. She was savoring her second cup when the butler came in. "You have a caller, Lady Westmorland," he said. "Lady Winston."

The teacup almost fell from her hands. "Who?" she repeated in alarm. "I mean . . . yes, of course. I shall see her." She set down her cup and rubbed her suddenly damp palms on her skirt.

"Oh my," murmured Lady Sidlow. "Should I send for the marquess?"

Georgiana chewed her lip. "No."

"As you wish." Lady Sidlow took another tiny cake and sat back.

She had accompanied Georgiana into Lancashire for propriety, and then stayed as an invited guest. Once Georgiana was married, Lady Sidlow had become a new woman, pleased to be free of responsibility. Every now and then her lips pursed up as before, when Rob and his brothers retold some daring adventure, but Rob had won her over with weekly bouquets delivered to her room—and a generous annuity.

Now Lady Sidlow sat by watching as Georgiana jumped up to pace nervously. Oh Lord. She felt the strongest urge to run into the garden and keep going, all the way to the seashore.

"I presume you told her," Lady Sidlow said.

"I sent her a letter," murmured Georgiana. The day before her wedding, she'd steeled herself and sent it. Kitty had never replied, and as a result Georgiana had never quite planned how she might react when next she met Kitty. She wet her lips. "What would my mother do?" she asked on impulse.

Becoming a daughter-in-law had made her more aware of how little she remembered her own parents, and she'd spent the last month asking Lady Sidlow about them, especially her mother. With Lady Sidlow's help and encouragement, she was using her winnings to locate and compensate the servants her mother hadn't been able to help escape Wakefield Manor. It must have infuriated Alistair, and Georgiana wouldn't spend a penny of his money on anything else.

Her former chaperone smiled and rose, just as footsteps sounded in the corridor outside. "She would be proud of you for acknowledging the truth to your friend." She left quietly, slipping through the door into the library.

"Sir Charles Winston," announced the butler, "and Lady Winston."

"Kitty," said Georgiana, gripping her hands together. There was a moment of stiff silence as they both curtsied, and Georgiana motioned for her guests to be seated. "And Sir Charles. How kind of you to call."

"Is it?" Kitty's eyes flickered over the room. It was restrained compared to the rest of the house, but it was still in a duke's castlelike home. Her gaze returned to Georgiana. "I received your letter."

"Oh? Excellent," said Georgiana, her cheer growing strained. Kitty was solemn and Charles looked as though he'd rather be stretched on a rack.

"It was quite . . . unexpected," Kitty went on. "We were all extremely astonished by it."

"I imagine so." Georgiana's smile was beginning to fade. "I am very sorry for . . ." She hesitated. ". . . many things."

Kitty nodded.

The moment of silence stretched, until Georgiana said, somewhat desperately, "I hope Mother Winston, Geneva, and Annabel are well?"

"Yes, they are." Kitty glanced at her husband, who was staring fiercely at the floor. "Charles," she hissed.

He started. "Yes, yes. Right." He cleared his throat. "Ah, Lady Georgiana—"

"Lady Westmorland," muttered his wife.

"Yes—right," said Charles, his face growing pink. "Lady Westmorland, I may have created an unjust impression in my letters, which Kitty tells me she made known to you." He glanced at Kitty, who nodded. "My conduct in the matter of a wager, over Osbourne House, was . . . not above reproach. I understand this now, and I do regret any false aspersions I may have . . . *inadvertently* cast against Lord Westmorland."

Georgiana just barely kept her mouth from dropping open.

Kitty smoothed her hands down her skirt. "I also regret any unkind things I said about Lord Westmorland."

"Of course," Georgiana murmured. There was another moment of awkward silence before she couldn't bear it any longer. "Why?"

Kitty started. "Why am I sorry?"

"Well . . . yes," Georgiana said, hesitating. "I understand you had valid reasons to be unhappy . . ."

"But not after what he did for Annabel," exclaimed Kitty before her husband leapt from his seat.

"It was all a monstrous misunderstanding," Charles declared forcefully. "Kitty, we should go."

"No," protested Georgiana in bewilderment. "What did you mean about Annabel?"

"Kitty," said Charles in desperation. His wife gave him a quelling look, and slowly the baronet sank back into his chair.

"You must know," Kitty told her, a faintly puzzled frown on her face. "Lord Westmorland put the deed to Osbourne House in trust for Annabel."

Now Georgiana's mouth did fall open, just a little bit. Rob hadn't said a word to her. "He did."

"We received the papers from the solicitor within days of your letter. Mr. Jackson agrees it is irrevocable, and all quite legal."

Georgiana looked from one to the other. "Then . . . the house is secured?"

Kitty nodded. "It cannot be disposed of until Annabel is of age, or marries."

Left unsaid was that Charles could not gamble

it away again. From the expression on his face, he knew this, and found it humiliating that Kitty knew it, too.

"It would have been better, perhaps, for him to have consulted us," Kitty went on. "But at the same time, we are all assured of a home until she is grown. Given what he might have done, it is a very generous arrangement."

I'm not taking their house, echoed Rob's voice in her memory. *That seems an end of the whole business, doesn't it?* That's why he'd been so confident Kitty would forgive her.

The man himself chose that moment to enter, coming in from the library door. Kitty and Charles looked up at the same time he saw them, and all three froze.

"See who's come to call," said Georgiana in the taut silence. "I was about to send for more tea."

Rob closed the door and came into the room. "Excellent."

"No," burst out Charles, staring at Rob with trepidation. "That is very kind, Lady Westmorland, but we must be on our way."

Rob ignored him and made a bow before Kitty. "Lady Winston. I trust you and your charming family are all well?"

"Yes, my lord, thank you." Kitty curtsied, then put one hand on his arm. "We've come to thank you for what you did, sir."

He smiled, darting a glance at Georgiana. "It was the properest thing to do. I hope it serves your family well."

Kitty smiled. "Yes, it will. Thank you."

"In turn I must thank you, for your kind and tender care during my convalescence. I am eternally grateful."

"It was Georgiana who cared for you," said Kitty with a wry laugh.

Rob glanced at Georgiana again, mischievously. "I am eternally grateful for her, too."

Kitty's face softened. "As you should be." She gave her husband a pointed stare. "Charles."

Wincing, Charles made his way to Rob, drawing him aside. They had a short conversation in voices too low for Georgiana to make out anything that was said, and then Rob nodded. Charles's shoulders sank in obvious relief, and they shook hands.

The Winstons took their leave, Charles trailing silently in his wife's wake. When the door closed behind them, Georgiana turned to her husband. "Why didn't you tell me you put Osbourne House into trust for Annabel?"

Rob put his hands on his hips in affront. "And spoil my rakish reputation? Why would I do that?"

She went up on her toes and clasped his face between her hands. "I already love you desperately. Rakish or otherwise."

"I will never tire of hearing that," he said with a wink.

"What did Charles tell you?"

He started to grin. "A story so ridiculous, even you couldn't make it up. Tom always wondered who gave me that thrashing in Maryfield. He thought Winston might have been behind it, and in a way he was. The night he lost the deed, Winston had a friend with him called Farley. Farley was so irate over what happened, he decided to hire some rough fellows to take that deed back for Winston—by apology, I suppose. The chaps he hired turned out to be a trifle rougher than he knew, though, and they went too far. Farley claimed he only wanted them to steal back the deed. Winston says he's mortified—even gone into hiding since he heard what happened."

Georgiana clapped one hand to her mouth. "But then . . ."

He nodded. "We stand here today, besotted husband and adoring wife, due entirely to the actions of a drunken fool and his idiot mate."

She burst out laughing.

Rob gathered her close. "I ought to send both of them my thanks, but I think instead I shall simply savor my good fortune, and lavish my appreciation on you."

She wound her arms around his neck. "Well, neither of us seem good at keeping to plans, but I think that is one we can both follow."

"For all the rest of my days," he said with a smile, and kissed her to prove it.

Author's Note

~~~

From the sixteenth to eighteenth centuries, English ships carried hundreds of thousands of slaves from Africa to the Americas and the West Indies. Slave trading was one of Britain's most profitable industries, particularly in the ports of Liverpool and Bristol, and many large British fortunes were built on slavery, either directly or indirectly. The wealthy plantation owners who relied on slavery and the merchants who profited by it used their money and political power to protect the trade.

After decades of work by abolitionists, Parliament passed the Slave Trade Act in 1807, outlawing the trade in slaves, though not slavery itself. This Act empowered the Royal Navy to patrol the coast of Africa, and to seize and fine captains discovered in violation. Many captains continued, though, drawn by the profits to be made and abetted by the merchants and investors who financed them. The Act applied only to British ships, so ships carried multiple flags and papers, claiming to be registered in countries where the slave trade was still legal,

and captains were known to throw captives overboard to reduce the amount they could be fined.

Not until further Acts in 1833 and 1843 did Britain abolish slavery within its empire, and then only
gradually, with exceptions, providing compensa-
tion for slave owners but none for the people freed
from slavery.

*Next month, don't miss these exciting
new love stories only from
Avon Books*

My Favorite Things: A Christmas Collection
   by Lynsay Sands
Full of dashing gentlemen who sweep women off
their feet, *New York Times* bestselling author Lynsay
Sands delivers *All I Want*, *Three French Hens*, and
The Fairy Godmother, three classic tales of Christmas
and love together for the first time ever in print!

The Duke's Stolen Bride by Sophie Jordan
To save her impoverished family, Marian Langley will
become a mistress. But she will not be just *any* mistress.
Marian intends to become so skilled, so coveted, that she
can set her own terms, retaining control over her body
and her fate. Only one problem remains: finding a tutor
like Nathaniel, Duke of Warrington …

Angel in a Devil's Arms by Julie Anne Long
How could the Duke of Brexford's notorious bastard son
return from the dead? The brutal decade since Lucien
Durand, Lord Bolt, allegedly drowned in the Thames
forged him into a man who always gets what—and
who—he wants. And what he wants is vengeance for his
stolen birthright … and one wild night in Angelique
Breedlove's bed.

REL 1019

New York Times bestselling author **Julia Quinn**

The Bridgerton Novels

On the Way to the Wedding
978-0-06-053125-6

Gregory Bridgerton must thwart Lucy Abernathy's upcoming wedding and convince her to marry him instead.

It's In His Kiss
978-0-06-053124-9

To Hyacinth Bridgerton, Gareth St. Clair's every word seems a dare.

When He Was Wicked
978-0-06-053123-2

To Sir Phillip, With Love
978-0-380-82085-6

Romancing Mister Bridgerton
978-0-380-82084-9

An Offer From a Gentleman
978-0-380-81558-6

The Viscount Who Loved Me
978-0-380-81557-9

The Duke and I
978-0-380-80082-7

At Avon Books, we know your passion for romance—once you finish one of our novels, you find yourself wanting more.

May we tempt you with . . .

- **Excerpts** from our upcoming releases.

- Entertaining **extras**, including authors' personal photo albums and book lists.

- Behind-the-scenes **scoop** on your favorite characters and series.

- **Sweepstakes** for the chance to win free books, romantic getaways, and other fun prizes.

- Writing **tips** from our authors and editors.

- **Blog** with our authors and find out why they love to write romance.

- **Exclusive content** that's not contained within the pages of our novels.

Join us at
www.avonbooks.com

AVON

An Imprint of HarperCollins*Publishers*
www.avonromance.com